# DUE
# DILIGENCE

OTHER BOOKS BY MICHAEL A. KAHN

*Grave Designs* (originally *The Canaan Legacy*)
*Death Benefits*
*Firm Ambitions*

# DUE
# DILIGENCE

*A Rachel Gold Mystery*

## Michael A. Kahn

A DUTTON BOOK

DUTTON
Published by the Penguin Group
Penguin Books USA Inc., 375 Hudson Street, New York, New York 10014, U.S.A.
Penguin Books Ltd, 27 Wrights Lane, London W8 5TZ, England
Penguin Books Australia Ltd, Ringwood, Victoria, Australia
Penguin Books Canada Ltd, 10 Alcorn Avenue, Toronto, Ontario, Canada M4V 3B2
Penguin Books (N.Z.) Ltd, 182–190 Wairau Road, Auckland 10, New Zealand

Penguin Books Ltd, Registered Offices: Harmondsworth, Middlesex, England

First published by Dutton, an imprint of Dutton Signet,
a division of Penguin Books USA Inc.
Distributed in Canada by McClelland & Stewart Inc.

First Printing, September, 1995
10 9 8 7 6 5 4 3 2 1

 REGISTERED TRADEMARK—MARCA REGISTRADA

LIBRARY OF CONGRESS CATALOGING-IN-PUBLICATION DATA:
Kahn, Michael A.
     Due diligence : a Rachel Gold mystery / Michael A. Kahn.
       p.   cm.
     ISBN 0-525-93743-9
     1. Gold, Rachel (Fictitious character)—Fiction.   2. Women
lawyers—Missouri—Saint Louis—Fiction.   3. Saint Louis (Mo.)—
Fiction.   I. Title.
PS3561.A375D84   1995
813'.54—dc20                                                95-9853
                                                              CIP

Printed in the United States of America
Set in Century Old Style
Designed by Eve L. Kirch

PUBLISHER'S NOTE
This is a work of fiction. Names, characters, places, and incidents either are the products of the author's imagination or are used fictitiously, and any resemblance to actual persons, living or dead, events, or locales is entirely coincidental.

This book is printed on acid-free paper. ∞

*For Jake "Shaq" Kahn*

A special thanks to Dr. Leonard B. Weinstock and Mark Zorensky—excellent tour guides through their respective fields of expertise. Thanks, Lenny. Thanks, Mark.

# PROLOGUE

*Down in the darkness it waits. Down in the subbasement of the Gateway Corporate Tower. From its open maw comes the stench of rotting flesh. Its single eye glows red.*

*The tenants of the Gateway Corporate Tower include lawyers and accountants, architects and insurance agents, advertising executives and business consultants. None have ever ventured down to the subbasement. None have ever imagined what is down there, waiting silently.*

THE trash chute of the Gateway Corporate Tower is essentially a 240-foot stainless steel tube that runs from the sub-basement to the top floor, eighteen stories above Olive Street. It drops through fifteen floors in a straight perpendicular near the north elevator shaft, veers north at a forty-five-degree angle through two levels of the aboveground parking garage and then makes a final, two-story descent, emerging at a steep angle through the ceiling of the subbasement near the northeast corner of the building.

*Motionless, it waits beneath the open end of the trash chute. By any standard, it is huge. Twenty-four feet from end to end, nearly eight feet wide, just shy of seven feet at its tallest point. It weighs at least fourteen tons, although, for obvious reasons, no one has ever tried to maneuver it onto a scale for a more precise measurement.*

The night cleaning crews cherished that chute. There was access to it on every floor, usually in a utility closet around the corner from the elevators. Better yet, the building's designers had specified access doors large enough to accommodate just about any form, shape, or quantity of trash that the office tenants and the ground-level restaurant and newsstand were likely to produce during a busy day. As a result, there was never need for a time-consuming trip down the freight elevator from the upper floors to the subbasement to unload a cumbersome cloth hamper. Just shove the trash down the chute and get on to the next office.

*It is squat and massive, with all that weight resting upon four small legs. Those legs seem almost dainty in contrast to the bulk they support.*

The eight-person night crew from Ace Office Maintenance arrived each weekday shortly after 5:00 P.M., started on the lower floors and gradually worked their way up, usually reaching the top floor a little after midnight.

The consulting firm of Smilow & Sullivan, Ltd. occupied the entire ninth floor. Those at the firm who regularly worked late knew that the cleaning crew reached their floor around nine o'clock and left before ten. The pattern held that night. The first two members of the night crew (Darlene Washington and La-Tisha Forest) got off the elevator on the ninth floor at 9:06 P.M. The last departing member of the night crew (Yao-Wen Hsieh) boarded the elevator for the tenth floor at 9:45 P.M.

The police eventually interviewed all eight members of the crew. All remembered seeing him up there, as did Cynthia O'Malley (who saw him in the hall) and Mr. Sullivan (who poked his head in his office on his way out). According to the night crew, he was definitely alive and hard at work when they left, and by then Cynthia and Mr. Sullivan were definitely gone. Yao-Wen Hsieh was in the firm's lobby vacuuming the carpet at 9:15 P.M. when Cynthia boarded the down elevator carrying her purse and jacket. Three members of the crew saw Mr. Sullivan. He arrived in his tuxedo straight from the Barnes Hospital fund-raiser around 9:30, picked up a few papers from his desk, and left ten minutes later. The time of Cynthia's departure and Mr. Sullivan's brief visit were both confirmed by the guard downstairs, who saw Cynthia sign out when she left and watched Mr. Sullivan sign in and out.

In short, according to the eyewitnesses and the sign-in sheet, there should have been only one person left on the ninth floor at quarter to ten that night. He was definitely up there.

Unfortunately, he was just as definitely not alone.

*Although it has stirred only once in the last twenty hours, it is ready. Day or night, summer or winter, it's always ready. It is, quite literally, programmed for vigilance. Its single red eye, hardwired into its tiny brain, never closes. And that brain—assuming that something so limited can still be called a brain—is primed to issue the one command that defines its existence.*

*The command—like the command issued from any brain—is just a weak electronic blip that travels quickly from brain to receptor. Here, that blip means "GO!" And here, the receptor is a crushing jaw, technically known as a power wedge. The power wedge is hidden within the open maw and aptly named: it can exert more than 122,000 pounds of force. Under that kind of pressure, a man's skull will crumple like a soft-boiled egg beneath the wheels of a Mack truck.*

He often worked late. It had been his style ever since joining the firm as the hotshot boy wonder out of Purdue seven years ago. His promotion to manager last winter had not diminished his capacity for long hours. He typically stayed late two or three

nights each week. On Saturdays—true to his nickname FILO—
he was usually first in and last out.

Looking back, Mr. Sullivan told the police, the young man had
seemed a tad jumpy that night, although, he cautioned, his ob-
servation was based on a conversation that lasted less than sixty
seconds. Nevertheless, Mr. Sullivan was on target. The young
man had been a tad jumpy. More than just a tad. Distressed was
a better word.

At 10:20 on the night in question he was standing at the work-
table just outside the copy room collating a stack of documents
to make a working copy to take home with him that night. The
hallway was carpeted, he was agitated, he hadn't been sleeping
well, and the document on top of the pile was clearly the most
troubling one—all of which may explain why he didn't hear the
approach.

The attack was swift, professional, and nearly painless—a powerful arm grabbing from behind, a sharp pressure on the side of
the neck, and then fade-out.

*Echoing down the steel tube comes the sound of an access
door opening.*

*It doesn't hear the sound.*

*It doesn't hear a thing. Unable to hear, or to even detect the
presence of sound waves, it remains unaware of the noise above,
unaware that something is about to come sliding down the tube.*

*But that doesn't matter. It's programmed for vigilance. It simply
waits. Patiently.*

Unconscious, he plummeted down the chute in total darkness.
The medical examiner surmised that he may have stiffened just
before his body hit the forty-five-degree bend, which would have
only made it worse. The impact shattered both ankles and splintered his right tibia, jamming shards of bone through the skin of
his lower leg. If he was unfortunate enough to regain consciousness during that descent, he surely lost it upon impact.

It took a full five minutes for his limp body to work its way through the bend in the tube. The blood helped lubricate the passage. Once through the bend, his body started sliding, feet first, down the tube, which passed at an angle through the two levels of the aboveground parking garage. His body gradually accelerated as it approached the final drop-off. Unconscious, he slid over the edge and plunged the final fifteen feet, landing facedown on top of several large bags of trash.

*The single red eye detected motion. The falling body briefly broke the narrow beam of red light when it dropped into the open maw—barely a flicker, far too quick to trigger the countdown.*

Perhaps it was the stench. Perhaps it was the pain. Perhaps it was the thud of yet another bag of trash landing on his back. Whatever the cause, he regained consciousness inside the chamber, according to the medical examiner.

It was pitch-black, the air heavy with the stench of putrefaction. The large bags beneath him felt like bunchy, crinkly cushions. When he opened his eyes, he saw the eye. It was directly in front of him, about two feet above his head. There was a thin beam of red light emanating from the eye.

He would have been confused, of course. In the total darkness, the red beam would have seemed almost unearthly. He may have reached up to pass his hand through the beam. It would have made a fuzzy red dot on his palm.

*The interruption is long enough to trigger the countdown: ten . . . nine . . . eight—*

He let his hand fall forward onto the bag of trash.

*—seven. The countdown stops. The timer resets.*

Somehow, despite the excruciating pain, he managed to pull himself into a sitting position. It took a long time, and the effort left him shaking and drenched with sweat.

*The sensor triggered the countdown: ten . . . nine . . . eight . . . seven . . . six—*

As he waited for his jagged breathing to return to normal, the intense pain muddling his thoughts, perhaps he looked down at the beam. The red dot would have been centered on his chest.

*—five . . . four . . . three—*

According to the medical examiner, he probably lunged toward the front wall, toward the single red eye.

*—two . . . one . . . zero.*
*The brain fires its one command: GO!*
*Exactly 2.5 seconds later, the power wedge system responds, precisely in accordance with the manufacturer's specs.*

He was leaning against the wall when the 35-horsepower engine kicked on with an electric growl. The noise came from somewhere just beyond the wall. At first he would not have realized the deadly relevance of the sound.

And then the lurch.

It would have seemed as if part of the wall was moving toward him—which is precisely what was happening. The lower half of the wall was actually the business end of the power wedge ram system, pressing toward him at the rate of two inches per second.

As the power wedge slowly shoved him backward into the bags of trash, he must have strained for the answer. The stench, the bags of trash, his plunge down the metal chute. *Where am I? What the hell is happening?*

Based on his final body position, he must have tried to shove the power wedge back, grunting and gasping, struggling to hold it at arm's length. But the trash behind him began to compress, to solidify. He arms strained against the advancing metal. Perhaps he screamed for help. The increasing pressure would have constrained his voice.

Eventually, his arms buckled.

*As designed by the mechanical engineers at the Vanguard Trashpacker Corporation, the compacting cycle on the Model 7800 lasts 42 seconds. The power wedge ram is designed to push forward 84 inches into the receiving chamber without stopping. That distance, in the industry jargon, is known as the "ram stroke." With 122,000 pounds of pressure supplied by the latest in hydraulic cylinder technology, the Model 7800's ram stroke is as close to unstoppable as modern engineering techniques can achieve.*

*On this occasion, the power wedge performs as designed. When it completes the 84-inch journey forward into the chamber, the gears shift and it slowly retracts until flush again with the rest of the front wall. The electric motor shuts off with a metallic shudder.*

*Other than the occasional crinkling sound of a bag of compressed trash expanding, there is no motion and there is no sound inside the compactor.*

Bags of trash continued to plunge down the chute from higher and ever higher elevations within the Gateway Corporate Tower. The mound grew closer and closer to the red beam until, around 12:30 A.M., a falling bag came to rest in the middle of the beam, triggering one last compacting cycle for the night.

The cleaning crew left the building at 1:05 A.M.

*Down in the darkness it waits. Down in the subbasement of the Gateway Corporate Tower. From its open maw comes the stench of rotting flesh. Its single eye glows red.*

# 1

CHAPTER

FRIDAY the rabbi slept late.

He was sleeping peacefully when I awoke a few minutes after seven o'clock. I glanced over and smiled. He was on his back, his chest bare. An arrow of curly black hair started at his navel and disappeared beneath the bedsheets, which were low on his slender hips. This was definitely not your grandfather's rabbi. He looked like a male model in one of those sexy ads for men's jeans. I turned on my side toward him, careful not to disturb his sleep. He had a delicious musky smell. It made me want to growl.

Rabbi David Marcus. My brilliant, gorgeous expert witness. He had been wonderful and masterful. In court, that is. Well, last night, too. I still couldn't believe that we'd known each other for less than a month.

I had called him three weeks ago because I needed an authority on the Holocaust to serve as an expert witness in a probate case on the trial docket for the following week. The decedent was Yetra Blumenthal, a survivor of Auschwitz who'd lost her husband and children in the death camps. She'd come to America after the Allies liberated Auschwitz, never remarried, and died childless and alone. In her will, she left her entire estate to the State of Israel. Unfortunately, the original document was never found—

only a photocopy of the will. Under Missouri law a photocopy isn't enough. I represented the State of Israel, which was the party trying to reinstate the missing will.

In my final trial preparations, I decided I needed an expert witness on the psyches of Holocaust survivors. A friend at the Jewish Federation told me to call David Marcus, the new assistant rabbi at Temple Shalom, a huge reform congregation in the western suburbs. "He's written a book on Holocaust survivors," she told me, "and he's a doll."

I had called him later that day. He was polite and low-key over the telephone and agreed to meet me the following afternoon. I offered to drive out to the synagogue, but he insisted on coming to my office in the city, explaining that he would be in the Central West End earlier that day anyway. I had assumed that he was coming to the city for the usual rabbinical visit with ailing members of the congregation who were in one of the hospitals along Kingshighway; it was only later that I learned that Wednesdays and Saturdays were his days to work in the shelter for battered women that he had helped establish.

I must confess that my preconceived image of Rabbi David Marcus was based in part on his profession, in part on his soft-spoken manner over the telephone, and in part on my grandfather's rabbi. I assumed he was short and overweight, with thick glasses (probably horn-rimmed, probably crooked), a wrinkled black suit, a baggy white shirt, an unkempt beard, and pudgy fingers.

Well, that was not the Rabbi David Marcus who arrived at my office that Wednesday afternoon. He was tall and good looking, with gentle brown eyes, dark hair, a strong nose, and large, powerful hands. The few points of overlap with my grandfather's rabbi were actually points of contrast. Both wore yarmulkes, although David's was small and embroidered. Both wore white shirts, although David's covered broad shoulders and a slender waist. Both had a slightly rumpled look, although David's look was rugged rumpled, as if he had paused at a playground on the way over to shoot some hoops. The image fit. Despite a slight limp, he moved across the room with the grace of an athlete.

I was strongly attracted to him from the start and had to force myself to remain in my professional role as attorney interviewing a prospective expert witness. It was quickly obvious that he not only possessed impressive credentials for the task but had a calm reassuring manner that would make him a compelling witness. Money was no issue, since he didn't want to be compensated for his testimony. And best of all, I told myself, given that the trial was just a week away, if I retained him as my expert witness we would have to spend many hours together between now and then.

We did.

My initial attraction continued to grow. David Marcus was an unusual man. Earnest and committed were adjectives that fit. He was serious about his Judaism, about his Holocaust studies, about his involvement with the shelter for battered women. He was no lightweight. But fortunately, he also had a sense of humor. Otherwise, as I told him after the trial, he'd be an insufferable bore.

"A bore?" he had repeated with a perplexed smile.

That was four nights ago. The trial had ended well, and we'd gone out to celebrate with dinner at Baliban's in the Central West End. We were walking back along Maryland toward my office to get our cars. I'd had one too many glasses of wine at dinner, and during dessert had had an almost overwhelming urge to lean across the table and kiss him. Really kiss him. A wine-spilling, silverware-clanking, busboy-blushing kiss. The urge passed somewhere between the first and second cups of espresso, leaving me almost ashamed for having such lustful thoughts about a rabbi, especially since I had no clear sense of what his feelings were for me.

"A bore," I had answered mischievously, looking up at him as we walked along. "You men don't seem to realize that a sense of humor is not merely vital. It's sexy."

"Sexy?" he repeated.

"Very."

He stopped to study me. "I don't think so," he finally said.

"Oh, no?" I responded, fighting back a smile. "And what do the great Talmudic rabbis have to say on the subject?"

"All I know is what this rabbi thinks." He put his arms around my waist and gently pulled me toward him.

"And what does he think?" I whispered, looking up at him.

He kissed me tenderly on my forehead. "He thinks your forehead is sexy." He kissed me on each eyelid. "He thinks you're sexy here, too." I shivered as he moved his lips down my nose. "And he thinks your nose is exquisitely sexy." He kissed me on each side of my nose and then pulled back. He stared into my eyes, and then dropped his gaze slightly to my lips. "And definitely here," he whispered. He leaned forward and kissed me on the lips. Our first kiss, slow and gentle.

I let it last until I could just sense that all of my defense systems were shutting down. I opened my eyes as I leaned back in his arms. "Maybe you're right," I said hoarsely. "That sure beats a joke."

Two days passed, and then a client called with a pair of box seat tickets to the Cardinals game that night. It was the first of May, and I hadn't been to a game since opening day. I called David, who seemed delighted to hear from me but unenthused about going to a baseball game.

"Come on," I told him. "They're playing the Pirates. Our seats are fabulous."

Reluctantly, he agreed to go.

*He probably doesn't like baseball,* I told myself after I hung up. Or maybe he didn't even understand how the game was played. *Don't forget,* I said, *you've never really known a rabbi before—at least outside of a synagogue. Don't assume a thing.*

But to my surprise, David Marcus turned out to be an extremely knowledgeable student of baseball. Several times during the game he quietly pointed something out that I never would have spotted on my own—a subtle shift in the infield alignment, a change in the pitcher's motion or the catcher's position, a batting strategy based on the next two players in the lineup.

On the way home from the game I made my decision. "Come on in," I told him when he pulled in front of my house. "I'll make us some coffee and you can meet Ozzie."

"Who is Ozzie?"

I raised my eyebrows impishly. "A gorgeous redhead I've lived with for the past seven years."

David and Ozzie hit it off immediately, although I must admit that I have yet to meet anyone who doesn't hit it off immediately with Ozzie. I've had Ozzie since he was six weeks old, and as far as I am concerned, he is the most lovable, gentle, loyal, and tolerant golden retriever in the Western Hemisphere.

When the coffee was ready, I let Ozzie out in the backyard and David brought the steaming mugs into the living room. When I came into the living room, he was kneeling next to the stereo system flipping through my old albums. *A good sign,* I told myself. He had ignored the rack of CDs.

"What are you in the mood to hear?" he asked.

"Your choice," I said.

Any lingering doubts vanished when I saw the album he selected: *The Greatest Hits of Smokey Robinson and the Miracles.* I knew then it would be a wonderful night, and it was. We kissed on the couch to "Shop Around." We made love on the bed to a medley that ended with "I Second That Emotion." We awoke at three in the morning and made love again, this time to our own music.

And now, at 7:15 in the morning, I gazed at my handsome sleeping rabbi. He had actually carried me from the couch to the bedroom last night, scooping me up as if I weighed nothing. I was surprised by his strength, but as I studied his bare arms and chest I could see how powerful they were. A weight-lifting rabbi? You could do worse. I stretched with contentment. You could do a whole lot worse than a strong, dark, and handsome rabbi who knew baseball, enjoyed good food, and could sing all the words to "Tracks of My Tears."

"Good morning, Rachel."

I turned to find him looking at me, a twinkle in his eyes. I leaned over and kissed him on the nose. "Good morning, David," I said, nuzzling against his neck.

An hour later, barefoot and wrapped in my terrycloth bathrobe, I came into the kitchen, fluffing my hair with a bath towel. The sight I found made me smile. David was dressed and at the kitchen table, reading the front page. Ozzie was curled on the floor at his feet. A fresh pot of coffee was on the counter and a basket of croissants, rolls, and Danish was on the table.

"Wow," I said as I joined him at the table. "Where did you get the goodies?"

He smiled. "The St. Louis Bread Company. I ducked out while you were in the shower."

I leaned across the table and kissed him on the lips. "Thanks." I sat back and ravenously surveyed the basket of pastries. I picked out a raspberry croissant, took a bite, and got up to pour myself some coffee.

"I thought rabbis only ate bagels," I said when I returned to the table.

"Not when we're romancing beautiful, long-legged attorneys." He winked. "There's a special exception set out in the Torah."

I reached for the sports page.

"By the way," I said a few moments later, "your friend never showed up."

David looked up from the newspaper. "My friend?"

"That guy you sent me. Bruce Rosenthal."

"He's not really a friend. He's a member of the congregation. He came to me Saturday morning after services. He was agitated, but didn't tell me much. From what he was willing to say, it sounded to me like he needed to talk to a lawyer. I suggested he give you a call. I thought he did."

"He did," I said. "He called last Thursday."

"Were you able to help him?"

I shrugged. "Not yet."

"What happened?"

"He was real nervous. He was calling from his car phone. He didn't want to talk about it over the phone, only face-to-face. 'Strictly confidential,' he told me, which was fine. Most new clients are reluctant to describe their problems over the phone, especially a car phone. We scheduled a meeting for eleven o'clock the next day—that was last Friday."

"And?" David said.

"I had to reschedule. He got to my office right on time, but I was still stuck in a court hearing downtown. I called him from court and apologized. We rescheduled the meeting for Tuesday morning at nine."

"What happened?"

I shrugged. "I have no idea. He never showed up, never called to explain, never called to reschedule. I haven't talked to him since last Friday. Has he said anything to you?"

David leaned back in his chair and scratched his neck pensively. "He was at Shabbat services on Saturday morning. I haven't talked to him since then."

I stood up with a shrug. "Well, let's hope his problem went away." I glanced up at the kitchen clock. "I'm going to get dressed. It won't take me long."

Five minutes later I was zipping my skirt when David Marcus came into the bedroom. I turned with a smile, which faded when I saw his ashen face. He was holding the newspaper in his hand.

"What's wrong?" I asked.

"Here." He handed me the paper. It was open to page three of the metropolitan section. He pointed to the headline at the top of the page:

LOCAL CONSULTANT DISCOVERED INSIDE TRASH
COMPACTOR; APPARENTLY DEAD FOR DAYS

I started reading the story:

The body of a 29-year-old engineering consultant was discovered yesterday afternoon when the contents of an industrial trash compactor container were dumped out at the Chain of Rocks landfill near Granite City, Ill. Workers at the site watched in horror and disbelief as a male corpse, still attired in a conservative business suit, came tumbling out of the compactor container along with dozens of large brown bags of trash.

Police at the scene identified the man as Bruce A. Rosenthal of Clayton, Mo. His employer had reported him missing the day before his body was discovered. A homicide investigation has commenced, according to Captain Ron Price of the St. Louis Police Department.

Rosenthal was employed as a manager at the engineering consulting firm of . . .

I looked up from the article. David was sitting on the bed, his head down. I glanced at my watch. I had to be downtown for a deposition in forty-five minutes, but I didn't want to act rushed. David was shaken by Rosenthal's death. I could tell that he was trying to shoulder some of the blame, as absurd as that was.

"You did what you could," I said.

He turned to me, puzzled. "Pardon?"

"He needed an attorney, not a rabbi," I explained. "I gather he wanted to talk to an attorney about a matter he was working on. I assume he had discovered something about one of his firm's clients and wanted to know who he could tell."

"Why do you say that?"

"You told me that he said he wanted to talk to an attorney about two things. One of them was the accountant-client privilege, right?"

"Right."

I scanned the rest of the newspaper article and looked up. "It says he had a degree in accounting. If he told you he had a question about the accountant-client privilege, I assume it had to do with one of his firm's clients. He must have learned something disturbing and wanted to know if he could tell anyone." I glanced down at the newspaper article. "He worked at Smilow and Sullivan, Ltd. An engineering consulting firm." I looked at David. "What kind of things does an engineering consulting firm do?"

"I don't know," he said with a frown. "He never told me." He shook his head sadly. "I never even asked."

"David," I said gently, "you did the right thing. Both of you decided that he needed to talk to an attorney. You're not an attorney. You gave him my name. You did exactly what he asked you to do. I was the one who wasn't able to make that first appointment. If anyone's to blame, it's me, not you."

He wasn't persuaded. I sat next to him on the bed and took his hand. "I'm sure the police will do a thorough investigation."

David sighed. "I hope so."

A few minutes later, we were in the front hall getting ready to leave. Ozzie was waiting at the front door, his eyes moving back and forth between David and me.

"What do you make of the other issue?" David asked.

"What issue?" I said, reaching for my purse.

"In addition to the privilege issue, Bruce told me he wanted to talk to an attorney about some sort of statutory limits."

"Do you remember what kind of statutory limits?"

David shook his head in frustration. "No."

"There are lots of possibilities," I explained. "The law books are filled with statutes that put limits on things—limits on the amount of damages you can recover, limits on the types of actions a board of directors can take without a shareholder vote, limits on the number of branch offices a bank can operate, and so on and so on. Unless you know who the client was, it'll be hard to figure out which statutory limits might apply."

I held the door open for Ozzie, who ran out, and then I locked it behind me.

"Where does Ozzie go during the day?" David asked.

"Next door." We watched Ozzie trot toward my neighbors' porch. "It's a great arrangement. They have adorable little twin girls. They're home all day with a babysitter. They love Ozzie, and he keeps them company."

Ozzie climbed onto my neighbors' porch and turned back toward me as he sat down. David's car was in the driveway behind mine. As we walked to our cars I tried to decide whether to raise the subject of when we'd see each other again. His distraction over Bruce Rosenthal's death made him seem distant. Having never before spent the night with a rabbi, I wasn't quite sure of the protocols.

David stopped when we reached my car and took my hand. "That was a marvelous evening, Rachel," he said softly. "When can I see you again?"

I blushed with pleasure and squeezed his hand. "Whenever you'd like."

He thought for a moment. "How about Sunday afternoon?"

"Sunday?" I repeated, mentally checking my calendar. "Well, I have a game—hey, how would you like to play softball on Sunday afternoon?"

"Softball?" he said with a frown. "I don't—"

"Come on, David. It won't be so bad. I'm on a coed team in the lawyers' league. We're going to be one short on Sunday. They'll let us play that way, but we could really use another man."

"I haven't played in a long time," he said reluctantly.

"Big deal. It's not like we're major leaguers out there. It's fun. My best friend Benny Goldberg's on our team. I really want you two to meet. We can all go out to dinner after."

He sighed in surrender. "Okay."

I stood on my toes and kissed him on the lips. "It's Diamond Number Two at Forest Park. The game starts at three-thirty."

He beeped his horn as he pulled away, and I honked back. Ozzie was curled up on my neighbor's front porch as I backed out of the driveway. I waved and called, "Bye, Oz." He lifted his head and his tail flopped three times on the porch.

I drove off with a feeling of total contentment, humming a Smokey Robinson tune, blissfully unaware that Bruce Rosenthal's grisly death had sounded the opening chords of a nightmare symphony.

# 2

CHAPTER

THE outlook wasn't brilliant for our Mudville nine that day. We were trailing 5 to 2 with just three innings left to play.

Our opponents were the coed team from the law firm of Crowley & Gillan, a products liability defense firm. Their players seemed determined to project the same tough-as-nails persona on the diamond as they did in the courtroom. They were a fierce and humorless group who argued every close call, slammed their bats in disgust whenever they made an out, exchanged brutal high-fives on good plays, and generally demonstrated how a group of obnoxious litigators can ruin a perfectly pleasant game. The Crowley & Gillan women were just as ferocious as the men. Their catcher was a good example: she stood nearly six feet tall, hit with power to all fields, blocked the plate like an offensive tackle, and from behind bore a striking resemblance to Philadelphia's John Kruk.

You can usually spot a serious team by their uniforms, and Crowley & Gillan was definitely a serious team. They had black-and-silver jerseys, black baseball pants, stirrup socks, and cleated Nikes. Their baseball caps featured a black-and-silver raider's logo, and their jerseys had each player's name in block letters on the back and the team name—the Defense Verdicts—in script on the front.

By contrast, we looked like a New Age softball "family" from the Lacto-Vegetarian League. I was on the pitcher's mound in my Chicago Blackhawks hockey jersey, faded Levi cutoffs, and Grateful Dead baseball cap. Playing first base was Benny Goldberg, looking, as he would say, "full figured but *très elegant*" in his Black Dog T-shirt, gray sweatpants, and Portland Beavers baseball cap turned backward. At shortstop, dressed in black with his long red hair pulled back in a ponytail, stood Donny Stockman, a flamboyant criminal defense attorney (and, thank heavens, a former varsity baseball player at Vanderbilt). At third base was Diane Correa-Valdes, a Hispanic labor attorney who was dressed for a role in a Janet Jackson music video.

But dress codes can be misleading, as Crowley & Gillan soon discovered. They had won the league championship last year and arrived that day with a definite attitude—two of the players had actually snickered when we showed up. But five innings later they were clearly unsettled by their mere three-run lead.

As I finished my warm-up tosses, Benny lumbered over to the mound.

"How you feeling, gorgeous?" he asked.

"I'm okay." I scanned the sidelines again. "I wonder where David is? He promised me he'd be here."

"Can you believe the women on that fucking team?" Benny said, shaking his head in disgust. "They have better builds than your new secretary. I hear their catcher got drafted by the Packers. I don't know about you, but I think a little chromosome testing might be in order."

"Let's go," I told him. "Get back in position."

"Hey," he said, stepping back to look at my legs, "you're kind of bossy for a chick in Daisy Dukes."

"Benny," I said in a warning tone. "Number one, these are *not* Daisy Dukes. Not even close. Number two, I'm bossy 'cause I'm the captain. Now get back in position."

He gave me a salute. "Yes, b'wana."

The first batter was a hot-tempered male outfielder. He swung for the fences and topped it instead, hitting a weak roller back to the pitcher's mound. I fielded it cleanly and easily threw him out. He slammed down his hat, kicked at the dirt, and shouted obscenities all the way back to the bench.

"Yo!" Benny shouted at their players. "Increase his medication."

Several of them glared at Benny, and I silently groaned. We surely didn't need to provoke them.

The batting order, as required by league rules, alternated male and female. A short, compact woman stepped up to the plate and stroked the first pitch to left for a single. She was forced at second on a fielder's choice ground ball to third base. The next batter hit a clean single to center, and there were runners on first and second.

I stepped off the mound to slow down the pace. Looking around, I saw David Marcus in the distance walking toward the field. My initial delight faded when I realized that he was wearing a white dress shirt, black baggy slacks, and dress shoes. His hands were empty—no baseball glove. Fighting my disappointment, I forced a cheerful wave. He waved back and quickened his pace, which only seemed to accentuate his limp.

I stepped back on the mound and focused on the next batter, a lean, intense left-hander with short blond hair and a flushed face. He cranked the first pitch foul down the right field line. That got Benny's attention, which was fortunate, because on the next pitch he hit a screamer right at Benny's head. Benny ducked out of the way but was able to knock down the ball with his glove. He picked up the ball and trotted over to first base for the third out.

David was waiting when I reached the sidelines. "Where've you been?" I asked him, trying to keep the edge out of my voice.

"I apologize, Rachel. I should have called. One of the residents at the Jewish Center for the Aged died on Saturday. Her funeral was this afternoon. I came here as soon as it ended."

"That's okay," I said, suddenly feeling frivolous standing there in my softball outfit.

He unbuttoned his cuffs. "Think I can borrow a glove?" He rolled up his sleeves. "I didn't realize until this morning that I don't have one anymore."

I found an old softball glove at the bottom of the equipment bag. It was small, beat-up and blue, but David didn't seem to mind. I introduced him to Benny, who offered to warm him up on the sidelines. Since I wasn't likely to bat that inning, I jogged across the field to the coach's box near third base. As I clapped in encouragement to our lead-off batter, I furtively glanced over to where David and Benny were playing catch. Over the course of the inning, I was relieved to see that David's throws and catches, initially awkward, were becoming more graceful.

We scored a run in the bottom of the fifth. In the top of the sixth I inserted David into the lineup at the bottom of the order and put him in right field, which seemed as close to being out of harm's way as one could get.

Neither side got a hit or a run in the sixth inning, and we took the field in the seventh and final inning still trailing by two runs. Their first batter—the huge woman catcher—hit a lazy fly ball to center field for the first out. The second batter grounded out to short. The next batter hit a slow roller between third and the pitcher's mound. I charged over, scooped it up barehanded, spun toward first, and fired a line drive five feet above Benny's outstretched glove. The runner took second on the error as Benny retrieved my throw. I stomped back to the mound, furious with myself.

"Shake it off, Daisy," Benny said as he tossed me the ball. "We'll get the next one."

Stepping in the batter's box was their first baseman, a tall, brawny guy who had already hit two line-drive doubles. I turned toward the outfield and motioned them back. I looked over at David out in right field, with his white dress shirt and street shoes and battered blue glove, and said a silent thanks that the batter was right-handed. But the batter must have spotted David, because he shifted his stance and lined the first pitch foul down the right field line. I glanced back at David, who nodded and took two more steps to the right. With growing concern, I turned to the batter, who was digging in at the plate and waggling his bat in a menacing fashion. His teammates were shouting encouragement.

"Please, God," I said under my breath as I threw the next pitch, aiming inside, hoping to force him to hit to left.

No such luck. He stepped back and lashed a line drive just over Benny's head and into the right field corner.

"Oh, no," I moaned, turning to watch. In my peripheral vision I saw the runner from second dashing toward third.

I was surprised to see that David had gotten a good jump on the ball, street clothes, limp and all. He reached it on the third bounce, just as the runner was rounding third and heading home on what should have been a routine, run-scoring double. David fielded the ball cleanly, pivoted, and threw home.

It wasn't until the umpire shouted "Out!" that any of us were able to grasp the sheer glory of David's play. In baseball jargon, he threw a frozen rope. In plain English, he hurled the ball on a line drive from deep right field all the way to home plate. Our amazed catcher caught the ball on the fly just to the third base side of home, where an equally amazed runner ran into the tag for the final out of the inning.

David received several congratulatory whacks on the back from our players and a kiss from me, but the celebration quickly faded as we returned to reality. It was our last time at bat, and we were still two runs behind.

Our first batter flied out to left field. I was up second and reached base on a throwing error. Our hopes started to build when Benny followed with a clean single to center field. I hollered encouragement from second base, but our next batter popped out to third base. We were down to our last out, still trailing by two. I watched nervously as David Marcus limped to the plate, pausing to tap the bat against the heels of his street shoes.

"Come on, David!" I called.

He assumed a batting stance that hardly looked intimidating. Indeed, it was remarkable how relaxed his stance looked: bat held low, wrists at about waist level, elbows not cocked. And yet, I realized after a moment, it was a stance that I had seen used before, most recently by the Cardinals third baseman Todd Zeile. "Please," I said under my breath.

David swung and missed the first pitch. The momentum of his swing and the slickness of his shoes made him spin and lose his balance. He staggered back two steps. Several of the fielders started laughing.

"Don't hurt yourself, Chester," shouted their cretinous first baseman.

David got under the next pitch and popped a fly ball into foul territory beyond third base. The third baseman, shortstop and left fielder all gave chase, but the ball drifted out of play into a row of high bushes.

"One more strike," yelled the second baseman as the players returned to their positions. They were pumped, sensing victory.

"Wait for your pitch, David," Benny shouted and looked over at me with a grin. Raising his eyebrows in appreciation, he put his fists together as if he were holding a bat and waggled his wrists.

I took a deep breath and nodded guardedly. Although the last foul hadn't been much of a hit, I had noticed—and so had Benny—that David was generating an awful lot of bat speed in his relaxed batting stance. All the whiplike motion and power in his swing was coming from his wrists. If he could time the pitch, he ought to get a hit.

I exhaled slowly, tensely, as I watched David step back into the batter's box. He fouled off two more pitches, both to the third base side, each harder than the one before it. The players on the other team were hollering for the kill, apparently oblivious to what David appeared to be doing at the plate. Although I couldn't tell for sure, it seemed as if he were intentionally fouling off pitches, as if he were taking a strange, high-risk version of batting practice in the bottom of the last inning. I glanced over at Benny on first base. He shrugged. David fouled off another pitch, again to the third base side. I studied him at the plate. As he got back into his batting stance, I noticed that this time he had shifted his feet slightly toward the right.

*This is the one,* I said to myself as I got ready to run.

The pitcher tossed the ball to the plate in a high underhanded arc. David followed it with his eyes, his legs bending slightly as the ball approached, his bat pulling back a little, his entire body seeming to coil just a bit. And then, like an eastern diamondback striking, he attacked.

Benny looked around the table with a big grin. "I've got it. We'll name ourselves the House of David."

David chuckled and shook his head as he put down his mug of root beer and picked up another fried onion ring. "My playing days are over."

"Over?" Benny said as he lifted his bottle of Budweiser. "Rebbe, you hit the living shit out of that ball." He took a swig of beer. "We're talking tape measure city. You cranked it, man." He sat back and belched.

"Oh, Benny," I said, grossed out.

"Excuse me, Daisy," he said in a lilting voice.

"Drop the Daisy, Goldberg," I said.

Benny Goldberg was fat and crude and gluttonous and vulgar. He was also brilliant and funny and thoughtful and savagely loyal. I loved him like the brother I never had, although I must admit that he in no way resembled the brother of my childhood daydreams.

David's towering home run had ended the game in classic

style, and the three of us went out for an early dinner at Seamus McDaniel's, a terrific Irish pub on Tamm Avenue in Dogtown. Benny had pressed David for details on his baseball background, since it was clear that he'd played some serious ball in his past. David was reluctant to talk about it, but finally admitted that he had played at San Diego State, had been drafted by the Reds, and had worked his way up to their Triple A team before his career ended in a terrible automobile crash that permanently crippled his right leg. Up until then, baseball had been his sole obsession. Severed from his moorings by the accident, he had drifted for years, holding various jobs, until he decided to study for the rabbinate. I knew there was much more to the post-baseball, pre-rabbi part of the story, but David was clearly uncomfortable talking about it, especially in a rowdy tavern. We didn't press him.

The waitress brought our dinners and set down another round of drinks—a longneck bottle of Bud for Benny, a Bass Ale on tap for me, a mug of root beer for David. As I thought back to our night at the Cardinals game, I realized that David had ordered only soft drinks that evening, too.

"Bruce Rosenthal's funeral is tomorrow," David said, poking at his salad.

"Where?" I asked.

"Columbus, Ohio. That's his hometown."

"Are you going?" I asked.

David shook his head.

"Who are you guys talking about?" Benny asked.

I explained.

"A trash compactor?" Benny said. "Jesus, who the hell did that to him?"

"We don't know," I said with a shrug. "According to David, he was awfully nervous about something he was working on. I assume that's what he wanted to talk to me about."

"I did some snooping around on Friday," David said.

"Oh?" I said, surprised. "Find anything?"

"Not really," he answered. "I spoke with the homicide detective on the case. The St. Louis one, that is. There's apparently a jurisdictional dispute—the crime was committed in St. Louis, but the body was found in Illinois, so both have opened an investigation. Anyway, the St. Louis homicide investigation is still in the early stages. They've talked to Bruce's mother and sister in Columbus, but neither knows a thing. Bruce wasn't close to his family."

"Did he have a girlfriend?" I asked.

David shook his head. "I don't think so. From what I've been able to gather, Bruce's sexual preferences went in other directions."

"Gay?" I asked.

"More than just gay," David said. "Apparently, Bruce frequented leather bars. He liked it rough. The detective said that, according to a few of Bruce's coworkers, he occasionally showed up at work with some pretty nasty looking bruises. About a year ago he came to work with a black eye and his arm in a cast. He refused to tell anyone how it happened and apparently never filed a medical claim through the office."

"Any chance that one of Bruce's boyfriends got angry," Benny said, "and decided to dump him . . . literally?"

"Possible," David said, "but not likely."

"Why not?" I asked.

"Bruce lived in the downstairs apartment of a duplex," David explained. "According to the detective, Bruce's entire apartment had been searched thoroughly long before the police got there. Very thoroughly. Mattress slashed, wallpaper ripped down. The place was trashed."

Benny nodded. "That sounds like more than just an old boyfriend looking for love letters."

"Do the police know what the searchers were looking for?" I asked.

"No," David said. "Nor whether they found it. The police assume that the break-in is tied to the homicide, but beyond that they're completely baffled."

"You said this guy lived in a duplex, right?" Benny asked. "What about his upstairs neighbors?"

"No help there," David said. "Two airline stewardesses. According to the police, they didn't see or hear anything unusual, but they haven't been around much. Both of them were out of town during most of last week."

"From what Bruce told you," I mused, "this probably had something to do with his work."

"That's what I told the police detective," David said. "He was planning to talk to one of the managing partners later on Friday. I've already made an appointment for tomorrow morning."

"An appointment?" I said. "Where?"

"Smilow and Sullivan."

"Is that where he worked?" Benny asked.

David nodded. "It's an engineering consulting firm. I'm meeting with Mr. Sullivan."

"Why?" I asked quietly.

David looked at me with sad eyes. "Because I need to. Whatever Bruce came across, whatever was bothering him, was obviously far more significant than I thought at the time."

"More than *anyone* thought," I said, "me included. You can't blame yourself for his death, David."

"I'm not, Rachel." He paused and then smiled sheepishly. "And don't worry, I'm not becoming a rabbi detective. I'll leave that to the mystery writers." The smile faded. "But I *was* Bruce's rabbi. He came to me with a concern. Whatever the police ultimately discover, I owe it to Bruce to at least make a few inquiries to try to find out what was troubling him."

"Let me warn you," I told him, "I've been there before, trying to put that kind of puzzle back together. It can be awfully frustrating."

David nodded. "I realize that. But I have to try. I've got a little to go on. He sent me some sort of list of names."

"Who did?"

"Bruce. Around the time I told him to contact you. He said he wanted me to keep the original. I'm embarrassed to say I forgot about it until yesterday."

"Whose names?" I asked, intrigued.

David shrugged. "I have no idea. I found the list at home yesterday."

"I'd like to see it," I said.

As we were leaving Seamus McDaniel's, Benny asked whether we wanted to join him down at Mississippi Nights on the Landing to hear a blues band that had been one of my favorites back when I lived in Chicago.

"Rats," I said, groaning. "I'd love to, but I've got a function tonight." I looked at David. "You should go, David. They're great. They used to play one Sunday a month at Biddy Mulligan's, which is this blues bar a few blocks from my old apartment in Chicago."

"I wish I could," he said, "but I've agreed to help out at a fund-raiser tonight."

"Oh?" I said curiously. "It's not the Armstrong fund-raiser, is it?"

He looked surprised. "Actually, yes."

I laughed. "Me, too."

"Oh, brother." Benny groaned. "Two Armstrong groupies? Folks, it's time to wake up and smell the coffee."

"Benny," I said with exasperation, "sometimes I can't believe you. Douglas Armstrong is good on every issue that counts, and he's been out there in front on most of them."

Benny looked at David and me. He smiled in resignation. "Now it all comes clear. You two are perfect for each other: a pair of mushy-headed, bleeding-hearted, tree-hugging, NPR-addicted, Sandinista-loving liberals." He placed his hand over his chest in mock rapture. "Is Saint Armstrong planning to announce his presidential candidacy tonight? Oh be still my heart."

I looked at David and sighed. "Benny's idea of a perfect presidential candidate is Vlad the Impaler."

"Now, now," Benny said, waggling his finger at me, "better heads on a stick than heads in the sand."

"Listen," I said, putting my arm around his ample waist, "while you're down at Mississippi Nights grooving on the music and plotting the return to power of your political mentor, Baby Doc Duvalier, don't forget your commitment for Tuesday night."

He paused, trying to mask the fact that he was drawing a complete blank. "I'm being committed?"

"The sooner the better. But until that blessed day arrives, you and I are supposed to be judges Tuesday night for Jennifer's government class." My niece Jennifer is in eighth grade at Ladue Junior High. Her government teacher was having his class stage a mock criminal trial in the County Courts Building, and Benny and I had agreed to act as judges. I raised my eyebrows sternly. "Remember, Uncle Benny?"

Benny snapped his fingers casually. "Of course I do. I thought you meant something else. I wouldn't forget that. Tell you what, I'll pick you up at six and we can prepare for the case over supper." He turned to David and put out his hand. "Well, rebbe, as the great Hasidic sage, Israel Baal Shem Tov, once said under remarkably similar circumstances, 'Awesome homer, dude.' "

As usual, Benny had exaggerated to the point of caricature. His Saint Armstrong bore little resemblance to the real U.S. Senator Armstrong. Douglas Armstrong, M.D., was a totally unsentimental liberal, a man of passion without a hint of sappiness, an enthusiastic deer hunter who had cosponsored every significant piece of gun control legislation during his years in the Senate, a physician who had led the charge on health-care reform, a hugely successful entrepreneur who refused to cross union picket lines, an indefatigable champion of freedom of choice who demanded that others respect his choices as well. His standard response to questions about his personal choices—whether they be a fondness for Cuban cigars, an occasional weekend gambling junket to Las Vegas, his African safari two years ago, or the ever-changing series of stunningly beautiful young women (mostly actresses and fashion models) who had graced his side and shared his bed during his years in Washington—was a blunt "None of your damn business." For a politician, it was an absolutely stirring performance.

Frankly, women—including this woman—found him stirring for an entirely different reason, as well. Douglas Armstrong was, to put it bluntly, a very sexy man. He looked the way a United States senator ought to look: tall and rangy, with close-cropped gray hair, dark blue eyes, and angular, almost severe, features— a face chiseled out of stone. He didn't merely look or act like a leader; he seemed the very embodiment of the word, which only enhanced his attractiveness. He was a widower. Edie, his wife of twenty-one years, had died of ovarian cancer two years before his first campaign for the Senate, and he had never remarried.

Ever since his reelection last year, when he defeated a conservative pro-life congressman from rural Missouri, the national media pundits had been commenting upon how "presidential" this Missouri senator seemed. Three nights ago, CBS Evening News did a feature on him that ended with Dan Rather observing, "For those who yearn for the promise of that brief, shining moment known as the Kennedy presidency, Douglas Armstrong must seem like Sir Percival himself, arriving at long last to reclaim the throne of Camelot."

Notwithstanding the growing national interest in him, Armstrong refused to make the politically safe choice when it clashed with his moral code. This evening's event was typical: he was the keynote speaker for a gathering on behalf of the Women's Reproductive Choice Clinic, a controversial abortion clinic that had been the focus of constant picketing and occasional blockades by various pro-life activists and one attempted bombing by persons unknown. The fund-raiser—complete with protesters out front, including two with large jars purportedly containing aborted fetuses—was precisely the sort of event that typical politicians avoid like the plague. Indeed, all had, I noted as I walked into the banquet hall. There was no elected official on the dais other than Senator Armstrong.

And certainly none could have matched his eloquence that evening. He had an unadorned, almost folksy speaking style— sort of the raspy country doctor come to town, but without a trace of the hick. His plain speaking style only magnified the power of his words as he described his own moral struggle with the abortion issue back in the early days of his medical practice and his eventual realization that the right choice for him (he chose not to perform the procedure) had no bearing on what was the right choice for anyone else. Neither he nor the government had any business making that choice for the one person most affected: namely, the pregnant woman.

When it was over, I joined the faithful up at the dais, crowding around him to shake his hand. As silly and childish as it may seem, shaking Douglas Armstrong's hand and looking into those cobalt blue eyes was just as exciting as the time, twelve years earlier, when I boarded the elevator at the Beverly Wilshire Hotel, at the end of a day of depositions and found myself alone for three floors with Robert Redford.

I hung around to help the other volunteers with the cleanup. Then I followed David in my car to his house, ostensibly to look at that list of names that Bruce Rosenthal had given him. The list was upstairs in his study. We got as far as the living room downstairs.

Maybe it was the thrill of shaking hands with Douglas Armstrong after the speech, or the lingering excitement over our come-from-behind softball victory, or just my growing infatuation with David Marcus, but by the time we reached the living room and David turned to ask if I wanted something to drink, I was in the grip of pure lust. Apparently, so was he. He paused in midsentence, his eyes shifting from my face slowly downward. Then he reached out, grasped me by the waistband of my skirt and pulled me against him. Pressing my face into the hollow of his neck, I inhaled deeply as he crushed me against him and yanked up my skirt from behind.

"Yes," I whispered.

Well, there are quickies and then there are quickies, but this was the quickie to end all quickies. We seemed to make love at warp speed. However long it took, it was totally focused and totally satisfying and, when it was over, totally relaxing.

As my senses gradually started functioning again, I realized that we were on the living room carpet, both of us still half-dressed. David rolled off me onto his back.

"That. Was. Wonderful," I murmured as my breathing slowed to normal.

He reached over and took my hand.

I smiled at the ceiling and gave his hand a squeeze.

An hour later, yawning and still tingling, I pulled up the covers of my bed and leaned over to set the alarm. The digital clock read 12:11 A.M. Just then the phone rang.

I lifted the receiver. "Hello?"

"I forgot to show you that list." It was David.

I leaned back against the pillow and smiled. "You showed me something much better."

"That was marvelous."

"Magical," I said dreamily. "You can just drop the list in the mail." I sighed. "I feel so—so peaceful."

"Sweet dreams, Rachel."

"Goodnight, David."

I gently replaced the phone and immediately fell asleep.

# 3

CHAPTER

TWO days later, the hand-addressed envelope bearing David's return address arrived in the morning mail, in the middle of a pile of attorney letters, court filings, bills, solicitations, bar association bulletins, and the rest of the daily postal impedimenta. Inside the envelope was a single sheet of bond paper and a small stick-on note from David. The note read, "Here's that list Bruce gave me." The document consisted of four columns of names:

| BETH SHALOM | | LABADIE GARDENS | |
|---|---|---|---|
| *P/S* | *P/A* | *P/S* | *P/A* |
| Abramawitz | Abrams | Allen | Bailey |
| Altman | Braunstein | Brown, A | Brown, R |
| Caplan | Cohen, M | Coleman | Carter |
| Cohen, S | Epstein | Jackson, R | Jackson, M |
| Freidman | Friedman | Johnson | Mitchell |
| Gutterman | Goldstein | Marshall | Perkins |
| Kohn | Gruener | Russell | Perry |
| Leiberman | Kaplansky | Shaw | Rivers |
| Perlmutter | Mittelman | Smith, B | Sleet |
| Rosenberg | Pinsky | Trotter | Smith, R |
| Rotskoff | Silverman | Washington, C | Washington, L |
| Schecter | Wexler | Young | Wells |

I stared at the list, waiting for something to click. Nothing did. Leaning back in my chair, I pondered the document. Beth Shalom sounded like the name of a Jewish synagogue, and the two columns of names beneath it sure fit. Abramawitz, Altman, Caplan, Cohen, Freidman, Gutterman—this was not the membership list for the First Baptist Church of St. Louis.

I buzzed my secretary on the intercom. "Jacki, would you bring in the Yellow Pages?"

"Be right in."

A moment later, my secretary came wobbling in on two-inch pumps and handed me the Yellow Pages.

"Thanks," I said. "Say, is that a new skirt?"

Jacki smiled demurely. "I bought it yesterday." She turned slowly. "What do you think?"

I nodded. "Very nice. Especially the pleats."

Two weeks ago I would have had trouble keeping a straight face, but I was starting to get used to my most unusual secretary. With maroon lipstick and nail polish to match the new skirt, Jacki Baird was probably the only legal secretary in town who had played linebacker on the varsity football team at Granite City High, was a member of the Panties-of-the-Month Club, could bench press 250 pounds and owned three blond wigs (including a Dolly Parton Deluxe).

At the time of our original job interview, Jacki Baird was Jack Baird—a night law school student at St. Louis University. Mr. Jack Baird had sandy brown hair, trimmed close, with long sideburns. He was in his early thirties, stood six feet three, weighed 240 pounds, had a slight beer belly and definitely had the look of a Granite City steelworker, which is what he had been for several years between high school and college. Although I was initially put off by the idea of a male secretary—particularly a massive former steelworker—he won me over during the interview. Part of it was his skill, including a typing score of ninety-three words per minute. Part was his knowledge of the law—always a big plus in a legal secretary. And part was his homely but totally earnest features, including the most soulful pair of brown eyes this side of a basset hound.

Jack Baird became my secretary six weeks ago. By noon on his first day I was ready to offer up a thanksgiving sacrifice to the Gods of the Legal Profession. He was everything a busy attorney dreams of in a secretary: efficient, smart, and skilled, with good judgment, plenty of initiative, and a working knowledge of state and federal court procedures.

Three weeks later, at the end of a busy Friday, a somewhat diffident Jack Baird came into my office to inform me of a detail about himself that he hadn't had the nerve to disclose during the job interview. To paraphrase the beer ad, it turned out that Jack Baird was everything I wanted in a legal secretary . . . and more. Specifically, he was a woman trapped in a man's body. And in exactly twelve months, he explained, he would be traveling to a hospital in Colorado for the two-and-a-half-hour surgical procedure that would complete Jack's transformation into Jacki. In order to qualify for the surgery, however, he was required (a) to live and work as a woman for a full year, and (b) to be on hormone therapy throughout that time. That meant, he had explained, that Jack was going to vanish forever over the weekend. He planned to spend Saturday and Sunday eliminating all traces —give away Jack's clothes, cut Jack's face out of all the pictures in the photo albums, take down all the books from the apartment bookshelves and add an "i" to the existing first name on the inside covers. With eyes averted he told me that he hoped that I would allow him to continue as my secretary, but that he would understand if I said no.

I thought he was joking.

When I realized he wasn't, I also realized that I was trapped. How could I reject him without despising myself? I'm no angel, and I was certainly not thrilled at the prospect of having a secretary who looked like Dick the Bruiser in drag. *Nevertheless,* I told myself, *how can I say no to him? Or her?* Jack had been a truly wonderful secretary during our three weeks together, and I had developed real affection for him. So I shrugged and I forced a smile and I told him that I was looking forward to meeting Jacki on Monday morning.

I feared that the metamorphosis would produce a brassy drag queen, but the buxom blonde who showed up for work on Monday morning was just as earnest and sweet as the ex-steelworker who had departed for good the prior Friday afternoon. And now, three weeks later, we were far enough beyond our initial awkwardness that I hadn't realized until after the fact that during our lunch today at a nearby restaurant the two of us had gone to the ladies' room at the same time. Nevertheless, I did realize it on our way back to the office. It was a bit unsettling.

"I assume you want to file those interrogatories today?" Jacki asked as I opened the Yellow Pages.

I nodded. "Let's serve them by mail."

She smiled proudly. "I already have the stamps on the envelopes."

As Jacki returned to her desk, I flipped to the heading for synagogues. There were listings for Beth Abraham and a Beth Hamedrosh, but none for Beth Shalom. On a hunch, I flipped back to the section on *Cemeteries, Jewish*. There was a Beth Hamedrosh Hagodol Cemetery, along with B'nai Amoona, Chesed Shel Emeth, Chevra Kadisha, but no Beth Shalom.

*Then again,* I reminded myself, *Beth Shalom could still be a synagogue or a Jewish cemetery—just not located in St. Louis.*

The other heading on the document was "Labadie Gardens." That sounded local. There was a street in north St. Louis called Labadie. There was also a small Missouri town west of St. Louis called Labadie. I stared at the name. Labadie Gardens didn't ring a bell. Maybe an apartment complex? Could these be lists of tenants? Again to the Yellow Pages, this time *Apartments*. There were listings for several Gardens, including one under L (Lavinia Gardens), but no Labadie Gardens. It was the same under *Cemeteries*: plenty of gardens—Bellerive Heritage Gardens, Chapel Hill Gardens, Laurel Hill Memorial Gardens, and St. Charles Memorial Gardens—but no Labadie Gardens. I flipped back to the listings for apartments. No Beth Shalom, either.

If Labadie Gardens were local, if it were indeed named after the street in north St. Louis, then it was probably located near its namesake, which would put it in a section of north St. Louis that had been black for as many years as I could remember. The names in the Labadie Gardens columns were not inconsistent with that location: Brown, Carter, Washington, Wells.

I closed the Yellow Pages and stared down at the list. Wherever and whatever Beth Shalom and Labadie Gardens were, I was completely stymied. The same was true for the headings above each column—"P/S" and "P/A." I couldn't even begin to guess what they meant, although I noted that Beth Shalom and Labadie Gardens each had a "P/S" column and a "P/A" column, and all four columns had the same number of names: twelve.

*Twelve?*

Mystified, I lifted the sheet of paper. It was heavy bond paper—an original document, not a photocopy.

*Twelve?*

The number meant nothing to me. The headings above the columns—"P/S" and "P/A"—meant nothing to me. The names Beth Shalom and Labadie Gardens meant nothing to me.

And yet this was the one document that Bruce Rosenthal had given to David Marcus. It obviously meant something to Bruce. Maybe David understood what it meant.

And even if he didn't, I admitted to myself, it was a good enough excuse to call him. I dialed his number at the synagogue and his secretary answered.

"This is Rachel, Liz. Is he in?"

"He hasn't come in yet, Rachel. Should I have him call you?"

"Sure. When do you expect him?"

"I don't know. I didn't see him yesterday and he hasn't called here this morning."

"Is he at home?"

"You might try him there. I'm just not sure. He could be doing a hospital visitation. One of our members had a bypass at St. Luke's last Friday, another one is getting chemotherapy at St. John's, poor thing. He could be seeing one of them. Or he might be at St. Louis U's library. He's been doing a lot of research there for a paper he's writing. When he calls in, I'll give him your message."

I tried David's home number and got his answering machine. I waited for the beep. "Hi, David. This is Rachel. I'm calling because I need the services of your impressive mental apparatus." I lowered my voice. "Come to think of it, I could use the services of another impressive apparatus. So give me a call, you sexy rebbe."

As soon as I hung up, the phone started ringing. I answered hopefully, but it was only my opponent in a securities fraud case, calling to complain about my response to his interrogatories.

"You call those answers, Rachel? Hell, I could get more information out of the Iraqi secret police."

"Well, then, serve a set of interrogatories on them."

"Come on, Rachel. Quit jerking me around."

"What?" I said angrily, suddenly back full-throttle in the practice of my learned profession. "*Me* jerking *you* around? How 'bout a reality check here, Jerry?"

# CHAPTER

IT was close to 9:00 P.M. and we were sitting in the car outside my sister's house. I placed my hand on his shoulder. "You were wonderful tonight."

"You sound surprised."

I shrugged. "To be honest, Benny, I had my concerns." I turned to watch my niece, Jennifer, who had reached the front porch and was ringing the doorbell. We'd given her a ride home. "However," I continued, "you were positively—well—"

"Judicial?"

"More than just judicial." I paused to wave good-bye to Jennifer as my sister opened the front door. I turned back to Benny and smiled. "Toward the end there I was ready to nominate you for the next opening on the Supremes."

Benny beamed.

He had been wonderful, too.

Thank God.

I'd had doubts from the moment he volunteered during the Passover seder dinner last month. We were all at my sister Ann's house: Richie and Ann, their two children, my mother, my Aunt Becky, Benny, and me. During dinner my niece Jennifer described the moot court project and said her teacher needed two lawyers to serve as judges.

"Could you be one of the judges, Aunt Rachel?"

"Sure," I told her. "I'd love to."

"Oh, great. It'll be so awesome having you there, Aunt Rachel."

"Yo, little woman," Benny said to Jennifer. "You need one more, right?"

She nodded uncertainly. "I guess so."

He raised his eyebrows and beamed. "You mean, 'I guess so, Your Honor.' Wait until you see me in my black gown." He turned to me, stroking his chin in feigned contemplation. "What do you think of pearls?"

I gave him a puzzled look. "What?"

"Pearls, dahling. With my black gown." He pretended to mull it over. "Yes," he said with a decisive nod. "Definitely pearls. And black pumps, of course."

Later that night, just after we'd opened the door for Elijah, I took Jennifer aside to assure her that Benny was only kidding about the pearls and pumps.

Still, I'd had my doubts up until the event itself. After all, putting Benny in a room with a group of junior high school kids sounded like a volatile formula. Even under normal circumstances, it didn't take much for Benny to assume the role of Id the Unchained.

But not so tonight. He'd been patient and courteous and helpful and impartial and logical—everything you always wanted in a judge but so rarely got. Ironically, Jennifer's classmates would have had a far more realistic view of the American judiciary with Id the Unchained as their judge instead of Mr. Justice Goldberg.

I leaned over and kissed him on the nose. "Thanks, Benny."

He shrugged, embarrassed by the praise. "I enjoyed it." As we drove off, he asked, "How's the rabbi?"

I realized that David had never returned my calls from that morning. That was odd. I wanted to hear his reactions to the list he sent me, and I wanted to see him. Mostly the latter. I hadn't seen or talked to him in two days.

"Hello?" Benny said to me.

"Would you mind swinging by his house?" I asked. "It's not that far out of the way."

"No problem. What's up?"

"Probably nothing. He sent me that list of names he mentioned the other night. I tried calling him about it today but couldn't find him."

*Two days,* I repeated to myself, feeling a little ripple of apprehension. But when we turned onto his street and approached his house, I was relieved to see his car in the driveway. Benny pulled in behind the red Saab. There was a faded Armstrong campaign bumper sticker on the rear fender. He'd be able to put a new one on before long, I thought. Just as soon as Douglas Armstrong officially launched his campaign for president.

"Thanks, Benny." I opened the car door.

"I'll wait to see if he can take you home."

As I approached the house, I noticed that the entire first floor was lit up. The second floor was dark. I rang the doorbell and waited. No answer. I rang it again and waited. From inside I could hear rock music blaring from the stereo system in the living room. The volume was turned way up. Probably too high to hear the doorbell. I reached for the brass door knocker. The force of the first rap pushed the door open slightly. I stared at the doorknob for a moment and then opened the door further.

Peering in, I called, "Hello? David?"

The music was too loud.

I stepped into the foyer. "David?" I shouted. "Hello! Is anyone there?"

I took three more steps into the house, far enough to see into the living room. All the lamps were on. The stereo was blaring the Rolling Stones' "Brown Sugar" into an empty room. Uneasy, I walked over to the stereo and turned off the power.

Dead silence. I waited, straining my ears.

"David?" I called. My throat felt pinched. "Hello?"

I walked around the first floor, moving cautiously from one brightly lit room to the next. All were empty.

I stopped at the foot of the stairs leading up to the second floor. Staring up into the darkness, I could feel my anxiety edging toward dread.

"What's up?"

I jumped at the sound of Benny's voice. He was standing in the foyer. I gave him a worried shrug. "I don't know. No one answers."

He joined me at the foot of the stairs.

"David?" I called.

No response.

I flipped on the light to the second-floor landing. Benny and I started up the stairs, stopping every few steps to listen. There was no sound other than the creak of the stairs. I reached the top and turned toward his room.

"Oh, no," I gasped, stumbling backward against a wall.

Spray-painted in black on the white wall outside David's bedroom was a dripping swastika. I stared in horror, my eyes darting between the black swastika and the closed bedroom door.

"David," I whispered, moving toward his bedroom. I stopped at the door, my heart pounding. I stared at the doorknob.

*Please, God,* I prayed, *please, please, please.*

"Wait," Benny said, stepping in front of me.

I stood behind him as he opened the door. The light from the hallway illuminated the darkened room.

All I could see from where I stood was the top of the headboard, which was splattered with reds and grays. On the wall above the headboard were the words *Die Nigger Lover* spray-painted in dripping black.

The earth seemed to shift on its axis.

"Oh God," I said as I staggered forward, grabbing Benny's right shoulder. "David. Oh God."

Benny blocked me with his body. "No," he said, his right arm reaching back roughly to push me behind him. He backed up and pulled the door shut. He turned to me, his eyes wide. "Call the police."

I tried to push around him toward the door.

"No," he said fiercely, grabbing me by the shoulders. "You can't help him, Rachel. Go downstairs. Call the police."

I stared up at Benny, tears blurring my vision.

"No, Rachel."

Slowly, I turned away.

# 5

CHAPTER

*IT just don't feel right.*

Of the thousands of words spoken on the subject of David's death during the dreary aftermath, it was those five that stuck.

*It just don't feel right.*

Even after the dramatic shootout that ended the murder investigation with the deaths of Eugene Worrell and five of his followers.

*It just don't feel right.*

Five words, uttered in the wee hours of that awful first night. Uttered at the bottom of the stairs by the white detective as I sat in the living room of David's house, staring at the wall.

"It just don't feel right."

The words had registered slowly, like a distant echo. I shifted my gaze from the wall to the man who had uttered them. He was the older of the two detectives, the white one, the one called Hank. He was short and chunky, with a large gray walrus mustache that covered his lower lip when his mouth was closed.

"Say what?" the other detective said. He was the black one, the skinny one with the goatee and shaved head, the one called Joe.

The older one tugged at his mustache and shook his head. He was bald, and there were large bags under his eyes.

After a moment, the black one shrugged. "Maybe."

During these bleak first days after David's death, I thought that my sense of incompleteness, of matters left unresolved, was caused, at least in part, by the way David's family handled the arrangements, which was basically to get his body out of St. Louis ASAP. Within hours of the autopsy, the corpse was on a plane to Phoenix for a private graveside funeral, family only.

Although there was a memorial service in St. Louis, it wasn't a real funeral. There was no casket; indeed, as I sat in the front row of the chapel, dazed, waiting for the eulogies to begin, I couldn't blank out the fact that David was already in the ground halfway across the country. Moreover, the combination of high-powered speakers, jostling Minicam TV news crews, and photographers with cameras set on autodrive seemed to heighten the unreality of the experience.

Although there was an impressive array of speakers, I remembered very little of what they said. In addition to the head rabbi and the president of David's congregation, those delivering eulogies included St. Louis Mayor Freeman Bosley, Jr., Missouri Congressman Richard Gephardt, and Senator Douglas Armstrong. The one thing I do recall was Senator Armstrong pausing to offer me his condolences. "I am sorry, Rachel," he said gently, taking my hand in his. "He was an exceptional human being."

I looked up, deeply touched by what he said.

The sense of incompleteness continued after the memorial service. Part of it was caused by the absence of the usual Jewish rituals and gatherings that help support the mourners and ease the pain. The family was in Phoenix, so there was no one sitting shivah in St. Louis. But most of the incompleteness was due to the fact that David's murderers were still at large.

That seemed to change dramatically a few days after the memorial service, the result of good luck and solid police work. The coroner had placed the time of David's death at approximately twenty-four hours before Benny and I found him. In cross-checking other police reports, the detectives came across a hit-and-run traffic accident report in David's neighborhood on the night he died, i.e., the night before I found him. A young couple returning from a party at midnight had been rammed by a rusted Buick Riviera as they passed David's street. The husband claimed he had stopped at the traffic sign and then proceeded into the intersection, at which point the Riviera ran its stop sign and hit them broadside. The Riviera backed up and pulled away with a squeal of its tires. Unfortunately, they weren't able to get the Riviera's license plate. All they could say for sure was that there were three men in the car: two in the front seat and one in the back.

Two days later, after every police department in metropolitan St. Louis had been faxed a description of the car, two officers found an abandoned Riviera in the Spanish Lake area. The car not only matched the description of the hit-and-run car but had paint chips on the front bumper that matched the paint on the other car involved in the hit-and-run. Although the license plates were gone, the police were able to trace the car by its vehicle identification number. It was registered in the name of Eugene Worrell of Jefferson County, Missouri.

Eugene Worrell was unmarried, thirty-one years old, and worked the day shift on the minivan line in the Chrysler plant in Fenton. Although he had been arrested only twice—a drunk-and-disorderly outside a tavern in Sunset Hills and an attempted statutory rape at a motel off Watson Road—there were detailed files on him maintained by several police departments, the St. Louis office of the FBI and the Eastern Missouri chapters of the NAACP and the B'nai B'rith Anti-Defamation League. This was because the United Auto Workers of America Local 325 was not the only organization to which Eugene belonged. He was also commandant of the Himmler Echelon, a small neo-Nazi group in Jefferson County that was loosely affiliated with the Aryan Nation.

According to the surviving members of the Himmler Echelon, Worrell swore he'd been framed. His "proof" was that he had personally reported his car stolen two days before it was discovered in Spanish Lake. In the aftermath of the shootout, the police dismissed the theft report as an inept attempt by a guilty man to cover his tracks. As for his claim that he'd been framed, it was precisely what one might expect from someone whose FBI personality profile included the terms "paranoid," "filled with rage," and "persecution complex (believes government out to kill him)."

In a hospital interview, one of the survivors said that Eugene Worrell had told his men of an anonymous midnight telephone call warning him that the police were coming to kill him. In response to the phone tip, Worrell gathered the rest of the Himmler Echelon at his house that night. They were armed and ready when the first squad cars arrived the following evening at dusk. Officers Dan Harter and Jimmy Engle got within ten yards of the front porch before an eruption of automatic gunfire literally knocked them off their feet, killing both immediately. It was not an astute strategic move. Two hours later, with police helicopters hovering overhead and dozens of squad cars surrounding the cordoned perimeter, a twenty-four-man SWAT team charged the house, backed by huge spotlights that virtually blinded the nine men inside. "It was like shooting fish in a barrel," one unidentified SWAT team member later commented. Fishing season lasted exactly one minute and twenty-seven seconds. By then, six of the nine members of the Himmler Echelon, including Eugene Worrell, were dead. The remaining three were wounded and disarmed.

The next day, at a press conference covered by the local and national media, the police officially announced the successful conclusion of their investigation into the murder of Rabbi David Marcus.

Case closed, bad guys caught, move on to the next one.

Except for me.

I was still haunted by a sense of incompleteness, of matters left unresolved. Those same five words stood out with graphic clarity.

*It just don't feel right.*

Which was why, two days after the big shootout, I was seated across the table from Detective Hank Nichols of the University City Police Department.

"Just a gut feeling," he said. He tugged at his walrus mustache and shrugged. "But sometimes your gut's wrong."

"Whether you were right or wrong," I said, "what didn't feel right to you?"

He stroked his mustache as he studied me. "Well," he finally said, "it didn't seem like the work of amateurs."

"What do you mean?"

"Your typical hate-crime perpetrators are amateurs—losers with guns. But that homicide"—he shrugged, puzzled—"it just didn't feel like the work of amateurs."

"Why?"

"That was professional work, Miss Gold. A quick clean head shot." He shook his head. "None of Worrell's people had that kind of training. Men like his, you expect sloppiness. You expect something like the traffic accident that night. That was pure amateur hour. But not the kill shot." He paused. "There were other things."

"Such as?"

"No fingerprints, no visible signs of entry. You'd expect both with amateurs."

"Anything else?"

"Well," he said uncertainly, "we checked that house pretty careful. I can't pinpoint why, but I just had the sense that the place had been searched. And if so, it was done by someone who took pains to make sure it didn't look like it had been searched."

"Was anything missing?"

He gave me a weary smile. "Hard to know what's missing unless you know what was there in the first place." He paused, his eyes far away.

"Why did it bother you that the place might have been searched?"

"Because it doesn't fit the MO of one of those skinhead groups. A hate crime is a lynching, Miss Gold. You either kill your man or you don't, but you don't go search his house."

"Maybe they were looking for money," I said.

"I suppose," he said without conviction. "We'll just have to see what turns up."

"Did you have any other suspects before you found out about the accident?"

He shook his head solemnly.

"If Worrell was the one who killed him, why would he report his car as stolen?"

"Stupidity. Maybe he thought it would make him seem innocent. I don't pretend to know how his mind worked."

"Did he have an alibi?"

"Not much of one. The three who survived, they claimed they'd all been playing cards that night in his basement." He shook his head. "Pretty lame."

I studied Nichols. "Detective, do you think Worrell and his thugs killed him?"

He thought it over and scratched his neck uncomfortably. "I just don't know, Miss Gold. Looking back, it sure seems more likely than not. You just don't ever know for sure. Some cases end like that."

I thanked him and drove back to my office.

I'd gone to the police station for reassurance. More than anything, I wanted to know that David's murder had been avenged. I'd gone to see Detective Nichols hoping for the closure I needed to get on with my life. He wasn't able to give me that.

*It just don't feel right.*

———

"For chrissakes," Benny said as he refilled my wineglass, "the only thing missing is a signed confession."

I picking moodily at my salad. "That's a big thing to be missing."

"Rachel, the reason he didn't sign a confession is that the cops blew his fucking head off before they could hand him a pen."

In an effort to cheer me up, Benny had invited me over to his apartment for dinner.

"What if Worrell and his men were set up?" I asked.

Benny looked at me as if I were crazy. "What makes you think they were set up?"

I shrugged. "Detective Nichols said that the murder looked like it had been done by a pro. What kind of professional hit man would be clumsy enough to ram into another car while leaving the scene of the crime?"

"But these weren't professional hit men, Rachel. They were slimeballs with room-temp IQs."

"Maybe. Or maybe they were professional hit men who wanted to make sure that someone would be able to remember that one particular car was in David's neighborhood on the night of the murder. What better way than to smash it into another car?"

"Which means you have to assume that your professionals really did steal his car."

"Right."

Benny raised his eyebrows. "Rachel, you're getting to sound like one of the Kennedy assassination conspiracy nuts."

"It's not far-fetched."

"Right," he said sarcastically.

"It's not," I protested. "If someone else wanted him dead, what better way to do it than to make it look like the crime was committed by a neo-Nazi group? And don't forget that anonymous telephone tip."

"Whoa," Benny said, signaling for a time-out. "Now you're saying that the phone call was part of the setup?"

"What better way to panic a violent paranoid into a shootout with the cops?"

"Wait a minute. Doesn't it make more sense that it was from a sympathetic cop involved in the investigation?"

"A cop?" I asked.

"Of course a cop. Is it beyond the realm of reason to suppose that there might be at least one rural Missouri cop who is sympathetic to the tenets of a white supremacist organization?"

I thought it over. "Maybe. But not necessarily. If someone wanted to blame David's murder on Eugene Worrell and then increase the odds that Worrell would be dead before his trial, you'd make sure someone told him that the government had framed him and was now coming to kill him."

"Someone?" Benny said. "Who's this mysterious someone who wants David Marcus dead? Oliver North? Ernst Blofeld? Come on, Rachel. He was a decent, good-hearted rabbi who once played minor league baseball. The only type of person with any reason to kill him would be a deranged, Jew-hating, lowlife piece of pond scum like Eugene Worrell."

"I know." I gave him a sad smile. "It's logical, it makes sense, it's probably true. But I'm not one hundred percent convinced, yet. I need to get to there, Benny. I have to find a way to get there. Otherwise it's just going to haunt me. I can't—help it." My eyes filled with tears. I used the napkin to wipe my eyes and blow my nose. "I owe it to him."

"Why?" he said gently.

I took a deep breath and exhaled slowly. "Because he was special. Because he would have done it if I were the victim." I paused, struggling to keep my composure. "If it turns out that Worrell was the killer, fine. But I have to know that for sure, and I don't, yet."

"So what are you going to do?"

"I'm going to try to eliminate the other possibility."

"What is the other possibility?"

"I'm not sure," I said. "All I know is that when Bruce Rosenthal came to David Marcus, he was extremely nervous and looking for an attorney. Someone killed him a few days later. When David decided to look into Bruce's death, someone killed him a few days later. If Bruce's death had nothing to do with David's death, then I suppose I'd be willing to accept that those skinheads killed David. But first I've got to satisfy myself that David's death and Bruce's death aren't connected."

"How are you going to do that?"

I looked at Benny and sighed. "I don't know."

# 6

CHAPTER

REVENGE of the nerds comes in two flavors: Ivy League and MIT.

The Ivy League version is downright creepy, as I witnessed one winter weekend during my second year at Harvard Law School. I went down to New Haven to visit a friend, and he took me to a Yale hockey game. Yale was playing the University of Connecticut, and the game was a mismatch. By the middle of the final period, UConn had built up a seven-goal lead. At that point, the Yale fans—a truly ragtag collection of sports geeks—started pointing at the UConn fans on the other side of the ice while chanting in unison:

*That's alright, that's okay,*
*You're going to work for us someday!*
*That's alright, that's okay,*
*You're going to work for us someday!*

The MIT version, while just as arrogant, is more pocket-protector arrogance. It's more Herbie Mintler, who sat across the aisle from me in high school geometry, his eyes distorted by the thick lenses of his hornrim glasses. Herbie Mintler, whose daily costume included an ill-fitting short-sleeved shirt buttoned to the collar and decorated with black-and-white photographic scenes of New York City and a pair of black slacks belted so high on the waist that when he walked it looked like his hips were fused to his rib cage. Herbie Mintler, who occasionally cleaned his ears with a paperclip during class and wiped the ear wax off on his slacks. Herbie Mintler, who averted his eyes and made an embarrassed grunt whenever I said hello to him in the hallways. Herbie Mintler, who graduated with the highest grade point average in the class, went on to MIT, and returned for our tenth reunion with a stunning brunette on his arm and a personal net worth, according to *Newsweek* magazine, in excess of $120 million (thanks to his ownership of two essential patents in the field of MRI technology).

Revenge of the nerds. Ivy League or MIT? Hiram Sullivan, managing partner of the engineering consulting firm of Smilow & Sullivan, Ltd., seemed a dangerous combination of both. A Ninja Nerd. He was in his early fifties and had the lean, wiry look of a man who swims forty laps every morning at dawn and hasn't eaten dessert in twenty years.

He squinted at me from behind his small wire-rimmed glasses and shook his head. "I've already answered that," he snapped. He had a cold, high-pitched voice. "The police asked me the very same question. I spent three hours with them. I provided answers to every conceivable question about young Rosenthal. As a matter of fact, I went down to the police station to answer them."

I tried an acquiescent smile. "That's why I came to your office, Mr. Sullivan. I don't want to inconvenience you, and I certainly don't want three hours of your time, sir."

He crossed his arms over his chest and leaned back from his big desk. "Three hours? You won't get three more minutes of my time, Miss Gold."

He was bald with a high forehead and visible blue veins at each temple. The veins were bulging at the moment. "I cooperated with the police," he continued, "because obviously we would like to see young Rosenthal's killer caught. But that is as far as our obligation reaches. I have no valid reason to talk to you. You are not the police, you are not the prosecutor. And—" he paused to squint at me "—you are not actually his lawyer. You conceded as much yourself, Miss Gold. You said he talked about retaining you, but he never did. You have shown me no letter of retention, no power of attorney. Young Rosenthal worked on a variety of important matters for this firm. Many are confidential. I cannot and will not divulge such information to a private individual with no official capacity in the matter. That is precisely what I told that unfortunate rabbi. That is what I am telling you as well. The police have my answers. You will just have to rely upon them to solve the crime. And now it is time for you to leave."

I tried another question, but that only made him more adamant. He wouldn't even tell me what David Marcus had asked him during their meeting. Frustrated, but not wanting to burn any bridges yet, I ended the meeting on what I hoped was a polite note. "Here's my card, Mr. Sullivan," I said, sliding it across the desk toward him. "I'm extremely concerned about Bruce Rosenthal's death, especially the possibility that it might be connected to Rabbi Marcus' death. I plan to keep asking people questions until I'm satisfied. Please call me if you have any information you're willing to share."

He frowned at my business card as if it were a dead mouse, and then leaned forward to press the intercom button on his telephone. "Donna, it's time for you to escort Miss Gold back to the lobby."

Fifteen seconds later, Donna marched into the room. She stood nearly six feet tall, with close-cropped blond hair framing a severe face. She looked like Central Casting's choice for the dental hygienist at the offices of the Marquis de Sade, D.D.S. The only accessories missing were the studded breastplate, the thigh-high leather boots, and the ominous coil of dental floss.

On the way down the hallway toward the reception area, Donna the Dominatrix and I passed an empty conference room.

I stopped with a flustered expression. "Oh, I just remembered," I said to her, "I'm supposed to call the court clerk about an oral argument." I pretended to check my watch nervously. Agitated, I turned toward the conference room. "Would it be okay if I called from here? It'll only take a minute."

She scowled. "Dial nine for an outside line."

I thanked her and went into the conference room, closing the door behind me. The telephone was on the credenza against the far wall. I picked up the receiver and dialed Sports Line. As the call went through, I opened the top drawer. As I expected, inside the drawer was a Smilow & Sullivan Office Telephone Directory. It consisted of two pages stapled together. All professionals were listed in one column, all secretaries in another, and all administrative and support staff in two others. It was dated in the upper right corner. As I had hoped, the Smilow & Sullivan directory was just like the telephone directory in the conference room of a typical law firm: it was about one month out of date. Peering down the column of engineers and accountants, I found him under the Rs:

| Roberts, Michael E. | (Mary G.) | x243 |
| Rosenthal, Bruce A. | (Karen H.) | x332 |
| Rucker, Carol B. | (Dixie C.) | x213 |

Karen H. was in the column of secretaries, under the H's:

| Harmon, Karen | x432 |

I heard the door open behind me. "Thank you so much," I said into the phone as I slid the directory back into the drawer. On the other end of the phone a voice was running through last night's American League box scores. I stared down at the name again: *Harmon, Karen.* "I'll be in the courtroom at two o'clock," I said into the phone, "and I'll be sure to notify the other counsel."

I hung up and turned toward the door, in the process sliding the drawer closed with my hip.

Donna stood there with her arms crossed, looking as if she'd like to polish my teeth with an industrial sander. I gave her my sweetest smile. "Thanks a bunch," I said.

She pivoted on her heel, marched me to the main reception area, and left me there. I spotted the visitors' telephone on a low table in the waiting area and waited until Donna was out of sight. Then I turned to the perky blond receptionist. "Would you mind if I used your phone to make a local call?"

"Go right ahead, honey."

"I'm not sure of the phone number."

"Here you go." She handed me the Southwestern Bell White Pages for Greater St. Louis. I flipped through the H's and found three listings for *Harmon, K*—one in Webster Groves, one in north St. Louis, and one in what sounded like an apartment complex way out west in Chesterfield. The third listing sounded the most likely. Pretending to use the listing as a reference, I dialed Sports Line again and engaged in what I hoped sounded like a conversation with a woman named Margi over the rescheduling of a lunch appointment. I hung up and returned the telephone directory to the receptionist.

"By the way," I said to her with a lively smile, "how's Karen Harmon doing these days?"

"Y'all know Karen?" she answered in a cheerful Southern drawl.

"Sure. Is she still in that apartment in Chesterfield?"

"Sure is. Matter of fact, Karen had me over last summer. Isn't that pool something?"

We talked long enough for me to change the topic from Karen Harmon's swimming pool to summer vacations down at the Lake of the Ozarks, which was the receptionist's favorite spot "in the whole wide world." My goal was to downplay the Karen Harmon aspect of our discussion so that I could leave without risking her calling Karen to come out to see her friend or asking me to leave a name and message for Karen. It worked. A visitor arrived, the phone started ringing, I left with a wave.

The following night at 6:30 I was sitting in my car in the parking area out front of the apartment and townhouse complex known as Tuscany Crossing. I'd been there for about forty minutes. I was waiting for the arrival of an emerald green Suzuki Sidekick (Missouri license plate number WGH 570), which Karen Harmon had financed with an automobile loan from Mark Twain Bank (on which she still owed $8,723.87 as of the end of last month). It's spooky how much information you can obtain on anyone with just a computer and a few commonly available data banks. In less than fifteen minutes, I knew the current balance on her Visa, MasterCard, Famous-Barr, Dillard's, and Discover credit card accounts, I knew the monthly rental payment on her apartment, and I knew the names and telephone numbers of the neighbors on either side of her.

But what I couldn't access on the computer was what she knew about Bruce Rosenthal. I just hoped Karen Harmon knew more about what her ex-boss was working on or worried about than Bruce's mother and sister did. Yesterday morning, after leaving the offices of Smilow & Sullivan, I had called Bruce Rosenthal's mother in Columbus to ask if I could meet with her and her daughter later that day. She reluctantly agreed to meet. I caught the noon Southwest Airlines flight to Columbus, rented a car at the airport, and drove out to her small frame house in the suburb of Bexley. Originally, I had considered just talking to them over the phone, but ultimately decided to make the trip. You can often get more out of a witness in person than over the phone.

Not this time though. It was a wasted trip. Thelma Rosenthal did not have a close relationship with her son, and neither did her married daughter, Robin Dahlberg. In fact, Bruce and Robin had not even talked since last Thanksgiving, when Bruce came in for the holiday weekend. That was more than five months ago. Although Bruce dutifully called his mother every Sunday, he talked very little about himself or his work. She had spoken with him briefly on his last Sunday, but the only personal part of the conversation she could remember was asking him whether he was dating any nice girls—a question that (as usual, according to her) made him sullen and even less communicative. Thelma Rosenthal had no recollection whatsoever of any conversation with her son during his last few months about any aspect of his work or anything that might have been disturbing him. I caught the last flight to St. Louis that night, crossed Thelma and Robin off my list, and circled Karen Harmon's name.

At 6:42 P.M., the green Suzuki convertible pulled into the lot and parked one row over from me. I watched as a striking redhead with long wavy hair got out of the car. She was carrying a gym bag, a purse, and clothes on a hanger. She was wearing white Reeboks and a Spandex exercise outfit consisting of a bright turquoise leotard cut high on the hips with a thong back over skintight navy bicycle shorts. Karen Harmon was pretty but not petite. She had large shoulders, large hips, large breasts. I judged her at my height, but twenty pounds heavier.

I got out of my car and walked quickly after her. When we were about ten feet apart, I called, "Karen?"

She turned with a tentative smile. "Yes?"

"I'm Rachel Gold. I was Bruce Rosenthal's attorney. I wonder if I could talk to you for a few minutes about Bruce."

She looked me over as she pondered the request. Fortunately, I had dressed for a court hearing that day and was wearing a conservative glen plaid suit, gold link necklace, and gold ropeknot earrings.

"Okay," she said with a congenial shrug. "I hope you don't mind if I eat while we talk. I just came from my aerobics class, and I'm starving."

Karen's little one-bedroom apartment was just as sunny and friendly as its occupant. There was a brightly colored crocheted afghan on the couch. On her bed was a homemade quilt and three stuffed animals. On the wall over the television was a framed "Ski

Utah!" poster. Over the couch was a framed poster of what appeared to be the Mormon Tabernacle in Salt Lake City. Scattered throughout the living room and kitchen and bedroom were about a dozen framed photographs of a pleasant-looking young man with thinning blond hair—on horseback, on a ski slope, sharing a milkshake with Karen, holding hands at the Arch.

The microwave oven dinged. I went into the kitchen, removed her Weight Watchers chicken mirabella from the microwave and placed it on the counter. A moment later Karen came in from the bedroom. She was wearing a robe, having changed out of her exercise clothes.

"Sure you don't want any?" she asked again.

"No, thanks."

"How about something to drink?" She opened the refrigerator. "Let's see, I have Diet Seven-Up and orange juice and Clearly Canadian." She turned to me. "I'm having a Diet Seven-Up. How about you?"

I smiled. "Okay. Same thing. Sounds good."

When we were both seated at the tiny kitchen table, I gestured toward one of framed photos of the blond guy. "Your boyfriend?"

She nodded radiantly. "William," she said, holding up her left hand to show me the modest diamond engagement ring.

"Congratulations."

"We're going to get married as soon as he gets back from Brazil."

"When's that?"

"Next December. I can't wait."

"Is he down there on business?"

"No, he's on a mission."

"Really?" I said uncertainly.

She noticed my expression. "For the church."

I recalled the Utah posters in the living room. "Ah, the Mormon Church?"

She nodded. "William's on a two-year mission in Brazil. It's already been more than a year."

As she ate dinner, we made small talk about life in Brazil and her wedding plans. Karen Harmon was an easy person to like: cheerful, outgoing, and warmhearted, with a bright, generous laugh. Almost reluctantly, I brought the conversation around to the purpose of my visit.

"I met with Hiram Sullivan yesterday morning," I said.

"Mr. Sullivan?" she said. "Really?"

I nodded. "He wasn't willing to tell me much about Bruce." I explained my interest in Bruce Rosenthal's death and my concern that it might be linked to another death. "Bruce was upset when he called me," I continued. "He wanted to talk to a lawyer. I think it had something to do with his work. Something he had discovered, probably about a client."

Karen nodded seriously. "Okay."

"Was he working on many matters the last month or so?"

Karen thought it over. "No," she said. "I think he was spending most of his time on the SLP deal."

"Good."

"Really?" She looked surprised.

"It narrows the hunt," I explained. "I was afraid you were going to tell me there were dozens of different matters."

"Well," she said with a frown, trying to remember, "there may have been one or two small projects, but nothing big. It was mostly SLP. If he was billing time to other projects, they'd show up on his time sheets. If it helps, I could check them for you."

"That would be great, Karen. Thanks."

"Sure," she said with a smile. "Actually, you're starting to get me kind of curious."

I shrugged good-naturedly. "It's contagious. You said he was working on the SLD deal."

"P, not D. SLP."

"What is it?"

She gave me a embarrassed look. "I'm not exactly sure."

"Is it confidential?"

"Oh, no. It's been in the newspapers, I think, or at least the

*Wall Street Journal.* I know, because Bruce had me make copies of some articles from the *Journal.* SLP is a foreign company. French, I think. Its initials are SLP."

"Was your firm doing work for them?"

She nodded. "They're buying a company or a division of a company here. It's called Chemitoc, Chemitac, Chemi-something."

"Chemitex Bioproducts?"

She smiled. "That's it."

"What was Bruce doing on the deal?"

"Some of the due diligence."

"Ahh," I said with a knowing smile.

*Due diligence.* Utter that dull gray phrase around a pack of corporate lawyers and watch them leer. That's because the final tab for the due diligence in a significant transaction will easily exceed ten million dollars. Those kinds of numbers enchant even the most somber of practitioners.

Due diligence is the stage in every corporate acquisition between the handshake and the closing, between the engagement party and the wedding vows, between that press release announcing the deal and the day the New York Stock Exchange opens with one less listed company. Due diligence is what squadrons of lawyers, accountants, and other specialists do to the books and records and the assets and liabilities of the target company during the months before closing. Think of it as a massive and extraordinarily expensive physical, with the target company face down and naked on the examination table for weeks, or even months. Usually, the patient checks out fine, and the deal goes through. But occasionally the head of the due diligence team removes his rubber gloves, steps out in the hallway, and grimly reports to the board of directors that, in the words of Gertrude Stein, his team has discovered that there is no there there, or even worse, that there is something rotten in the division in Denmark. That's when the spin doctors put out the carefully worded release explaining that, after lengthy and careful consideration, the board of directors had concluded that the goal of maximizing shareholder value blah blah blah.

"Where was Bruce doing the due diligence?" I asked.

"In town. Chemitex is south on Hampton Avenue. Bruce spent a lot of time down there over the past two months."

"What sort of due diligence?"

"I'm not sure. You see, he was a chemical engineer *and* he was an accountant. Sometimes they had him do engineering stuff, sometimes accounting stuff, sometimes both." She raised her eyebrows. "He was really smart."

"What kinds of things did you do for him?"

"Some typing, some filing, answering the phones—you know, secretary stuff. I had two other bosses, too. It keeps you busy."

"Did he have you do any typing or filing on the SLP deal?"

She frowned in thought. "Not much typing. Just an occasional dictation tape or letter, but that's all. He had a laptop computer that he took with him everywhere. As for filing, he kept his SLP documents in the file drawers in his office and did most of the filing, but I helped keep them organized."

"Was that typical?"

"Sort of, at least on the big due diligence projects. When they're over, I usually have to type up all the reports and memos to the file, but I don't do much while they're still going on. That's 'cause the guys are usually out of the office reviewing the documents at the business site."

"Is the SLP deal still going on?"

"Oh, yes. Definitely."

"Are there others at the firm working on it?"

"I think three others. But none of them had Bruce's background."

"What do you mean?"

"He was the only chemical engineer working on it. He was the only one reviewing the drug files."

"Is someone taking over his part of the due diligence?"

"I don't think so. At the end of last week I was told to pack up his files and ship them off to the lawyers for SLP."

"Did anyone tell you why?"

She smiled at my naïveté. "No one tells secretaries why. But I asked around 'cause I was curious. I heard that SLP decided to have its own scientists review Bruce's files instead of postponing the whole deal to wait for another chemical engineer to get up to speed. It would have taken a long time. Bruce had been working on it for almost two months."

"Did Smilow and Sullivan save a copy of Bruce's due diligence files?"

She shook her head. "There were thousands of documents." She paused, her forehead wrinkling in thought.

"What is it?" I asked.

"I don't know," she said tentatively. "He missed three days of work before we found out he was dead. None of us knew anything was wrong at first. I thought maybe he was busy down at Chemitex and too busy to call. Anyway, I went into his office that first day to straighten up." She paused. "His due diligence files were a mess."

"That was unusual?"

She nodded. "Definitely. Remember, Bruce was an engineer *and* an accountant. He kept everything in that office neat and organized. That's why I remembered about those due diligence files. I straightened them as best I could. I thought to myself that maybe he came in that morning real early looking for something in a big hurry and made the mess. At least, that's the way it looked—like someone searching for something in a big hurry."

"Was anything missing?"

"I wouldn't have been able to tell, Rachel. There were so many documents to begin with, including a bunch written in scientific gobbledygook. I tried to put the files back together that first day. Bruce didn't come in the next day. That's when I started to get nervous. Finally, Mr. Sullivan had us report him missing. The police talked to me. I answered their questions, told them what he was working on, showed them his office. I was really worried by then. Having the police there made it seem serious. After they left, I went back into his office to look around. The first thing I noticed were those due diligence files."

"What?"

"They were messed up again—even more so than the first time. Maybe the police did it, but I don't think so."

"Why?" I asked.

"Nothing else in his office was messed up. Just those darn files."

"What kind of documents were in those files?"

"A real mishmash. Bruce's work papers and spreadsheets, of course, and then gobs and gobs of photocopies of company documents. That's how Bruce did due diligence on these deals. He would go down to the company, dig into their files and start tagging documents to be copied. Hundreds of documents. Then he'd come back to the office with all those copies and stay there till midnight sorting them and marking them up and arranging them in different folders and typing notes and comments on his laptop."

"Do you remember what kind of documents he copied?"

She shrugged. "Not specifically. They were mostly the usual types he'd copy when he did due diligence—memos, lab reports, scientific stuff, correspondence, financial records."

I leaned back, trying to make sense out of what she had noticed about the state of his files. According to the police detective I had spoken with earlier that day, Bruce Rosenthal had most likely been assaulted in the firm's offices late at night and then shoved into the trash chute, feet first. Judging by the extent of the fractures in his leg bones, he had fallen a good distance, which meant he probably had been dumped into the trash chute opening on the Smilow & Sullivan floor.

There was, I realized, an innocent explanation *and* there was a far darker one for the condition of Bruce's due diligence files. The innocent explanation was that Bruce himself had messed up his files the first time, looking for something in a rush, and the police had messed them up the second time. The darker explanation was that whoever killed Bruce had gone into his office the first time, probably right after he dumped the body down the chute, looking for a specific document or, more likely, a specific group of documents. A day or two later, the killer discovered that he may have missed one or more of the key documents, so he sneaked back into the office to search again.

I looked at Karen. She was wiping her eyes. "Are you okay?"

She nodded her head, sniffling. "I was just thinking about poor Bruce. He wasn't real friendly, but he never did anything nasty to me. And even if he had, no one deserves to die that way."

I handed her a tissue. When she got her emotions back under control, she made us both some herbal tea. We took our mugs to the living room.

I took a sip of tea and asked, "During the last few weeks, did he mention any concerns or worries?"

She shook her head. "No."

"Where did Bruce keep his due diligence notes?"

"Mostly in his laptop computer. He took it with him just about everywhere—to job sites, to meetings out of the office, on business trips. Sometimes he dictated his notes into one of those portable recorders. But when he did that, he always had me type them up right away. He'd make corrections and have me copy the corrected version onto a disk so that he could load it into his computer."

"Did he ever have you do that on the SLP deal?"

"A few times."

"Do you remember what you typed?"

"No, but I might recognize it if it's still in his computer."

"Where is his computer?"

"Probably at the office."

"Really? The police didn't take it?"

She shook her head. "We made them a copy of everything on the hard drive. I heard that Mr. Sullivan didn't want them to take the computer. Those things cost thousands of dollars, you know, and he's a real penny-pincher."

I leaned forward. "Karen, do you think you could get me a copy of whatever files are in his computer?"

"Well," she said hesitantly, "I guess so."

"Maybe there's something in there that will tell us what he was so worried about."

"I can try tomorrow," she said.

I took out one of my business cards, wrote my home phone number on it, and handed it to her. "This is my office number, and this is my home number. Don't tell anyone at the office why you want his computer files. If you get asked, have a cover story ready."

"Okay."

"One last thing," I said, reaching into my briefcase. "There was a list Bruce gave my friend. I'm not sure what it is, but maybe you typed it for him. Or maybe he found it on his SLP due diligence. Here's a copy." I handed her the list. "I have the original."

I came around behind so that I could look at the list too:

| BETH SHALOM | | LABADIE GARDENS | |
|---|---|---|---|
| *P/S* | *P/A* | *P/S* | *P/A* |
| Abramawitz | Abrams | Allen | Bailey |
| Altman | Braunstein | Brown, A | Brown, R |
| Caplan | Cohen, M | Coleman | Carter |
| Cohen, S | Epstein | Jackson, R | Jackson, M |
| Freidman | Friedman | Johnson | Mitchell |
| Gutterman | Goldstein | Marshall | Perkins |
| Kohn | Gruener | Russell | Perry |
| Leiberman | Kaplansky | Shaw | Rivers |
| Perlmutter | Mittelman | Smith, B | Sleet |
| Rosenberg | Pinsky | Trotter | Smith, R |
| Rotskoff | Silverman | Washington, C | Washington, L |
| Schecter | Wexler | Young | Wells |

She studied the list and then looked over her shoulder at me. "I don't recognize it."

"You don't think you typed it?"

She shook her head. "I don't remember ever using that font."

"Have you seen that font on other documents?"

She frowned as she examined the document. "I can't tell for sure. I can't remember if I ever saw it in any of the due diligence files. Gosh, I wish we still had those files."

I came back around to the couch and started getting my things ready. "You said you were told to send those files to SLP's lawyers. Do you remember who the lawyers were?"

"No, but I can find that out real easy tomorrow. I still have a copy of the Federal Express receipts in the file. I'll check them in the morning and give you the name when I call on the computer files."

She walked me to the door.

"Karen," I said, putting my hand on her arm, "I really appreciate all the time you gave me." I gave her arm a squeeze. "You've been very helpful."

"You don't need to thank me, Rachel. It was just terrible what happened to Bruce. I feel sick whenever I think about it. If I can help you find who did that to him, that'll be thanks enough."

# 7

CHAPTER

LATE night was the worst time. During the days I kept busy, sometimes frenetically so, and most days I could sustain the momentum well into the evening—a noisy dinner with the radio tuned to NPR; walking and grooming Ozzie; doing a load of wash; vacuuming the rug; straightening the house; writing a letter to a friend. A little Ted Koppel, a little David Letterman, and, then, finally, unavoidably, lights out. Once upon a time I fell asleep within seconds of clicking off my reading light. Now the light served the same function as a campfire on the African savanna: it kept the hurtful things at bay. When the light went out, the memories and the pain crept in close. Often it took more than an hour to fall asleep.

The mornings seemed to fit a pattern: I would awake, and for a fraction of a second it was all just a nightmare. David was alive! And then reality would yank me back down. From there it would take a conscious effort to marshal the will to restart my day. But I would do it each morning, and as soon as my bare toes touched the carpet, Ozzie would scramble to his feet on the floor near the bed, his tail wagging furiously, and I would feel the adrenaline start to flow. By the time I left the house, I was usually dialing my after-hours answering service on my portable phone to pick up messages from clients.

This morning's messages included a frantic call from Sara Allen, the head of a small advertising firm that I represented. I felt my pulse quicken. The day's distractions had begun. I called her on my way to the office and learned that her firm had just been served with court papers filed by one of the major St. Louis advertising firms. True to form, the big boys had retained one of the largest and most expensive firms in town, and the signature block on the motion listed seven attorneys on the case. Their court papers included a motion for a temporary restraining order, a forty-seven-page supporting brief, and a notice informing us that the motion would be heard that morning at ten o'clock in Division Five of the Circuit Court of the City of St. Louis. Seems that the big boys were miffed over the recent loss of a lucrative account to my client, which was a four-person ad agency whose managing partner was, of all things, a woman.

"Forty-seven pages," I said with a chuckle. "Perfect."

It was a crucial strategic error. Asking a state court judge to read a forty-seven-page brief was asking for trouble. It was the equivalent of asking the judge to grab a shovel and head for the Augean stables. He'd refuse, and you'd rile him in the process.

"But seven attorneys!" she moaned.

"Relax, Sara. I'll meet you in the courthouse lobby at quarter after nine."

"Relax?! Rachel, we're going into court against seven lawyers!"

"I know those guys. Think of them as redcoats. Big, lumbering, conventional redcoats. Sara, we're the Green Mountain Girls."

It wasn't a complete rout, but the redcoats were in disarray by the time the judge denied their motion for TRO at 11:30 A.M. "Gentlemen," he warned them, "I don't see much here besides a bad case of sour grapes, and last time I looked there's no cause of action in Missouri for sour grapes unless you're in the winery business. If your people want a trial on the merits, I'll give you a setting for next month, but if I were you, gentlemen, I'd try to talk some sense into them."

Sara was delighted. She insisted on treating me to a victory lunch at Union Station. I got back to my office at one-thirty that afternoon. Jacki seemed a little frazzled as she handed me my telephone messages.

"You feeling okay?" I asked her.

She heaved a giant sigh. "It's the hormones. I feel like I'm riding the Screaming Eagle at Six Flags."

"What's the doctor say?"

She fanned herself with a legal pad. "He says it can take a couple months to get the dosage right."

I gave her a sympathetic smile. "Hang in there, kiddo."

I leafed through my telephone messages as I walked into my office. There were four of them. One was from Karen Harmon. I returned her call first.

"Here's the story so far," she said in a conspiratorial voice. "I found Bruce's computer in the supply room. I made a copy of all the files in the hard drive."

"Great."

"It's four disks. You want me to mail them to you?"

"No. I'll send a messenger. Leave them in an envelope at the reception desk."

"No problem."

I thought back to my encounter with Hiram Sullivan, chairman of Smilow & Sullivan. "Just to be safe, don't put my name on the envelope. Instead, put, um, Professor Benjamin Goldberg, Washington University School of Law. I'll make sure the messenger knows to ask for that envelope."

She giggled. "This is fun."

"Did you find out anything else?"

"A couple of things. I checked Bruce's time sheets. He worked most of the last two months on the SLP deal. By the way, SLP stands for—I'm not sure how to pronounce it—Société Lyons Pharmaceutique." She spelled it for me.

"Got it," I said as I scribbled the name onto my legal pad.

"That's why we just call it SLP," she said with a laugh. "Anyway, he spent most of his time on that deal. About six weeks ago he billed a couple of hours to an intellectual property audit we did for Naiman Electric. Three weeks ago he billed about eight hours over three days to a personal matter for Mr. Sullivan."

"What type of matter?"

"I can't tell from his time sheets. He didn't describe what he did for Mr. Sullivan."

I paused to jot down: *Sullivan—"personal" matter? 8 hrs.*

When I finished, I asked, "Would it be a problem to make me a copy of his time sheets for his last two months?"

"Not at all. I'll put them in the package along with the disks."

"Great. By the way, who is the Smilow of Smilow and Sullivan?"

"Oh, he was a sweet old man. He died a couple months after I started work here."

"When was that?"

"About two years ago."

"How did he die?"

"It was so sad, Rachel. He was down in Miami on a consulting project. He was out walking one night after dinner and someone shot him."

"Who?"

"They never caught the person. It was a drive-by shooting. The police said it was probably one of those drug wars." She sighed. "He was a nice man."

I was taking notes as she talked.

"One more thing," she said. "I found those Federal Express receipts. The ones for the files that I shipped to SLP's lawyers. It was a lawyer in Chicago. His name is Barry Brauner and he's at the firm of—"

"Scott, Dillard and Marks," I said.

"That's right. You know him?"

I groaned. "I'm afraid so."

"He has the documents. According to my inventory list, he also got a set of disks with a copy of the information on Bruce's computer. I guess someone made a copy for him. Anyway, I sent everything up there exactly a week ago."

I told Karen that I would have a messenger service send someone down within an hour to pick up the package for Professor Goldberg. Which got me thinking about the real Professor Goldberg. I gave him a call. His secretary said he was teaching his advanced antitrust seminar but ought to be back in the office in twenty minutes.

I looked down at my notes. *Société Lyons Pharmaceutique?* I flipped through my Rolodex and called Bob Ginsburg—a law school boyfriend turned investment banker at Bear Stearns. We had survived a brief romance that, in classic Cambridge style, got derailed over politics. He was a conservative Republican—one of those pro-life, pro-death types—who was, in that absolutely maddening fashion typical of conservative Republicans, lots of fun, very sweet, and wonderfully thoughtful when not enmeshed in the Cause. We parted friends, and over the years he'd been a terrific source of the types of information that investment bankers possess.

I reached Bob Ginsburg's secretary. She said he was on the other line and took my number. I returned the other three telephone calls. During the third call, which was with a gabby bankruptcy attorney in Kansas City, Jacki walked in with a note that read: *Mr. Ginsburg is on line 1.* I covered the mouthpiece and told her to tell him I'd be with him in a minute or so. I finally got rid of the bankruptcy attorney and took Bob's call.

As I hoped, he knew all about the Société Lyons Pharmaceutique and their acquisition of Chemitex Bioproducts. "Sure," he said. "Heller ran that company into the ground. I think SLP may be getting a good deal."

"Who's Heller?"

"Sammy Heller. He was chairman of Chemitex Industries until they filed for bankruptcy last year in Detroit."

"Chemitex Industries is the parent company?"

"Right. Just another victim of the eighties. Once upon a time, back in the seventies, Sammy Heller had a nice little company in Michigan called the Pontiac Chemical Corporation. Ironically, they manufactured solvents, which was just about the last time Sammy was solvent. He got hooked up with a couple of renegade investment bankers who'd left First Boston. They had him form a holding company called Chemitex Industries and took him on a buying spree—junk bonds up the wazoo and all kinds of weird financings."

"I sense a bankruptcy on the horizon."

"Bingo. As the cash flow got tighter the bankers started squeezing him. When the notes and bonds began coming due, they sent in their workout goons to stop the hemorrhaging. When that didn't work, they started foreclosure proceedings and Sammy filed Chapter Eleven."

"Is the company still in bankruptcy?"

"Yep. There's been a trustee appointed to sell off each of the operating companies."

There was a sudden banging noise from the other room. It sounded like a file drawer slamming shut.

"Goddammit!" Jacki hollered. Then another bang. "Oh, shit!"

"Hang on, Bob." I stood up and put my hand over the mouthpiece. "Jacki?" I called.

"Sorry," she answered in a subdued voice from the other room.

"Are you okay?"

I heard a sigh. "I'm fine."

I leaned forward, trying to peer around to Jacki's secretarial station, but I couldn't see her. "You sure?" I asked.

Another sigh. "Yes."

I sat down and uncovered the phone. "Sorry, Bob. Go ahead."

"Is anything wrong?"

"I don't think so." I looked down at my notes. "You were saying that the French company is buying Chemitex Bioproducts out of the bankruptcy?"

"Right. There may be some real value there, too. Pierre Fourtou—he's the chairman of SLP—has become a real bottom fisher in the States. He's bought three or four companies out of bankruptcy in the last few years. Chemitex Bioproducts might be a gem. It used to have a good name. You know who founded it, don't you?"

"No, who?"

"Your hotshot senator, the Great White Liberal Hope of the Democratic party."

"Douglas Armstrong?" I said, flabbergasted.

"You got it. Chemitex Bioproducts used to be called Armstrong Bioproducts. Once upon a time Douglas Armstrong was a fine, upstanding businessman, before he fell into the clutches of you bleeding-heart liberals."

"Don't start that again, Robert," I said with grudging good humor, recalling our Cambridge days. "Armstrong's company, eh? I knew he once had a pharmaceutical company, but I didn't realize it became Chemitex Bioproducts."

"Armstrong was in the Senate by then. Sammy grabbed it in a hostile takeover in late 1987 and changed the name to Chemitex."

"Listen, Bob," I said as I jotted down notes, "you guys do mergers and acquisitions. I'm trying to get a sense of what's typical. Does it sound normal for a chemical engineering consultant to spend two months doing due diligence on this deal?"

"Well, for some deals that might be overkill, but not for SLP."

"Why do you say that?"

"Pierre Fourtou's lieutenant is a guy named Levesque. René Levesque. He has final say on all the deals, and he's supposed to be an absolute data demon. They call him the Doctor of Due Diligence. Every deal takes longer when he's involved because of the amount of information and the level of detail he demands."

"Would a chemical engineer be competent to do due diligence on a pharmaceutical company's files?"

"A pharmacologist might be more familiar with certain aspects of the files, but someone with a chemical engineering background could handle it with the right reference materials."

"What kind of due diligence would he do?"

"Think about it. What are a pharmaceutical company's biggest assets? The drugs it already has on the market and the drugs that are still in the development phase. Everyone knows what drugs are on the market. In Chemitex's case, their Hope Diamond is still Phrenom."

"That's theirs?"

"You bet. It's what Douglas Armstrong founded his company on, and it's still a popular treatment for arthritis. But everyone already knows about Phrenom. You wouldn't need to do much due diligence on that drug beyond checking the sales numbers and evaluating the trends. The crucial due diligence is to figure out whether Chemitex has something big in the works. To do that, you have to examine the R and D files, evaluate the trade secrets, figure out what's in the works. We did some work with McNeil Pharmaceutical last year—"

"I'm sorry, Bob. Can you hold a sec?"

"Sure."

There was an odd snuffling noise coming from the other room. I listened for a moment. "Jacki?" I called.

No response, just more snuffling. Then the sound of her blowing her nose. I set the receiver on my desk and walked to the doorway. My secretary was hunched forward, her shoulders shaking. "Jacki, what's wrong?"

She turned toward me. Her mascara was streaked down her cheeks and her wig was slightly askew. She shook her head in frustration as she stood up. "Look," she sobbed, gesturing toward her leg.

I moved close enough to spot the tiny run in her stocking. It was just below the knee, along the calf of one of her massive legs.

"I'm so damn clumsy," she said, her lips quivering. "This is the third pair of pantyhose today. The third! They cost me four dollars each."

"It's not so bad, Jacki," I said gently. The poor thing looked like she was on the verge of estrogen shock.

"Maybe not yet," she moaned, waving her arms, "but just wait. In an hour it'll be all the way down to my toes."

I kneeled by her leg and studied the run. I looked up with a smile. "We can stop it."

She gave me a puzzled look.

"Do you have some clear nail polish?" I asked.

Jacki thought for a moment and shrugged helplessly. "It's at home."

"Check the bathroom down the hall," I said as I stood up. "I think I left some in the medicine cabinet."

She blew her nose. "What do I do with it?"

"I'll show you." Then I remembered Bob Ginsburg. "Good grief." I hurried back to my desk. "I'm sorry, Bob."

"What's happening out there?" he asked.

"My secretary had a problem. It's okay."

"What kind of problem?"

"Well, uh, with her pantyhose."

"Pantyhose?"

I giggled. "Just a run."

"Just a run? Hey, tell her I'll buy her a new pair. She sounds sexy."

"What?" I said in surprise.

"I love her voice. Deep and husky."

"She's not your type, Bob."

"How do you know?"

"Trust me."

"Describe her."

I chuckled. "Well, she's tall."

"Blond?"

"Actually, yes."

"Sounds better every minute. Built?"

I chuckled. "You mean chest size?"

"Well, sure."

"Big."

"How big is 'big'?"

"At least forty-two inches."

"Praise the Lord."

I could barely keep from laughing. "Tell you what, Bob, I'll fix you two up next time you're out here."

"You're a true pal, Rachel."

"Don't thank me, yet. Meanwhile, back to business. You were telling me about some work you did with a pharmaceutical company."

"Oh, yeah. The due diligence stuff with McNeil Pharmaceutical. Do you know anything about the economics of the drug industry?"

"Not really," I admitted, taking notes.

"You can't sell a new drug in the United States without first going through an incredibly rigorous system of approvals supervised by the Food and Drug Administration."

"I knew that much."

"Well, that's where the economics come in. On average, it takes eight to ten years and fifty to eighty million dollars to bring a new drug from the original concept through the FDA process to the market."

"Wow."

"Exactly. Moreover, the odds against a new drug surviving all the way are steep. The guys at McNeil had statistics showing that only one out of every four *thousand* drugs that undergo preclinical testing ever makes it to the market. Even if you get past the preclinical phase to the human testing stage, which is pretty far down the process, your odds of making it to the market are still only one of five. You know what that means?"

"I'm not sure," I mumbled as I finished scribbling: *1 out of 5 —human testing to market.*

"It means that you've got to do some serious due diligence before you have a sense of what a pharmaceutical company is really worth. For example, you need to find out the status of the IND applications."

"The what?"

"IND. It stands for Investigational New Drug."

"Let me write that down."

As I was scribbling, Jacki came in. "I found it," she whispered, holding up a bottle of clear nail polish.

"Bob, can I have one more pantyhose timeout?"

"No problem. Tell your secretary I'm falling in love long distance."

I rested the receiver against my neck. "Here's how you do it," I said to her, reaching for the bottle of nail polish. I unscrewed the top. "Come closer." She did. I slid out the brush and leaned toward her leg. "Just like this. Put a little dab at the end of the run. Let it dry. It'll keep the run from getting any longer." I leaned back with a smile, screwed on the top and held it out to her. "There. All done."

Jacki gave me a look of gratitude as she took the bottle of nail polish. "Thanks so much, Rachel." She glanced down at the stocking. "That's wonderful."

I lifted the receiver to my ear. "I'm back," I said to Bob.

"Wow, that's better than phone sex."

"Back to business, stud." I glanced at my notes. "IND. You said it stands for Investigational New Drug. What's that?"

"Okay. When a drug company has finished all of its preliminary testing on animals and wants to move to the next stage of the approval process, which is testing the drug on humans, it files an IND application with the FDA. Among other things, the IND describes the drug and the human testing the company proposes to do. Accordingly, part of the due diligence is to review the pending IND applications. That will give you a sense of what the company might be able to bring to market four to six years down the road."

There was more. According to Bob, the due diligence should also include a review of the NDAs, or New Drug Applications, which is the final step in the FDA approval process, filed after the proposed drug has passed the human testing stage and is ready to bring to market. In addition, the due diligence should include a review of the R&D files to determine whether there are any projects or proposals that might be worth pursuing. As Bob explained, Chemitex might not have had the capital to pursue some of the concepts still stuck in R&D, while SLP has money to burn. For an information fanatic like Levesque, two months spent reviewing IND, NDA, and R&D files would be money well spent.

I thanked Bob for his help, told him I would buy him dinner next time I was in New York, and promised to introduce him to Jacki when he came to St. Louis. I was organizing my notes when Benny returned my call. I filled him in on what I had learned that afternoon. He offered to drop by the library to try to locate the newspaper article on the Miami shooting death of the Smilow of Smilow & Sullivan.

"If I find it," he told me, "I'll drop it off at your house on my way home."

"Better yet, stop in for dinner. I'll get us some Chinese takeout."

"You got a deal, gorgeous."

"Bring your portable computer."

"Oh?"

"Bruce's secretary made me a copy of everything off the hard drive of his computer. I'm sending a messenger down to pick up the disks. Maybe the answer is on one of those disks."

# 8

CHAPTER

BENNY leaned back and rolled his eyes in ecstasy. "Oh, God, that's good."

I winked. "What did I tell you?"

"What's it called?" he asked.

"Kung Pao Squid. Try the Fresh Clam with Ma-La Sauce." I slid the white take-out carton toward him. "It's even better than the squid." Using my chopsticks, I leaned over and lifted out a squid. I popped it in my mouth and chewed slowly, savoring the tastes.

"Where is this place?" he asked.

"In Olivette. Across from the bowling alley."

I watched as Benny spooned some of the Fresh Clam with Ma-La Sauce onto his plate. We were having dinner at my house. Benny shoveled in a mouthful, chewed for a bit, and gave me a look of appreciation.

"Good, eh?" I said.

He swallowed and nodded. "Excellent find, dude."

"I take that as a compliment," I said with a tolerant smile, "even though it comes from a man whose idea of a great Oriental experience involves a set of pulleys and a heavily sedated JAL stewardess."

"A man can dream, can't he, Miss Gold?"

Ozzie sat in the corner of the kitchen, intently watching us eat. He was a big fan of Chinese food. Although he preferred Cantonese over Szechuan style, I was sure he wouldn't let provinces get in the way of leftovers.

I took a sip of beer and glanced down again at the copy of the newspaper article Benny had brought with him. It had appeared on the front page of the *St. Louis Post-Dispatch* almost two years ago, under the headline:

ST. LOUIS ENGINEER KILLED IN MIAMI CROSS-FIRE
WHILE WALKING BACK TO HOTEL AFTER DINNER

The article described the shooting death of Milton Smilow, one of the name partners of Smilow & Sullivan.

"I don't like it," I said.

"What's not to like?" Benny asked as he twisted off the cap of another Dixie beer.

"It says here that Hiram Sullivan was with him in Miami up until the shooting."

"So what?" Benny leaned over, scanned the article upside down. He pointed to a paragraph in the middle of the story. "Sullivan said that when they left the restaurant Smilow decided to walk back to the hotel instead of riding in the cab with him."

"I still don't like it."

"For chrissakes, Rachel, you think Sullivan shot his own partner from the cab? Come on! Read the papers, watch the news. It's open season on visitors to Miami. It's like a fucking video game come to life down there. And anyway, what's his motive?"

I shrugged. "I don't know. I just don't like him, I guess. He was a total jerk when I went to see him."

"Just because he's an asshole doesn't mean he's a killer."

"At this point, Benny, everyone's a suspect. Listen to this: you saw that Bruce's time sheets showed that he did eight hours of work on some personal matter for Sullivan, but there's no evidence of what he did."

"Big deal. Think back to when we were associates at Abbott and Windsor. Remember some of the personal family bullshit the partners made us do? Traffic tickets, insurance claims. Shit, do you remember that uncontested divorce I handled for Bryce Carville's second cousin? The babe who married the sailor?"

I laughed at the memory. "How old was she?"

"Nineteen. Showed up at court with a wad of chewing gum in her mouth, a skirt slit up to her *pupick*, four-inch fuck-me pumps, a skintight turtleneck, and no bra."

"You loved it."

"Me? You should have seen Judge Diener. When she sashayed up to the witness stand, I thought that horny bastard's eyeballs were going to pop out of his head on springs."

"It worked, didn't it? He gave her the divorce."

"The divorce? Hell, by the time she was done he would have given her his pension. The guy had a major husky under his robe."

I smiled at the memory. "What a great case."

"But," said Benny, jabbing his finger at me for emphasis, "none of that showed up on my time sheets. All I wrote down was 'Bryce Carville—personal matter.' Assuming consulting firms are the same as law firms, there's your reason for no description of what he did on Hiram Sullivan's personal matter."

"But there's one difference," I said. "When you handled that divorce, you had a file. There were divorce papers in there, correspondence, research memos." I gestured toward Benny's laptop computer, which was near me on the table. "Bruce's computer files are on those four disks. I've looked through them all. There's nothing on any personal matter for Sullivan in there."

Benny shrugged. "So maybe what he did for Sullivan didn't require a computer. Or maybe he didn't save the files. According to his time sheets, he worked on the project off and on over a three-day period about three weeks before he died, right? Presumably, he started and finished the project during those three days. So even if he did use the computer, maybe he just deleted the files when he was done."

"Or maybe someone else did." I pulled his computer to me and turned it on. "I spent two hours going through these files at work this afternoon," I said. "Bruce Rosenthal was an organization and classification fiend." I gestured toward the screen. "He's got directories and subdirectories and sub-subdirectories and sub-sub-subdirectories. Every file and every document is neatly arranged. This disk," I said, holding up the one Karen had marked DISK 2, "has the directory and all the subdirectories for the SLP deal. Presumably, it should have everything he did on the deal." I inserted the disk, typed DIR, pushed the ENTER key and looked over at Benny. "But I don't think it does."

"Really?" He came over to my side of the table. "What makes you say that?"

"A couple things. First of all, let me show you how this is organized." I pointed to the screen, which showed one directory:

CHEMITEX          <Dir>

To the right of CHEMITEX <Dir> was the date (2/16) and the time (8:45 am) that the directory was created.

"Now look at the subdirectories within the SLP directory."

I typed the instruction again and pushed ENTER. That gave us access to all the Chemitex files. Now the screen showed the following:

FINANCIAL          <Dir>
IND-PENDING        <Dir>
NDA-PENDING        <Dir>
R&D-LAB            <Dir>

"Okay," he said uncertainly.

I said, "The first one—FINANCIAL—has his due diligence on

the Chemitex financial records. Look." I typed the List Files instruction for the FINANCIAL subdirectory and pushed ENTER.
The screen filled with three rows of sub-subdirectories, all clearly
having to do with the books and records of Chemitex Bioproducts—depreciation, state taxes, federal taxes, cash flow, receiv-
ables, payables, assets, etc.

I returned to the prior screen:

| | |
|---|---|
| FINANCIAL | <Dir> |
| IND-PENDING | <Dir> |
| NDA-PENDING | <Dir> |
| R&D-LAB | <Dir> |

"What's this one?" Benny asked, pointing to the IND-
PENDING directory.

"That's for all the pending IND applications."

"Great," he said sarcastically. "What the hell are IND applications?"

"IND stands for Investigational New Drug. When a pharmaceutical company has finished all of its preliminary testing on
animals and wants to move to the next stage of the approval process, which is testing the drug on humans, it files an IND application with the FDA. So this," I said, pointing to the
IND-PENDING directory, "is for all of Chemitex Bioproducts'
pending IND applications." I looked over my shoulder at Benny
and winked. "I've been doing my homework."

"What a total babe you are."

I entered the IND-PENDING directory. "See?" I said. "There
are five IND applications in that directory. Those are the ones he
reviewed." I returned to the prior screen.

"What are these directories?" he asked.

I explained what an NDA was and showed him that the NDA
directory included the two pending new drug applications that
Bruce had reviewed. I returned to the main screen. "This," I said,
pointing to the R&D directory, "is presumably for all of the re-

search and development files." I typed instructions to reveal the contents. "But look." I pushed ENTER.

We were staring at a blank screen.

"Empty?" Benny asked.

"Completely."

Benny scratched his chin. "Maybe he never got around to this part of the due diligence."

"Wrong. I have his time sheets. Bruce actually spent most of his time on the R and D stuff."

"Maybe he didn't use the computer for that part."

"I doubt that. His secretary said he took his computer with him everywhere." I took the photocopies of Bruce's time sheets off the chair next to me and handed them to Benny. "Look how the dates on his time sheets match up with the dates on these files. According to the computer, what's the date he created the directory for the financial records of Chemitex?"

Benny squinted at the screen. "February sixteenth."

"Now look at his time sheets. What's the entry for February sixteenth?"

Benny read from the time sheet for that date: "Chemitex Acquisition—Commence examination of financial books and records—eleven hours."

I had him page slowly through the time sheets so that he could see the correlation between certain key dates in the computer records and dates in the time sheets. For example, the time sheets showed that on February 22 Bruce stopped reviewing financial records and started reviewing pending INDs. That was the same date he created the IND directory in the computer. So, too, the date he stopped reviewing INDs and started reviewing NDAs was the date he created the NDA directory.

"Okay," Benny said, "but what's the point?"

"Here's the point. According to his time sheets, what did he do on March fourth?"

Benny read the entry. "It says he started examining the Research and Development files."

I pointed at the screen. "And that's the date he created the R and D directory, right?"

Benny looked at the screen and then back at the time sheets. He started flipping through the time sheets, nodding his head. "That's all he did for the remaining weeks—examine R and D files."

"Exactly. That's the point. Bruce spent more time on the R and D files than on any other phase of his due diligence, but look—" I pressed the key to display the contents of the R&D directory. The screen showed no contents. "See," I said, pointing. "There isn't one file in that directory."

Benny squinted at the screen again, and then down at the time sheets.

"Jesus," he finally grumbled as he placed the time sheets back on the table. "Someone erased the files?"

I nodded. "Definitely."

Benny gave me a puzzled look. "Who?"

"There are only two possibilities: either the person who killed him that night or someone at Smilow and Sullivan."

Benny walked over to the refrigerator and took out two more bottles of Dixie beer. He handed me one and sat down at the table across from me. He unscrewed the cap, took a big gulp of beer, and frowned at me. "Why?" he said.

I shook my head. "Don't know enough, yet."

"Where else can you look?" he asked.

"The documents Bruce copied from the Chemitex R and D files are the best bet."

"Where are they?"

"All the documents Bruce had copied were sent to Chicago. For all I know, they're over in France by now."

"What else?"

"I don't know. His computer files were deleted. His apartment was searched." I sighed in frustration. "Even if Chemitex would let me look at their original files, which I'm sure they won't, I wouldn't even know where to begin. If Bruce spent six weeks looking through those files, there must be tons of records down there."

"You're right," Benny said grimly. "You don't know enough to make sense out of the files. Even if you got lucky enough to stumble across a key document, you'd probably not realize it. And you're right about them not letting you look through those records. They must be filled with trade secrets."

"It's maddening," I said. "Bruce was clearly upset about something, yet everything that could tell us what that was is gone, except for the list he gave to David."

"You showed that list to his secretary?" Benny asked.

I nodded.

"She didn't recognize it?"

I shook my head. "No. I was hoping that maybe she typed it." I stopped. "Typed it," I repeated. I smiled at Benny. "Yeah."

"What?"

"Her computer, Benny."

"Huh?"

"There might be R and D records in *her* computer. She said that sometimes she typed tapes that he dictated. The stuff she typed for him might still be in her computer."

I found Karen Harmon's number in the telephone book. Fortunately, she was home. I explained what I was looking for and the missing computer files.

"I definitely typed tapes for him on the SLP deal," she said.

"He spent the last six weeks going through the R and D files," I said. "Those are also the only due diligence materials that were erased from his computer. Did you type any tapes during those last six weeks?"

She paused for a moment. "I'm pretty sure I did."

"Would those documents still be in your computer?"

"Oh, rats," she said. "I don't think so, Rachel. I'd type it, he'd edit it, and then I'd retype it in final form and copy it onto a computer disk for him. The whole process would take a few days, especially when he was out of the office. After that, though, I didn't see much reason to keep the document in my computer. Every couple weeks, I'd go through my computer files and delete whatever I didn't need. I'm pretty sure I deleted all those documents."

"Darn," I said, disappointed.

"But wait," she said. "I bet I could still find them, or at least some of them."

"Where?"

"At the end of each day we have to make a backup copy of our computer files. We do what they call an on-site backup during the week, but every Friday we have to do a full off-site backup."

"What's that mean?"

"Each secretary copies all of her computer files onto specially labeled disks. The firm collects them and stores them somewhere off the premises just in case a fire or other disaster destroys our original computer records. Rachel, I bet some of the documents I typed from Bruce's dictation tapes are still on one of those backup disks."

"How do you get them back?"

"I'll just ask. The gal in charge of our computer systems is the one who takes care of the off-site storage. I'll have her get me my old backup disks tomorrow. I'll give you a holler if there's anything on them."

"That's great, Karen." I paused. "You need to be careful, though."

"Why?"

"Just like I said before. Hiram Sullivan doesn't like me poking around. You could get in a lot of trouble if he found out you were helping me."

"I'm not afraid."

"You need to be cautious, Karen. When you ask for those backup disks, be sure you have a plausible explanation for why you need them."

"I'll pretend that I accidentally deleted one of the documents. It's happened before."

"Good. Keep me posted."

"Well?" Benny said after I hung up. He was in the process of cracking open his fortune cookie.

I shrugged. "We might still get lucky."

Benny read his fortune. "Ahhh," he said with a smile. "Talk about luck."

"What's it say?"

In a silly Chinese accent he read aloud, "Soon you will savor pleasures of heavily sedated JAL stewardess in Hong Kong basket."

I broke open my fortune cookie and pulled out the fortune. "Ahhh. 'Soon obnoxious friend will receive full frontal lobotomy he so urgently requires.' "

# 9

CHAPTER

KAREN called the following morning with news that she had been able to retrieve two documents from Bruce's R&D directory: one created two weeks before his death, the other about a week before his death. She had printed them both for me. I worked out the pickup arrangements and then called down to the clerk's office at the U.S. District Court to leave a message for Jacki, who was on her way there to file a brief for me. Jacki called ten minutes later, and I told her to drop by Smilow & Sullivan for a package that would be waiting out at the front desk with her name on it.

As I waited for Jacki's return, I pulled out the folder of materials she had copied for me last night at the St. Louis University Law School library after her evening class. I had asked her to find me some information on Phrenom, the drug Bob Ginsburg had described as the crown jewel of Chemitex Bioproducts. Jacki had copied the relevant pages from the *Physicians' Desk Reference*. I skimmed through the listings for Phrenom Injection, Phrenom Capsules, and Phrenom Tablets, all three of which were also identified by their generic name: Phenylpyrrole Sodium. According to the heading entitled "Indications and Usage," the drug was to be used for "the relief of symptoms associated with the following conditions, but only after other therapeutic measures have been tried and found unsatisfactory: active rheumatoid arthritis, active juvenile rheumatoid arthritis, active osteoarthritis, and acute attacks of degenerative joint diseases of the hips and knees."

I had also asked Jacki to find me some biographical materials on Douglas Armstrong's days as head of what had then been known as Armstrong Bioproducts. She had photocopied seven pages from a *New Yorker* profile that ran several months ago. I settled back to read it. Most of the story was already familiar to me—and no doubt to thousands, or even millions, of others. Indeed, Jacki's cover note to me stated that Armstrong had also been profiled in recent issues of *Vanity Fair, People*, and the *New York Times Sunday Magazine*. Obviously, the senator's spin doctors and PR flacks had been hard at work getting their candidate ready for the big announcement.

According to the article, Douglas Armstrong was a thirty-three-year-old physician when he founded Armstrong Bioproducts in 1970. During the early 1960s, young Dr. Armstrong had spent three years in the Peace Corps stationed in Costa Rica. He worked in a clinic in the poor section of San José and his wife Edie taught mathematics in a village school outside of town. He had long been intrigued by botanical drugs, and on many weekends he traveled into the rain forests with Indian guides to gather samples of the plants that formed the basis of many of the folk cures of the country.

One folk medicine that had particularly fascinated him was the tuber of the peloto plant, which grew only in the Monteverde Cloud Forest. Although the tubers had an extremely bitter carrot flavor that made them nearly inedible, they were nevertheless eaten raw by the women in the tribe. As Armstrong observed, all of the women shared one thing in common: a total absence of any symptoms of rheumatoid arthritis, a painful and crippling form of arthritis that afflicts millions of women every year, most of whom develop it between the ages of thirty and fifty.

His fascination with native pharmacology remained strong after he returned to the United States. In 1970, he mortgaged everything he owned to start Armstrong Bioproducts. His goal was to replicate and manufacture in the laboratory the more promising botanical drugs he had observed in the rain forests of Costa Rica. He was convinced that somewhere within the bitter tubers of the peloto plant was the active ingredient of a powerful arthritis medicine that could bring relief to millions of people, if only he could figure out how to isolate it and produce it in large quantities in a laboratory.

The early years at Armstrong Bioproducts were lean ones. Twice creditors of the company tried to force it into bankruptcy, and both times the company fought them off with the brilliant legal maneuverings of Armstrong's attorney, Sherman Ross. Operating on a shoestring budget, Armstrong and his small staff of researchers worked on isolating the active ingredient in the peloto tubers. In 1977, the company received FDA approval for Phrenom Injection—the drug that transformed the fortunes of Armstrong and his company almost overnight. He took the company public in 1979 and, in the six hours it took for the initial public offering to sell out, he went from a net worth of $57.25 to a net worth of $12 million.

Eighteen months later, his wife of twenty-one years died of ovarian cancer. Their marriage had been an extraordinarily close one, the intimacy actually enhanced by Edie's inability to have children. Her death threw him into a depression that lasted nearly a year. "I lost my bearings when I lost Edie," Armstrong told the reporter for the *New Yorker*. When he regained them, he announced his candidacy for the U.S. Senate, sold all of his holdings in Armstrong Bioproducts, crisscrossed the state of Missouri in a marathon campaign, and won his very first election by an astonishing fifty-eight percent of the vote.

The article made a passing reference to Sammy Heller's hostile takeover of Armstrong Bioproducts several years later. According to the reporter, Douglas Armstrong was no longer a shareholder of the company at the time. As I was making a note to do some further checking on Sammy Heller, the outer door opened and Jacki came in, grousing under her breath. I heard her fumbling around in the other room.

"Hello?" I called.

"Shit, shit, shit, shit," she grumbled as she walked into my office, hunched over. She had the package from Karen in her left hand. Her right hand was clutching her left breast.

I stood up, worried. "Jacki, are you okay?"

"No."

"Is it your heart?"

"Hah," she laughed derisively. Her blond wig was slightly askew. She placed the manila envelope on my desk. "Here's the package from Smilow and Sullivan." Still bent over, she turned to go.

"Wait a minute, Jacki. Tell me what's wrong."

"Never mind."

"Jacki!"

She froze. After a moment, she turned to face me, her right hand still clutching her left breast. Her eyes were red.

"Tell me, Jacki," I said gently.

She sighed, blinking back the tears. "If nothing else, I've got one helluva defective products claim." She was wearing a long-sleeved navy blue shift with a white sailor collar. The shift was cut loose and ended just below her knees. "You ready for this?" she asked.

She straightened up and moved her hand away from her left breast. I stared at the fabric, half expecting to see blood or an alarming discoloration, but there was nothing visibly amiss. Then I heard a faint clattering, as if someone were dropping tiny pebbles to the floor. I leaned forward over the desk to look at the floor. There were about twenty little black and white pellets scattered on the floor around her feet. They were dropping down, one by one, from under her dress.

"What are those?" I asked.

"Birdseed."

"Birdseed?" I repeated.

"Watch this." She placed her hands on her hips and wiggled her upper torso vigorously. When she stopped, I watched in astonishment as the birdseed came tumbling down in a torrent. When the downpour ended, there was a pile of birdseed on the floor between her legs and dozens of loose seeds strewn on the floor around her.

Slowly, I moved my eyes upward, battling against the urge to grin. Afraid I'd lose it if we made eye contact, I paused at her chest level. Her left boob had disappeared.

*Birdseed?* I glanced down at the floor and then back at her missing boob. I could feel my lips quiver.

*Please God, don't let me laugh.*

I heard a chuckle. I looked at Jacki's face. Her eyes were shiny with tears but she was smiling. "Can you believe this?" she asked. "Birdseed falsies. They're supposed to look and move like real ones. I pay extra for them and then the damn seam rips. Thank God I'm not outside, or I'd be fighting the pigeons off my chest. It would have been a scene out of Hitchcock."

"Oh, Jacki," I said, aiming for sympathy and almost getting there.

I started giggling, and then both of us exploded with hysterical laughter. We laughed so hard that we ended up on our hands and knees on the floor, tears on cheeks. It was just what the doctor ordered. Both of us needed a good belly laugh.

Twenty minutes later, when we'd cleaned up the birdseed and Jacki had headed back to the lingerie store like a Marine commando on a search-and-destroy operation, I settled in my chair and opened the package Jacki had picked up from Karen Harmon, the one containing the two documents she had typed from Bruce Rosenthal's dictation tapes.

Both documents were still in rough-draft form and consisted of sentence fragments, key words, and other notes that no doubt had made far more sense to Bruce than me. Reading through them, I could almost hear Bruce dictating the entries as he paged through the R&D files at Chemitex Bioproducts.

The first document was dictated about two weeks before he died. It appeared to be notes of his review of laboratory research files on various attempts to develop antiseptics, fungicides, and psoriasis agents. His notes summarized the contents of those files in a neutral, dispassionate tone, and ended each section with the phrase: *"Not promising."* In all five pages, he raised only one question, and that was in the section on fungicides:

- *Need to check PDR—didn't Squibb solve this problem w/Myco products?*

The other document, dictated eight days before he died, appeared to be notes of his review of laboratory research files on arthritis medications. Like the first document, it began in a neutral, dispassionate tone. The first section covered research on steroids and ended with the phrase, *"Not promising."* The second covered something called "Newer NSAIDs" and ended with the same phrase. But the final area, which started at the bottom of page four under the heading "Other" and ended on the following page, consisted entirely of a series of increasingly agitated questions and comments:

- *Primax? Where?*
- *Cross-referenced materials not there—Filing glitch?—Need to locate—Need to ask*
- *What's going on with Guillain B?*
- *Where are Primax files???—must find*
- *Be sure to look for LGB—Sounds like typical G-B syndrome*
- *Cross-reference to Phase Two Trial?—Need to check date— Phase Two Trial?—Not possible!?*

Those were the last words in the document: *"Not possible!?"*

Karen called while I was still pondering Bruce's list of questions and comments.

"What do you think?" she asked.

"I'm baffled. Do you know what any of these abbreviations stand for?"

"Such as?"

"LGB?"

"No."

"PDR?"

"I think so. There's a big fat book called the *Physicians' Desk Reference.* Bruce has a copy in his office. So do some of the other guys. When they talk about it, they call it 'the *PDR.*'"

"I know the book," I said, making a note. "What about Primax?"

"I've never heard of that."

"How about NSAIDs?"

"Sorry."

"That's okay. This stuff could be a big help, Karen. At least now I have something more to go on. Bruce seemed disturbed by what he had found in those last files."

"You can say that again."

"I assume that whatever bothered him would bother someone else with a background in pharmacology or chemistry. What I need to do," I mused aloud, "is to get my hands on the files that bothered Bruce, and then turn them over to an expert that I trust to explain them to me."

"I'm already working on it," Karen said proudly.

"What do you mean?"

"I called down to Chemitex just before lunch. I talked to one of the girls who helped coordinate copying documents when Bruce was down there going through their files. I told her that I needed another set of the R and D documents that they copied for Bruce if it wasn't too much trouble. She said she'd check to see if the documents they copied for him were still tagged."

"Karen, I appreciate your help, but you really shouldn't have done that. You could get in a lot of trouble."

"Don't worry. I followed your advice: I have a story all set if anyone asks."

"Okay, but I really don't want you doing anything more without clearing it with me first. I know you want to help, and you've been terrific so far, but you're too visible down there. First of all, you could get fired." I paused, lowering my voice. "Second of all, I don't know what we're dealing with. I'm assuming that something Bruce was involved with at the office got him killed. It could have been completely unrelated to this Chemitex due diligence, but probably not. You've already gone way beyond the call of duty, Karen. If Chemitex sends you those documents, that'll be fabulous. But if not, don't worry about it. I'll find another way to get them. It's really better for you to keep a low profile for a while."

"Okay," she said dejectedly.

"Don't be down, Karen. You've done a terrific job so far. You've given me plenty of great leads. Let me run them down, see where they lead. I'll figure out our next move. I promise I'll let you know everything I find. Okay?"

She sighed. "Okay." She sounded a little more chipper.

"Your fiancé would be proud of you."

It was almost one o'clock when I hung up. I stood and stretched as I gazed out my office window. It was a beautiful spring afternoon in the Central West End—a perfect day for walking. I strolled down Maryland to the Saint Louis Bread Company, picking up the current issue of the *Riverfront Times* on the way. I bought myself two sourdough rolls and a cup of espresso and took my tray out to one of the sidewalk tables. I munched on my rolls and read the paper and sipped my coffee and tried to pretend that I was on the Left Bank in the 1920s, waiting at the Café du Dôme on the Boulevard Montparnasse for Ernest and Gertrude and Alice and Scott to arrive. But I couldn't concentrate on the newspaper or the fantasy because I couldn't keep Bruce's series of questions out of my mind:

- *Primax? Where?*
- *Cross-referenced materials not there—Filing glitch?—Need to locate—Need to ask*
- *What's going on with Guillain B?*
- *Where are Primax files???—must find*
- *Be sure to look for LGB—Sounds like typical G-B syndrome*
- *Cross-reference to Phase Two Trial?—Need to check date— Phase Two Trial?—Not possible!?*

I finished my espresso, stuffed the newspaper into my briefcase, and walked down Euclid to the library of the St. Louis College of Pharmacy, which was on the block just east of Children's Hospital. The librarian pointed me toward the *Physicians' Desk Reference.* I took the thick volume over to a study carrel and tried to make sense out of Bruce's notes.

I started with what I hoped would be the easy part, and I was right. The earlier of Bruce's two documents had contained only one question:

- *Need to check PDR—didn't Squibb solve this problem w/Myco products?*

"PDR" meant *Physicians' Desk Reference,* and Squibb was the pharmaceutical company. As for the "Myco line," the *Physicians' Desk Reference* listed various Squibb medications starting with the prefix "Myco"—Mycolog Cream, Mycostatin Oral Suspension, Mycostatin Oral Tablets, Mycostatin Pastilles, and Mycostatin Vaginal Tablets—all for treatment of yeast infections. Based on Bruce's notes, the folks at Squibb had apparently overcome the obstacle that had stymied the Chemitex scientists.

Next on my list was "NSAIDs," which turned out to be short for a broad group of medications known as nonsteroidal anti-inflammatory drugs. NSAIDs ranged from over-the-counter products such as aspirin and ibuprofen to others available only by prescription, such as Tolectin, Butazolidin and Phrenom, the crown jewel of Chemitex Bioproducts.

I pulled out the second dictation document, the one with all the questions and comments. "Primax" sounded like it might be a drug. I searched through every index in the *Physicians' Desk Reference*: the manufacturer's index, the product name index, the product category index, the generic and chemical name index, even the discontinued products index. No Primax anywhere.

"Guillain B" sounded less like a drug than a name—a French name, to be specific. Nevertheless, I searched for it in all the indices. No Guillain listed in any index. I glanced back at Bruce's question: *"What's going on with Guillain B?"* The name certainly sounded French. I wrote a reminder on my legal pad: *Be sure to look for someone named Guillain B at Société Lyons Pharmaceutique.*

I looked back at Bruce's questions and comments: *"Be sure to look for LGB—Sounds like typical G-B syndrome."* I found no LGB in the *Physicians' Desk Reference*. I glanced back at the note I had just made: *Be sure to look for someone named Guillain B at Société Lyons Pharmaceutique.* I looked over at Bruce's comment: *"Be sure to look for LGB."* I added the following to my note: *Look for someone with initials LGB.*

I could only guess at Bruce's references to "Phase Two Trial." It was a term I had heard in connection with class actions and mass tort cases, including ones involving pharmaceutical companies. Bruce seemed quite agitated over the subject: *"Cross-reference to Phase Two Trial?—Need to check date—Phase Two Trial?—Not possible!?"* It made no sense at all. I wrote a note on my legal pad: *Check litigation reports on SLP and on Chemitex Bioproducts.*

On my way out of the library I dropped by the general reference section on a hunch. They had complete sets of *Sorkins' Directory of Business and Government* and *Standard & Poor's Register of Corporations, Directors & Executives.* Neither had a listing for any business called Primax or LGB. The *Standard & Poor's* entry for Société Lyons Pharmaceutique listed its five top officers. No Mssr. Guillain B, and no one with the initials LGB. But then again, I reminded myself, the list in *Standard & Poor's* included only the top five officers of the company. LGB and/or Guillain B could be somewhere else within the company, such as head of R&D. Or, for that matter, he or she or they could be within Chemitex Bio-products. The French heritage of St. Louis was still evident in the names of its streets (Bellefontaine, Chouteau, Debaliviere) and its suburbs (Creve Coeur, Des Peres) and its inhabitants (including, perhaps, Guillain?).

It was close to six o'clock when I got back to my office. My secretary was gone and my message light was blinking. I pressed the play button and waited for the tape to rewind:

"Rachel, this is Karen Harmon." She spoke in a hushed voice. "I'm in really big trouble. Mr. Sullivan found out about my call down to Chemitex for those R and D records and he's totally furious with me. He had me in his office for a half hour ranting and raving. It was just terrible. I was crying and apologizing like crazy, but don't worry, I never told him about you or us. I don't think I'm fired, but I'm not exactly sure. He told me to report to work tomorrow morning. He has meetings out of the office in the morning, but I'm supposed to report to his office right after lunch and he'll decide what to do with me. Anyway, I've got my aerobics class tonight, which is good, and then I'm going to just try to get my mind off all this stuff for a while. I'm just going to veg out. I'll call tomorrow after I see Mr. Sullivan. Phew! Some day, huh. Bye-bye, Rachel."

I grabbed the phone and dialed her home number. It rang four times and then her taped message started. I checked my watch. It was almost six-thirty. She was still at her aerobics class. I waited for the beep.

"Karen, this is Rachel. I feel just awful. Please call me at home tonight if you want to talk about it. And don't worry about that jerk Sullivan. If he fires you tomorrow, you can come work for me until you find another job. Please call if you need someone to talk to."

I called her again at nine o'clock, but got the answering machine. I hung up without leaving a message. I called again just before bed. Once more I got the answering machine.

"Karen," I said after the beep, "this is Rachel. If you're there, please pick up the phone." I waited. Nothing. "Call me when you get home. I don't care how late it is. Call me, Karen."

I clicked off the reading light. It took a long time to fall asleep.

# 10

CHAPTER

THE Honorable Kevin "Mad Dog" Madigan, the spooky and senile United States District Judge for the Eastern District of Missouri, once told me that during World War I the second lieutenants in the Romanian army had to wear lipstick and rouge and were required, in Mad Dog's words, "to perform infamous crimes against nature upon their commanding officers." If that's true, then Barry "Brown Nose" Brauner would have flourished in the old Romanian military.

Not because he was gay, which he wasn't, at least to my knowledge. And not because he performed infamous crimes against nature upon his commanding partner, which he didn't, at least to my knowledge. No, Barry Brauner would have flourished because he was the consummate second lieutenant, and every major American law firm needs a supply of consummate second lieutenants. As the old saying goes, behind every great rainmaker is a Barry Brauner.

The rainmakers are the Great White Hunters of the law firm, the ones who bring in the big clients and the big fees. For the ambitious young associate at any major law firm, an understanding of the subtle nuances of the rainmaker/lieutenant relationship is a far more essential piece of knowledge than an understanding

of the subtle nuances of, say, federal securities law. That is because most partners in most major law firms are merely glorified
employees—the legal profession's equivalent of middle management, and thus vulnerable cogs in the law firm machinery. By
contrast, the rainmakers own the machinery, and their lieutenants
run it.

In the Abbott & Windsor lingo, a rainmaker is a BSD, the
acronym for Big Swinging Dick. Barry Brauner's BSD was Amory
Brewster, former head of A & W's mergers and acquisitions department, now the managing partner of the new Chicago office of
Scott, Dillard & Marks. Brewster's surprise move to Scott, Dillard
after more than two decades at Abbott & Windsor rated a page-
two blurb in the *National Law Journal* ("L.A. Powerhouse Ac-
quires Acquisition Maven To Anchor Windy City Office") and a
feature article in *The American Lawyer* ("Brewster and the
Friendly Takeover: A Merger Made In Heaven?"). The *National
Law Journal* feature mentioned that Brewster had taken along "a
junior partner from Abbott & Windsor." Although the junior partner was not identified in the article, any lawyer, paralegal, or secretary who had ever worked at the Chicago office of A & W at
any time during the past ten years immediately knew who it was.
Just as Richard Nixon required a Haldeman and Henry VIII required a Cromwell, Amory Brewster required a Brown Nose
Brauner.

As with any BSD/lieutenant relationship, Brewster and Brauner had struck the usual Faustian bargain. Brewster gave his lieutenant a partnership in the firm, a nice share of the profits, and
a membership in the Union League Club. Brauner gave Brewster
his immortal soul.

Back when I was a young associate in Chicago at Abbott &
Windsor, there was no lieutenant as masterful as Brauner, and
none as despised. He was a virtuoso at positioning himself to get
all credit and avoid all blame. Even worse, he had an uncanny
ability to detect an associate's Achilles' heel and exploit the tac-
tical advantage such knowledge conferred. So, too, he had no

qualms about manipulating the lives of those he summoned onto one of the matters for his BSD's clients. By virtue of his BSD, Barry Brauner had the power to destroy a young career. Accordingly, every aspiring A & W associate knew that a summons from Brauner was a command from on high, even when that summons arrived—as so often it did—at five o'clock on a Friday afternoon or on Thanksgiving morning or on the day before the associate's two-week vacation. "Mr. Brewster needs this on his desk the day after tomorrow," he would tell you in that serene but ruthless tone, adding, "and I assured him that you would meet the deadline." There was no escape hatch for those who hoped to become partner someday.

Brauner was, in short, a thoroughly creepy person. Because I had been in Abbott & Windsor's litigation department back then, I never had to work for him. Although I had my own lieutenants to serve, I was always grateful to be outside Barry Brauner's sphere of influence.

*No longer,* I thought glumly as I sat in Brauner's office, waiting for him to finish the third leisurely telephone call he had taken, in true lieutenant form, during our meeting. The firm of Scott, Dillard & Marks occupied several floors near the top of the Sears Tower, and Barry had an east exposure with a dramatic view of the Loop and Lake Michigan. The only personal touch in an otherwise austere office was a framed photograph of his somber wife and two children. The photographer had shot them in a serious pose, staring off to the left, as if watching Barry leave the studio to return to the firm.

Barry Brauner was grayer and balder than during my Abbott & Windsor days, but otherwise looked the same. Although Benny usually referred to him as "that sawed-off piece of shit," I had forgotten how short Barry really was. I was five feet seven, and he was several inches shorter than me. Although he compensated in subtle ways (his desk chair seemed a little higher than normal, and mine felt a tad lower than usual), he wasn't one of those swaggering bantam roosters or pint-sized popinjays one so often encounters in the courtroom. Indeed, I couldn't recall him ever raising his voice. Early on in his career, Barry Brauner had perfected the ability to smile while projecting an aura of menace from beneath his hooded eyes. The talent had served him well.

He ended the telephone conversation and shifted his gaze toward me. "The documents are now in France," he said quietly.

"Come on, Barry," I said with a trace of irritation, "we were both weaned at Abbott and Windsor. They taught us never to work without a net. I assume you made a complete copy of all the documents before you shipped them to France. All I'm asking is to let me look through the documents that relate to the research and development files."

"Now, Rachel," he said calmly, "you know I can't do that. These documents are extraordinarily confidential. Your Mr. Rosenthal had to sign a strict nondisclosure agreement before he was allowed to look at any of them."

"I'll be happy to sign one."

He sighed and shook his head. "I couldn't even think of raising the subject with my client."

"Why not?" I persisted. "What if those documents hold the key to Bruce Rosenthal's death? After all, he was working for your client at the time. Wouldn't your client want to help bring his killers to justice?"

"Now, Rachel," he said with a patronizing chortle, "since when did you become Nancy Drew? As for the documents, the idea that they might contain a clue to Mr. Rosenthal's death is pure speculation. I could never advise a client to let you rifle through highly confidential materials on so tenuous a link. Moreover, my client has very little discretion in this matter. Indeed, Société Lyons Pharmaceutique isn't actually the real party in interest, yet. Don't forget, the deal won't be consummated for at least another month. Until then, the documents are the property of Chemitex Bioproducts, and thus they are the ones with the final say on the subject." He shrugged. "You see? My hands are tied. Obviously, you are free to try to persuade Chemitex Bioproducts of the merits of your position."

I had only one trump card left, and now was the time to play it. "I know," I started in a slow, even voice, "and you know I know, that somewhere in this firm is a complete set of the documents Bruce Rosenthal selected. I'm here, and your client is across the Atlantic Ocean in France. What I see today they'll never have to know about."

"Good heavens, Rachel, you—"

"Shut up, Barry. It can be done quietly and with discretion, or I can make it noisy and disruptive. That's your choice. You stonewall me today and I will personally write a letter to Mr. Pierre Fourtou, the chairman of your client. I'll tell him what I know and why I believe that there could be information in those due diligence files that relates to the death of one of his U.S. consultants. I'll send copies of that letter to the chairman of the FDA, to the science editors of the *New York Times* and the *Washington Post*, and"—I paused for full effect—"to your boss, Amory Brewster." I leaned back in my chair and crossed my arms.

He was deadpan up until the last name, which triggered a tic on the right side of his mouth. To a true lieutenant like Brown Nose Brauner, an irritated BSD was a far more intimidating prospect than a team of investigative reporters and a suspicious regulatory agency.

We stared at each other for a long time, and then he turned toward the window overlooking the Loop. He gazed out the window as he rubbed his chin. I waited. Eventually, he turned toward me. "I can't let you see the documents," he said.

"That's just great," I said in disgust as I stood up.

"Wait a moment, Rachel. I have a proposition."

I looked down at him. "What?"

"Please, sit down."

I remained standing. "Just tell me."

He leaned back in his chair. "I can't let you see the documents.

It would violate our agreement with the client and, just as important, our agreement with Chemitex Bioproducts. If Chemitex discovered that breach, they could call off the deal and sue my client, this law firm, and me. Nevertheless, I am willing to push the limits of the express language of that agreement. Although I can't let you see the documents themselves, I can have the documents searched for you. Our paralegals have prepared a comprehensive computerized index. You tell me what you're looking for, and I can have the answer to you within hours."

"I'm not completely sure what I'm looking for."

"That's okay," he said with what he must have hoped was a reassuring smile. It looked more like a grimace. "You tell me what you're looking for at this stage, Rachel, and I'll get back with the answer. If you have followup questions, I'll have the documents searched for them as well. Fair enough?"

I stared down at him. It wasn't much of a proposal, but it was better than nothing, and it would sure yield quicker results than any other option I had at the moment.

"Well?" he asked.

"I'll give it a try. But if I don't like the results, or if I think you're holding out on me, the deal is off."

He uncapped his Mont Blanc fountain pen and reached for a legal pad. "Where do we start?"

"Primax," I said. I spelled it for him.

He looked up with a curious expression. "What is it?"

"I have no idea. But whatever it is, it seemed to bother Bruce."

"How do you know that?"

"Trust me," I said. I didn't want to reveal any more than I had to.

"Okay," he said. "Anything else?"

"Yes. Guillain."

"Who or what is that?"

I shrugged. "Check the documents. If you draw a blank there, have someone check your clients' list of employees. He or she might work for your client. Guillain is probably a first name. Last name begins with a B. Also, check for someone with the initials LGB."

He finished writing and looked up. "Is that it?"

I mulled it over. "One more thing." I reached for my briefcase and removed a photocopy of the Beth Shalom/Labadie Gardens list. "See if there's any reference to this." I handed him the document.

He studied it with a frown. "Where did you get this?" he finally asked, still studying the document.

I shook my head. "Just tell me what's in the files."

He looked up at me. "Whose document is this?" he asked, clearly bothered.

"Why, do you recognize it?"

He stared at the Beth Shalom/Labadie Gardens list for a moment. "No," he said without looking at me.

I couldn't tell whether to believe him or not.

"I'm going back to St. Louis this afternoon." I placed a business card on his desk. "Call me as soon as you have any answers."


For most of the short flight home I stared at the set of questions that Bruce had dictated during his due diligence review of the R&D files. His reference to "Phasc Two Trial" reminded me of one of the items that Bruce had apparently wanted legal advice on, namely some sort of statutory limits. If the "Phase Two Trial" was in fact a litigation matter, presumably one that arose out of a pharmaceutical matter, then perhaps there was a statute that limited the amount of damages that could be recovered in such a case.

*"Need to check date"* could thus mean the date the statute was enacted. The insurance industry lobbyists in several states had been able to get statutory damage limits enacted in a variety of products liability and medical malpractice contexts over the past several years. I scribbled a note to myself to check the Missouri statute books for statutes that limited the amount of damages a plaintiff could recover in such a case.

It was close to five o'clock when the plane landed in St. Louis. I called my secretary from a pay phone in the terminal to see whether I had any message from Barry Brauner. No word from him, but plenty of nonurgent messages from others, all of whom could wait until tomorrow.

"What about Karen Harmon?" I asked.

"No word from her, Rachel."

I dialed Karen's home number and let the phone ring until her answering machine clicked on. I hung up without leaving a message. I checked my watch. 5:03 P.M. Maybe Karen hadn't lost her job after all, I thought. Maybe that jerk Hiram Sullivan decided to give her a second chance. I might still be able to catch her at the office. I dialed the number.

"Karen Harmon, please," I said when the Smilow & Sullivan receptionist answered.

"Oh." There was a pause. "Are you a friend?" she asked awkwardly.

I gripped the receiver and closed my eyes. "What happened to Karen?"

"Well, she's—oh, God, I'm so sorry. Karen's dead."

CHAPTER

AT 9:50 that night, I was standing in the lobby of the Berkeley Police Station waiting for Patrolman Dan Roland. According to the desk sergeant, Roland would be out of roll call any minute.

What I knew so far I had learned from the Missouri Highway Patrol, which had ceded jurisdiction to the Berkeley police. According to the Highway Patrol, Karen Harmon was killed instantly when her car hit a bridge embankment on Highway 170 out near the airport. The one-car accident occurred around midnight, which was about seven hours after Karen had left the message on my answering machine.

I turned at the sound of voices and footsteps. Several uniformed cops were walking out of a large room down the hall. Each was carrying a briefcase and a shotgun.

"Danny," the desk sergeant called to one of them. "Got a lady over here to see you about that traffic fatality last night."

Patrolman Dan Roland turned toward me. He was tall and stocky, with sleepy eyes and a neatly trimmed blond mustache.

"Ma'am?" he said in a polite but neutral tone. He was in his twenties.

I introduced myself, explained that I was an attorney, and told him I wanted to talk to him about the accident. He nodded and set the briefcase on the ground between his feet. He placed the shotgun next to it.

"What would you like to know, ma'am?"

"To begin with, how it happened."

He nodded, crossing his arms over his chest. "It appears that the driver lost control of the vehicle. She wasn't wearing a seat belt at the time. The force of the impact threw her body through the windshield and against the concrete embankment."

"How did she lose control of her car? Was there something wrong with it?"

He shook his head. "I don't think so, ma'am. The decedent appeared to be intoxicated."

"Karen was drunk?" I asked in disbelief.

He nodded firmly. "That's my conclusion, ma'am. We won't have the blood alcohol count until the autopsy results are in, and that won't be for at least a week, but she appeared to be intoxicated at the time of the accident."

"Why do you say that?"

He raised his eyebrows. "It seemed pretty obvious, ma'am. There was a strong odor of alcohol in the vehicle interior and on the decedent. There was an empty bottle of rum and an empty bottle of Diet Coke on the floor of the vehicle. Judging by the damage, the vehicle impacted the embankment at a speed in excess of fifty miles an hour. There were no skid marks in front of the collision site." He paused, a hint of sadness showing through his cool facade. "She's my third one, ma'am, and they all pretty much look the same. The last two had blood alcohol counts between point-one-eight and two. I'm assuming hers will be up in that range."

"What if it isn't?"

He frowned. "I'm not following you, ma'am."

"Did you know she was a Mormon?"

"No, ma'am."

"Her religion prohibits alcohol."

He nodded slowly, his face expressionless. "Okay."

"Doesn't that bother you, Officer?"

He tugged at his mustache. "She appeared to be intoxicated, ma'am. That happens sometimes, even to Mormons." He took a small notebook out of his breast pocket and clicked his ballpoint pen. "I might put that information into a supplemental report." He jotted something in the notebook.

"What about the car?" I asked. "Are you going to examine it?"

"We've looked in the vehicle, ma'am. That's where we found the empty bottles."

"No, I mean the engine, the steering device, the accelerator. What if someone tampered with the car? What if it was sabotaged?"

As I asked the questions and watched his reactions, I realized it was pointless to try to convince this local patrolmen that what appeared to be a routine drunk driving fatality on a stretch of interstate that ran through his town might actually be connected to two completely different deaths in two other jurisdictions, especially given that I hadn't yet been able to find any hard evidence of a connection between any of the deaths.

"Well, ma'am," Patrolman Roland said, "we don't normally do much with the vehicle in an accident of this type. The vehicle was pretty much totaled. In fact, it may have already been hauled off for scrap." He paused to make a note. "If you give me your name and telephone number, ma'am, I'll certainly be happy to call you with her blood alcohol count when it comes through."

Hiram Sullivan answered the front door in his bathrobe and slippers.

"I want to talk to you," I said.

"Do you have any idea what time it is?" he snapped. "It's almost eleven o'clock."

"So what?" I said through clenched teeth. "What did you do to Karen?"

He stared at me, his eyes narrowing.

A woman called from the second-floor landing, "Who is it, Hi?"

He turned toward her voice. "Go back to bed. I'll be up in a minute." He turned back to me and crossed his arms. "I should have known," he said, grimly shaking his head.

"What are you talking about?"

"Karen acted quite improperly when she requested those documents from Chemitex, and she was punished accordingly for her misconduct."

"You think death is an appropriate punishment?"

"Don't be absurd, Miss Gold. I am referring to the disciplinary action for her misconduct. She had a ludicrous excuse, claiming that she wanted a backup set of documents. Obviously, I regret her unfortunate death. My firm mourns her demise. However, we certainly will not accept any blame for it. People who drink and drive must accept the consequences of their behavior." He narrowed his eyes. "So it was you, eh? She was trying to get those documents for you?"

"Why is everyone so uptight over those documents?"

"I certainly can't speak for others, Miss Gold. My firm is concerned because we assumed certain confidentiality obligations with respect to those documents. Unlike some people, I happen to take such obligations quite seriously."

The conversation was going nowhere. Barging in on him was a stupid idea—an angry, impulsive act that was looking dumber every moment. I decided to end with a shot from left field. "What was Bruce doing for you before he died?"

He took a step back. "What?"

I stepped forward. "He was working on a personal matter for you. What was it?"

"How do you know that?"

"Answer my question. What was he doing for you?"

Hiram Sullivan scrutinized me as he got himself under control. "A personal tax matter," he said calmly. "Good night. Leave now or I shall call the police."

He closed the door in my face. I heard him turn the deadbolt lock.

"How 'bout some more wine?" Benny asked.

"I've had enough," I said, wiping my eyes. Frustrated and depressed, I'd come directly to Benny's place after my encounter with Hiram Sullivan. Thank goodness he was home, and alone. Two glasses of wine and a half a box of Kleenex later, I was almost under control again.

I blew my nose. "I think I'm becoming emotionally unstable," I said.

"You're not. You've been under incredible pressure. A new client dies, your boyfriend gets murdered, now this girl dies. And meanwhile, you've been running around like crazy trying to find a link. People are stonewalling you. Rachel, you're allowed to get upset. You're allowed to cry."

I wiped my eyes with a tissue. "She was a good kid, Benny."

"You really liked her. I could tell."

"If they killed her . . ."

"Rachel, it doesn't sound like anyone killed her."

"Benny, she was a Mormon. They're not even allowed to drink a Coke."

"Rachel, we're Jews. We're not supposed to eat pork. Where do barbecue rib restaurants always locate? Near Jewish neighborhoods. Go figure."

"But I think she was an observant Mormon."

"Hey, I know some observant Catholics. They go to mass every weekend. And guess what? They have two kids. You think they're keeping the numbers down with just rhythm? Look, Karen got in big trouble at work, she was upset about it when she called you, her boyfriend is down in some dirtball village in South America, and she's all alone up here. Is it so crazy to think she might try to cheer herself up with a drink or two?"

"But it wouldn't be hard to fake the whole thing," I said. "You could force her to drink that stuff, or just inject her with grain alcohol. Then knock her out, stick her in the car without a seat belt, toss in the empty bottles, wait until there's no traffic, fiddle with the accelerator, and let it rip. The car gets totaled, she gets totaled, the whole incident gets filed away as just another drunk driver fatality."

"Well, the cop told you he'd file a supplemental report."

I rolled my eyes. "Big deal. Even if he does, no one's going to pay any attention to it. And when the autopsy report comes back with a high blood alcohol count, they'll close the file." I sighed in exasperation. "It's driving me crazy."

"What else can you do now?"

"I'm going to try to talk to someone at Chemitex tomorrow morning."

"Who?"

"I'm not sure, yet. I want to find someone in research and development, preferably a science type. I'm getting nowhere dealing with smoothies."

"Speaking of smoothies," Benny said, "did you see who's coming to town tomorrow?"

"Who?"

"Saint Armstrong. They had a blurb on the ten o'clock news. He's holding a press conference down at the Old Courthouse at two-thirty."

"Really? On what?"

"No one's sure, but the speculation is that he's going to announce he's running for president. A two-thirty press conference is just in time for the national news."

"At the Old Courthouse?"

Benny nodded.

I thought it over. "I'm going to go down there."

He snorted. "Am I surprised?"

"No, not for that. Maybe he can help."

"Help what?"

"With Bruce's death, and all the rest."

Benny gave me a dubious look. "Pardon?"

"It was once his company, Benny. He must still have influence there."

"Rachel, he's ancient history down there. Shit, he probably hasn't owned any stock for more than a decade."

"Benny, he founded the company. He must know plenty of people down there. It's worth a shot."

"Don't get your hopes up, kid."

# 12

CHAPTER

I decided to bluff my way in, so I spent the first hour of the morning at the public library looking through the past ten editions of *Sorkins' Directory of Business and Government*. When I closed the current edition, I was convinced that Otto Pritzner was my man. He had been the head of research and development at Chemitex Bioproducts for the past six years. Prior to that, he had worked in their research laboratories. I called Chemitex Bioproducts from the library and confirmed (a) that he was still head of R&D, and (b) that he was in the office today.

Before heading down to Chemitex, I called my office for messages. There was one from Brown Nose Brauner and one from Bob Ginsburg. I called Brauner first.

"We're not turning up much, Rachel."

"Tell me what you found."

"No match on Guillain or LGB. Just a couple of obscure references to Primax."

"Give me the specifics."

"To begin with, there is no Primax file. At least none in the documents this Rosenthal fellow copied. The references to it appear in two of the older files, but they're vague and don't make much sense. For example, it's not even clear what Primax is."

"Describe the references."

"I can't tell you that, Rachel."

"Come on, Barry. If the references are in older files, it can't be that important to your client."

"That's where you're wrong. The age of the file has no bearing on its potential value."

He was probably right. His statement was consistent with what Bob Ginsburg had told me: a project abandoned five years ago by Chemitex for lack of funds might be worth resurrecting, especially if scientific advances in the interim had solved a problem that had once made the project seem unpromising.

"I'm disappointed, Barry."

"Give me a few more days, Rachel. Perhaps I can get you the clearance you want. What do you say to that?"

"I don't know." I didn't believe him. It sounded like a stall tactic. "I'll think about it."

"I'll get back to you in a day or so, Rachel. Oh, one more thing."

"What?" I said cautiously. When a consummate lieutenant like Barry Brauner reaches the end of a discussion and then acts like he just remembered one more item, it's time to get wary.

"That list you gave me."

"What about it?"

"We're having a hell of a time running it down. Where did you get it?"

"To quote you, Barry, 'I can't tell you that.' "

"That's not fair, Rachel. You want answers from us. We'll have better luck giving them to you if we know where it came from."

"You get me clearance to look at those files and then I'll tell you exactly where I got that list."

"Well, I don't—"

"That's my proposal, Barry. Work on it."

I tried Bob Ginsburg next, but his assistant said he was on an international conference call that would probably last for another hour. I said I would try him again later.

I told his secretary I was a close friend of Robin Dahlberg, the sister of Bruce Rosenthal, and that I wanted to talk to him about Bruce. It was enough to get me into the office of Otto Pritzner, Director of Research and Development at Chemitex Bioproducts.

I had expected someone matching Pritzner's career, i.e., a lifetime beneath the fluorescent lights of a laboratory. Instead, I found a gruff but good-natured drill sergeant in a crisp white short-sleeved shirt and a narrow black tie. He had a gray crewcut, crinkly blue eyes, a neatly trimmed mustache, even white teeth, and a Teddy Roosevelt smile.

"Terrible thing about your friend's brother," he said with a frown when I introduced myself. "Hope they catch the bastards and fry 'em."

I thanked him and explained that I had come to see if he could help me make sense of what Bruce had been concerned about during his last weeks.

"Bruce told Robin that he was looking through files down here," I said. "Something about the sale of your company."

Pritzner nodded and explained the transaction and Bruce's role in due diligence. He also explained his own background. Otto Pritzner had been with the company for fifteen years—all the way back to the time of the Doc which is what the oldtimers called Douglas Armstrong.

"Have the police talked to you about Bruce's death?" I asked.

"Nope. I know they talked to Mr. Carlson, and I think they talked to Mr. Andrews, but no one else that I know of."

Ronald Carlson was the president of Chemitex Bioproducts and Howard Andrews was general counsel. I had concluded that neither of them was worth my time: even if they agreed to talk to me, they wouldn't tell me anything important. That's why I chose Otto Pritzner. I thought I stood a better chance with someone who wasn't experienced at answering inquiries from people outside the company.

"You said Bruce seemed concerned about us?" Pritzner asked.

"He seemed bothered by some of the stuff in the R and D files."

"Such as?"

"Robin didn't understand a lot of what Bruce said to her. It was all kind of technical. She does remember some names. One sound French: Guillain. I think it's a first name. The last name begins with a B. Another could be just someone's initials: LGB. Do you know anything about them, or it?"

"Them," he said with a smile, "*and* it."

"What do you mean?" I said, trying to mask my delight at finally finding someone who knew something.

"Guillain was a French doctor: Georges Guillain. His research partner was Jean Barré. The *it* is the disease named after them. Back around World War One, they described a rare disease that's been known ever since as Guillain-Barré syndrome." He gave it a French pronunciation, with a hard "g": gee-LAN bär-RAY.

"Actually," he continued, "some call it Guillain-Barré syndrome, and some call it Landry-Guillain-Barré syndrome. LGB for short."

"What kind of disease is it?"

"It affects the nervous system."

"Is it fatal?"

"Usually not, but it can be. The early symptoms are numbing or tingling in the arms and legs. Sometime it progresses to temporary paralysis. In rare cases where the paralysis progresses enough to cause respiratory or circulatory problems, it can be fatal. Do you remember the problems with the swine flu vaccine?"

"Vaguely."

"Back in 1976 there was a big scare over what many medical researchers predicted would be a particularly virulent strain of influenza that winter. It got nicknamed the swine flu. One of the pharmaceutical companies developed a swine flu vaccine, and the federal government arranged for mass inoculations across the country, especially of children and older adults. Unfortunately, there was a rare side effect no one predicted: Guillain-Barré syndrome. Some of the patients developed it, and some of them died from it."

"What caused the disease?"

He shook his head. "No one is sure. For the most part, the victims were perfectly healthy before the inoculation."

"Is there a cure?"

"I don't think so. As I recall, most doctors believe it's caused by a virus. There've been different treatments over the years, but none are sure cures. Usually, the disease runs its course and the patient recovers."

"But not always."

"No, not always."

"Was someone at Chemitex working on a cure for Guillain-Barré?"

Otto Pritzner rubbed his chin and frowned. "I don't believe so. At least not recently."

"What do you define as recently?" I asked.

"At least the last six years. That's how long I've been head of R and D. Before that, well, I guess it's possible. I don't recall hearing any of the others talk about it, but it's certainly possible."

I opened my briefcase. "Robin found this in her brother's papers." I pulled out a photocopy of the Beth Shalom/Labadie Gardens list. "Do you know what this is?"

He studied the document. "No. Can't say that I do."

"Bruce had you copy a lot of documents from the files, didn't he?"

Otto chuckled. "You can say that again. I was afraid we were going to burn out that copy machine. We had two secretaries designated to do the copying, and he kept those poor gals running eight hours a day."

"Did you keep track of what you copied for him?"

"No, can't say that we did. He'd bring them a file with those yellow stickers on every page he wanted copied, and they'd remove the stickers as they made the copies. Then they'd refile the originals and give him the copies."

I gestured toward the Beth Shalom/Labadie Gardens list. "Do you think that was copied from one of the files?"

He studied the list again. "Hard to say." He started to hand it back to me.

"Keep it," I said. "It's a copy. I'd be grateful if you'd show it to some of the others here. Maybe one of them will recognize it. Anything you learn might be helpful."

"Good thinking." He smiled and placed the document on his desk. "I'll ask around."

"Thanks."

I glanced down at my list of topics. Next on the list was *Phase Two Trials*. "Dr. Pritzner, has—"

"Please, call me Otto."

I smiled. "Okay. Otto, has the company been involved in any big litigation over one of its products?"

"Well, the folks to talk to for that would be our lawyers. I try to steer clear of the legal stuff."

"I understand," I said with a sympathetic smile. "I realize that pharmaceutical companies get named in lots of malpractice cases. That's not my focus. I'm thinking more in terms of one of those big class action lawsuits that sometimes get filed against a pharmaceutical company over one of its products. Like the Dalkon Shield case?"

He shook his head and chuckled. "Nope. Thank goodness, we've been able to dodge that bullet so far."

I nodded as I looked down at my notes. "One more thing. What do you know about Primax?"

I looked up when he didn't answer right away. He was studying me, his face blank. I waited.

"Nothing," he finally said.

I tried to ignore the tension in his voice. "Do you have any idea what it is?"

"No," he answered forcefully.

I stared at him. He looked down at his desk and moved a pencil over to one side. "Have you ever heard of Primax?" I asked.

He continued to look down. "No."

I scrutinized him for a moment. "You're sure?"

He nodded curtly, checking his watch.

I handed him my business card as I stood up. "Thanks, Otto. I know you're a busy man, and I appreciate the time you've given me. If you think of anything else, please give me a call."

He stood up to shake my hand. "I'll keep that in mind," he said, just a little less tense than before.

I picked up lunch on my way back to my office. It was almost one-thirty. Armstrong's press conference was in one hour. I was even more anxious than before to talk to Armstrong. I needed help breaking the code of silence, and he might have the influence to do it.

I ate at my desk while I pondered the Primax puzzle. At least I had solved the Guillain-B puzzle. I reached for Bruce's list of questions:

- *Primax? Where?*
- *Cross-referenced materials not there—Filing glitch?—Need to locate—Need to ask*
- *What's going on with Guillain B?*
- *Where are Primax files???—must find*
- *Be sure to look for LGB—Sounds like typical G-B syndrome*
- *Cross-reference to Phase Two Trial?—Need to check date— Phase Two Trial?—Not possible!?*

"Primax" and "Phase Two Trial" were still a mystery, but now I knew that "Guillain B," "LGB," and "G-B syndrome" all referred to Guillain-Barré syndrome, aka Landry-Guillain-Barré syndrome, aka LGB syndrome. Unfortunately, Bruce's references to the disease were still opaque. What he had found in the R&D files having to do with Guillain-Barré? Was someone working on a cure? Was someone studying the disease? Had someone misidentified another disease as Guillain-Barré syndrome, or vice versa? And why did it make him so agitated?

As I was pondering these questions, Jacki returned from the library and came into my office. I filled her in on what I had learned about Guillain-Barré and told her of Otto Pritzner's odd reaction when I had mentioned Primax.

"How about you?" I asked. I had sent her off to the library to hunt down information on Primax. "Any luck?"

She shook her head. "Nothing. I checked all the reference books, all the guides to periodicals, and I even ran it through Nexus. Whatever it is, I can't find any information on it whatsoever."

I leaned back in my chair. "That's strange."

She nodded. "It sounds like a brand name for a drug, doesn't it?"

"It does," I said glumly, and then I made the connection. "Jacki, you're right," I said, sitting up.

"What?"

"It sounds exactly like a brand name."

"Okay," she said uncertainly.

"What if it is? Or was?"

"What?"

"Jacki, what's the very first thing a company does when it comes up with a new brand name?"

She shrugged. "What?"

"It applies for a trademark registration."

"Really?"

"Absolutely, and if Primax is a brand name that means we can at least find out who owns it."

"*If* they registered it," she cautioned.

"If it's a drug product, I bet the name is registered. Pharmaceutical companies are obsessed with trademarks. They make sure they get the brand names registered with the U.S. Trademark Office as early as possible. If Primax has anything to do with pharmaceuticals, it'll be registered."

"Do you have to go Washington, D.C., to find out?"

"Not anymore. It's all in computer data bases. We can access them right here from my computer."

I glanced over at the clock on my desk. It was already ten after two. I had just twenty minutes to get downtown for Senator Armstrong's press conference. "Jacki," I said, standing up, "I have to run. We can check the trademark stuff when I get back."

# 13

CHAPTER

THE Old Courthouse in downtown St. Louis, now operated by the National Park Service, was a bustling site of justice, commerce, and drama years before Abraham Lincoln became president. Slaves were sold from the white step blocks of the east portico, while on the west side a struggling farmer named Ulysses S. Grant, on the verge of bankruptcy, freed his only slave. In fact, the Old Courthouse had a cameo role in the origins of the Civil War: it was the site where a black slave named Dred Scott filed a lawsuit seeking his freedom—a lawsuit that would eventually reach the Supreme Court.

Built during the height of the Greek Revival era of architecture and topped with an Italian Renaissance cast-iron dome, it looks more like a state capitol than a courthouse. A broad stairway of granite leads up to the portico, which is supported by six massive Doric columns. The best view of it is facing east from the small park across Broadway. From there, the Old Courthouse is perfectly framed by the Gateway Arch, a gleaming steel parabola that rises in the background 630 feet above the levee of the Mississippi River. It's the postcard view favored by the camera crews from the networks and CNN, all of whom were crowded in the park facing the Old Courthouse as I jogged toward them.

Parked behind the camera crews and talking heads were the Minicam vans and equipment trucks and uplink satellite disks and miles and miles of wire. In front were the print reporters and photojournalists. All were jockeying for position in front of the makeshift podium erected near the top of the broad flight of stairs leading to the massive doors at the courthouse entrance. Senator Armstrong had not yet appeared.

Near the podium were three youngish men in suits and loosened ties huddled in conversation with a harried-looking woman in a wrinkled gray dress. She was holding a clipboard and seemed to be in charge. I recognized her as Diane Raney, Armstrong's press secretary.

Other than Sherman Ross, who was nowhere in sight, Diane was probably the best person for me to approach for an audience with Armstrong, and this might not be a bad time to ask her. But as I pushed through the crowd of reporters, Diane turned from the three men, shouted something to another young aide standing off to the side, and then walked quickly up the stairs. A uniformed police officer pulled open one of the courthouse doors as she approached. Frustrated, I watched her disappear inside.

As I turned to ask one of the reporters about Armstrong's itinerary for the rest of the day, I was astonished to see who was standing right next to me scribbling notes in a steno pad.

"Flo?" I said with delight.

She looked up with a Hollywood double-take, her eyes widening as she broke into a big grin. "Rachel Gold!" she bellowed. "Goddam, how you doing, girl?"

We gave each other a big hug. I stepped back to admire my best friend from law school. Florence Shenker was as *zaftig* as ever—a big, robust woman with high cheekbones, full lips, and the beginnings of a double chin. She had thick curly black hair, fiery brown eyes, and a lusty, wonderful laugh.

"What are you doing here?" I asked her.

"The usual: getting quotes from uptight suits, fighting with editors, and keeping a lookout for the last normal single man in

America. What about about you? What are you doing in St. Louis?"

"I live here."

"I thought you were up in Chicago. What happened?"

"My father died."

She winced. "I'm sorry, Rachel."

"Thanks. My mom was in bad shape emotionally, my best friend had just moved down to teach law at Wash U, and I guess I was kind of in the mood for a change." I shrugged. "So, here I am."

"How's Sarah doing?"

"Better," I said with a smile. "She's off on a one-month cruise of the Far East with Aunt Becky. That's her sister."

"Searching for knishes in Korea, eh?"

I laughed. "If there are any over there, those two will find them. But what about you? I thought you were with a newspaper in Detroit."

"I moved to D.C. six months ago to take a job with the Washington bureau of the *Chicago Tribune*."

"What do you cover?"

"Mostly old, ugly white guys in plaid suits or black robes."

"Huh?"

"The courts and the Senate Judiciary Committee."

I paused. "Is Douglas Armstrong on that committee?"

"No. We drew straws for the likely presidential candidates. I have Armstrong and Dole."

I raised my eyebrows. "So he's really going to announce today?"

"Naw," she said with a weary roll of her eyes. "I couldn't get Diane Raney to confirm one way or the other yesterday. She probably didn't know herself. The one calling the shots these days is Sherman Ross, the little putz."

"So if he isn't announcing today, what's he going to do?"

She chuckled and shook her head in grudging admiration. "The son of a bitch doesn't shy from controversy. He's unveiling a public school bill that has something in it to piss off everyone. It would simultaneously eliminate the use of busing to desegregate schools *and* require all public schools within each metropolitan area to be funded equally from a combined city-suburb tax fund."

"Which means?"

"That the inner city schools would be funded at precisely the same level as the schools in the wealthiest suburban community—same teacher salaries, same programs, same extracurricular activities."

I nodded. "I like it."

"Sure," Flo said sardonically, "but he'll never get it off the ground. Rush Limbaugh is already putting on the warpaint."

"Armstrong's no pushover," I said.

"No question about that. Ted Koppel has him booked tonight on *Nightline* to talk about it, and I'm sure Armstrong will be impressive. But on this one I'm afraid he's tilting at windmills."

"So how long are you in St. Louis?"

"I'll cover this speech, stay overnight, maybe do a piece on the southern Illinois court system for the Sunday paper and head back tomorrow night."

"Are you free for dinner?" I asked.

"You bet I am. What's it been for us? Six years?"

"At least." I touched her hand. "Flo, it's so great to see you."

She threw an arm around my shoulder. "Same here."

One of the huge courthouse doors swung open and Diane Raney walked quickly across the staging area toward the place where two of the three youngish men in suits and loosened ties were still huddled in conversation.

I turned to Flo. "I came here to talk to Armstrong." I pointed to Raney. "Is she the best person to see about that?"

Flo looked at me with surprise. "What do you have to talk to him about?"

"It's a long story. I'll tell you over dinner tonight."

Flo looked back toward Raney and the two men. "Forget

Raney. See the guy with the brown hair talking to her? That's Mitch Kinsock. He handles Armstrong's schedule. Talk to him."

Just as I started to push through the crowd of reporters, the courthouse doors swung open and Senator Douglas Armstrong emerged, along with the mayor of St. Louis, the mayor of East St. Louis, and the commissioner of suburban St. Louis County. Armstrong towered over the three local officials. The 35mm cameras all around me were whirring and clicking as Armstrong strode toward the podium, trailed by the other three men, two black and one white. He paused and surveyed the crowd without a smile.

*The man definitely has charisma,* I said to myself as I stared up at his ruggedly handsome face. It was thrilling to see him up close and in person. I felt a little like one of the schoolgirls at a Beatles concert.

"Let's get to the point," he started briskly. "The system has failed twice. It failed a black man named Dred Scott, who came to this very courthouse seeking equality nearly one hundred and fifty years ago. That time the court said no. One hundred years later, a little black girl from Topeka, Kansas, came to another courthouse, the big one in Washington, D.C. She came seeking equality in education. That time the court said yes." He paused. "But it didn't matter. The system failed again. We're no closer to equality in education today than we were back then. I know it. You know it. So let's be honest with one another. It's time for a change . . ."

We touched our glasses of Singha beer.

"To friendship," I said.

"And to normal men who don't live at home with Mom," Flo said with a wink. "May they seek us in droves."

"Hear, hear," I said with a laugh as we clinked our glasses again.

Flo and I were having dinner together at the Thai Cafe on Delmar. Benny was supposed to join us, but hadn't yet arrived. I was glad he was running late, since it gave us a chance to catch up on each other's lives.

We had met our first day of law school, a pair of Jewish girls with little in common but our religion. Flo was the brassy Brooklynite who arrived at Harvard ready to coldcock the first professor who tried to pull a Socratic number on her. I was the polite one from St. Louis who arrived at Harvard wondering how in the world a product of a midwest public school system would survive at the alma mater of Oliver Wendell Holmes, Louis Brandeis, and Felix Frankfurter.

Flo was in my section first year, and she quickly organized an all-woman study group that met once a week at her apartment in Somerville. The five of us gathered every Wednesday night over pizza and wine in her cluttered living room. We'd spend the first hour or so trying to make sense out of that week's caseload in Torts, Contract, and Civil Procedure. Once that was out of the way, the wine having taken effect, we would spend the rest of the evening laughing and commiserating over life as a female 1L at manful and manly Hahvahd.

After her second year, Flo landed a coveted summer clerkship at Silverstein & Candicci, the hottest law firm in L.A. and one of the premier merger and acquisition firms in the country. The firm, headquartered in Westwood with a branch office in Newport Beach, had a prominent role in virtually every significant corporate takeover battle during the 1980s. Nevertheless, at the end of the summer Flo shocked them (and us) when she rejected their offer of permanent employment (starting salary: $76,000 plus bonus) for a job with the staid downtown L.A. firm of Fowler & Graves—a 174-lawyer firm that (by choice) represented no client in the entertainment business and, to this day, still does not have enough Jewish lawyers for a minyan.

"Why?" I had asked in astonishment back then when I learned of her decision.

"I spent a whole summer with berserk Jews and Italians," she had explained, referring to the lawyers of Silverstein & Candicci. "They may be brilliant and they may be out there on the cutting edge of the law, but three months of listening to those testosterone-crazed geeks screaming and cursing and pounding on tables and savaging each other was too much. I felt like I was back in Brooklyn. Forget it. I want a firm filled with nothing but uptight, repressed, anal retentive WASPs—the kind of lawyers who would rather die than have a confrontation. You know why? 'Cause when I go to the office I want some goddam peace and quiet."

The theory was better than the reality. Flo lasted three years in the medical malpractice defense group at Fowler & Graves. Bored out of her mind, she returned to her first love: journalism. She landed a job on the business page of the *Dallas Morning News*. From there she went to the Washington office of the *National Law Journal*, but had a falling out with the bureau chief after just a year. She quit that post and took a job as the national legal correspondent for the *Detroit Free Press*, which is when I lost track of her. And now she was back in D.C., covering the legal beat for the *Trib* and, judging by the stories she had told me that afternoon, loving it.

"I think it's great that you're on your own," she said to me. "How'd you ever get the courage to leave Abbott and Windsor?"

"It wasn't that hard." I shook my head at the memories. "After a few years, I was really starting to get fed up with big firm hicrarchies. I realized that even if I hung around long enough to become a partner there, I'd still be taking orders from jerks on cases that I couldn't care less about. I mean, how excited can you get representing some huge defense contractor in a highly technical dispute with a subcontractor over a payout under a government contract?" I sighed. "So I left."

"Sounds like my final days at Fowler and Graves. I woke up one morning, looked at myself in the mirror, and said, 'Florence, honey, life is too short to spend it taking shit from these assholes.' So I put on a pair of jeans, a Grateful Dead T-shirt, and sandals, drove down to the office, and resigned."

"Regrets?" I asked.

"Hell, no. How 'bout you?"

"Not yet." I smiled. "I'm having fun."

Flo leaned back. "You look great, Rachel."

"You, too."

"No, I mean *great* great. You were practically the homecoming queen of Harvard Law School, and now you look even better. You must have to fight them off."

I laughed uncomfortably, not sure what to say.

"I'm amazed you're not married," she said.

"Bad timing," I said with a shrug. "It's either been the wrong guy at the right time or the right guy at the wrong time."

"Last time I saw you, you were living with that studly Northwestern professor. What was his name?"

I looked down. "Paul Mason," I said softly. "We broke up."

"Oy, that sounds bad."

I nodded, still remembering the pain of discovering how he had betrayed me. It unfolded like a scene out of a soap opera. I had come home early one afternoon, stopping on the way to pick up a loaf of crusty French bread, a large wedge of cheddar cheese, and a bottle of chilled white wine. It was going to be a romantic surprise. We would build a fire and start with a picnic on the rug in front of the fireplace. Instead, I found him up in the bedroom with one of his students. I later learned that Paul had escorted a procession of coeds up to the bedroom during his Tuesday and Thursday afternoon "office hours."

"Fucking intellectuals," Flo said with disgust. "The professors I've dated have been among the nastiest, most self-centered men I've ever met. Second only to surgeons. You know what I want?"

"What?"

"A blue-collar worker. A guy who punches a time clock and makes an honest living with his hands. I'm beginning to think that my Mr. Right is a big strong steelworker."

I laughed. "My secretary is a big strong former steelworker."

"No kidding?"

"Problem is, he's in the process of becoming Miss Right."

Flo rolled her eyes heavenward. "Terrific. See what I mean? Find a good one, and next thing you know he wants to put on lipstick and cut off his johnson."

"All rise."

I turned toward the unmistakable sound of Benny's voice just as he arrived at our booth, out of breath. "What a fucked-up day," he said, panting. "Jesus, I feel like I ran a hundred feet. My heart is beating like a rabbit's."

"Benny," I said, gesturing toward Flo, "you finally get to meet my best friend from law school."

Flo stood up and put out her hand. "Glad to meet you, Benny."

As Benny reached for her hand I waited for the usual snappy rim shot. Instead, I heard a subdued, almost klutzy, "Me, too."

I looked up in surprise at the two of them standing there. Benny seemed transported, and Flo was actually blushing. It lasted only a moment, and then they both took their seats, just a little awkwardly. Benny sat on my side of the booth, facing Flo.

"The beer's good," she said, sounding more girlish than I had ever heard her sound in my life.

"Great," Benny answered, just a tad too cheerfully.

It was almost a scene out of *Ozzie and Harriet* (Episode 42: "Ricky Falls In Love"), except that Benny was wearing a Beavis & Butt-head T-shirt under his sports jacket.

Another round of Singha beers helped break the spell, and before long the three of us were laughing and talking.

"So," Benny asked, "did the great and mighty Armstrong announce his candidacy today?"

"No," I answered. "Flo said that Sherman Ross decided it's better to hold off for another few weeks."

"Once he announces," Flo explained, "he goes under a media microscope. Every thing he says or does will get scrutinized. This way he can pick his moments in the spotlight and then scurry offstage for a while."

Benny turned to me. "You have any luck with him?"

"Maybe tonight," I said. "Flo told me to ask Mitch Kinsock after the speech. He's one of his aides. At first Kinsock was kind of rude." I paused to wink at Flo. "But when I explained that I needed to speak with his boss about a possible link between his former company and at least one and possibly three recent homicides, Mitch suddenly became Mr. Congeniality. I have a private appointment with the senator at eight o'clock tonight down at Channel Two."

"Why there?" Benny asked.

"He's doing a *Nightline* with Ted Koppel. I guess they're going to film him from there." I checked my watch. "So let's order." I looked over at Benny, trying to mask my smile. "Flo is staying down at the Marriott. If I'm running late, do you think you could possibly give her a ride down there?"

"No problem," he said with genuine conviction.

# 14

MITCH Kinsock was waiting in the lobby of Channel
Two. He ushered me back to an empty office. "The senator will
be down in a few minutes, Rachel. Would you care for coffee or
a soft drink?"

"I'm fine."

Ten minutes later, there was a knock at the door.

"Come in," I said.

The door opened and Senator Douglas Armstrong entered,
followed by Sherman Ross.

"Hello, Rachel," Armstrong said. He took my hand in his right
hand and covered it gently with his left as he leaned down. "How
are you holding up?"

I smiled sadly, touched that he had remembered. "The nights
are worse than the days."

He nodded compassionately. "I know. I remember. The pain
will diminish with time, but it never vanishes. Nearly twenty years
later, and I still mourn for my Edie."

There were tears in my eyes. I started to reach for my purse
to get a tissue.

"Here," he said, handing me his handkerchief.

I wiped my eyes and nose on the soft cotton, inhaling the masculine, comforting scent of his cologne.

After a moment Armstrong said, "Rachel, this is Sherman Ross. He's my chief of staff. More important, he's the man who keeps me in line."

Sherman Ross had been in the background, leaning against the beige wall, almost invisible in his gray suit, white shirt, and gray patterned tie. He was short and lean, with a bald head, bushy black eyebrows, and dark probing eyes. At the mention of his name, he moved forward to shake my hand. "I am delighted to meet you, Rachel," Ross said in the soothing, neutral tone of a virtuoso legal counselor. Although Armstrong towered over his attorney, Ross seemed to radiate authority almost equal to that of his client.

Just as Douglas Armstrong looked presidential, Sherman Ross looked perfectly cast for the role of special counsel to the president. It was easy to picture him at a meeting in the Oval Office —a motionless predator seated in a warm corner of the room, keeping a cool vigilant eye on his client. I knew some of his background. Ross had started off as a criminal defense attorney fresh out of law school at St. Louis University. He began handling white-collar cases during the heyday of the Antitrust Department's criminal prosecutions in the early 1970s. As a result, he found himself spending more and more time with the business elite of St. Louis, who were sufficiently impressed with their savage but savvy antitrust defender to begin seeking him out for advice in other areas of the law. Sherman Ross' influence within those circles expanded quickly. While the Fortune 500 companies that were headquartered in St. Louis might allow one of the staid downtown firms to handle the daily legal grist of the corporate mill, when the CEO needed the advice of a true counselor, more often than not you could find the corporate limo parked on a particular side street in Clayton, idling outside the small building that housed the offices of Sherman Ross & Associates.

Back in the early, hungry days of Armstrong Bioproducts,

Ross' brilliant and bold maneuverings kept the fledgling company out of bankruptcy. Douglas Armstrong and Sherman Ross formed a lifetime bond. Indeed, rumors of Armstrong's presidential ambitions began to pick up when Ross left his firm last year and moved to Washington to become the senator's chief of staff.

Armstrong pulled up a chair and said, "Rachel, I understand you think there may be some skulduggery involving my old company?"

I nodded. "You're familiar with the SLP deal?"

"I am. As you may know, I sit on the Senate Commerce Committee, which is monitoring the transaction because of the foreign investment issue."

"One of the chemical engineers hired by SLP to perform the due diligence on Chemitex's R and D files apparently found something in there that disturbed him enough to want to talk to a lawyer, namely me."

"He found something in the R and D files?" Armstrong asked.

"I think so."

"What did he tell you he found?"

"We never met. His name was Bruce Rosenthal. He was killed before we got to meet."

Armstrong raised his eyebrows. "Killed?"

I nodded. "In a ghastly way. Someone dropped him nine stories down a trash chute and into trash compactor, where he was crushed."

Armstrong gasped. "Good God." He turned toward Ross, who had silently withdrawn to the corner. "Did you hear that, Sherm?"

Ross was leaning against the wall, his arms crossed. He gave a noncommittal nod.

Armstrong turned back to me. "Do you have any idea what the poor man found at my company?"

"Douglas," Ross interjected in a soft but firm voice, "it's not your company anymore."

Armstrong nodded without turning toward Ross. "You're right." He gave me a rueful smile. "At Chemitex, I mean."

I shrugged. "I'm not sure. I think it was something in the R and D files."

Ross interjected. "Why do you say that?"

I looked toward him. "His apartment was searched after he was killed. Also, his secretary thinks his office may have been searched." I explained my unsuccessful efforts to obtain a copy of the documents Bruce had photocopied from the R&D files.

"But how do you pinpoint the R and D files as the source of his concern?" Armstrong asked.

I explained my review of the files from Bruce's laptop computer.

It was obvious from Armstrong's expression that he didn't know enough about computers to understand what I was saying. Fortunately, Sherman Ross did. He asked, "How can you tell there were ever any R and D materials on the hard drive?"

"His secretary typed some dictation tapes on his R and D review. She gave them to him in disk format to load onto his computer. She still had copies of two of the documents she had typed for him."

"Where is this young lady?" Armstrong asked.

"Dead," I said.

Armstrong sat back and crossed his arms over his chest. "How?" he asked quietly.

"A one-car accident. The police think it was drunk driving. I have my doubts." I explained them.

Armstrong shook his head. "This is terrible, Rachel. How can I help?"

"I need access to the R and D files. Specifically, the documents Bruce copied. I need to find out what got Bruce so upset. Let me give you an example. In the dictation tape his secretary typed, he was all worked up about something called Primax."

"Primax?" Armstrong repeated with a frown. He turned to Ross. "Ring any bell, Sherm?"

Ross looked at Armstrong and then at me, his hooded eyes expressionless. "No," he said.

Armstrong turned back to me. "What is it?"

"I have no idea. But Bruce must have, and something about it seemed to bother him. What was that something? I think the answer could be in those files. He also mentioned Guillain-Barré syndrome. He found something in those files having to do with that disease. Was someone doing research on it? If so, what about that research made Bruce so upset?" I paused to reach into my briefcase. "And here's another thing. Look at this document." I handed Armstrong the Beth Shalom/Labadie Gardens list.

He leaned back in his chair and squinted at the list. Ross stepped forward and peered at it over Armstrong's shoulders. After a moment Ross looked at me. "Where did you get that?"

I explained the Bruce-to-David-to-me chain of custody.

Ross nodded. "Who are those names?"

I shrugged. "I don't know. Somehow, Bruce got hold of the original document. Not a copy. I have to believe that document is somehow connected to what Bruce was so upset about. That's why I need access to those files."

Ross looked up from the list. "How do you know that document came from Chemitex's files?" he asked.

It was a fair question. I didn't have a good answer. "I don't," I conceded. "But everything else points to Chemitex."

Ross studied me with curiosity. "Why are you so obsessed with this?"

I took a deep breath and exhaled slowly. "Because David Marcus was special. I'm haunted by his death."

Armstrong reached over and covered my hand with his. "I understand," he said gently.

I shook my head. "It's more than just that. The cause of his death haunts me, too."

Ross said, "It is my understanding that his murderers were killed by the police."

I sighed. "Probably. But even the homicide detective on the case has doubts. His initial reaction was that David had been killed by professionals."

"Professionals?" Armstrong looked surprised. "Who would have a motive to kill him?"

"That's what I'm trying to find out." I paused, momentarily overwhelmed by frustration. I looked at Ross and then Armstrong. "I know I'm getting consumed by this, Senator. But I have to run it down." I looked into his eyes. "You know why your wife died. I don't know why David died. Maybe it *was* just a hate crime, but I have doubts. Those doubts are like a hole in the middle of my heart. If I don't do everything I can to put the doubts to rest, I'll never be able to get on with my life." I shrugged helplessly. "That's why."

Armstrong nodded. "I understand." He turned to Ross. "We've got to be able to do something here, Sherm."

Ross studied me. "How late will you be up tonight?"

"Probably until midnight."

He nodded pensively. "I'll look into it."

There was a knock at the door. Diane Raney, Armstrong's press secretary, poked her head in. "They need you in makeup right now," she said to Armstrong. "And then Ted Koppel wants to go over the program schedule."

Armstrong nodded. "Fine," he said wearily as he stood up.

I stood up. "Thank you, Senator. Good luck tonight."

He chuckled. "I'm sure old Ted and I will be chewing on each other before we're five minutes into the show." His expression got serious. "We'll do what we can, Rachel."

Sherman Ross let Armstrong go first. Ross paused at the door and turned to me. "Midnight?"

I nodded.

"I'll contact you before then."

I took a detour by my office, took care of some paperwork, and got home around ten o'clock. For the first time in at least a week I was feeling a glimmer of optimism. I tried Benny, but got his answering machine.

I waited for the beep. "So how'd you like Flo? Isn't she great?

Give me a buzz when you get back. I had a great meeting with Armstrong. I think he's going to help me out."

I made a cup of tea and read through the mail. Afterwards, I took Ozzie for a long walk. I checked the message light on my answering machine when we got back. No message. I smiled at the thought of Benny and Flo together. They really seemed to hit it off at dinner. I dialed his number again and waited for the beep.

"Benny," I said in mock alarm, "it's almost eleven o'clock. Are you still with Flo? Before you two start getting serious, I better remind you: she's old enough to be your wife. Worse yet, she's probably smarter than you. I thought you liked your women fresh out of high school and unburdened by the distractions of intellect. Call me, dahling."

I curled up on the couch and read two more chapters of Edith Wharton's *The House of Mirth*. Just as I closed the book and stood to get undressed, the phone rang.

I answered on the second ring. "Welcome home, lover boy," I said mischievously.

"Uh, Rachel? This is Sherman Ross."

"Oh," I said, flustered and embarrassed. "I thought you were someone else."

"Is this a good time for us to talk?"

"Sure."

"I am calling from the car. We are in your driveway. Perhaps you could join me out here."

Surprised, I peered out the living room window. Sure enough, there was a stretch limo with the lights on idling in my driveway. "I'll be right out."

A few minutes later I was seated across from Sherman Ross in the back of the limo.

"The senator is in an awkward position on this matter," Ross started off, his tone solemn. "Far more awkward than he himself realizes or wishes to admit. There are many people out there, including a significant number of Republicans and Democrats, who view Douglas Armstrong as a threat to the status quo and, not surprisingly, as a dangerous candidate for the presidency. The media spotlight is becoming increasingly intense, and will continue to intensify. As a result, every act or omission by the senator is magnified. It is within that context, and with an awareness of those risks, that I am attempting to fulfill his request that we help you."

"Spoken like a true lawyer," I said, only half in jest.

He ignored the comment. "Do you know Harold Henderson?"

I shook my head.

"Harold is the St. Louis Chief of Police. I spoke with him an hour ago. As I suspected, he knows nothing about the Rosenthal homicide. I suggested that it might be prudent for him to take a more active interest in the case to insure that the investigation remained vigorous. I also spoke with a member of the legal team representing the parent corporation of Chemitex Bioproducts. As you know, the parent is in a bankruptcy proceeding. I suggested to them that before the hearing on the sale of Chemitex Bioproducts occurred, it would be prudent to have someone review the R and D documents that are now in the hands of SLP's attorneys in Chicago."

He paused to take a sip of mineral water. "It will no doubt take at least a week or so before we begin to see any results from the suggestions I've given to these people. You will need to be patient, Rachel."

"Okay," I said, a little disappointed.

Ross gazed at me, his eyes cold. "I will not allow Douglas Armstrong to become more involved in this matter. The stakes are high, especially given the ease with which the media can be manipulated. This is a turning point in Douglas Armstrong's political career. He cannot risk being portrayed as meddling in an ongoing local police investigation, especially given his opponents' efforts to paint him as soft on crime. Similarly, any effort by the senator to interject himself into the affairs of his former company could be used by his opponents—unfairly, of course—as evidence that he is still financially involved with that company while holding public office." He paused again to set his glass back into the rack.

"Frankly," he continued, "we have already done far more than I believe we should have. I have bowed to the senator's wishes on this matter I assume we can count on your total discretion." He slipped a card out of his vest and handed it to me. "You can call me at this number day or night. They will know how to reach me."

I reached for the door. "Thank you."

"Good evening, Rachel."

# 15

CHAPTER

THE word "brand" comes from the Anglo-Saxon "bær-non," which means "to burn." The first trademarks were just that—markings burned into the hides of cattle and other animals, a practice traced back as far as ancient Egypt. During medieval times, trademarks became a symbol of responsibility as the powerful guilds of Europe required their members to each use a unique mark. That way a defective product could be traced back to its maker. A trademark was thus the highly personal symbol of a single worker: when his life ended, so did his trademark. By the middle of the twentieth century, however, it had metamorphosed into the multibillion dollar world of brand-name marketing—a world where a single word, such as Xerox or Corvette or Chanel or Kodak, can be worth hundreds of millions of dollars.

Like any piece of extraordinarily valuable property, a trademark must be guarded from theft and destruction. Few are more sensitive to this than the pharmaceutical industry. Indeed, the sorry experience of one drug company has become the textbook example of what happens when you don't protect your trademark. Back in 1899, the Bayer Company of New York began selling a patent medicine made from a drug known as acetyl salicylic acid. To help promote the medicine under a snazzier name, the company's marketing gurus coined the trademark "Aspirin." For seventeen prosperous years, the Bayer Company sold acetyl salicylic acid under the trademark Aspirin throughout the United States. But when the patent expired in 1917, competitors flooded the market with their versions of the drug, all under the name Aspirin. The Bayer Company ran to federal court. Screaming infringement, it sought an order forcing its competitors to use another name to describe their version of the drug. Too little too late, announced U.S. District Judge Learned Hand, and in one swoop of the judicial pen, the trademark Aspirin became the common noun aspirin.

The pharmaceutical industry learned its lesson. These days, each company guards its own trademarks (such as Tylenol or NyQuil) with a pack of snarling attorneys. All of which told me that if Primax was a brand name coined by a pharmaceutical company, there was an excellent chance that the company had registered the name with the U.S. Trademark Office. Even if the drug itself was no longer in use, the trademark and its last known owner ought to show up in the federal Trademark Register.

It was the morning after my midnight limo meeting with Sherman Ross. I was seated in front of my computer terminal on the credenza, waiting for the computer to confirm that I had accessed the data banks containing information on each of the millions of trademarks in the Principal Register of the U.S. Trademark Office. When the computer advised that it was ready for my first trademark search request, I decided to warm up with a trademark I already knew about: Phrenom. According to Bob Ginsburg, Phrenom was the crown jewel of Chemitex Bioproducts. Just as important, it was the drug that had quite literally saved Armstrong Bioproducts in 1977. I typed in the letters P-H-R-E-N-O-M and pressed the ENTER key.

The screen went blank for a moment as the computer searched the trademark files, and then the following information appeared on the screen:

### PHRENOM

INTL CLASS: 5 (Pharmaceuticals)
U.S. CLASS: 18 (Medicines & Pharmaceutical Preparations)
STATUS: Renewed
GOODS/SERVICES: Pharmaceutical - Namely, an anti-
 inflammatory preparation for the treatment
 of rheumatoid arthritis, osteoarthritis, juve-
 nile rheumatoid arthritis. Generic name:
 Phenylpyrrole Sodium
REG. NO.: 1,214,321
REGISTERED: November 1, 1974
FIRST USE: June 1, 1974
FILED: June 1, 1974
ORIGINAL REGISTRANT: Armstrong Bioproducts, Inc.,
 St. Louis, Missouri, USA
ASSIGNEE: Chemitex Bioproducts Corporation,
 St. Louis, Missouri, USA
 Recorded: December 29, 1987
 Brief: Acquisition effective December 17, 1987
LAST LISTED OWNER: Chemitex Bioproducts Corporation,
 St. Louis, Missouri, USA

I read through the information to familiarize myself with the format. Most of it was unexceptional, although I noted with curiosity that Armstrong Bioproducts had filed and obtained the trademark registration for the name Phrenom in 1974, which was three years *before* the FDA issued its final approval for the drug. According to Bob Ginsburg's explanation of the FDA approval process, the drug would have been in the late stages of preliminary testing or the early stages of human testing when Armstrong Bioproducts registered the Phrenom trademark. Then again, that only underscored the importance of the trademark: years before the drug was approved, Armstrong Bioproducts had already secured its rights in the name.

I pushed the PRINT SCREEN button.

"Rachel?"

I turned away from the credenza. Jacki was standing in the doorway with a forlorn expression on her face and one of her black pumps in her hand. I looked closer. The shoe was missing the heel, which was in her other hand.

I leaned back from the computer and gave her a sympathetic sigh. "Oh, Jacki, another one?"

"I can't stand it," she said, her lips quivering. "This is the fourth time in three weeks."

I looked back at the computer screen for a moment and then at my secretary. The trademark search could wait. "Come on," I said. "Let's talk."

"No, you're busy."

I gave her a mock stern look. "Come in here, Jacki."

She padded in barefoot and took a seat across the desk from me. Looking down at the broken heel, she shook her head. "I paid seventy-five dollars for these pumps. You'd think that when you pay that kind of money you'd be buying quality."

I didn't have the heart to tell Jacki that when you're six feet three inches tall and weigh 240 pounds, it isn't enough to pay for quality in your pumps. You also need to pay for space-age alloys and industrial-strength epoxy.

I mulled it over for a moment. "Look," I said, leaning back in my chair and holding up my feet. She frowned at my shoes, which were simple black leather flats.

"You're in law school, Jacki. Someday you're going to be a professional. A professional, uh, woman. Being a woman is hard enough. Being a woman attorney is even harder. You're going to have to work at making people take you seriously. That means you're going to have to dress like a woman, not a bimbo."

"A bimbo?" she said with a pained expression.

"Look at me. I'm five feet seven. If I don't need heels for

height, you surely don't. Save your pumps for when you go out at night. They're too uncomfortable to wear around the office anyway. Believe me, you want to be comfortable at your job." I leaned forward with a reassuring smile. "Go over to Pappagallo on your lunch hour. Get yourself a nice pair of flats. They're classy, and you'll love them."

She stood up, her eyes watering. "I'll do that." She paused at the door and turned back. "I want to be a woman, not a bimbo."

"I know you do. Don't feel bad, Jacki. Remember, the rest of us got to start off as girls. We had mothers or older sisters to teach us what to wear and how to dress and how to act. You didn't. You've been at it for just a month. You're doing fine."

She straightened her back. "If you see me in anything bimbolike, please tell me."

I was tempted to mention her makeup, which she apparently applied with a trowel, but I recalled how embarrassed she was by her five o'clock shadow, which usually arrived three hours early. She used the makeup to conceal her whiskers. So instead, I nodded. "You've got a deal, Jacki."

"Thanks." She returned to her desk to work on the interrogatories I'd given her earlier in the day.

Smiling, I turned back to the computer screen and typed in a new search request: PRIMAX. I pressed the ENTER key and waited as the screen went blank. After a moment, the computer informed me that it had found three registrations for Primax. After running through a 1963 registration for a car wax and a 1992 registration for a saw blade used with concrete and core drilling machinery, I called up the third Primax registration:

### PRIMAX

INTL CLASS: 5 (Pharmaceuticals)
U.S. CLASS: 18 (Medicines & Pharmaceutical Preparations)
STATUS: Canceled

GOODS/SERVICES: Pharmaceutical - Namely, an anti-
inflammatory preparation for the treatment
of rheumatoid arthritis, osteoarthritis, juve-
nile rheumatoid arthritis. Generic name:
Primillamine acid
REG. NO.: 1,214,328
REGISTERED: November 1, 1974
FIRST USE: June 1, 1974
FILED: June 1, 1974
CANCELED: May 8, 1975
Reason: Request of registrant.
ORIGINAL REGISTRANT: Armstrong Bioproducts, Inc.,
St. Louis, Missouri, USA
LAST LISTED OWNER: Armstrong Bioproducts, Inc.,
St. Louis, Missouri, USA

I leaned back in my chair and frowned at the screen. I glanced
over at the Phrenom information I had printed out. Armstrong
Bioproducts had filed its trademark applications for Phrenom and
Primax on the same day, June 1, 1974. Almost a year later, it had
canceled the Primax registration.

I printed out the information and typed in a request for all
trademarks registered to Armstrong Bioproducts or Chemitex
Bioproducts. The search located twenty-seven other trademarks.
Twenty-three were still active, four were canceled. The four canceled trademarks were Depran, Enval, Immunin, and Zepronal.
Each was the name of a different type of drug: Depran was the
name of an anticoagulant, Enval a salve for eczema, Immunin a
platelet inhibitor, and Zepronal a diuretic. I compared the product
descriptions of the four canceled trademarks to the product descriptions of the company's twenty-three active trademarks. For
two of the four, the company had another trademark for a drug
whose description was precisely the same as the one for the canceled trademark. For the other two, there was no overlapping
product description among the active trademarks.

I leaned back in my chair, trying to make sense out of the trademark puzzle. There could be a benign explanation for those four canceled registrations. And for Primax. In the situation where there was only one trademark for a particular product description and that trademark registration had been canceled, it could be that the company registered the trademark while its new drug application was pending before the FDA, but thereafter the FDA refused to approve the drug. Where there were two trademarks for the same product description, one of which was subsequently canceled, it could have been that the company registered both names because it couldn't decided which it liked better. After the FDA approved the drug, the company chose one name and discarded the other.

Presumably, there were other explanations as well, some benign and some ominous. Was Primax just the abandoned brand name for what became Phrenom?

I frowned at the screen. It was getting even more confusing.

Jacki buzzed on the intercom line to tell me that Benny Goldberg was on line one. She was giggling as she told me. I lifted the receiver. "Are you harassing my poor secretary?"

"I beg your pardon. We were having a medical discussion on the salutary effects of female hormone injections."

"In English, please."

"I asked her if she'd started growing tits yet."

"Benny, that's horrible."

"Hey, what's the big goddam deal? I've started growing them, too, for chrissakes, and I'm not taking any hormones."

"That's because you need to lose some weight."

"Real sensitive, Miss Buns of Steel. And anyway, never underestimate the raw sexual stamina of a full-figured man."

"Speaking of which," I said with a smile.

"Huh?"

"So?"

"So?" he repeated. "What's that supposed to mean?"

"It means 'tell me.' "

"Tell you what?"

"Tell you what?" I mimicked. "Come on, Benny. For starters, tell me what you did to my sweet, shy, defenseless girlfriend."

"Flo and I had a very pleasant time."

"Um-hm," I said, grinning. A flustered Benny Goldberg was such a rare event that I couldn't resist. "A little more specific, Professor."

"I told you, we had a very pleasant time."

"Come on, Benny. We're buddies. You can tell me."

"Tell you what?"

"You know."

"No, I don't know." He was struggling to remain dignified. "What is it you want to know?"

"Well," I said demurely, "for starters: did you guys do it?"

"I cannot believe this."

"Is that a yes?"

"No. Absolutely not."

"Really?"

"Really."

"My, my," I said in wonder. "I guess it must have been the novelty of being with a woman your own age."

That put him into his Jackie Gleason mode. "One of these days, Rachel . . . to the moon!"

We both laughed.

"Isn't she great?" I asked.

"Definitely. We went over to the bar at the Hotel Majestic and talked until midnight."

"Is she staying around another day?"

"I wish. She's driving over to the east side this morning to research her story and then she's flying back to D.C. tonight."

"When are you going to see her again?"

"I told her I might go up there to visit in a few weeks. Once I get the exams graded."

"That's wonderful." I was genuinely delighted, for Benny and for Flo. Especially for Benny, whose idea of the perfect mate too often seemed to be a dumbed-down, underage version of a Dallas Cowboy Cheerleader.

"Yeah," he grudgingly agreed. "So tell me about last night. Is Armstrong going to help you?"

"A little," I said. I described my meeting with Armstrong and Ross down at the television station and my subsequent meeting with Ross in the limo in my driveway.

"Fucking politicians," Benny said in disgust.

"I can sort of understand their concerns," I said. "Ross is putting on the brakes. I got the sense that Armstrong was more eager to help, but Ross is the one keeping his eye on the prize."

"Don't be naive, Rachel. Both of them have their eye on the goddam prize. Armstrong wants to be president at least as much as Ross wants to be chief of staff."

"I'm not giving up on them. Ross told me he's pulled some levers behind the scenes. He said to give it a couple weeks' time. I've got nothing to lose."

"True."

"Listen to what I found," I said, gathering the trademark printouts and my notes. I explained what I had discovered about Primax and the other trademarks.

"What's it all mean?" he asked when I was through.

"I'm not sure, yet."

"What about Guillain-Barré? Do one of those other drugs cure it?"

"I don't think so," I said, "but I'm not sure. I thought at first that Primax might be the one, but it looks like it's another arthritis drug. In fact, it sounds almost the same as Phrenom. And maybe it is. Maybe they registered two names for the same drug and later decided to go with Phrenom."

Benny said, "If your theory is right about the lag time between the name and the FDA approval, you need to look at the FDA files. That'll tell you a lot more about Primax."

"Good idea. Do we know any good lawyers in Washington, D.C.?"

"We know someone even better."

"Who?" I asked.

"A brilliant reporter with a law degree and a great set of knockers."

"Ah, yes," I said with a smile. "She'll be back in D.C. tonight, right?"

"Right."

"Benny, would you do me a really big favor?"

"Anything, my dear."

"Would you be a love and give Flo a call tonight to see if she could help us out over at the FDA?"

"It would be my pleasure, Rachel."

"You're sure I'm not imposing, Benny?"

"Not at all, my dear. Not at all."

# 16

CHAPTER

WHEN the going gets tough, the tough go shopping. At least I do.

At four-thirty that afternoon, fed up with trying to unravel the Primax puzzle and the rest of Bruce Rosenthal's due diligence jottings, I left my office, hopped in the car, and headed west to Town and Country Centre, my favorite shopping mall in metropolitan St. Louis.

I realize, of course, that the very notion of a glitzy suburban mall with glassed-in elevators and piped-in music might seem to be anathema for someone educated near the ten-ring circus of Harvard Square and trained in the flamboyant urban funk of Chicago, but I can't help myself. When I'm feeling blue, nothing beats a couple of hours in a sunny mall with cascading waterfalls, hanging sculptures, lush floral plantings, patterned marble floors, dramatic skylights, food courts, espresso bars, a Bloomingdale's, a Saks Fifth Avenue, a Famous-Barr, three bookstores, and dozens of specialty shops.

I know, I know. Call me an embarrassment to the Ivy League, but don't forget to call me when Banana Republic has a sale. Which, in fact, they did. Forty percent off on leather bomber jackets, thirty percent off on hiking shorts, fifty percent off on selected jeans. Such deals! Such bargains! What a pleasure it was to concentrate on denim and khaki after a steady dose of Guillain-Barré syndrome, Phrenom Injection, and the Principal Register of the U.S. Trademark Office.

I didn't zero in on him until I was having dinner at Pizzeria Uno's in the upstairs food courtyard around six-thirty. I had turned to gaze out the window toward Athlete's Foot and Blockbuster Music across the way when I saw him. He was standing in the smoking area over by the interior mall entrance to Saks. I studied him carefully. He was tall and lanky, with longish red hair that was parted in the middle and fell over his forehead. He was dressed in black—tight black jeans, a black leather jacket over a black T-shirt, black boots.

With a tiny shiver of recognition, I realized that I had seen him more than once over the past couple hours. He had been outside Banana Republic peering in through the window while I was trying on jeans. He had been leaning against the glass wall of Talbots and leafing through a magazine when I came out of the Mrs. Field's with a chocolate chip cookie. Later, he drifted into the National Geographic store when I was in there mapping out my fantasy trip to Belize.

I chewed on a slice of pizza as I stared at him. He was wearing dark aviator sunglasses and smoking a cigarette. He seemed to be observing me, but it was hard to tell with the sunglasses. As I watched, he turned slowly and strolled away. By the time I finished my meal and paid the bill, he was nowhere in sight.

I was edgy, and I was angry with myself for being edgy. After all, I had nothing to be defensive about. I wasn't wearing a micromini or a tiny tube top or spiked hair or thigh-high leather boots. I was just an ordinary shopper, wearing a fleece gray cowl-neck chemise, a black belt, black stockings, and sensible black flats. Out of all the comfortably dressed woman browsing through the mall with a shopping bag in each hand, how was it that I got picked out by my very own rebel without a cause? He was probably lurking out there right now, lighting up another Marlboro and practicing a semiarticulate opening line.

*The hell with him,* I said to myself as I headed down the corridor toward the garden courtyard area and my favorite store, Graphic Traffic. Fifteen minutes later, I had forgotten about him as I moved around the store, looking at the wearable art and handpainted crafts with a blend of enchantment and envy—enchanted by the creations, envious of the creators' talents.

But when I stepped back out, there he was, over near the escalators by Maverick Jewelers. I turned in the other direction and walked rapidly down the main corridor in the direction of Bloomingdale's, took the escalator up to the second level, and ducked into the Barnes & Noble. I walked back to the mystery section and turned into the aisle between the bookshelves, my heart still racing. Killing time and trying to get calm, I pulled out a paperback edition of Grisham's *The Pelican Brief.* I studied the cover photo of Julia Roberts. I thought back to how wonderful she had been in *Mystic Pizza,* still one of my favorite movies. I turned it over and looked at the picture of John Grisham. I didn't get the point of the unshaven look: if you're going to go to all the trouble of getting dressed up and traveling to the studio to pose for your portrait, who's going to believe you forgot to shave? I put the book back in the shelf—I had long ago vowed to avoid suspense novels written by attorneys.

I checked my watch. I'd been in the bookstore for ten minutes. I moved to the front of the store and, feigning a casual attitude, I strolled out and down the corridor toward Famous-Barr. No sight of him. I paused at the entrance to Victoria's Secret, wondering whether there really were women out there who thought in terms of matched sets of underwear. I told myself that I probably moved in the wrong circles.

I slowly turned 360 degrees. No sight of him.

Feeling better, I continued down the corridor and went into Abercrombie & Fitch. Immediately I was back to planning my fantasy vacation to Belize. As I pretended to select the appropriate tropical outfits, David Marcus unexpectedly popped into my thoughts. I thought how wonderful it would have been to go to Belize or Costa Rica with David, and immediately a wave of sadness washed over me. Blinking back the tears, I turned to leave.

That's when I spotted him. He was inside Abercrombie & Fitch, two rows over, trying on safari hats. I left the store and moved hurriedly toward the escalator. Halfway down I looked back. He was leaning on the railing overlooking the escalators.

My first thought was to flee, to run for my car.

But then I realized how foolish that was. First of all, I couldn't be certain that he had any dangerous intentions. He just could be one of those creepy but harmless followers. And if he was creepy and dangerous, running to my car was the dumbest thing I could do. He'd either grab me in the parking lot, or follow me home.

I got off the escalator at the first level and walked quickly toward the atrium area where there were escalators down to the lower level. I stepped onto the down escalator.

Trying to find a security guard wasn't the answer, either. He would disappear into the crowd until the guard left. Same with calling the police. He'd be nowhere in sight when they arrived. And what could I tell them, anyway? That a man seemed to be following me at a distance?

I got off the escalator at the lower level and walked briskly toward the ticket window to the Wehrenberg Theaters.

"One," I said, sliding a ten-dollar bill through the opening.

"To which picture, ma'am?"

"Doesn't matter. Just give me one fast."

I grabbed the ticket and change and moved inside. I ducked around the corner just as he stepped off the down escalator. I couldn't tell whether he had seen me. I moved down the carpeted hallway past the first two screens and went into the third. I found a seat halfway down the center aisle on the left. Putting my shopping bags on the seat next to me, I sat numbly, staring at the screen.

After maybe ten minutes, I realized I was watching an Arnold Schwartzenegger film. Despite the tension, or perhaps because of it, I grinned. What a surreal place Hollywood must be. Where else could a man named Arnold Schwartzenegger become an action movie star under his real name?

Each time the theater doors opened, I spun around. It was never him. I stayed through the end of the movie and filed out with the rest of the crowd, glancing furtively around.

*Damn.*

He was seated on the plaza across the way at the Northwest Coffee Co. Still wearing dark sunglasses, he was sipping a cup of coffee as he surveyed the throng emerging from the theater.

My mind was racing.

*Lose him,* I told myself. *Start moving around and lose him.*

I edged toward the glass elevator and squeezed on with a large group of buzzing and laughing moviegoers. I hunched down, trying to disappear in the middle of the crowd so that he wouldn't be able to tell whether I got off at the first or second level. The elevator stopped at the first level. I moved to the side to let the crowd out and then wormed my way back into the middle of the mostly new group. I hunched down as the doors closed.

The elevator stopped at the second level. I got off with the rest of the crowd. Directly ahead was the corridor leading to the covered bridge to the parking garage. On one side of the corridor was a Champs, on the other side a Crate & Barrel.

I got my bearings. My car was on the opposite side of the shopping center, down on the parking lot in front of Saks. Saks was to the left. I turned that way and walked briskly down the main mall corridor, passing the J. Crew on my right, the Eddie Bauer on my left, trying to formulate a plan of action. Up ahead on my right was another corridor leading to the parking garage. On the left was the second level entrance to Saks.

*Lose him in the parking garage,* I decided, and turned right.

As I broke into a sprint toward the covered bridge I saw a sign on the left for restrooms, telephones, and lockers. The arrow was pointing down a hallway that was just before the bridge to the parking garage. I looked back as I jogged toward the bridge, my shopping bags banging against my legs. No sign of him. I cut left down the narrow hallway. The doors to the men's and women's restrooms were on the left side about twenty feet down the hallway. To my right, across from the restroom doors, was a pillar that protruded about a foot into the hallway, just enough to screen me from view. I backed against the wall on the far side of the pillar. I looked down. I was concealed, but the bulky shopping bags weren't. I peered around the pillar and down the hallway toward the corridor that connected the mall to the parking garage. No sign of him. I glanced down at the shopping bags and then across the hall at the door to the women's restroom. I took a deep breath and quickly stepped forward, kicking the door open with my foot. As it swung wide, I heaved the shopping bags inside and ducked back against the opposite wall behind the pillar.

I counted to ten and quickly peered around toward the main corridor on my left. No sign of him. Across the hallway to the left of the restroom doors was a metal door with the words THE MUSEUM CO stenciled in black. To the right of the restroom doors was a metal door with the word CAPEZIO stenciled in black. They must have been the back, or freight, entrances to the stores. About ten yards further down to the right, the hallway was barred by a large metal door with the words NO ADMITTANCE stenciled in black.

I tried to visualize a blueprint of the mall. The building was the length of several football fields. I was standing in a corridor that ran along the back, or west, side of the building. My position was a little to the south of the halfway point of the structure. Saks was on the front, or east, side of the mall. That meant that my corridor didn't connect to Saks. Presumably, my corridor continued on the other side of the door marked NO ADMITTANCE—continued on until it ran into Famous-Barr at the end of the mall, which was too far south. But there might be a stairway along that corridor at the south end that would lead across and down to the first level, and then I could dash through Saks and out to the parking lot.

It was worth a shot.

I peered around the pillar again, staring toward the bridge that connected the mall to the parking garage. Just as I did, he jogged by, heading toward the garage. I jerked back, banging my head against the concrete.

*Shit.*

*Wait. He's out in the parking garage now.*

*Now!*

I spun right and sprinted toward the NO ADMITTANCE door. I turned the knob and shoved hard against the metal door. The force made the door swing open all the way and bang against the wall as I ran through the doorway and down the narrow corridor. The freight entrance to Famous-Barr was about seventy-five yards ahead. I passed a freight elevator on the left and then several metal doors, each with the name of the store stenciled in black: FOOT LOCKER, CRAYOLA KIDS, D.O.C., BENNETTON. The linoleum floor was shiny with wax. I slid to a stop at the end of the corridor in front of the large door bearing the legend FAMOUS-BARR. I grabbed the doorknob.

"Shit," I hissed as I twisted and yanked. The door was locked.

I turned.

I couldn't believe what I saw.

Back at the far end of the corridor, the large metal door that I had shoved open was still open.

I started running back down the corridor, trying each back door along the way. Each was locked.

I stopped in front of the freight elevator and peered through the glass window. I jammed my thumb against the down button. I heard the elevator gears shift somewhere below. I squinted through the window, trying to spot the elevator car. The cables started to vibrate and then move.

"Come on," I pleaded, glancing back toward the open metal door. "Come on."

I could hear the tired whine of the elevator car slowly rising on the cables.

"Come on, come on."

As the top of the elevator car rose into view, I turned to look down the corridor. I caught my breath as he stepped back into view, returning from the garage.

Just as the elevator car clunked into position, he turned and stared at me. We were maybe forty yards apart.

He started toward me at a deliberate trot until he reached the open metal door. Without breaking stride, he reached out and yanked the door closed behind him. Then he broke into a sprint, his red hair flying.

We were twenty-five yards apart when the elevator door slid open. He reached into his jacket and pulled out what looked like a gun or a knife. I ducked onto the elevator and banged furiously on the button for the lower level. The elevator door slowly slid closed. It clanged shut just as he reached the elevator. I flinched as his face suddenly appeared in the window. As the elevator started to descend, he glared down at me through the reinforced glass. Then his head jerked from view.

"Oh, my God." I was shivering. "Oh, my God, oh, my God."

The elevator descended at an infuriatingly leisurely pace. I stared at the floor indicator above the elevator door, tapping my foot anxiously. After what seemed like an hour, the light blinked from 2 to 1. As the elevator passed by the first floor landing, light came through the window and I winced, afraid that his face would abruptly appear. I jammed my thumb hard against the button for the lower level.

"Hurry," I pleaded. "God, hurry."

Finally, the elevator reached the lower level and shuddered to a halt. The door slid open and I stepped out into a small area. To my left was a door marked STAIRS. To my right was a long narrow corridor. From somewhere up above, I heard a metal door open. Then there was the clattering sound of footsteps coming down the stairs. It had to be him.

Cradling my purse under my arm like a football, I sprinted down the corridor, which opened onto a concrete loading dock area. I could go right or left. To my right there were four parallel loading docks, all positioned at a forty-five degree angle to the underground service tunnel that ran through the center of the mall. A large Saks truck was parked in position at the far dock. Beyond the loading dock area to the right, the concrete slab narrowed into an elevated walkway that ran along the side of the building for fifty yards and then curved out into another loading dock area. To my left, the slab narrowed and ended. The service tunnel curved out of sight to the left.

I chose right. I jogged past the four loading docks and continued along the pathway, pausing to try the doors marked MALL STORAGE, ELECTRICITY, GENERATOR ROOM, GAS METERS, WATER VALVE ROOM. Each was locked.

Back in the distance I could hear the sound of a metal door swinging open, then footsteps charging down the corridor. Up ahead, just before the next loading dock area, was a large trash compactor. It was twenty feet long, maybe four feet high.

I turned back. He wasn't visible yet. I looked around frantically. There was nowhere else to hide. I tossed my purse into the open top of the compactor and climbed in after it, landing inside on several large, bunchy bags of trash.

# 17

CHAPTER

THE stench was powerful.

Fighting back thoughts of Bruce Rosenthal's final moments, I grabbed my purse and crawled over the bags toward the other end of the long container. When I was far enough back to be invisible from the opening, I turned toward the front and waited, my knees pulled up to my chin. I tried to breathe through my mouth to minimize the putrid smells.

After a few minutes, I heard footsteps from a distance. The metal container was a good sound conductor. The footsteps were heavy enough to be boots. I listened, straining my ears. I heard several quick steps, then a pause, then several more steps, then another pause.

Perhaps he was trying each of the doors I had tried.

His steps grew louder as he approached the trash compactor from the rear. I listened as he walked the length of the container, passing my position on the way. He stopped at the front end. I held my breath.

A hand appeared at the top of the opening, and then the other hand. I saw a glint of metal in the second hand. He was resting his hands on the top of the container opening. I remained motionless, silently begging him to move on. He leaned over and squinted into the container, his red hair falling over his face. I didn't move, praying that I was far enough back to be shrouded in darkness.

He straightened up. His hands withdrew. I heard him move down the length of the container toward the back. I listened as the footsteps grew fainter.

When they faded away altogether, I exhaled slowly and waited. A few minutes passed in silence. I heard the distant growl of a truck engine starting up, followed by the noise of shifting gears. As the engine noise grew louder, I suddenly realized that the truck was inside the service tunnel somewhere south of my position. It was moving north toward me. But by the time I made the connection—namely, that the driver could be my rescuer—the truck had already rumbled past the compactor on its way out of the mall.

"Damn," I mumbled as my spirits fell.

More silence. Ten minutes passed. Then the crackle of automobile wheels on cement.

I clambered over the garbage bags toward the opening, but by the time I got to my feet the vehicle was disappearing into the northern end of the tunnel. I could just make out the two red bubbles on the roof. I realized that it must have been mall security, or maybe the police.

The realization triggered a wave of hopelessness. If that vehicle really was mall security or the police, they were probably on their evening rounds. That meant they might not be back through the tunnel for hours.

Standing chest high in the opening of the trash compactor, I scanned the area. No sight of him.

I knew I couldn't remain there. I had to start moving, to get out from the underground portion. Just as important, I had to get myself into a position where I could flag down a truck or other vehicle that might come through the tunnel.

As quietly as I could, I climbed out of the compactor container.

Standing on the cement platform looking out over the service road, I got my bearings. The service tunnel ran south to north underneath the middle of the mall. The freight elevator shaft was roughly two-thirds of the way down the mall structure, which meant that I had started off in the underground section closer to the southern than the northern end of the mall. After getting off the elevator, I had moved further south. The underground service tunnel was a one-way road. The entrance was at the southern end of the mall. The choice seemed obvious: the quickest and safest way out was to keep moving south.

The elevated concrete pathway wrapped around the corner of the loading deck and terminated in a short stairway down to the road level of the service tunnel. I went down the stairs and inched along the wall until I was facing south. The tunnel was dark beyond the loading dock. The only illumination was an occasional weak overhead light.

He could be down there waiting, or he could be coming up from behind. Based on the sound of his footsteps when he walked away from the compactor, he was heading north. Moving south still seemed the best idea for me.

*Seemed*, I reminded myself.

If I was wrong, I told myself, if he was actually somewhere farther south in the tunnel, I would need a hiding place if he turned and came back. I looked around. I didn't see any doors or openings on either side of the tunnel. A few yards ahead, set in the wall near the ground, was something I first mistook for a small steering wheel. As I kneeled to look closer, I saw that the steering wheel was actually the locking mechanism for a circular hatch, like one on a submarine, except set in the wall. There were yellow warning stripes on the hatch. A small yellow sign bolted to the wall above the hatch read:

WARNING: ACCESS TO STORM CULVERT
OPEN ONLY WITH EXTREME CAUTION!

I put my hands on the wheel and tugged counterclockwise. The wheel initially resisted, but then turned smoothly. I retightened it and stood up.

Peering down the tunnel, I saw another hatch set in the wall about twenty yards further south. The tunnel curved to the right beyond that, so I couldn't tell whether there were other hatches.

It hadn't rained for at least a week, I told myself as I started walking forward along the tunnel wall. That meant that the storm culvert might be a good hiding place.

As I continued to walk south down the tunnel, I could feel the slight incline in the road. That was a good sign, because it meant that the service tunnel was beginning to return to street level, which meant I was getting closer. Anticipation got the better of me, and I started to run. As I rounded the corner I could see the tunnel entrance off in the distance.

*Yes!*

But as I got closer, I saw that the entire entrance was blocked by a steel-barred gate. I stopped in front of it. It was one of those motorized gates that slid up and down like a flexible garage door. I peered through the gate toward the entrance ramp. Getting in was easy. There was an electric eye device out there, along with one of those cardkey boxes. Getting out at this end was another story. I put my hands on the cross-hatched steel and tried to pull the gate up. It wouldn't budge.

I stared through the gate, my hands resting on the steel bars. I felt like a prisoner.

There had to be a way to open the gate from the inside. I looked around. Over on the wall near the gate was a control panel. The button marked CLOSE GATE was just that: a simple black button. But the one marked OPEN GATE required a key.

I turned around and faced north into the service tunnel as I tried to organize my thoughts. I had two choices: (1) I could wait here in the hopes that a truck or a security car would eventually come down the ramp and open the gate in time to save me, or (2) I could go back into the service tunnel and try to reach the elevator. The advantage of waiting by the gate was that I could get out the moment the gate opened. The disadvantage was that if he showed up before a vehicle did, I would be trapped. If I headed back into the tunnel, though, there were two advantages: there were other escape routes and there were more places to hide if he showed up. The disadvantage was that he was probably in there somewhere.

I turned back and peered through the gate.

*If he's somewhere down in the tunnel, which he probably is, and if he's heading my way, which he eventually will, I certainly don't want to end up against this metal gate like a cornered rabbit.*

I turned around, my back against the gate, and took a deep breath. The panic and the raw fear had faded. I seemed to be running on a combination of adrenalin and autopilot.

*Okay,* I said to myself as I slipped off my shoes and shoved them into my purse.

I started down the slope, back into the underground service tunnel. I was walking quickly but cautiously in my stocking feet, trying to make as little noise as possible.

I heard the first sound as I came around the curve. It was a metallic clanking noise, as if someone were trying to open a locked door by yanking on it. The clanking was off in the distance, somewhere back near the second loading dock area.

Silence for a moment. Then more clanking, this time just a little closer.

It had to be him. I remembered all those locked doors near the second loading dock. He must have first searched for me in the north end of the service tunnel and was now working his way back.

I spun around. The entrance gate was no longer visible. I turned back at the faint sound of boots on concrete. I concentrated, trying to reconstruct the layout in my mind. He was crossing the loading dock, still out of view around the next bend. We weren't more than fifty yards apart. Soon he'd be coming down those stairs and heading north toward me. My eyes darted around the tunnel. One of the storm culvert hatches was a few feet in front of me.

I heard him coming down the stairs. In just moments he would round the curve.

I knelt by the hatch, grabbed the locking mechanism, and yanked counterclockwise. It didn't budge. I yanked again as hard as I could, grunting from the effort. Nothing.

I stood up, gasping, and started to back up along the wall. The footsteps were approaching. I turned and ran south toward the next storm culvert hatch.

This one turned.

I spun the wheel as fast as I could for several rotations. The locking mechanism clicked and the hatch swung free on its hinge, opening out from the wall like a small door.

The footsteps were closer.

Without even looking, I scooted feetfirst through the opening into a corrugated metal tube and turned to close the hatch. There was a handle on the inner side of the hatch, but no locking mechanism. The best I could do was pull it closed. When I let go of the handle, it opened slightly, creating a gap of a couple inches. I tried again to pull it shut, with the same result.

*Forget the hatch,* I told myself. *Just move!*

It was pitch-black inside the tube. I could hear the noise of moving water below me. It sounded like a creek. I reached forward in the dark and found the edge of the tube. I turned and crawled backward, blind, to the edge of the tube. I lowered myself slowly, feetfirst. My stocking feet touched the slanted side of the culvert. It was slick and oily. I could hear scurrying, scrabbling noises beneath me.

*Rats,* I told myself with a shudder.

I kept lowering myself until my arms were fully extended and I was hanging from the edge of the tube by my fingers. My feet were in the water now. It was icy cold. I could hear his footsteps. They were practically even with the hatch. I took a deep breath and let go.

I slid down the greasy side of the culvert and into the water, banging my wrists hard against the concrete as I struggled to regain my balance. The water came up to my thighs. Fortunately, the bottom of the culvert was flat, which enabled me to stand.

The metal hatch banged open above me. I took a quick breath and ducked under the water. Using my hands, I pulled myself forward down the culvert, trying to keep my body submerged as I moved along.

I scuttled along underwater with my eyes closed tight, bumping into glass bottles and tree branches and other junk scattered along the bottom. I was literally blind and deaf in the icy water. I kept flinching at the thought of a knife or a bullet ripping into my backside. When my lungs were about to explode, I carefully raised my head, quickly exhaled and inhaled, and ducked under water again.

I got about ten feet further before I banged into a large object. I tried moving right, and then left. It was too big to get around under water. Slowly, I lifted my head and turned to stare back in the direction I had come. It was too dark to see a thing. I turned toward the object that had blocked my path. Feeling around it, I realized it was a metal shopping cart on its side, slick with algae.

I raised my head to look beyond the cart. I could see light in the distance. The storm culvert emerged from beneath the shopping center about fifty yards further down. I was almost there.

Using my hands for balance, I climbed around the shopping cart. There was a sudden explosion behind me and I spun around just as something zinged off the concrete to my left. A second of silence, then the panicked squeals of hundreds of rats. There was a quick flash of light, then another roar of gunfire, followed by a splash in the water in front of me.

He was shooting at me from the edge of the tube above the culvert.

My last shred of control vaporized. Hysterical, I turned and started running and splashing and stumbling through the water toward the opening ahead. He fired again, this time high and wide. I tripped over a heavy object and fell forward into the water. As I struggled to my feet, he fired, missing again. I staggered on, sobbing for air, as I got closer to the opening.

Gasping, I emerged from the culvert into a swampy area behind the mall below the parking area. I scrambled up the gravel embankment and onto the dry grass. A chain-link fence separated me from the parking lot. Exhausted and soaking wet, I lurched toward the fence and grabbed the chain links for support. I glanced back toward the culvert, half expecting him to emerge with a fresh round of ammunition.

*Don't stop now,* I told myself.

Totally fatigued, I looked up. The fence was about seven feet tall. I looked down at my bare feet. Where were my shoes? Reaching for my purse, I realized it was gone. It must have fallen off in the storm culvert.

I looked up at the fence again.

*You can do it, Rachel.*

The fence seemed as tall as Mount Everest.

*Just do it, goddammit.*

I reached up, grasped hold of the chain links, and started up the fence. As I swung my second leg over the top of the fence, I saw the flashing red light of a police car as it pulled onto the grass near the fence.

"Thank God," I said as I pushed off the fence and collapsed on the ground.

# 18

CHAPTER

"WHAT the hell is going on in St. Louis?" Flo asked.

I gave a weary groan. "Crazy, huh?" I cradled the phone against my shoulder as I reached for my coffee mug.

"I just talked to Benny. It's totally outrageous. Have they caught him?"

"Not yet."

"What do the police say?"

"They're working on several different scenarios."

"What are they?"

"One: a rapist. Two: a stalker. Three: a serial killer. Four: none of the above."

"Great," she said contemptuously. "In other words, they have no idea. Are they city cops?"

"No, suburban."

"Even better," she snorted. "I covered that beat in Detroit for a year. Your typical suburban cop couldn't find his own asshole with a map."

"Benny probably has more details. He met me at the police station last night and asked most of the questions. I was kind of woozy."

"I'm not surprised."

"Flo, Benny was a doll. He refused to let me go home alone. He spent the night on the couch. Don't tell anyone, though. He said it'll ruin his image. Actually, you're going to ruin his image."

"Me?"

"The last time he fell for someone his own age was in kindergarten."

"It's a little early for either one of us to be falling for the other."

"He said he's going to visit you in D.C."

"I'm not holding my breath."

"I think he really likes you."

"We'll see."

"Do you like him?" I asked.

"He's okay," she said without a lot of conviction.

"What's wrong with him?"

"I like him and all. It's just that he's . . . I don't know."

"He's what?"

"Well, overly polite."

"Benny?" I asked incredulously. "Overly polite?"

"He's considerate and all, but almost too much so. From what you told me about him, the last person I expected was Mr. Goody Two-Shoes."

"Oh, my God, Flo. He's not like that at all. I've never seen him like that. He must have been nervous. In reality, Benny's incredibly obnoxious. I promise. He's one of the crudest people I've ever met. Once you get to know him, you'll see that he can be vulgar beyond belief. Trust me on this, Flo. You've got to give him another chance."

"We'll see. But enough about me. How do you feel?"

"Sore."

"Did you catch a cold from all that water?"

"No, and I'm not complaining, believe me. I'm glad to be alive. In fact, I'm going into the office in about a half hour. It'll get my mind off all this."

"Not a bad idea. Listen, Benny called me yesterday afternoon. He had some questions from you about the FDA."

"Oh, right. What did you find?"

"Plenty about the process, nothing about specifics."

"What do you mean?"

"According to Benny, you want to see the FDA files on Chemitex Bioproducts and Armstrong Bioproducts, right?"

"Right."

"Forget it."

"Really?"

"Really. I was on the phone for over an hour this morning with an attorney in the general counsel's office. There are two relevant FDA filings for each drug. The first is the Investigational New Drug Application. Known for short as—"

"—the IND," I said.

"Right. That's what you file when you're ready to start testing your drug on humans. Among other things, the IND describes in detail how you are going to do each of the three phases of human testing."

"Three?"

"That's what the guy told me. You start with phase one clinical trials. That's where you test the drug for side effects, usually on thirty or forty healthy volunteers. Then you move to the phase two clinicals. That's where you test it on people who have the target ailment. If it passes phase two, you move to the phase three trials and test the drug on a few thousand patients over a couple year period. If the drug passes all three phases, you're ready to file—"

"—a New Drug Application," I said.

"Yep. But that one wouldn't be as helpful to you. Apparently, the NDAs are humongous—hundreds and hundreds of thousands of pages of documents, most of them highly technical."

"So how do I get a hold of an IND?"

"You don't," Flo said.

"Why not?"

"The FDA won't let you see them. They treat the IND as a trade secret of the applicant."

"What about an FOIA request?" I asked. The Freedom of Information Act is a federal law that requires various governmental entities to turn over gobs of information if requested to do so by a member of the public.

"Nope," Flo said. "INDs are specifically exempted from FOIA. Same with the NDAs."

"Rats," I said glumly. "No way Chemitex will let me see them voluntarily. Sherman Ross said he made some inquiries for me, but I'm not optimistic."

"There's another possible route," Flo said, "but it's a long shot."

"It's probably my only shot. Tell me."

"I asked the guy to describe a typical IND."

"And?"

"They all start off with the FDA Form 1571."

"Which is?"

"A two-page, fill-in-the-blanks federal form."

"Okay."

"But the rest of the IND is usually one volume of text and test data, and that's the key."

"What's the key?"

"The length. I asked the lawyer pointblank: do the drug companies ever have their applications professionally printed?"

"And?"

"Not often these days, he told me, but it was more common back before most companies had sophisticated in-house word processing capabilities."

I smiled. "You're a genius, Flo."

"I admit it, counseler."

"I'll start working the phones as soon as I get to the office."

"Call me if you score a direct hit."

Before leaving for the office, I took out the second of the two documents that Karen Harmon had typed from the tapes Bruce Rosenthal had dictated during his review of the Chemitex R&D files. It was the document with the baffling series of questions on Primax and Guillain-Barré and the hitherto cryptic "Phase Two Trials." I glanced at Bruce's questions:

- *Primax? Where?*
- *Cross-referenced materials not there—Filing glitch?—Need to locate—Need to ask*
- *What's going on with Guillain B?*
- *Where are Primax files???—must find*
- *Be sure to look for LGB—Sounds like typical G-B syndrome*
- *Cross-reference to Phase Two Trial?—Need to check date— Phase Two Trial?—Not possible!?*

Thanks to Flo, I had a good idea what "Phase Two Trial" probably meant, at least generically. How it related to whatever had agitated (and probably killed) Bruce was still a mystery.

Jacki was at lunch when I got to the office. I flipped through my phone messages and glanced at the mail. Nothing that couldn't wait.

I took out the Yellow Pages and flipped to the heading for Printers. I was expecting six or seven listings. Instead, there were nine *pages* of listings. But as I went down the columns, name by name, I saw that I could eliminate many that were obviously geared toward the walk-in trade and ordinary customers looking for a wedding invitation, stationery, or business cards. A major pharmaceutical company was not likely to have a formal FDA filing handled by Sir Speedy Prints or Tommy's Print & Copy Corner. But even after eliminating the obvious ones, I still had more than fifty companies to call. With a deep breath, I lifted the receiver, checked the listing and punched in the number for Ace Printing Company.

I was up to Chesterfield Graphics Corp. when Jacki returned

from lunch. She was surprised to see me and came rushing into my office.

"Oh, Rachel, how are you feeling?"

"Much better."

"You should have stayed home for a day. You need your rest after that dreadful night."

"I'm okay, Jacki. Really I am."

She crossed her beefy arms and frowned with concern. "Maybe, but I'm still going to send you home early."

I smiled. "Yes, ma'am. In fact, you can help me get out of here early." I handed her the Yellow Pages. "I've been calling printers, and this is as far as I got." I pointed to Chesterfield Graphics. "I need to find which of these companies has ever printed FDA filings for either Chemitex Bioproducts or its predecessor, Armstrong Bioproducts. So far, I'm zero for eight."

She lifted the Yellow Pages and frowned at the listings. "I'll start right in."

"Use a little indirection. A pointed question might put them off. I told the ones I called that a client of mine in the pharmaceutical business needed to have an Investigational New Drug Application printed. I asked whether they had ever done one before. So far, no one has."

She was taking notes. "An Investigational New Drug Application?"

I nodded. "If you find one who's done it before, ask them for references of pharmaceutical companies that they've done work for. If they don't mention Chemitex or Armstrong on their own at that point, you can ask them."

Jacki finished taking notes and nodded. "I'll start now."

"Thanks."

She paused at the door and turned to face me. "Rachel, did you happen to come back here last night before you went to the mall?"

"No. Why?"

She looked perplexed. "I always turn off my computer at the end of the day. I would have sworn it was off last night when I locked up. Yours, too. But they were both on when I got here this morning. Odd, isn't it?"

I nodded uncertainly. "Maybe you forgot. I usually turn mine off when I leave, but I honestly can't remember whether I did yesterday."

"Maybe, but I know I looked in your office before I locked up. I could swear your computer was off, too." She paused. "And another thing."

"What?"

"I was catching up on my filing this morning. Were you in the file drawers yesterday?"

I felt an icy finger on my spine. "I don't think so."

"Hmmm," she said with a puzzled frown. Although her personal life was in disarray, Jacki was a stickler for order at the office, especially in the file drawers. I realized early on in our relationship that I should let her do all of the filing.

"What?" I asked.

"Things are out of order," she said. "I thought you might have gone into the drawers yesterday looking for some document and forgot to put things back in the right place." She heaved a sigh. "Oh, well, it's probably the darn hormones again. I woke up at two in the morning with my nipples on fire." She left my office shaking her head and returned to her desk.

I sat there motionless, absorbing the clear import of what Jacki had noticed. I carefully surveyed the top of my desk, looking for something askew. I couldn't tell for sure. There were always piles of documents on my desk. There happened to be four of them this morning. As far as I could remember, there were four when I left yesterday afternoon. Whenever Jacki was the last to leave at night or the first to arrive in the morning, she would neatly square each pile. All four piles were neatly squared. I couldn't remember for sure what had been in each pile, and thus I couldn't tell whether any of them had been disturbed or rearranged. The same was true of the drawers of my desk and credenza. Jacki maintained all the really important files in her filing cabinet. The few files in my credenza were a real hodgepodge of documents —my TWA Frequent Flyer materials, the documents from my house closing, sets of local rules from the various federal district courts in Illinois, Missouri, and Arkansas, a miscellaneous collection of photocopies of judicial decisions that I had at one time or another thought worth saving, copies of some of the briefs I had filed over the years. Nothing essential, nothing I had looked at recently, and thus nothing I could say for sure had been disturbed or rearranged since yesterday afternoon.

Then there were the contents of my briefcase, including all my notes and photocopies of materials from my ongoing investigation. But my briefcase had been with me the whole night. It had been locked in the trunk of my car while I was at Town & Country Centre, and it remained there until I opened the trunk much later that night with the set of keys from my waterlogged purse, which the police fished out of the stormwater culvert under the shopping mall. I brought the briefcase into my house when Benny and I came home from the police station.

As for any other valuable documents . . .

I glanced at the heavy, squat safe, which sat in a corner of my office. I went over and kneeled in front of it. It was a banged-up relic that I had bought at a garage sale from a retired criminal attorney. I examined the combination dial and the handle and the other parts for signs of tampering, but the safe was already so battered it was impossible to identify any new marks. I turned the combination and opened the safe. Everything that was supposed to be in there was, and in the right order. I removed the original of the Beth Shalom/Labadie Gardens list from the top shelf of the safe and then closed the door and spun the dial to lock it.

I went back to my desk and, for the umpteenth time, studied the list:

| BETH SHALOM | | LABADIE GARDENS | |
| --- | --- | --- | --- |
| *P/S* | *P/A* | *P/S* | *P/A* |
| Abramawitz | Abrams | Allen | Bailey |
| Altman | Braunstein | Brown, A | Brown, R |
| Caplan | Cohen, M | Coleman | Carter |
| Cohen, S | Epstein | Jackson, R | Jackson, M |
| Freidman | Friedman | Johnson | Mitchell |
| Gutterman | Goldstein | Marshall | Perkins |
| Kohn | Gruener | Russell | Perry |
| Leiberman | Kaplansky | Shaw | Rivers |
| Perlmutter | Mittelman | Smith, B | Sleet |
| Rosenberg | Pinsky | Trotter | Smith, R |
| Rotskoff | Silverman | Washington, C | Washington, L |
| Schecter | Wexler | Young | Wells |

Although it still didn't make any sense to me, for a brief moment there seemed to be something different about the list. Then I realized it was just the paper. For the past week I had been handling and passing out *photocopies* of the list. I hadn't touched the original in more than a week, and the original was typed on heavy bond paper.

*Bond paper?*

I leaned back and held the list up to the light overhead. I could detect the outline of a watermark in the center of the page. I tilted the page slightly to focus the light on the watermark.

Stunned, I lowered the page.

After a moment, I held it up to the light again. The watermark consisted of an oval with a symbol in the middle. The symbol was a stylized rendering of a mortar and pestle, the emblem of the pharmaceutical industry. The oval was formed out of two words, the letters curving around the circumference. The top half of the oval was the word "Armstrong," and the bottom half was the word "Bioproducts."

I allowed the significance of the watermark to sink in. The list of names—the only original document that Bruce Rosenthal had given to David Marcus for safekeeping—had been typed on bond paper bearing the private watermark of Armstrong Bioproducts.

"Rachel?"

I started at the sound of the voice, and then smiled sheepishly at my secretary. Jacki gave me a troubled look. "You're a little jumpy today."

"Sorry."

"After last night, you're entitled. Well," she smiled proudly, "I think I found your printer."

"Oh?"

"Here." She handed me a slip of paper. "LaSalle Press. It's over on St. Charles Rock Road east of the Inner Belt. That's the address and phone number."

"Who'd you talk to?"

"The proprietor, I think. He sounds like an older guy. His name is Harry Beckman."

"What did he say?" I asked.

"He said he used to print materials for FDA filings, but that he hadn't done one for years. I told him I needed references. He had to search through his files. It took a while. He said he printed a few INDs for Monsanto back in the 1960s and several for Armstrong Bioproducts back in the 1970s."

"Yes!" I said, delighted. "That's terrific, Jacki. Did he sound friendly?"

She thought it over, moving her head from side to side. "Mostly, he sounded old."

"I like old." I stood up and stared at the address on the slip. "You're wonderful, Jacki. Wish me luck."

# 19

CHAPTER

I PEERED through the window of LaSalle Press. Although the yellowed placard on the door read OPEN, there was no sign of life within. I tried the door. It was open, so I stepped inside the storefront office. A mechanism on the door rang a distant bell.

As I waited at the counter, I looked around. LaSalle Press was at least a decade past its prime. Everything seemed old and worn, from the dull paint job on the walls to the two dented metal desks on the far side of the counter to the rust-stained light fixtures overhead. A faded sign on the wall announced LaSalle's fortieth anniversary. From the dates on the sign, the fiftieth anniversary was just two years off.

There was the sound of someone clearing phlegm from his throat, and then Harry Beckman emerged from the back, an unlit cigar stuck in the corner of his mouth. He was short, thick and slightly stooped with age, and his bald head was sprinkled with age spots. He was wearing a wrinkled white shirt that was too large for his neck and a maroon tie that was too short and too wide for any recent decade. Several stubby red pencils stuck out of the side pocket of his vest. His rumpled slacks were bunched in folds at the tops of his scuffed black shoes.

Removing the cigar from his mouth, he squinted at me. "Yes?"

I introduced myself and explained that my secretary had called earlier regarding his experience on print jobs for pharmaceutical companies.

"Right, right," he rasped, with a hint of a smile. There were flecks of tobacco on his lips and on his chin. "Well, come on around and have a seat."

I joined him by one of the metal desks on the other side of the counter. There was a nameplate on the desk that read H. BECKMAN. I glanced at the other desk. That nameplate read MRS. BEAM.

"She's at home," he said, gesturing toward the other desk with his cigar. He took a seat behind the desk, wincing as he sat down. "Her damn arthritis is flaring up again." He jammed the cigar back in his mouth. "Now run this story of yours by me again, young lady." His eyes were clear blue and seemed amused.

I explained that I represented a pharmaceutical company that needed to have an IND printed and that my job was to help select an appropriate printer. I thought my delivery was excellent.

When I finished, Harry Beckman crossed his arms over his chest and grinned, exposing an uneven set of tobacco-stained teeth. "Young lady," he said in his gravelly voice, "you'll do better if you don't try to shit a shitter. I'm not completely senile yet. You know and I know that you're not here looking to get an IND printed. No one sends those goddam things to outside printers anymore. And even if they did, let's face it—" he paused to survey the room "—this place is no longer on anyone's short list. I haven't done that kind of work in more than a decade."

He took the cigar out of his mouth and squinted at me. "Now, I probably ought to run you out of here for trying to trick an old man like that. But, what the hell? We're not busy this afternoon. Hell, we're not busy this year." He winked at me. "And you're just about the prettiest thing I've seen in here since a gal about three years back came in for some wedding invitations, and if a compliment like that is considered politically incorrect these days, well, that's just too goddam bad, 'cause when you get to my age, you can say whatever the hell you want."

He pointed the cigar at me. "You came here looking for something. Tell me what you need. Maybe I can help."

"Okay, Harry," I said with a smile. I couldn't disguise my amusement. It was like talking to someone out of *Guys and Dolls*. "I need to know as much as I can about every IND that you printed for Chemitex Bioproducts and Armstrong Bioproducts."

He studied me for a moment. "Why?"

I pondered the question. "I'm not sure," I finally said. "And I'm not sure how much I should tell you. Three other people tried to find out information about those companies, and all three are dead. Last night, someone tried to kill me. Quite literally, Mr. Beckman, I'm beginning to think that the less you know the better."

He tugged at his ear and frowned. "What exactly are you looking for here?"

"Whether you printed an IND for a drug called Primax. Also, whether you printed an IND for a drug for treating Guillain-Barré syndrome. If the answer to either is yes, I'd like to see the INDs."

He studied me for a moment. "If memory serves, those things are confidential."

"They are," I conceded. "Or at least they once were. The documents I'm looking for go back to the 1970s. Whatever was once secret about them must be old news by now."

He nodded and stood up with a wince. "Well," he said as he gestured toward the nameplate on the other desk, "let's hope Mrs. Beam did her usual thorough job of keeping track of old records."

Thirty minutes later, a baffled Harry Beckman was on the phone with the woman he called Mrs. Beam.

"They're gone, Mrs. Beam. Not lost. Not misplaced. Just plain gone."

We were standing in the file room in back. There was an open file drawer in front of us. According to Mrs. Beam's meticulously organized filing card system, all materials printed by LaSalle Press for Armstrong Bioproducts and Chemitex Bioproducts were supposed to be in File Drawer 78. According to the hand-printed file card, the contents of File Drawer 78 contained the paperwork for a variety of printing jobs over the years, including: three annual reports of Armstrong Bioproducts (1978, 1979, and 1980); form invoices for Armstrong Bioproducts and Chemitex Bioproducts; stationery, envelopes, and business cards for both companies; and five different INDs for Armstrong Bioproducts (covering the period 1974 through 1981). The annual reports were there, as were the invoices, stationery, envelopes, business cards—including the backup paperwork and samples of each finished product. But all five INDs were missing, paperwork and all.

"Now why in hell would I remove them, Mrs. Beam?" he said in exasperation. "Excuse me. I didn't mean to curse." He glanced over at me and rolled his eyes. "Yes, Mrs. Beam. Very good. Certainly. I'll see you tomorrow, Mrs. Beam."

He hung up and frowned at me. "That's the damndest thing," he grumbled, indicating the open file drawer. "Some son of a bitch must have come in here and cleaned out the INDs."

"Do you have any idea when?"

He snorted and shook his head. "Sometime over the past fifteen years, I guess. Last one was printed when?" He glanced down at the file card. "1981, eh? Well, they were all there in that drawer back in 1981."

"Could I see the file card?"

He handed it to me. The work orders were listed in chronological order. The first entry for an IND was in mid-1974. It read:

- *7/12/74 IND (Phrenom)—*
  *Galleys: 8/26—Final: 9/13*
  *Invoice: 9/30—Paid: 11/10*

The very next entry was for Primax. It read:

- *7/12/74 IND (Primax)—*
  *Galleys: 8/28—Final:*
  *Invoice: 10/30—Paid: 12/29*

"What does this mean?" I asked Beckman, pointing to the two entries.

He glanced at the card and nodded. "For this first one, Phrenom, we got the job on July twelfth. It must not have been a rush, because we didn't send them galleys until August twenty-sixth. We did the final version on September thirteenth, billed them for the job on September thirtieth, and they paid November tenth."

"But what about the one for Primax?" I asked.

He studied the card for a moment and grunted. "I guess we never did it in final form. Billed them, though, and they paid."

"Why didn't you do it in final form?"

He squinted at the card and shook his head. "Don't know. They must have canceled the order."

The other three INDs on the card resembled the entry for Phrenom; i.e., they were done in draft form and final form and presumably filed with the FDA. One of them was for Depran, a drug whose name Armstrong Bioproducts had trademarked in 1978 and canceled in 1979. If my earlier hypothesis was correct, the FDA never approved the drug. One of the other two INDs was for a drug with a familiar name. I think my internist had once prescribed it for me. The last was for another drug that had showed up on my trademark search.

"This is so maddening," I said in frustration as I slid the file drawer closed. "Somebody is going to an extraordinary amount of effort to hide something."

"And trespassing on my property in the process," Beckman growled.

When I was back in the front office area packing up my briefcase to leave, I remembered the Beth Shalom/Labadie Gardens list of names on bond paper. Harry Beckman was in the printing business. He might be able to help.

"Mr. Beckman, what do you know about watermarks?"

"Watermarks?" He bit the end off his chewed-up cigar and spit the chunk into the trash can. "A fair amount, I suppose. Why?"

"First of all, what exactly are they?"

"Watermarks? Well, I guess you could describe them as images that are inside the paper. A watermark is only visible when you hold the paper up to the light."

"How are they made?" I asked.

"Genuine watermarks are made at the paper mill when the paper is wet and being formed. You etch the pattern onto a special plate and then attach that plate to a cylinder that's known as a dandy roll. When the paper goes under the dandy roll, the pattern gets stamped right into the fibers." He sat down in his chair. "A watermark is like an indelible fiber fingerprint. You can't alter or remove it without destroying the paper."

"What's the purpose of it?"

He looked around the top of his desk and found a blank sheet of bond paper. He held it up to the light and squinted at it. "Here," he said, handing it to me. "Look."

I held the paper up to the light. Near the middle of the page was the following watermark:

**Strathmore Bond**

25% COTTON FIBER USA

I lowered the paper and looked at Beckman.

"That," he said, indicating the paper, "is the paper mill's watermark. It tells the world that Strathmore manufactured the paper. Then you've got your private watermarks."

"What are they?"

"Well, if you're a corporation or a bank or a fancy law firm and you're willing to pay for it, you can have your own private watermark put on your stock of paper."

"Why would a company do that?"

He shrugged. "Some do it for security purposes, especially for stock certificates, letterhead, business forms, and other important papers. Some see it as a mark of distinction, a status symbol. Others see it as a marketing tool."

I paused, weighing the options. *Why not?* I reached into my briefcase and removed the list of names on the original bond paper with the Armstrong Bioproducts watermark. I handed it to him and said, "I assume this is an example of a private watermark."

He held it up to the light and examined it. "Yep."

"Is there any way to date that?"

He frowned. "What do you mean?"

"How can I find out when that paper was made?"

He held it up to the light and examined it carefully. He shook his head. "Sometimes paper with a private watermark is dated. Not this one, though. The paper mill might have a record on it, but that's a long shot. Hell, there hasn't been an Armstrong Bioproducts for what? Ten years?"

"Can you tell which paper mill made it?"

He held the page up to the light again and squinted at it. "Nope. Say," he mused, "didn't they change logos?"

"Pardon?"

He stood up. "Come with me."

I followed him back to File Drawer 78. He flipped through the various folders, mumbling to himself, and then stopped. "Ah-ha!" he said triumphantly.

"What?"

He pulled out the Armstrong Bioproducts 1979 Annual Report and pointed to the cover page. "Note the logo," he said.

I nodded. "Same as the watermark."

"Exactly." He handed me the 1980 Annual Report. "Compare."

I raised my eyebrows. "A new logo."

He grinned broadly. "Yep."

The new logo design was completely different. Gone was the mortar and pestle with the company name arranged in an oval shape. Instead, it had been replaced by a streamlined motif in which a silver Gateway Arch served as the letter "A" in Armstrong.

"Here," he said, pointing to stationery with the same logo. He studied the file card. "We printed that batch of letterhead in 1981."

"So the old logo was changed in 1980," I said. "That means my list was typed before then."

He nodded. "Narrows it down a little for you."

"Who was your contact at Armstrong?"

"Our contact," he repeated, trying to remember.

"Was it Douglas Armstrong?"

"No." He chuckled. "I would have remembered him."

I flipped to the back page of the 1979 Annual Report, where it listed the officers and directors of the company, and handed it to him. "One of these?"

He looked down the list. "Lee Fowler," he said with a nod. "I remember dealing with him."

I came around to peer over his shoulder. Lee Fowler was listed as Chief Financial Officer. "Anyone else?" I asked.

"Oh, yeah. I remember Peter." He was pointing to Dr. Peter Todorovich, Director of Research. "He was the contact on a couple of printing jobs, too." Beckman ran a thick finger slowly down the rest of the list. When he reached the bottom he shook his head. "Just Lee and Peter. I don't recognize the others."

"Could you make me a copy of this page?" I asked. "It's a good source of names."

He waved his hand dismissively. "Just take the original. I've got too much crap in those filing cabinets. It's time to get rid of this old junk."

I put the materials in my briefcase and thanked him for his time and effort.

"Young lady," he said with a grin as he jammed his unlit cigar back in his mouth, "it was my pleasure. I've always been a sucker for a pretty gal with long stems. Those legs of yours remind me of Cyd Charisse, and that's one hell of a compliment in my book. Good luck."

I had to smile. He was a character. "Thanks, Harry."

As I walked out the door he called me. "Hey."

I turned.

He pointed the cigar at me. "You be careful."

"I will, Harry."

I drove home from LaSalle Press. I parked in my driveway and walked next door to pick up Ozzie. Julie and Jill, the little twins, came to the door with Ozzie standing between them. I patted Ozzie on the head and kneeled in front of the girls.

"Hi, girls. Big day?"

Julie nodded. "We went to the playground."

I widened my eyes. "You did? How come you didn't invite me?" Last Sunday morning I had taken them to the Shaw Park with Ozzie.

Julie giggled. Jill, the shy one, smiled bashfully.

"What else did you guys do?"

"We watched the telephone truck," Julie said.

"Cool," I said, turning to Jill. "Where was it?"

Jill put her thumb in her mouth and pointed with her other hand toward my driveway. I looked to where she was pointing and then back at her.

"The telephone truck was in my driveway?" I asked.

Jill nodded.

"All afternoon," Julie added.

"Where were the telephone workers?"

"We're not sure," Julie said. "They went in your backyard and we didn't see them for a long time. Rachel, if they gave you new phones, could me and Jill have one of the old ones?"

I stood up and stared at my house.

*The telephone company? All afternoon?*

I went into their house and borrowed the kitchen phone. It took me ten minutes to get through to someone at the phone company with access to the service records.

"Give your address and telephone number again," she said.

I did.

She came on the line after about a minute. "I'm sorry, Miss Gold, but we have no record of any service call at that address today."

"What about in the neighborhood? Maybe there was a problem in the outdoor lines."

"No, ma'am. Nothing in the area."

"Are you sure?"

"Yes, ma'am. The last service call in your neighborhood was four weeks ago, and it was two blocks over."

I slowly hung up the phone and turned toward the breakfast room window. The window had a clear view of my backyard and the back of my house. I stared at my house.

*What is going on?*

# 20

CHAPTER

THE last cop left my house at 6:50 P.M. His final words to me were, "The little girls could have been mistaken."

I nodded silently and closed the door behind him. There had been as many as eight police officers in my house, including someone from the bomb squad. They had searched every floor and every room. Nothing was missing, nothing seemed out of place. The police left one by one, and now there were none.

Just Ozzie and me. He was standing by his dinner bowl when I came back into the kitchen.

"You hungry, Oz?" I said, scratching him on his head.

He wagged his tail in response.

I filled up his bowl with dog chow, patted him on the head and went over to the sink to fill the teapot with water. I put the pot on to boil and slumped into a chair at the kitchen table.

Absently watching Ozzie wolf down his food, I took stock of my situation. It was now apparent that something bad had occurred at Armstrong Bioproducts, probably back in the 1970s, and that one or more persons were determined to keep it secret. Bruce Rosenthal had discovered what that secret was, or had at least stumbled upon a trail that would lead to the secret, and now

Bruce was dead. David Marcus was dead. Karen Harmon was dead. And now someone had tried to kill me.

Whoever was responsible for Bruce Rosenthal's death had also caused his apartment to be searched. Whoever was responsible for David Marcus' death had probably caused his house to be searched as well. Yesterday, someone had searched my office. Today, from what the twins had observed, someone had searched my house. I glanced over at my briefcase. In there was the Beth Shalom/Labadie Gardens list of names, typed on bond paper. It had been created sometime before 1980 and contained what Harry Beckman referred to as "an indelible fiber fingerprint" identifying it as a product of Armstrong Bioproducts. It was an original document. An original piece of evidence.

Discovered by Bruce, now dead.

Given to David, now dead.

Given to me.

The teapot began to whistle. I filled a mug with boiling water and added a Red Zinger teabag. When the tea was brewed I went back to the table. Ozzie had finished dinner and was lapping up water from the other bowl. When he finished he padded over and sat in front of me. I scratched him behind the ears as I considered my situation, evaluating every option, from relying on the police to fleeing the country. Sunlight seemed the best option. As long as the secret remained secret, those seeking to conceal it had an incentive to silence me. As long as no one else knew that a secret existed, the concealers could eliminate potential exposers by dropping them into trash compactors or rigging automobile accidents or faking hate crimes or, in my case, staging a shopping center abduction and homicide. As long as no one knew about the secret no one would ever make a connection between the killings. But once the secret was exposed, the incentive to silence me would disappear. Indeed, the risk of silencing me would suddenly become too high.

Feeling edgy, I checked my watch and decided to go for a jog. As I changed into my jogging sweats in the bedroom, I realized that I probably had more than enough information to interest a good investigative reporter right now. Flo Shenker was the obvious choice, given the Douglas Armstrong connection. Although I hated the thought of the political damage he might suffer by being associated with a scandal involving his former company, it seemed unavoidable. In fact, it was an added reason to pick Flo. Since she would be the only one working on the story, she would in all likelihood scoop everyone. As a result, her stories would set the tone and define the relevant universe for all subsequent coverage. That was the best Douglas Armstrong could hope for. Flo was brilliant and she was fair. Although the Douglas Armstrong angle was the hook to get her involved, if it turned out that he knew nothing incriminating, Flo would make that clear in the story.

And it was possible he knew nothing. Armstrong had maintained his medical practice during the early years of Armstrong Bioproducts. He could have been busy treating his patients and completely oblivious to whatever shenanigans were going on in the lab or elsewhere. Indeed, he might even be able to work with Flo to help expose the secret. *Talk about sunlight,* I thought with a smile, imagining a big news story followed by a U.S. senator demanding a full investigation.

Back downstairs in the kitchen, I found Flo's business card in my purse. I checked my watch. It was close to 8:30 at night in Washington, D.C. Flo had written her home telephone number on the back of her card. I lifted the receiver to dial the number. I paused. The dial tone sounded a little odd. I hung up and lifted the receiver again. The same, slightly off-key dial tone. I dialed the number anyway. It rang several times. There was a metallic clicking sound on the line. The sound continued when her answering machine came on.

I hung up before the beep and stared at the phone, confused. I lifted the receiver and got the odd tone again. I studied the receiver, trying to remember suspense movies I had seen. How could you tell if your phone was tapped? I unscrewed the mouthpiece and looked inside. There were different pieces of metal and colored plastic and tiny strands of different colored wires. I couldn't tell whether anything didn't belong in there. I replaced the mouthpiece and hung up the phone.

*Assume it's tapped,* I told myself.

*Okay, so now what?*

I sat at the table, trying to formulate a plan. After a while, the outlines of one began to take shape. I went upstairs to my bedroom and found my sunglasses. Back downstairs, I got Ozzie's leash out of the pantry. The sound brought him into the kitchen. He gave me a curious look, since I rarely put him on a leash.

"You're sticking with me, pal. I'm getting too paranoid." I scratched him on the head. "We did this once in Chicago. Remember?"

We got in the car. I glanced in the mirror as I pulled out of the neighborhood in the direction of the nearest Walgreens. "Damn," I groaned.

There was a car about a hundred feet behind me. I stared hard at the headlight configuration, trying to memorize it.

I took a roundabout, zigzag route to the Walgreens. The headlights remained in my rearview mirror. By the time I pulled into a parking space, I had my plan. I turned to Ozzie.

"Get up here."

He scrabbled over the seat while I put the sunglasses on my lap. I turned back to look toward the street as I fastened the leash to Ozzie's collar. I couldn't spot the headlights, but I was certain he was out there waiting. I wound the end of the leash in my hand to shorten its length. I wanted Ozzie with me at all times, and this was the only way I could take him into the store.

"Okay, Oz. I expect an Academy Award–winning performance."

We got out of the car and I put on my sunglasses. Using the shortened leash, I held Ozzie to my side in a manner I hoped would make him pass as a seeing-eye dog. We got into the store with no problem. I walked over to the pay phone, careful to act tentative enough to remain in my blind woman role. I dropped in a quarter, dialed Benny's number, and turned back toward the doors as the phone began to ring. Two teenage girls walked in, giggling and sipping Diet Cokes.

Benny answered on the third ring. "Talk to me."

"Benny, I need help."

"What's wrong?"

"I can't tell you now. Here's what I need. Go by my sister's house. We're almost the same size. Borrow some clothes for me. Two or three outfits, all completely different styles, okay? Including shoes. And be sure to get some underwear and stuff. All I've got on are my running clothes."

"Rachel, tell me what's wrong."

"I'll tell you later."

"Is that motherfucker after you again?"

"Just listen to me," I said fiercely. "Put her stuff in something I can carry. Maybe a backpack."

"Okay."

"Once you have everything, call a cab. Put the backpack in the trunk of the cab, give him some money, and tell him to go to Town and Country Centre."

"Why there?"

"Benny, just listen me. I don't have time to explain. Tell the cabby to wait right outside the far south entrance." I checked my watch. "Tell him he has to be there by nine o'clock. Okay?"

"Fine. I'll have him meet me at your sister's house."

A short burly black man in a Dr. Dre sweatshirt came in. He had a thick mustache and a smooth, shaved head. He scowled at me for a moment and then moved on into the store.

I waited until he was out of earshot. "Last thing," I said to Benny. "Ozzie."

"What about him?"

"Go to the Famous-Barr at Town and Country tonight after nine. I'm going to leave him in men's suits."

"Leave him? How?"

"Just go up there and ask for him. I'm hanging up. Oh, wait. One more thing. Call Flo."

"Flo?"

"Right. Tell her I'm going to call her tonight at her office."

"When?"

"Before midnight. Tell her I don't want to call her at home. Have her go to her office. Okay, I'm hanging up. Benny, you're a love. Thanks."

"Wait. Where are you going?"

"I'm not sure."

"How can I contact you?"

"You can't. I'll contact you. It's better that way. Good-bye, Benny."

I hung up and tried to scan the store unobtrusively—not an easy task for a blind person. I noted the black man walking toward the checkout line with a liter of Pepsi and a pouch of pipe tobacco.

I found a shopping cart after pretending to grope my way toward it. I moved up and down the aisles slowly, occasionally fumbling against the merchandise, as if trying to feel the items. I had a short but crucial shopping list: a good pair of scissors, one scarf, a hair dryer, a pair of glasses, and two different hair dyes (blond and red, both of the temporary variety—if I had to change hair colors twice, I didn't want to end up bald in the process). Although I had doubts about being able to find an appropriate pair of glasses, I was able to get everything on the list, including a weak pair of reading glasses that were round enough to pass for regular glasses. I headed for the checkout line.

When I stepped outside into the dark, the sunglasses made me nearly blind. I slid them down on my nose and peered over toward my car. The doors were closed and it looked empty. I approached it cautiously, glancing around the parking lot for the familiar headlights. I didn't spot them.

"You see anyone?" I asked Ozzie.

He just looked at me and wagged his tail.

I smiled and scratched his head. "You were wonderful, Oz. Definitely best supporting actor material."

I walked around the car once to make sure no one was hiding anywhere inside or out. I put the shopping bag in the backseat and had Ozzie get up in front with me. I checked my watch. 8:21 P.M. Forty minutes to go.

Starting the car, I realized I needed cash. If I was going to disappear, I couldn't use credit cards. Too easy to track. There was a branch office of my bank down the block with a drive-thru ATM machine. I pulled up to the machine and withdrew the maximum four hundred dollars. 8:27 P.M. I needed to enter Town & Country no later than 8:45 P.M.

I didn't spot the headlights until I was on the Inner Belt heading south toward Highway 40. I was in the middle lane, the headlights were one car back in the right lane. They stayed there all the way to the Highway 40 exit, and then took up a position one car back in the middle lane. I took the Town & Country Centre exit, and so did the other car. I entered the huge mall parking lot and drove around to the north side of the Centre. I found a parking spot near the main entrance to Bloomingdale's. Slinging my purse over my shoulder, I grabbed the shopping bag in my left hand and Ozzie's leash in my right. I stepped out of my car and looked around. No sign of the headlights, but I was sure he was out there watching. I leaned inside the car and got the sunglasses.

"Okay," I said to Ozzie as I closed the door and put on the sunglasses. "It's show time."

We moved briskly toward the entrance, slowing as we reached the bright lights. I shortened the leash, pulled Ozzie close against me and stepped toward the revolving door into Bloomingdale's. The clock overhead read 8:47.

*Perfect.*

We drew stares as we moved through Bloomingdale's—a confident blind woman striding through the aisles with her extraordinary guide dog. I was tempted to freak out one of the gawkers by pausing to remind her that it was impolite to stare at blind people.

I stepped into the enclosed mall area without turning back. He could be in one of two places: trailing behind me through the mall or sitting in his car waiting for me to return. It didn't matter which. No one was going to bother me in the open so long as Ozzie was at my side.

At 8:57 I entered Famous-Barr, took the escalator up to the second level and followed the sign to men's suits. I slowed as I entered the area, noting with grim amusement how a thirtyish male salesman simultaneously stared at me and backed away as I approached. He stepped between two rows of suits as I came down the main aisle.

*Too bad, jerko.*

When I was even with where he stood, I stopped and spun toward him. "Sir?"

He flinched. "Er, yes?"

"Can you tell me where the lady's room is?"

"Sure. Uh . . ."

I held my hand toward him. "Just point me in the direction."

He took it gingerly and pointed. "Down there and to the right."

"Thank you so much."

"No problem," he said with a self-congratulatory smile over the minuscule "good deed" he thought he had just performed.

I handed him Ozzie's leash. "His name is Ozzie. Be a doll and watch him for me."

"Well," he stammered as he took the leash, "you know, I—"

I looked down at Ozzie. "Ozzie, stay," I said in a stern voice. I turned to the salesman with a smile. "Thanks so much."

I headed off briskly in the direction he had pointed me, the Walgreens bag in one hand while I pretended to use the other hand for guidance. I turned right at the end of the aisle. When I got beyond his line of sight, I started running toward the escalator.

That's when I spotted him—the guy who had stalked me through the mall yesterday. He was over in the shirt section, dressed in a navy blue sweatshirt, faded jeans, and Reeboks. His red hair was hidden beneath a Detroit Tigers baseball cap. I saw his gaze shift momentarily toward the men's furnishings section. I looked, too. Standing by a rack of ties was the same burly black man I had seen at the Walgreens.

I took the down escalator two steps at a time, not bothering to look back. The south exit was directly ahead. The clock above the revolving doors showed 9:07 P.M. As I pushed through the doors I had a horrible thought: *What if the cab isn't there?*

But it was, thank God. Parked along the curb over to the left, the engine idling. I ran to it and hopped in back.

"Go!" I told the driver.

"Where to?"

"Just get us out of here," I yelled, panting. "Hurry."

As he pulled away, I turned to look out the back window just as the two men came bursting through the revolving doors. I slid down out of view, my pulse hammering furiously.

# 21

CHAPTER

I WAITED for a response. "Well?" I finally asked.

"Someone's trying to cover up some bad shit," Flo said.

"That's what I think," I said. I had called her long distance from my room at the Airport Hilton to explain my predicament.

"You think the coverup goes all the way back to the seventies?" Flo asked.

"Everything seems to point that way, including what Bruce told David Marcus. David must have misheard him. I don't think Bruce wanted to see a lawyer about 'statutory limits.' I think he wanted to see a lawyer about the 'statute of limitations.' He wanted to know whether a crime from back then was still considered a crime."

"So what's the crime?"

"I don't know, but I'm getting close, Flo. I know I'm getting close. Think the *Trib* will be interested?"

"Interested? Good God, Rachel. Does the wild bear shit in the woods? An exclusive with the possibility of an Armstrong connection is going to give every one of these editors a huge hard-on. Hell, I wouldn't be surprised if my bureau chief starts dry humping the water cooler."

"Perfect. What's the *Trib*'s Federal Express account number?"

"Hang on." A moment later she read it to me. "What are you sending me?"

"Original evidence."

"Of what?"

"It's that sheet of paper with the four columns of names and the private watermark. The one Bruce gave to David. Whatever it shows, it's clearly significant. There's a Fed Ex mailbox in the hotel lobby. You'll have it tomorrow. Put it somewhere safe, Flo."

"Will do. How do I contact you?"

"You can call me here tonight." I gave her the phone number. "Ask for Elizabeth Bennett."

She chuckled. "A wonderful novel."

"I'm her tonight."

"Check out of there tomorrow," she said.

"I plan to. I'll find somewhere else for tomorrow night."

"Good. If they've done all that you think they've done over the past month, you can't take any chances. You've got to keep moving."

"I know," I said. "But it also means I've got to close the loop on this soon. I'm running out of time."

"I'll join you tomorrow. How can I help tonight?"

"Can you get your hands on a St. Louis telephone directory from the seventies?"

"Sure. If we don't have one here, they'll have one in Chicago. What do you need?"

"There are two names at the top of these lists I'm sending you. One is Beth Shalom."

"A synagogue?"

"Maybe. The other is Labadie Gardens." I spelled Labadie for her. "I couldn't find a listing for either in my telephone book, but I didn't know that the list was created sometime in the 1970s. Since Armstrong Bioproducts was a St. Louis company, the odds are that Beth Shalom and Labadie Gardens are St. Louis names."

"I'll get on it now. I'll call you back if I find anything."

"Thanks, Flo."

"You be careful, Rachel."

Ninety minutes later, I turned off the hair dryer and studied myself in the bathroom mirror.

"Well," I said with a smile, "we'll finally get to see whether they really do have more fun."

Gone were my shoulder-length natural brown curls, replaced by short blond hair, straightened with help from the hair dryer. I turned to check out the sides and back. It wasn't bad for a home cut. A little punky, but that was good. It increased the contrast with the old me, which meant it improved the disguise. I put on the pair of glasses from Walgreens and looked at my reflection, full face and both side profiles.

*Interesting.*

A few minutes later, I was back in the bedroom sorting through the outfits that Benny and my sister had packed for me when the phone rang. I straightened up and stared at it. Only one person was supposed to know the number. I moved quickly to the door and peered through the spy hole. No one out there. I went back to the nightstand and lifted the receiver.

"Hello?" I said warily.

"Greetings, Miss Bennett," said Flo. "It's me."

"Thank God," I said with relief.

"I'm flying to St. Louis late tomorrow afternoon. I just got the green light from my bureau chief."

"Is he okay?"

"Believe it or not, he used to be the editor of the Tempo section. I was worried he might turn out to be some weird hybrid of Sydney Omarr and Ann Landers, but he's pretty cool, and he's got brass balls. If this thing leads where it seems to be headed, Rachel, we're going to need a bureau chief with brass balls."

"When's your plane get in?"

"Around seven-thirty."

I mulled it over. "Stay at the Hyatt at Union Station. And rent a car. Check in. I'll come by around nine."

"Good. You'll stay with me."

"Maybe," I said.

"Definitely," she ordered. "Two is better than one."

It sounded appealing. It would be good to have company on this case. "Flo, if you leave before my package reaches you tomorrow, be sure to have someone looking out for a Federal Express package from St. Louis."

"I will. Speaking of St. Louis, I found an old phone book. 1977."

"And?"

"Bingo."

"Tell me."

"Nursing homes."

"Really? Both?"

"Yep. Beth Shalom was on Union Boulevard. Labadie Gardens was on Labadie."

I let the information sink in. "So the names on the lists must be residents of the nursing homes."

"All dead by now, no doubt."

"Probably," I conceded.

"We need to find someone who'll talk."

"That's a place where I need your help," I said.

"Good. Go ahead."

"I have four possible sources. I need you to locate three of them. The printer told me he dealt with two people at Armstrong Bioproducts. One was Lee Fowler, the chief financial officer. He's the one I've found. There's a listing for him in the phone book, and I'm going to try to contact him tomorrow. The other guy was the director of research back then. His name is Dr. Peter Todorovich." I spelled the last name. "He's probably the best source. Problem is, he's not listed in the phone book. I have two other possibilities. Their names appear in the company's 1979 annual report. One is Gerald R. Tuck, vice president of marketing. The other is the vice president of operations. His name is, I swear,

Ronald McDonald. Neither one is listed in the phone book. The way people in business move around, the odds are that each is now working for another company outside St. Louis."

"I'll find them, Rachel."

"Thanks."

There were three separate locks on the hotel door, and I made sure all were locked before I got ready for bed. Sitting on the edge of the bed, I thought again of poor Benny. He'd really come through for me tonight, and he was probably worried sick. I wanted to reassure him, but I didn't want to risk calling him at home: if they had tapped my home phone, his was the next logical one to tap. I dialed his office number. I got his answering machine at the office and waited for the beep:

"It's me," I said. "I'm okay."

I paused, trying to think of what else I could tell him. But as I did, another image flashed into my mind: a pair of intruders, each wearing rubber gloves, each holding a flashlight, listening to my message in Benny's darkened office. Maybe they were standing there right now, staring at each other over an open file drawer, waiting for me to continue talking.

"Sorry I couldn't say good-bye," I said, "but my plane was late. I'll be out of town for a few days. I'll call you when I get back." I paused. "I'll miss you, Benny."

I replaced the receiver and turned off the lamp.

# 22

CHAPTER

MY first stop the next morning was the downtown offices of the United Way of Greater St. Louis. I traveled there by a sufficiently roundabout route to confirm that I wasn't being tailed. I started with a hotel van to the airport. I walked quickly through the main terminal, drawing plenty of stares on the way. Benny had certainly made an interesting selection of outfits for me. Today I was wearing one of the ensembles my sister takes on her annual trip to Las Vegas: a gold turtleneck, a red leather miniskirt, sheer black pantyhose, and black pumps. With my new blond hairdo and sunglasses, the one person I definitely did not resemble was Rachel Gold, attorney at law.

The young taxi driver at the airport seemed to concur. From his rearview-mirror gape as I slid into the backseat, I got the sense that, if asked, he would have guessed that I was a member of an even more ancient profession. I had him take me on a circuitous route from the airport through several side streets in University City and then up Hanley Road to the Interco Tower in Clayton. Every block or so I would turn to look out the rear window. No car seemed to be following us.

I got out at the Interco Corporate Tower, walked through the building to the other side, and flagged another cab at the Holiday

Inn across the street. Once again Ann's outfit was a distraction. This driver, a swarthy man with a thick black mustache, grinned and leered at me throughout the drive. I was tempted to take his name and file a complaint, but I didn't feel like digging out a pen and pencil to write it down, and without that I'd never be able to remember either his first or last name, both of which were at least ten letters long and seemed to consist entirely of consonants and chemical symbols from the table of elements. Instead, I ignored him on the ride and paid exactly what the meter showed when we reached my destination downtown.

As I entered the United Way office on Olive, I reviewed my cover story, which was fairly straightforward. I was Liza Bennett of Los Angeles. I was born in St. Louis but moved to L.A. with my family when I was five. This was my first trip back, and my mother had asked me to try to track down two people. One was her Aunt Betty, who used to be at a nursing home called Beth Shalom. The other was Lucille Evers, a black woman who had helped raise my mother and whose last known residence was at Labadie Gardens.

I assumed that the United Way had provided funds to the two nursing homes, and thus would have someone who knew what had happened to them. I was wrong and right. Both Beth Shalom and Labadie Gardens were private and operated for profit; as such, neither had received any money from the United Way. However, someone at the United Way knew what had happened to both. Her name was Sarah Jennings and she was in charge of the older adult services division. She was a sturdy, heavyset black woman in her early sixties.

"Many years ago," Sarah Jennings said with a sad shake of her head, "Labadie Gardens was owned by one of the north side Baptist churches. Either First Baptist or Mt. Zion. It was a fine, respectable home. But back in about 1977 a man named Lombardy bought it. James Lombardy." She gave an angry snort. "He was a bad man. Squeezed every last penny out of those poor old black folks while running that place right into the ground. Lord have mercy."

"What happened?"

"In 1980, just around the time the state was about to step in, he showed up one morning and closed the place down. Just like that. Honey, it was a sorrowful spectacle—all those old people kicked out of there, some with no place to go. The bastard just closed it down and left town."

"Where did the residents go?"

"All over town. We helped get them placed in the other homes." She shook her head at the memory. "My goodness, it was a mess. Right in the middle of it all, the place burned down."

"Was anyone killed?"

"No, praise the Lord. But all the records were destroyed. We didn't have medical records on most of those folks. Some of those poor darlings couldn't even remember their own names, or who their children were. Oh, it was just a pitiful situation."

I scratched Labadie Gardens off my list. With the records gone, there was no way to trace a thing.

Sarah Jennings had slightly better news on Beth Shalom.

"Old Mordecai Jacobs," she said with a big grin.

"Who's that?"

"One of the most unforgettable characters I ever met." She leaned back in her chair with a chuckle. "He started off in the rag business, I think. Made a lot of money at it, too. He was a regular character, honey. A real live P. T. Barnum. You ever hear of the Gutmann Cavern?"

"Related to the old brewery?"

She nodded. "Mordecai bought that old property, and all them caves underneath. He turned those caves into a regular tourist attraction."

"Really?"

"My heavens, child. The Gutmann Cavern Tour? Ask your momma. It was a big deal back in the early sixties."

"What happened?"

"Oh, the usual. The Highway Department purchased the land for part of an expansion. They knocked down Mordecai's building and closed off the cave." She fondly shook her head at the memory. "But it was sure something while it lasted."

"How was Mordecai Jacobs connected with Beth Shalom?"

"He sort of adopted it back in about 1970 or 1971."

"What do you mean by 'adopted'?"

She smiled. "He became its sugar daddy. It was a Jewish nursing home. One of those real orthodox ones—kept kosher, all that stuff. Problem was, it was run by a couple of orthodox rabbis from the old country. She chuckled. "Those rabbis didn't know a balance sheet from a ballerina. The creditors put Beth Shalom in receivership, but Mordecai came to the rescue. He bought it and kept pumping money into that place until he found out he had lung cancer."

"When was that?"

"Oh"—she frowned, trying to remember—"about 1984 or 1985, I think. When Mordecai found out he was dying, he put all his affairs in order."

"What did he do with Beth Shalom?"

"He contacted the Jewish Federation and arranged to have Beth Shalom merged into the Jewish Center for the Aged."

"How long did that take?"

"Oh, not long. Maybe six months. By then Beth Shalom was in a dangerous neighborhood and the families were afraid to visit the residents. So once the deal was done, the residents were transferred out of there pretty quickly. Before he died, Mordecai donated the building to the neighborhood. It's a community center, now."

"Were the records transferred to the Jewish Center for the Aged?" I asked.

Sarah Jennings shrugged. "You'd have to ask them, honey. I don't know."

———

The Jewish Center for the Aged, known for short as the JCA, is out in the western suburbs. But because I was still paranoid about being followed, the first leg of my journey was east. I took the Metro Link over the Mississippi River, caught a cab back across the river and out west to the County Courts building in Clayton. I walked into the building and through metal detectors, took the elevator up to the top level, worked my way around to the back entrance, and flagged a cab, which took me west to the JCA.

The director of the JCA was a pudgy balding man named Mark Levine. He couldn't have been more friendly or less informed. He also couldn't have been more distracted. That was largely my fault. Judging from his slack-jawed expression and a suddenly distended vein in his right temple, the distraction was due to my punky blond hairdo, Ann's red leather miniskirt, and the low-slung chair across from his desk—a treacherous combination that made it impossible to find a comfortable sitting position that didn't, in the process, remind Levine of the Sharon Stone police interrogation scene in *Basic Instinct*.

Eventually, with the help of a strategically placed briefcase, I found a PG-13 position on the chair, and Levine's throbbing vein receded. Wiping some spittle from the corner of his mouth, he explained apologetically that he was new to the job and to St. Louis, having moved here just three months ago from a similar position in Cleveland. As a result, he was even less familiar with Beth Shalom than me.

"Liza—may I call you Liza?" he asked with a furtive peek toward the area covered by my briefcase.

I stared at his face until his eyes returned to mine. Embarrassed, he looked down at the appointment calendar on his desk.

"Certainly," I answered, aiming for a friendly but firm tone.

"I have a lunch meeting that I can't get out of." He checked his watch. "As soon as I get back, I'll have my assistant start digging through those records to see what we can find out. Call me around three. I should have something by then." He hesitated, this time his eyes glancing down to my chest and then back up again. "Perhaps we can get together after work and I can show you what I have, uh, or what I found."

There was, of course, a gold band on the ring finger of his left hand. I thanked him and, ignoring his last suggestion, told him I would call around three.

I got as far as the parking lot when I realized I didn't have a car. Turning back to call myself a cab, I was surprised to see Mark Levine burst through the front door.

"Oh, good," he said, panting. "I thought you'd already left."

"That was fast," I said with an expectant smile.

He laughed and shook his head. "No, no. I won't get to that until after lunch. But in the meantime, I thought you might want to talk to Matilda Jackson."

"Who is she?"

"One of our finest nurses," Mark said. "But more important for you, Matilda used to work at Beth Shalom."

"Really?"

"That's what my secretary just told me. She said that when Beth Shalom merged into the JCA, three of the nurses came over. Matilda is the last one still here."

"Would she be willing to talk to me?"

"I don't see why not. She's on her lunch break now. Come on back. I'll introduce you before I leave."

Matilda Jackson leaned back in her chair and smiled at the memory.

"Oh, Mr. Mordecai Jacobs was a fine figure of a man," she said. "Carried a pearl-handled cane and wore rattlesnake cowboy boots." She stared at me solemnly, as if bearing witness. "He knew Dr. King, praise God. That's the truth. Mr. Mordecai Jacobs went to Washington in 1963 to march with Dr. King. He carried a picture of the march in his wallet. He showed it to me on many an occasion." She gave me a proud look. "Mordecai hired me, you know. I was the first black nurse to ever work at Beth Shalom. Mordecai hired me in 1972 and told me that I had an equal opportunity to excel. I believed the man, and the man was true to his word, praise God. In 1981, he promoted me to the position of head nurse." She smiled again, her eyes far away. "Oh, yes, Mr. Mordecai Jacobs was a fine figure of a man."

"Is his family still in St. Louis?" I asked, taking notes.

"I believe Mrs. Jacobs is still alive, bless her soul. They never had any children, though."

"Do you remember her first name?"

"I most certainly do. Clara. Mrs. Clara Jacobs."

I jotted down the name and looked up at her. "I have a list, Mrs. Jackson, and it appears to include residents of Beth Shalom." I handed her a copy. "I wonder if you recognize any of the names in those first two columns."

She put on her reading glasses and studied the document. "Oh, yes," she said with a smile. "Mrs. Caplan, Mrs. Friedman. Oh, Mrs. Gutterman, what a darling she was. And Shirley Lieberman, my, my. She used to love to play poker." As her eyes moved down the list, she cooed and chuckled at her memories of the people.

"Were they all women?" I asked.

She looked down both columns. "I can't say they all were. There was a Mr. Mittelman and a Mr. Schecter, but their wives were there, too. Oh, and Wexler—that must be Rabbi Wexler. What a sweetheart he was. But wait a minute, his wife was there, too. Lenore Wexler." Her happy expression shifted to sorrow. "Oh, poor Mrs. Wexler. She was one of them."

"One of who?"

"Oh, it was that terrible summer."

"What terrible summer?"

She shook her head sadly and heaved a sigh. "When they all died."

I felt a shiver down my spine. "Tell me about it," I said quietly.

"It was so tragic." She sighed. "The first two died on Friday around sundown." She paused. "Are you Jewish, honey?"

I nodded.

"Well, then you know that the Jewish sabbath starts at sundown on Friday. Beth Shalom was strictly orthodox, which meant that we couldn't transport these two bodies to the funeral home until Sunday. That was a real problem, because it was so hot and humid that weekend. We had to move the bodies to the coolest place in the building." She shook her head at the memory.

"Where was that?" I asked.

"The barber shop. It was on the basement level and there were two window air conditioners. We moved the first two bodies down there on Friday night. There were two barber chairs, and that's where we put them, each covered with a sheet."

I waited silently, caught up in the tale.

"Later that night, the third one died. Another woman. We moved her down there, too. There were no empty barber chairs left, so we sat her up on one of the three waiting chairs. The fourth died the next morning, and then the fifth died Saturday night. Five deaths over one Sabbath." She raised her eyebrows and sighed heavily. "When the men from the funeral homes arrived on Sunday afternoon, there was a corpse on every single chair in that barber shop. I'll tell you, honey, it's a sight my eyes will never forget."

The eerie image of the shrouded barbershop quintet held us both rapt. After a moment, I asked, "What did they die of?"

She squinted, trying to remember. "I don't recall the exact cause. There were respiratory problems, circulatory problems, muscle problems. It just sort of swept through the home. Several others came down with the disease that week. Some of them died, others recovered. I swear, I have never had a week like that in my life."

"When did this happen?"

"In the summer. I know that, honey, because it was so hot."

"Which summer?"

She scratched her chin as she mumbled under her breath, trying to place it in relation to other events. "Arthur was born that year . . . no, that was the year before . . . we had that picnic over at the Alton Locks . . . no, that was the next summer . . ." Finally, she looked up with a helpless shrug. "It was either the summer of 1973 or the summer of 1974. I can't be sure which year, but it was one of those two for sure."

I referred back to the list. "And you think Mrs. Wexler was one of the people who died that weekend?"

She nodded sadly.

"Any others on the list?"

She looked down the list again, shaking her head. "My memory just isn't what it should be, honey. Maybe Mrs. Gutterman. Maybe Mrs. Silverman. I just can't be sure."

I thanked Matilda Jackson for her help and walked back to the front of the building. From a pay phone in the lobby I called for a County Cab.

"Destination?" the dispatcher asked.

"The St. Louis County Library on Lindbergh," I said.

Matilda's memory would serve as my compass to navigate through the official records.

# 23

**W**ITH the *Post-Dispatch* indexes for 1973 and 1974 on the table to my right and the rack of microfilm to my left, I looked down at my photocopy of the Beth Shalom/Labadie Gardens lists. I started alphabetically with the A's. The first "A" was Abramawitz.

Matilda vaguely recalled summer as the time of year. Specifically, she recalled hot and humid. In St. Louis, that narrowed it to May through September. I checked the obituaries for that period during 1973. None for Abramawitz. I checked the obituaries for 1974. None again.

The next "A" was Abrams. I checked the obituaries for May through September of 1973. There were two Abrams—one on May 8 and one on July 3. I jotted down the dates. I checked the obituaries for 1974. There was one Abrams: August 26. I wrote the date on my pad.

I reached over and sorted through the microfilm rack. I found the reels for the first half of May 1973, the first half of July 1973 and the second half of August 1974. Starting with May 1973, I threaded the microfilm and advanced the reel to the front page of the May 8 issue of the *Post-Dispatch*, pausing to check the weather forecast: a high of 82° with a chance of afternoon show-ers. *Possible.*

I advanced the reel to the obituaries and funeral notices. I found my first Abrams under the funeral notices:

ABRAMS, TYRONE R., Blessed with the Sacraments of Holy Mother Church, May 2, 1974, 89 years, beloved husband of the late Gertrude, loving father of Thomas and Catherine, grandfather, brother-in-law, father-in-law, uncle, relative and special friend.

Funeral Tues., 9:30 A.M. from HOFFMEISTER COLONIAL Mortuary, 6464 Chippewa at Watson, Tues., 9:15 A.M. with Mass celebrated at the Church of Annunciation, 10 A.M., Internment Resurrection Cemetery.

Whatever else he had been during his nine decades, Tyrone Abrams clearly had never been a resident of Beth Shalom.

Nor had the second Abrams, whose obituary appeared in the July 3, 1973, issue of the *Post-Dispatch.* Randall Abrams, age 20, had died in an automobile crash on Highway 70 while home for summer vacation from Drake University.

The third Abrams obit was Monday, August 26, 1974. The front page of that day's *Post-Dispatch* had an appropriate weather forecast: hot and humid, with a high of 101°. I advanced the reel to page 4 of Section B and found the funeral notice:

ABRAMS, RUTH S., August 23, 1974, beloved wife of the late Milton, dear mother of Karen and Lee, beloved grandmother of Cory, Kelly, Lara, and Kyle, dear sister of Jack (Rose) Sanders and the late Ida Turner.

Funeral service Tues., 2 P.M., at RINDSKOPF-ROTH Funeral Chapel, 5216 Delmar Blvd. VISITATION 1:30 P.M. Burial at Chesed Shel Emeth Cemetery. Contributions preferred to Beth Shalom or a charity of your choice.

*Bingo.*

I studied the funeral notice. Ruth Abrams had died on August 23. Her notice was in the August 26 edition of the *Post-Dispatch*. I glanced up to the top of the page. Monday, August 26, 1974. So Ruth had died on the prior Friday. Was she one of the three who had died that Friday? I skimmed through the rest of the funeral notices. Sure enough, I found the other two: Thelma Friedman and Anna Mittelman. I also found Lenore Wexler, who had died on Saturday, and Margaret Cohen, who had died on Sunday.

Ruth, Thelma, Anna, Lenore, and Margaret. Five elderly women, who spent their last weekend together, covered with sheets and propped silently on the chairs as the Beth Shalom barber shop air conditioners rumbled.

I glanced down the Beth Shalom/Labadie Gardens list and placed check marks by their names:

| BETH SHALOM | | LABADIE GARDENS | |
|---|---|---|---|
| *P/S* | *P/A* | *P/S* | *P/A* |
| Abramawitz | Abrams✓ | Allen | Bailey |
| Altman | Braunstein | Brown, A | Brown, R |
| Caplan | Cohen, M✓ | Coleman | Carter |
| Cohen, S | Epstein | Jackson, R | Jackson, M |
| Freidman | Friedman✓ | Johnson | Mitchell |
| Gutterman | Goldstein | Marshall | Perkins |
| Kohn | Gruener | Russell | Perry |
| Leiberman | Kaplansky | Shaw | Rivers |
| Perlmutter | Mittelman✓ | Smith, B | Sleet |
| Rosenberg | Pinsky | Trotter | Smith, R |
| Rotskoff | Silverman | Washington, C | Washington, L |
| Schecter | Wexler✓ | Young | Wells |

I leaned back in my chair and stared blankly at the screen of the microfilm reader. There were four obituaries grouped above the funeral notices. One of the headlines caught my eye:

LUCILLE WASHINGTON;
LONGTIME TEACHER

I glanced at the list. Sure enough, there was a "Washington, L" in one of the Labadie Gardens columns. I read the first paragraph of the obituary:

> Lucille (Henson) Washington, a former teacher and reading specialist in the St. Louis Public Schools system, died Sunday (Aug. 25, 1994) at the Labadie Gardens Nursing Home after a brief illness. She was 76.

I carefully reviewed the rest of the funeral notices on the page, looking for any other matches with the names on the two Labadie Gardens columns. There were none.

I read through the Lucille Washington obituary again. It seemed an unusual coincidence—a name from one of the Labadie Gardens columns just happened to show up on the same page of funeral notices as a name from a Beth Shalom column. Slowly and methodically, I advanced the reel forward to the obituaries and funeral notices for each successive day in August and then for each day in September. The "coincidences" continued.

Each time I found a match, I photocopied the page and checked off the name on the Beth Shalom/Labadie Gardens list. I located a total of fifteen, all of whom had died between August 23 and September 4, 1974. The pattern looked strange. To double-check the results, I expanded my search to include the entire year of 1974. To my surprise, the expanded search did not add a single name from the Beth Shalom/Labadie Gardens list. When I finished, I looked at my results:

| BETH SHALOM | | LABADIE GARDENS | |
|---|---|---|---|
| *P/S* | *P/A* | *P/S* | *P/A* |
| Abramawitz | Abrams✓ | Allen | Bailey✓ |
| Altman | Braunstein✓ | Brown, A | Brown, R |

| Caplan | Cohen, M✓ | Coleman | Carter✓ |
|---|---|---|---|
| Cohen, S | Epstein | Jackson, R | Jackson, M✓ |
| Freidman | Friedman✓ | Johnson | Mitchell |
| Gutterman | Goldstein | Marshall | Perkins |
| Kohn | Gruener | Russell | Perry |
| Leiberman | Kaplansky✓ | Shaw | Rivers✓ |
| Perlmutter | Mittelman✓ | Smith, B | Sleet✓ |
| Rosenberg | Pinsky | Trotter | Smith, R |
| Rotskoff | Silverman✓ | Washington, C | Washington, L✓ |
| Schecter | Wexler✓ | Young | Wells |

I stared at the list, trying to make sense of it. In a period of less than two weeks, fifteen people out of forty-eight on the list had died. At two separate institutions, the only people on the list who died were under the column headed "P/A" Indeed, if you focused only on the "P/A" columns, fifteen out of a total of twenty-four had died—eight at Beth Shalom and seven at Labadie Gardens. More than half of the names on each column.

And all fifteen were women.

And all were listed on a document bearing the private water-mark of Armstrong Bioproducts.

Obviously, all fifteen women—eight Jews, seven blacks—had something in common. Something important. And fatal. Fatal to them and, for different reasons, fatal to at least two men: Bruce Rosenthal and David Marcus.

I gathered my notes and photocopies, stuffed them in my brief-case, and went over to the pay phone. It was quarter after three. I dialed the number of the Jewish Center for the Aged.

"Mark Levine," I told the receptionist.

"Hi," he said cheerfully. "How are you?"

"Fine," I said in a businesslike tone. "What did you find?"

"How about we meet somewhere to talk?"

"How about we start by you telling me over the phone what you found?"

There was a pause. "Okay. Well, there's a problem."

"What's the problem?" I asked.

"The Beth Shalom records don't go back before 1981."

"Why not?"

"I'm not sure. It merged into the JCA in November of 1984. Apparently, the older records weren't among the files transferred in the merger."

"Were they destroyed?" I asked.

"I honestly don't know. We followed the paper trail back to 1981. That's where it ends."

"Damn," I said in frustration.

"I thought Matilda might know the answer," he said, "but she doesn't. However, she did say that Mrs. Jacobs might know. In fact, she says that the records might be stored in the basement of the Jacobs' home."

"Does Mrs. Jacobs still live in St. Louis?"

"Matilda thinks so."

"Does she know where?"

"No."

"Do you have her number?"

"I don't, and neither does Matilda. Apparently, it's unlisted."

"One more question," I said.

"That's what I'm here for."

"Do you have physicians on your staff?"

"No. We have a contract with Mt. Sinai Hospital. They provide our doctors."

"How long has that been the case?"

"For a long time. Nursing homes don't generally have their own physicians. They usually contract with a hospital."

"Would that be the same hospital where one of your residents would be taken if they needed hospitalization?"

"That's usually how it works."

I thanked him for his help, declined his invitation to "brainstorm" together over a drink after work, hung up the phone, and stepped back into the main area of the library. I surveyed the crowd, searching for someone who might seem out of place among the retirees leafing through magazines, the mommies on the carpet in the children's section reading books to their children, the earnest young men in business suits hunched over thick books in the reference section. One or two looked up at me curiously, but none appeared sinister.

I went over to the medical reference section. As long as I was in a library, I should try to fill in the gaps in my knowledge of Guillain-Barré syndrome. I found a listing in a medical encyclopedia and photocopied all three pages on the subject.

I checked my watch: almost four o'clock. I might have enough time. There were two cabs at the taxi stand outside. I got into the backseat of the first one. The driver glanced at me in the rearview mirror and then spun around with a leer.

"Ah, hello to you, my dear lady. Again it is that we meet."

"Oh, no," I groaned. It was the same swarthy man with the thick black mustache and all-consonant names. I yanked open the door. "Forget it, creep," I said, slamming the door closed behind me.

"But lovely lady," he called after me.

I walked back to the second cab, opened the front passenger door, and leaned in. The driver was an old black man reading the newspaper.

"Do you know where the Bureau of Vital Statistics is?" I asked.

He neatly folded his newspaper. "Would that be county or city, ma'am?"

"City."

He nodded. "I certainly do. Hop in." I got in back and he pulled away from the curb, swinging wide of the first cabbie, who was now standing outside his cab and shouting at me in some guttural language.

# 24

CHAPTER

AT three minutes to five, the clerk at the Bureau of Vital Statistics handed me a payment receipt and an envelope containing certified copies of two death certificates.

"When will the other thirteen be ready?" I asked.

"Check back tomorrow morning at eleven. They'll be waiting up here."

I thanked her, put the receipt and the envelope in my briefcase, and walked out of the building onto Grand Avenue. The rush-hour traffic was in full force. I was meeting up with Flo at nine o'clock, which was four hours away. I turned and walked toward the Fox Theater, reviewing my list of things to do. It was too late to find someone to look through records at Mt. Sinai Hospital, but it could be a good time to make contact with Lee Fowler, the former CFO of Armstrong Bioproducts, who might be getting home from work soon.

By the time I reached the Fox, I had concluded that today's disguise had too many drawbacks. Although I might get past someone looking for Rachel Gold, I was hardly inconspicuous. Blondes may not have more fun, but they sure have more hassles. Especially blondes in miniskirts and pumps, to judge from the wolf whistles, stares, and lewd comments flung my way from passing cars or from bystanders across the street.

The Fox Theater was open. I ducked into the women's room to change. So long as I was lugging around my entire wardrobe, such as it was, I might as well get into something a little less flamboyant. A little less was about as far as I could get. I chose my sister's skintight black jeans and red cotton turtleneck. My footwear selection was limited to the black pumps I had worn during the day or my Nikes. I stuck with the pumps. I paused to look in the mirror, surprised again by the sight of a blond, straight-haired Rachel Gold. The hair was starting to curl in the humidity, but the color and the length were enough to even throw me off.

I hailed a cab in front of the Fox and gave him Lee Fowler's address. I had debated whether to call in advance, but my paranoia was such that it seemed safer, albeit ruder, to show up without warning.

Settling back in the seat, I tore open the envelope containing the two death certificates that the clerk had been able to locate and copy before closing time. The first was for Ruth Abrams. Date of death: August 23, 1994. Residence: Beth Shalom Retirement Home. Under the section CAUSE OF DEATH there were two lines, one for Immediate Cause and the second for Underlying Cause. On Ruth Abrams' death certificate, the Immediate Cause was "Respiratory Failure" but the Underlying Cause apparently wasn't certain. The physician had filled it out as follows:

*Diphtheritic Polyneuropathy?*

Near the bottom of the form was a space labeled NAME OF ATTENDING PHYSICIAN IF OTHER THAN CERTIFIER. In the space was the name George McMillan.

The second death certificate was for June Bailey. Residence: Labadie Gardens Nursing Home. June had died later that same week. My eyes moved slowly down the form, stopping at the CAUSE OF DEATH section:

Immediate Cause: *Respiratory Failure*
Underlying Cause: *Guillain-Barré syndrome? Porphyria?*

I looked down to the final section for the identity of the attending physician. I stared at the name: Peter Todorovich.

I looked out the window as the cab turned onto Kingshighway.

*Peter Todorovich?* The 1979 annual report of Armstrong Bioproducts listed a Dr. Peter Todorovich as the Director of Research. How many Dr. Peter Todoroviches could there be in one city? Perhaps Todorovich, like his boss at Armstrong Bioproducts, had maintained his medical practice during the early, lean years of the company. Perhaps Todorovich had been one of the physicians provided by whichever hospital Labadie Gardens had its medical contract with.

One of Flo's assignments was to find where Todorovich was today. That assignment suddenly seemed much more important. I was anxious to hear what she had found.

I looked again at the cause of deaths on the death certificates. The diseases sounded familiar. I opened my briefcase and removed the pages I had photocopied from the medical encyclopedia. I read through them as the cab headed toward the Fowler residence.

Guillain-Barré syndrome (aka Landry-Guillain-Barré syndrome aka Guillain-Barré-Strohl syndrome aka acute idiopathic polyneuritis) was part of a family of diseases of the peripheral nervous system that also included such mouthfuls as porphyric polyneuropathy, diphtheritic polyneuropathy, and acute idiopathic hepatitis with polyneuritis. According to the photocopied materials, the first signs of the diseases are tingling in the ends of the arms and legs, sometimes moving up the entire limbs, sometimes leading to paralysis, sometimes leading to severe circulatory and respiratory problems, sometimes leading to death. The causes of the diseases are unknown and there are no known cures, although most patients fully recover.

The Fowler residence was a stately, two-story brick house on Aberdeen, a quiet street just off Skinker. The streetlights were on. I gave the driver some extra money and asked him to wait. My heels clicked along the front walk as I strode toward the front porch. I rang the doorbell, which set off a musical series of chimes inside. I turned back toward the street as I waited. It was the kind of neighborhood where people parked their cars in their garages. There were few cars on the street, and none near the Fowler house except for my cab.

I turned as the door was yanked open by a well-dressed woman in her sixties holding a highball glass containing what looked like a martini with an olive. The force of the opening door jolted her slightly, causing some of the drink to slosh over the top of her glass and onto the terrazzo floor.

"Yes?" she said in a two-pack-a-day rasp, ignoring the splatter at her feet. I could hear a television blaring somewhere in the back.

"Hi," I said in my friendliest voice. "I'm Elizabeth Bennett. Is Mr. Fowler in?"

She stepped back and gave me the once-over. Her narrow, angular face was tanned and leathery and unusually taut. It was a face that had survived thirty winters in Boca Raton and a truly epic face-lift. Indeed, the skin was so tight that it gave her a look of surprise, quite literally over the results of her plastic surgery.

"Elizabeth, huh?" she snorted. She took a gulp of her drink. "What's he call you? Lizzy? Or maybe Liza? Were you the one he was with last weekend?" Her words were slightly slurred.

"Excuse me, ma'am," I said politely. "I've never met your husband. He has no idea who I am. I came here to ask him some questions."

She gave me a dubious look. "Questions?"

"Is he here?"

She thrust her chin forward belligerently. "Questions about what?"

I wasn't prepared for the hostility and distrust. I had to choose my words carefully, sensing that if I told her it involved a "personal matter" she would slam the door in my face. The way she was acting told me that Lee Fowler wasn't home yet. The alcohol was making her angry, but it also might make her talkative if I could get inside before her husband got home.

"I wanted to ask your husband about his years at Armstrong Bioproducts."

"What do you want to know about?"

"What it was like back in the early days."

"Why do you want to know that?"

I had three alternative cover stories. I decided which version she would be most likely to respond to. "I'm a freelance writer," I said. "I'm doing some background work on Douglas Armstrong for *People* magazine. Your husband worked with the senator back then, right?"

She nodded slowly, frowning. "You've never met Lee?"

"Never. I don't know where he works or what he does. I don't know what he looks like. I didn't even know he was married until you opened the door. Were you married to him back then?"

"Yes."

"Great. So you knew the senator in the early days?"

She smiled. "Oh, yes," she said with a conspiratorial wink. "I've got some juicy inside stories, too."

"Wonderful. Would you mind sharing some with me?"

She opened the door wider. "What's your name again?"

"Elizabeth."

"Well, come on in, Elizabeth."

Within twenty minutes, it was clear that Donna Fowler had no "inside" information about Douglas Armstrong, Armstrong Bioproducts, or her husband's role back then. But I let her continue to talk and drink, hoping a gem might slip out. None did. I learned that Lee Fowler joined the company in January of 1973 and remained there until Douglas Armstrong resigned to run for the U.S. Senate. Since then, Fowler had held finance positions at Monsanto and Mallinckrodt, and three years ago joined the St. Louis office of an investment banking firm. The firm had a client list from around the world. As a result, Fowler was on the road a lot. In fact, he was returning from out of town tonight.

Her memories of the early days were hazy. She remembered that Douglas Armstrong and Peter Todorovich had gone to Costa Rica. She didn't know what ever happened to Peter, although, she said in a stage whisper with arched eyebrows, "I think he was a queer." She didn't like Sherman Ross, who was "always lurking around that place." Her dislike seemed to stem, at least in part, from her husband's belief that Ross had blocked his progress in the company. She was fond of Armstrong's wife Edie, and she started crying when she talked about Edie's death from cancer.

As she regained control of herself, I checked my watch. I'd been listening to her for almost an hour and had learned little of any relevance. Lee Fowler apparently was not the type who talked about his work at home. Donna Fowler had only the vaguest sense of what her husband had done during his years at Armstrong Bioproducts.

"I'm sorry," she said, wiping her face with a tissue.

"I understand," I said gently, trying to mask my growing impatience. I had too much yet to do. While her husband might be able to help me, Donna couldn't.

"Have my stories helped?" she asked.

"Very much." I decided to take a wild stab before leaving. "Donna, did your husband ever tell you about a drug called Primax?"

She looked up with a curious grin. "Primax? Why does everyone all of a sudden want to know about Primax?"

I sat back in surprise. "Who else?"

"There was a man."

"Who was he?"

She shook her head. "I can't remember his name."

"Did he call you?"

"No, he came here one afternoon."

"When?"

"Oh, maybe a month ago."

"Was he a rabbi?"

She gave me an incredulous look. "A rabbi? Oh, no. But he did have a Jew name."

"Rosenthal?" I asked, ignoring her crude choice of words. "Bruce Rosenthal?"

She tilted her head, trying to remember. "Maybe that's it."

"He wanted to know about Primax?"

"Yes. He wasn't a writer like you. He said he was doing some . . . what did he call it? It was part of some deal."

"Due diligence?"

She smiled and nodded her head. "Right. Due diligence. That's it. Said he wanted to know about Primax. He also had a list he showed me."

"This?" I asked as I reached for the Beth Shalom/Labadie Gardens list and handed it to her.

She put on her reading glasses and nodded. "I think that's it. I don't remember these check marks, though."

"What did he want to know about the list?"

"I can't remember. I told him I'd never seen it before, and I hadn't."

The phone rang. I waited while Donna went into the kitchen to answer it. The television in the background was too loud to hear all of her side of the conversation. It sounded like her husband. I heard the word Primax a couple times.

*So Bruce Rosenthal had visited Donna Fowler.*

Was I now retracing his steps? Was I getting warmer?

Donna came back in with a big smile. "That was Lee," she said. "His plane just landed. I told him that if he hurried home he could talk to you." She paused and rolled her eyes. "He said he had to stop off at the office, but that he'd be here in about an hour. Is that too long?"

Stalling, I checked my watch. On the one hand, I wanted to talk to her husband. On the other hand, I wanted to go off somewhere for a while and sort through what I had just learned.

"Tell you what," I said. "I have to leave now, but I'll try to come back."

"You sure?" She seemed disappointed.

"I have another appointment, but I should be done in an hour."

"Where is it at?"

"Well," I said, my mind going blank.

"Don't worry," she said. "It's just that Lee seemed like he wanted to talk to you. I thought that if you couldn't stay, he'd know where to reach you."

"Oh," I said, a red flag popping up. "Don't worry. He won't need to contact me. I'll be back."

I said good-bye to her at the front door, relieved to see that the cab was still waiting for me.

# 25

CHAPTER

I DECIDED to hole up for the hour at Blueberry Hill Restaurant and Pub in the University City Loop. As I had hoped, there was a big weeknight crowd of mostly college students jammed into the front area around the bar. I squeezed past the throng near the bar and walked through the restaurant area and back to the dart room. There was a game in progress at every board, and over in the pinball area there were one or two intense players at each machine. The cigarette smoke made my eyes smart. I moved back to the restaurant area and found a secluded table beyond the booths by the window facing the street.

I didn't realize how hungry I was until the waitress arrived. The only thing I'd eaten all day was a bagel and coffee for breakfast. I ordered a cheeseburger, fries, and a Coke. As I settled back and peered out the window at the passing sidewalk traffic, the waitress placed a longneck bottle of Bud Light in front of me.

"No," I explained, "I ordered a Coke."

"I know, honey. The guys over there sent it."

I turned to where she gestured and found myself staring at what looked like the front four of the Green Bay Packers. They were squeezed into a booth—four humongous guys with crew cuts and grins. Each was holding a bottle of Bud Light. Simultaneously, all four tilted their bottles in my direction, as if about to propose a toast.

*Great,* I groaned. *Just what I need.*

I held my beer toward them with a weak smile. "Thanks, fellas."

They gave a raucous chorus of cheers and then turned back to their conversation.

"Who are they?" I asked the waitress.

She gave a weary shake of her head. "Damned if I know."

Ten minutes later, she returned with my food and another complimentary brewsky from the boys. She gestured toward them. "Joe says they're from KU. He says they're on the football squad."

"They're a long way from home."

She rolled her eyes. "They tend to wander when you turn off the electric fence."

I held the bottle up and tilted it toward them in acknowledgment. That triggered another burst of cheers, punctuated with a manic round of high fives and table poundings. It sounded like an entire cattle drive.

I stared out the window as I ate, trying to concentrate on my situation. To return or not to return, that was the question. The fact that Bruce Rosenthal had made contact with Donna Fowler, and probably her husband as well, was both encouraging and creepy. Encouraging because I seemed to be on the right track. Creepy because Bruce had asked about Primax and he had asked about the Beth Shalom/Labadie Gardens list and now he was dead.

*And you're seriously considering going back to that house tonight?* I told myself.

But there wasn't any direct evidence linking the Fowlers to Bruce Rosenthal's death. Just coincidence. Sure, he had asked about Primax and the list, and later he was killed. But he had apparently asked the same questions of others, too. Moreover, if Lee Fowler were guilty, why invite me back tonight? Could it be that he was innocent himself but had guilty knowledge that he wanted to get off his chest?

*Wishful thinking,* I told myself as I peered out the window and took a sip of my Coke.

That's when he passed in front of the window. The guy with the long red hair.

Choking on the soda, I stood up and pressed my face against the window to watch him. In disbelief, I saw him turn into Blueberry Hill.

*Oh, shit,* I groaned silently as I turned away from the window.

I glanced around in dismay. *But you don't look like Rachel,* I reminded myself.

*Who are you kidding? Blond hair, and all of a sudden you're someone else?*

Any moment he would drift into the restaurant area and stop to survey the crowd. The dart room was too far. I'd never make it. My eyes stopped at the table of jocks. I moved quickly toward them.

"Guys, can I squeeze in?"

They looked up, momentarily perplexed, and then they all grinned. Two scooted over to make room for me. I scrunched in with my back to the restaurant entrance.

"I need help," I said in a low voice. They leaned forward. I looked around the table at each of them. "There's a man following me. He just came in the building." I slid lower in the booth. "He'll be in here any second. He has long red hair, parted in the middle, and he's wearing a black leather jacket. He's already tried to kill me once. I've got to get away from here."

"Hell, darling," one of them said gallantly, "I'll take you anywhere you want to go."

I shook my head. "You'd only get in trouble. All I need is someone to slow him down long enough for me to get away."

The two guys across the table looked up past me and became still. Their eyes moved slowly to the left.

"Him," I whispered.

They nodded, still tracking him with their eyes.

After a moment, one said, "He went in the dart room."

"Who the hell is that sumbitch?"

"I don't know," I said.

"Well, he just went down the stairs to the dance floor."

"C'mon, boys," one of them said as he stood up. He checked his watch. "Time to kick some butt." He looked down at me with a wink. "You got nothing to worry about, little lady. We're the fucking Jayhawks."

I watched as three of the four squeezed out of the booth and lumbered toward the stairway—over seven hundred pounds of prime Kansas beef. Two of them were banging their fists into their palms.

The fourth guy waited for me to scoot out of the booth. His neck was larger than my waist. "Come on, ma'am," he said, glancing longingly toward his companions, who were disappearing down the stairs. "I'll walk you out." He gently put his hand under my elbow.

In less than a minute I had flagged a cab cruising east on Delmar. I opened the car door and turned to my hulking escort. "Thanks," I said, holding out my hand.

"No problem." He awkwardly shook my hand.

As the cab door closed, he turned and charged back into Blueberry Hill. My cab continued east on Delmar, catching every stoplight on the way to Skinker. As we slowed for the light at Skinker, two squad cars with sirens blaring zoomed past us heading in the opposite direction toward Blueberry Hill.

*If I live through this,* I told myself as I turned back, *I'm a Jayhawk fan for life.*

"Go slow," I said to the driver as we turned off Skinker onto Aberdeen. There seemed to be a few more cars parked on the street than before. The Fowler house was two-thirds of the way up the block on the right.

I leaned forward to peer out the front window. "Put on your brights."

There was a car parked on the left side, two houses before the Fowler house. The high beams from the taxi illuminated the windows of the parked car. There was someone on the driver's side. As we passed the car, I strained to see in the window. Although his features were cloaked in darkness, I recognized the Dr. Dre sweatshirt. It was the black man who had spotted me in Walgreen's and later chased me through the shopping center.

"Go!" I shouted to the driver.

I turned to look back as we zoomed off. The other car pulled away from the curb with the headlights off.

"Oh, no," I groaned, still watching out the rear window.

"Where to?" the driver asked.

I was surprised by the voice. I hadn't realized the driver was a woman. I moved to the side for a better look. She was a stout woman in her late forties with short black hair and crow's feet around her eyes. She was wearing a white, short-sleeved bowling shirt. There was a wedding ring on her plump left hand.

"Uh, downtown," I said.

"Where downtown?"

"I don't know. Just head in that direction."

I checked my watch, my mind racing. It was almost nine o'clock. Flo would be in her room at the Hyatt by now. But I couldn't go directly there. He'd see me go in. I'd be a sitting duck if they knew where I was. They could simply post people round the clock and wait for me to emerge.

The headlights flicked on behind us. It was the same headlight configuration as the car that had followed me last night. *Last night?* It seemed like last year.

I evaluated my position as we got onto Highway 40 at Forest Park. There was only one person in the tail car. My advantage, though slim, was that I had only me to worry about. He had me and his car. That meant that if I suddenly got out of the taxi, he had to get rid of his car *and* follow me. An office building with two entrances might work. But at this time of the night, there was probably only one entrance open. A shopping center? The only one downtown, St. Louis Centre, was probably closed for the night by now. A big hotel? Possibly. But at a hotel he'd have an easier time dumping his car.

"Is there anything at the convention center?" I asked the driver.

She nodded. "Auto show. Tonight's opening night."

"Perfect. Let's go there."

"You got it."

I looked out the rear window. He was right behind us.

"You trying to shake that guy?" the driver asked.

I turned toward her. "I'm trying to get to the Hyatt without him finding out. If I can lose him at the convention center, I might be able to reach the Hyatt without him knowing."

There was a burst of static over her dispatch radio. I stared at it.

"If you tried to contact someone over that radio," I asked, "can the signal be picked up by others?"

"Yep."

"Oh," I said glumly.

"What do you need?"

"I need to find out the room number of a friend of mine who's staying at the Hyatt, but I can't risk anyone eavesdropping on the conversation." I had an idea. "Listen, if I went in one entrance at the convention hall and hung around for ten minutes or so, would you have enough time to call the Hyatt from a pay phone and then pick me up at another entrance?"

"Sure."

"Let's do it."

She stopped at the intersection just east of the main entrance to the convention center.

"I'll meet you there," she said, pointing at the main entrance. She turned right and headed north down the street toward the side entrance. Three-quarters of the way down the block she started to brake. She looked at me in the mirror. "Ready?"

I nodded. My free hand was on the door handle.

She stopped the taxi. "Go!"

I yanked open the door, ducked out, and sprinted up the stairs toward the side entrance. As I pushed through the revolving door I saw my taxi pull away. The tail car hesitated in the middle of the street.

I ran down the enormous hushed hallway toward the auto show area, passing people heading in and people heading out. My feet and ankles were killing me. There's a reason why joggers don't wear pumps.

I passed an entire squad of high school cheerleaders who were leaving the showroom area laughing and swishing their pom-poms. I turned down another main hallway. Sashaying toward me were three Hooters girls, dressed in knee-high white boots, white fishnet pantyhose, white short-shorts and Hooters tank tops. Off in the distance was the entrance to the auto show. I looked back. The black man wasn't in sight. I continued toward the auto show signs.

As I approached the entrance, I slowed to a walk. My breath was coming in jagged gasps. The large placard in front of the entrance read:

*OPENING NIGHT—BY INVITATION ONLY*

There were two entrance gates. A severe-looking woman was checking passes at one. A middle-aged man was checking passes at the other. I moved toward the man.

He gave my blond hair and tight jeans an appreciative look. "Do you have your pass, young lady?" he asked with a flirtatious wink.

*Perfect.*

I gave him a perky, wide-eyed expression. "I jes' can't believe myself sometimes," I said with a syrupy twang. "I'm Cheryl Ann, honey. You know, one of them Hooters girls." I gave him a saucy swing of my hip. "Well, I must have got myself so worked up over the hot cars y'awl have in there that I plumb forgot my boots and little shorts in the changing room." I rolled my eyes and shook my head. "Have you ever?" I put my hand on his wrist and asked, "Honey, can I jes' scoot myself back there real fast and get my stuff?"

He chuckled. "Why certainly, Cheryl Ann. Go ahead."

I crinkled my nose at him. "Well, aren't you a sweetie pie? What's your name, darlin'?"

He blushed. "Fred."

"Well, thank you, Fred. Next time y'awl are down at Union Station, y'awl better come by Hooters and see me, you hear?" I blew him a kiss as I wiggled past. "Bye-bye."

I moved quickly into the huge showroom area. It was filled with hundreds of automobiles, pickup trucks, and vans, grouped by manufacturer. The Dodge section was to my left. Further off in the distance was the BMW section. To my right was a display of dozens of conversion vans.

I needed to figure out which exit from the showroom area would lead me to the main entrance of the convention center. As I stood there in the middle of the showroom, trying to get my bearings, I started to feel exposed, vulnerable—as if I had a bull's eye painted on my back. I opened a side door to one of the conversion vans, stepped inside, and closed it behind me. It was extraordinary roomy inside. The roof of the van was high enough for me to stand. There were shades on the windows and soft music coming from the stereo speakers. I sat down in the nearest captain's chair and mentally retraced my steps through the building, trying to pinpoint my position. I peered through the blinds toward the BMW section. The exit beyond the BMWs ought to lead to the main entrance.

As I surveyed the crowd through the blinds, the black man in the Dr. Dre sweatshirt passed directly in front of me. My head jerked back. I let the blinds close and crawled toward the front of the van. Crouching low, I watched him through the windshield. He moved toward the center of the showroom. Using the sleeve of his sweatshirt, he wiped the perspiration from his face. There was a bulge under the front of his sweatshirt. He looked to his left, scrutinizing the crowd, and then to his right. The BMW section was to the left. He moved off to the right.

When he disappeared from view, I yanked open the van door and hopped down. Inching toward the front of the van, I peered around the hood toward the right. I saw his glistening bald head off in the distance, moving away.

I started in the opposite direction, walking briskly toward the exit sign beyond the BMW section. My gait quickened as my anxiety continued to build. I cringed once, half expecting to feel a bullet rip into my back. I reached the exit and stared down the vast hallway. The rotunda was visible in the distance at the end of the hallway, maybe one hundred yards away.

I turned to look back, adjusting my backpack. My feet were killing me. As I scanned the crowd, I slipped off my pumps and shoved them into my purse. I didn't see him, and then I did. He was over to the left, maybe seventy-five yards away, moving along the edge of the showroom. For one horrible second our eyes met.

I whirled and sprinted down the hallway, my briefcase in one hand, my purse slung over my shoulder. The purse swung wildly against my hip as I ran barefoot toward the rotunda that loomed up ahead. It seemed to take forever until I reached it. I burst through the door into a drizzling rain. My cab was idling on the street in front of the entrance. I jumped into the back seat as it pulled away with a screech.

I looked back. No sign of him. I continued to stare, sweaty and flushed, until the cab turned and the convention center disappeared. I slumped back against the seat. I was getting sick of this chase routine.

# 26
CHAPTER

FLO stood in the doorway, obviously baffled.

"It's me," I said.

Her eyes widened. "Holy shit." She grabbed my arm and yanked me into her hotel room. After triple-locking the door, she turned to me. "You okay?"

I shrugged. "I'm alive."

"You weren't followed?"

"I don't think so."

She checked me out from blond head to high-heeled toe. "Rachel Gold in fuck-me pumps." She chuckled, shaking her head. "If only those goobers on the Harvard Law Review could see you now."

"The man who invented these . . ." I grumbled as I kicked them off.

". . . ought to be whipped like a circus monkey," Flo said.

". . . for starters."

"Right on." Flo walked over to the miniature refrigerator. "Here," she said, handing me a bottle of Amstel Light. "You look like you could use one."

"Thanks." I twisted off the cap and tilted the beer to my lips.

"What happened to you tonight?"

I told her. When I was finished, Flo shook her head and said, "You've got to extricate yourself from this."

"I can't anymore."

"Why not? I can poke around some to see whether there's a story."

I shook my head helplessly. "I can't, Flo. I'd love to, but I'm in it too deep. I'm a target. In fact, I'm probably the main target. People are definitely trying to kill me, and they're definitely going to keep on trying. My only hope is to solve this fast and turn it over to the press or the police or both. Otherwise, I'm dead." I stood up and turned to her. "Those are my options. Solve it or die. I don't want to die."

She stared up at me, her lips pursed. After a moment, she nodded decisively. "Then let's solve it, goddammit."

I smiled wearily. "My thought exactly."

"So fill me in."

I opened my briefcase and walked her through what I had discovered since we spoke last night and how it seemed to fit into what I already knew.

Flo listened intently. When I finished, she stared down at the two death certificates. "Guillain-Barré," she mused. "What about the other thirteen?"

"Won't know that until tomorrow. The clerk said they'd be ready before noon."

She reached for the Beth Shalom/Labadie Gardens list and asked, "The only deaths were women?"

I nodded. "All fifteen."

"What about the ones that didn't die during that period? The ones that got sick but recovered. Are they women, too?"

"I don't know. That's why I need to talk to Mordecai Jacobs' widow. The medical files on these people are the key to everything. If he saved the old files from the Jewish nursing home, maybe she'll know where they are."

"What about the Labadie Gardens medical records?"

"Gone," I said. "Destroyed in the fire." I picked up the death certificate for June Bailey. "But look at this." I pointed at the entry for attending physician: Peter Todorovich. "He may be far better than the files. Were you able to locate him?"

"Forget about him," she said grimly.

"Why?"

"He's dead."

"Oh, no. When? How?"

"In 1983. Two bullets in the chest."

I sat down on the edge of the bed, numb. "What happened?" I asked quietly.

Flo sorted through a folder and pulled out a photocopy of a newspaper article from the *St. Louis Post-Dispatch.* "In 1981," she said, "he left Armstrong Bioproducts to return to private practice. Two years later, while leaving Powell Hall after a symphony concert, he was robbed and killed."

"Did they catch the killer?"

Flo shook her head. "Nope."

I leaned against the dresser and crossed my arms. "Do you think it was staged?"

She shrugged. "We'll never find that out."

I shook my head in frustration. "Oh, brother."

"Let me see those Bruce Rosenthal questions again."

I handed them to her and stared at the document over her shoulder:

- *Primax? Where?*
- *Cross-referenced materials not there—Filing glitch?—Need to locate—Need to ask*
- *What's going on with Guillain B?*
- *Where are Primax files???—must find*
- *Be sure to look for LGB—Sounds like typical G-B syndrome*
- *Cross-reference to Phase Two Trial?—Need to check date— Phase Two Trial?—Not possible!?*

"Well," she finally said, "we found someone on that list who died of Guillain-Barré. Maybe two."

"And maybe more after we get the other death certificates."

"And presumably the LGB here"—she pointed—"refers to the same thing."

I nodded. "And I assume the phase two trial refers to the second phase of human testing. Isn't that what the guy at the FDA called them?"

Flo nodded. "Yep. Once the FDA approves your Investigational New Drug application, you start with the phase one clinical trials on a small group of healthy people to determine whether there are any side effects. Once you get past that phase, you move to phase two clinicals on a large group who have the target disease."

"So," I said, pointing to the *Phase Two Trial* reference in Bruce's notes, "he thinks the dates are out of whack."

She studied Bruce's notes. "For Primax?"

I shrugged. "Makes sense, doesn't it?"

Flo looked at me with a frown. "Except Armstrong Bioproducts never filed its IND for Primax. Right?"

I nodded. "They got as far as the galley proofs, but never went to the final version."

Flo shook her head. "So what's going on? Where the hell is Primax?"

I stared intently at the Beth Shalom/Labadie Gardens list. And then, finally, another piece of the puzzle dropped into place. "Hmm," I mused. "I wonder . . ."

"What?"

I reached for my pile of papers. "Wait."

I found the trademark registration printouts for Phrenom and Primax. I held them side by side. Then I looked down at the Beth Shalom/Labadie Gardens list. "Good God," I said.

"What, Rachel?"

I pointed to the Beth Shalom/Labadie Gardens list of names. "Do you know who these people really are?"

"Who?"

I shook my head in wonder. "These are the people in the phase two trials."

"Of what?"

"Of Phrenom and Primax."

Flo looked down at the list and then back at me. "Huh?"

"Look at this trademark printout for Phrenom," I said, handing it to her.

She studied it. "Okay?"

"Do you see the generic name for Phrenom?"

Flo read, "Phenylpyrrole Sodium."

"Now look at the trademark registration printout for Primax."

"It's a registered trademark?" she said with surprise as she took the printout.

"Was." I showed her the entry. "It was canceled in 1975. What's the drug's generic name?"

She read aloud, "Primillamine Acid."

"So Phrenom is Phenylpyrrole Sodium, and Primax is Primillamine Acid."

"Okay," she said uncertainly.

I handed her the Beth Shalom/Labadie Gardens list. "Take a careful look at this list."

I came around to look with her:

| BETH SHALOM | | LABADIE GARDENS | |
|---|---|---|---|
| *P/S* | *P/A* | *P/S* | *P/A* |
| Abramawitz | Abrams✓ | Allen | Bailey✓ |
| Altman | Braunstein✓ | Brown, A | Brown, R |
| Caplan | Cohen, M✓ | Coleman | Carter✓ |
| Cohen, S | Epstein | Jackson, R | Jackson, M✓ |
| Freidman | Friedman✓ | Johnson | Mitchell |
| Gutterman | Goldstein | Marshall | Perkins |
| Kohn | Gruener | Russell | Perry |
| Leiberman | Kaplansky✓ | Shaw | Rivers✓ |

| Perlmutter | Mittelman✓ | Smith, B | Sleet✓ |
| Rosenberg | Pinsky | Trotter | Smith, R |
| Rotskoff | Silverman✓ | Washington, C | Washington, L✓ |
| Schecter | Wexler✓ | Young | Wells |

Flo studied the list for nearly a full minute before it clicked. She looked at me, her eyes widening. "You think?"

I nodded. "What else could they stand for? According to the trademark registration materials, Armstrong Bioproducts filed its registration papers for Phrenom and Primax on the same day. They also had drafts of IND applications at the printers for both drugs around the same time, too. That tells me that they were working on the two drugs in tandem, right?" I pointed at the headings on the lists. "P/S has to stand for Phenylpyrrole Sodium and P/A must be Primillamine Acid."

"Let me get this straight," Flo said. "If you're right, then the people in the first column at each of these nursing homes were getting Phrenom."

"And the other group was getting Primax."

"But these people," she said, pointing to the fifteen names I had checked off, "were dead by . . . when?"

"They all died between August twenty-third and September fourth, 1974."

She stared at me. "According to the printer's records, neither of the INDs had been filed with the FDA by then. In fact, the IND for Primax was never filed."

I nodded.

She looked back at the list. "Which means," she continued, "Jesus, Rachel, these were illegal human tests."

"Exactly. Don't you see? That's what got Bruce so agitated. Look at his notes on the phase two trials. He said he needed to check the date on them, right? Because the date he had found was, quote, 'Not possible!?' He thought there had to be a mistake on the date of the clinical trials because he knew the INDs hadn't been filed yet."

Flo sat down and shook her head in wonder. "This is some major league heavy shit. Illegal drug tests? Resulting in deaths? Involving Senator Armstrong's former company? Former? Hell, this was back when he was running the damn place." She looked up at me.

"What else do you need?" I asked.

She shook her head and whistled. "You're talking about a United States senator and a presidential candidate. I'll never get this story into print without confirmation."

"I understand that," I said calmly. "What else do you need?"

Flo chuckled. "A witness would sure be nice."

"We're running out of them," I said. "Todorovich is dead."

"As for Fowler," Flo said, "something tells me he's not going to be on Team Tribune."

"What about the other two names I gave you on the phone last night?"

Flo shook her head. "Nothing. Tuck works for the European division of Toyota. I wasn't able to get through to him today, but he doesn't seem like a good bet. I checked his employment history with Armstrong Bioproducts. He didn't join the company until 1979. That was five years after these deaths. And he was only there for three years."

"How about Ronald McDonald?"

Flo smiled. "Poor guy ought to legally change his name, eh? He lives near D.C. Works for a small munitions manufacturer in Arlington. I talked to him this morning. He claims he never knew a thing about the research and development side of the company, and I believe him. He joined the company in 1978 to head up their pharmaceutical production. His whole existence at Armstrong revolved around cutting costs and increasing production quotas. He was basically a glorified plant manager. Did it for seven years. Strike him from the list. Who's left?"

"Douglas Armstrong," I said flatly.

"Don't forget his mouthpiece."

I gave a rueful laugh. "Sherman Ross? Forget it. He won't talk."

"And he sure as hell won't let Armstrong talk."

I pointed to the list. "Which brings us back to the medical records."

"*If* there are any left."

"That's what I'm going to find out tomorrow morning," I said. "Let's hope Mrs. Jacobs has those files in her basement."

"It's a long shot," Flo said dubiously.

"It's just about our only shot."

We divided up our tasks for the following morning. I would concentrate on Mordecai Jacobs' widow, and Flo would try to tie up the loose ends from today, which included obtaining the remaining thirteen death certificates and talking with someone at Mt. Sinai Hospital about any contractual arrangements it had with Beth Shalom or Labadie Gardens back in the mid-1970s.

It was close to midnight when we finished, and we were both starving. Flo called down to room service and had them deliver a huge quantity of shrimp cocktail and fried calamari, along with a bottle of chilled white wine. I hid in the closet when room service arrived. Just in case.

When the bottle was uncorked and the wine poured, Flo raised her glass in a toast. "To Colonel McCormick and his wonderful expense account. May that anti-Semitic, racist, right-wing prick rot in hell."

"Here, here," I said as we touched glasses.

We pigged out on the room-service goodies. Before long, the bottle of wine was empty and we were giggling like the school girls we once were. It was sheer bliss to be able to forget, even momentarily, David's death and my predicament.

It was nearly two in the morning when we started getting ready for bed. Flo was brushing her teeth over the bathroom sink. I stood next to her, staring at my face in the mirror.

"Time for another change," I said with a sigh.

Flo rinsed her mouth. "Huh?"

"They know my disguise." I touched my hair. "It's time to become a redhead." I turned my head to the side. "I should shorten it, too." I looked over at Flo. "Could you help cut it?"

Flo wiped her mouth with a face towel and grinned. "Sure."

We brought a chair into the bathroom. I sat in front of the mirror with a towel draped over my shoulders while Flo intently snipped away.

I looked at her in the mirror and grinned. "Remember that old guy you shocked at the job interview?" I said.

Flo leaned back with a chuckle. "Oh, yeah. Macklind Moore. What a putz."

"Which firm was it?"

"One of the Wall Street firms. Packard, Johnson and Marlin, I think. Moore was one of the partners they sent up for the on-campus interviews."

"Senior partner, right?"

Flo nodded as she cut another lock of hair. "Oh, yeah. Part of the Harvard old boy network. Believe me, the guy richly deserved getting mind-fucked. It was a pleasure."

Flo's interview incident quickly became a legend among the women at Harvard Law School. Ironically, it was the lawyer, and not Flo, who made the story public. Macklind "Mac" Moore filed a written complaint with the Placement Office about Flo's "unlady-like misconduct." It blew up in his face. The Placement Office backed Flo and issued Moore's firm a warning letter. A junior associate at the firm leaked the letter to *The American Lawyer*, which did a delicious hatchet job.

"What exactly did Moore ask you?" I said. Although I knew the story by heart, I loved to hear her tell it.

Flo snorted with amusement. "Well, we were about fifteen minutes into the interview. He'd already asked the usual ignorant, sexist questions, like whether I planned to get married and have children and how they could count on my dedication to the law. I'd decided by then that I wanted no part of him or his bullshit firm. 'Young lady,' he said, 'do you type?' I gave him a look like I couldn't believe what I'd just heard. 'Pardon?' I said. He gave me a stern frown. 'I said, do you type?' Well, I'd about had it with that old fart anyway, so I figured, what the hell? I stood up and very calmly said, 'Yes, sir, as a matter of fact, I do type. I also fuck. But I don't do either at the office.' And then I walked out on him."

Laughing with delight, I held up my hand. Flo put the scissors in her other hand and slapped me five.

After she finished snipping, I took a shower and shampooed my poor hair three times. I'd dye it red in the morning.

There were two double beds, and we each took one.

"Flo?" I said in the darkness a few minutes after she'd clicked off the reading light.

"Um-hm?"

"Whatever happens tomorrow, you're the best."

"You ain't so bad yourself, Red."

"Goodnight, Flo."

"Goodnight, Rachel."

# 27

CHAPTER

BY the time I arrived at Clara Jacobs' apartment door the next morning at ten, I was a close-cropped redhead wearing heavy mascara and round glasses. I looked even less like myself than I had as a blonde.

Although Clara Jacobs' number was unlisted, I knew it wouldn't take long to locate her. To the people who raise funds for charitable or nonprofit organizations, a wealthy widow is the equivalent of a beautiful woman in a singles bar. Before long, any self-respecting fund-raiser knows her name and phone number. I had acquaintances at the Jewish Federation and the United Way. It took just two phone calls to find the telephone number and address for Clara Jacobs.

The address was the first indication of a problem. To my dismay, Clara Jacobs no longer lived in an eight-bedroom home on the grounds of the Golden Bough Country Club. Instead, she lived on the seventh floor of an apartment building on Union Boulevard just north of Forest Park. As nice as her new address might be, it no longer included a giant basement where her husband could have stored records from his various business ventures, including the Beth Shalom Retirement Home. In fact, now I had to hope that he had never stored any documents at home, since

I knew full well what she, or any reasonable widow, would have done with a basement full of moldy old records from her husband's defunct businesses when it came time to move to a new residence.

The wheelchair was the second indication of a problem. I had arranged the meeting over the telephone with her housekeeper, who seemed quite reluctant to let me see Clara Jacobs and skeptical about my proffered reason, namely, that I was researching a biography on Mordecai Jacobs. She told me I'd be disappointed, but I assured her that I would be thrilled just to meet Mrs. Jacobs. The housekeeper met me at the door. She was a heavyset, stern black woman in a starched white uniform and thick-soled white shoes. She placed me in a dimly lit sitting room and returned five minutes later with Mrs. Jacobs, who was seated in the wheelchair and wrapped in an old gown. With her unkempt white hair, gnarled fingers, and milky brown eyes, Clara Jacobs reminded me of a fairy-tale crone.

The lipstick was the third indication. Clara Jacobs had applied maroon lipstick at what appeared to be a thirty-degree angle from the actual line of her lips. As a result, the thick red smear started below her lips to the left, crossed her mouth at a diagonal, and ended above her lips to the right.

The housekeeper stood directly behind her charge, her meaty arms crossed, an implacable look on her face. It soon became clear that Clara Jacobs no longer had all of her oars in the water. Indeed, after thirty minutes of watching in frustration as each of my questions about the whereabouts of her husband's business records triggered another rambling and largely unintelligible response, it was apparent that all her oars were overboard and the rudder had broken off. Eventually, Mrs. Jacobs' answers became briefer. Her words began to slur. Finally, right in the middle of her description of a delicious dinner she and her husband had once had at Smith & Wollensky in New York City, her head slumped forward.

Dismayed, I watched until she started to snore, and then I

looked up at the housekeeper. "How long have you been with Mrs. Jacobs?" I asked softly.

The housekeeper stared at me for what seemed a long time before she answered. "Thirty-three years."

"Can you help?"

Her stare turned to a frown. "You ain't writing no biography."

I nodded. "I'm not. What I'm doing is trying to save my life. It's a long story. Someone killed my boyfriend and killed another man and killed his secretary and now they're trying to kill me. That's why I need your help. I need to find the Beth Shalom records, and I need to find them fast. It's my only hope."

Her arms still crossed over her chest, she said, "How'm I supposed to believe that?"

I fumbled in my purse. "Look," I said, pulling my driver's license out of my wallet. I handed it to her.

She studied my picture and then me. In the wheelchair beneath her, Mrs. Jacobs was snoring loudly.

"That was me," I said, "just three days ago. Look what I've done to my hair, to my face, to my clothes. I'm in hiding." There was a catch in my voice. I struggled to control my emotions. "People are trying to kill me. Those records could save my life."

I fought back the tears, my lips quivering. I felt as if I was at the bottom of a deep, deep well. "Please help me. Please."

The housekeeper stared down at me as I wiped my nose with a tissue.

"Please," I repeated.

After a moment, she uncrossed her arms. "Okay," she said. "Okay."

Flo and I met two hours later in a room at the Seven Gables Inn in Clayton. My level of paranoia was so high that I had insisted we switch hotels that morning. Tonight would be the Seven Gables. If there was a tomorrow, we'd be somewhere else.

"Who goes first?" she asked as she poured herself a cup of

room-service coffee. She was sitting on the bed near the night-stand.

"You," I said, taking the coffee pot from her. I was at the small table in the corner of the room. "What did you learn at the hospital?"

Flo shook her head. "Not much. I talked to a woman in the administrative office at Mt. Sinai Hospital. She thinks the hospital had contracts to provide physicians to both Beth Shalom *and* La-badie Gardens back then, but she isn't sure. Records that old are kept in off-site storage over in Illinois. She agreed to retrieve them for me, but they won't be delivered to the hospital until the day after tomorrow."

I poured cream in my coffee. "Labadie Gardens, too?"

"That's what she said."

There was a knock at the door. We stared at each other. I carefully placed my coffee spoon onto the table and stood up.

"Who is it?" Flo called as she signaled me to hide in the closet. She took a step toward the door.

A male voice answered, "Special delivery for Miss Shenker."

Flo and I exchanged troubled glances. I shook my head. She frowned and turned toward the door. "What do you have for me?" she called.

The male voice answered, "The man of your dreams."

"What?" Flo said.

"Jesus, Flo," he answered, "open the fucking door. It's Benny. If that's not enough, how about this: I've got something out here specially for you, and it's thick and hot and juicy."

Flo peered through the peephole. "Son of a bitch," she mumbled, a grin spreading on her face. She unlocked the door and pulled it open as I came around to see.

In walked Benny Goldberg. He was carrying a large white bag with the Posh Nosh Deli logo on the side.

"Ladies," he said with a smiling bow as he put the bag down. The delicious smells of Jewish deli foods began to fill up the room.

"Oh, Benny," I said with a mixture of joy and concern. I gave him a hug.

He leaned back and inspected me curiously. "Interesting new look, dahling. Love the hair. What'd you do? Trim it with a Weed Whacker?"

I gestured toward Flo. "My personal hairdresser," I said.

Benny put his hand over his heart. "My apologies, mademoiselle."

"Accepted," she answered with a good-natured smile.

"How's Ozzie?" I asked.

"Ozzie's fine," Benny said. "But I've been a fucking wreck, thanks to you." He turned to Flo. "Did you hear what she had me do?"

Flo nodded.

"How did you find us?" I asked him.

"Hey," he said with feigned irritation, "just because I look like a Chippendale dancer doesn't mean I think like one, too."

"How?" I repeated.

"I was motivated, that's how. For chrissakes, Rachel, you call me on the run from a pay phone, have me send a bag of your sister's clothes in a cab to the same goddam shopping mall where someone tried to kill you, leave your dog with some total douche bag in men's suits, and then drop off the face of the fucking earth. I've been going ape shit ever since."

I gave him a kiss on the cheek. "I'm sorry, Benny, but they're trying to kill me."

Flo was frowning. "How did you find us, Benny?"

"Through your office," he said. "When I couldn't find Rachel, I tried to contact you at the *Trib's* D.C. office. They told me you were in St. Louis."

"They told you that?" Flo asked, outraged.

"Well," Benny said with a sheepish smile, "I fibbed a little about who I was."

"Oh?" Flo said, her eyebrows raised.

"Hey," Benny said with a shrug, "you'd be amazed what people will tell to your gynecologist."

"Go on," I said, secretly pleased that Benny was finally allowing Flo to see his crude side.

"After that," Benny said, "it was easy. I called around to the St. Louis hotels." He turned to Flo. "I found out that you were registered at the Hyatt. I got there early this morning and followed you from there to here. And now, ladies." He paused to lift the Posh Nosh bag by the handles. "Shall we dine?"

Benny had outdone himself. The mouth-watering smells of corned beef and fresh rye bread and tangy brown mustard and dill pickles and vinegary coleslaw simultaneously lifted my spirits and reminded me of how ravenous I was. As promised, he did indeed have something thick and hot and juicy for Flo—specifically, a hot pastrami sandwich on rye. He had a smoked turkey with lettuce on pumpernickel for me. For himself, a typically gluttonous extravaganza: a mammoth corned beef, chopped liver, and sliced Bermuda onion sandwich on rye, slathered with Thousand Island dressing. Benny had thought of everything, including cans of Dr. Brown's cream soda to wash down the lunch, three large slices of apple strudel for dessert, and three large cups of fresh hot coffee from Starbucks.

I filled Benny in as we ate. I was anxious to find out about the rest of Flo's morning. "What about the Bureau of Vital Statistics?" I asked her as I spooned some more coleslaw onto my plate. "Were the death certificates ready?"

"All thirteen."

"And?"

Flo raised her eyebrows as she wiped her mouth with a napkin. "Very interesting."

"Tell me."

"The immediate cause of death for all thirteen was respiratory failure. The underlying causes ran the gamut, but all within the pattern." She looked over at her notes. "Three Guillain-Barré syndromes, two porphyrias, one diphtheritic polyneuropathy, two aspiration pneumonias, and the rest acute peripheral neuropathy."

"I love when you talk dirty," Benny said.

"Shush," I said to him. Turning back to Flo, I asked, "Any more Peter Todoroviches?"

She nodded. "He was listed as attending physician on three more Labadie Gardens residents."

I whistled. "Oh, brother."

"But," Flo said with a triumphant grin, "I save the best for last."

I gave her a puzzled look. "What?"

She glanced down at her notes. "Guess what Sarah Braunstein, Thelma Kaplansky, and Kay Silverman had in common?"

"I give up," I said.

"The same person was listed as their attending physician." Flo was grinning. "And it wasn't Peter Todorovich."

I gave her a baffled frown. "Then who? Oh, no. Douglas Armstrong?"

She nodded.

"Douglas Armstrong?" Benny repeated.

"I can't believe it," I said.

Flo handed me the stack of death certificates. "See for yourself."

Benny leaned over to look with me. Sure enough, Douglas Armstrong was listed as the attending physician for all three women.

I looked up at Flo and shook my head in wonder. "Him, too?"

"So it appears," she said.

"Him what?" Benny asked.

"We're not sure," I said. "All we know is that Armstrong and Todorovich were at Armstrong Bioproducts at the time, were also on staff at Mt. Sinai Hospital, and were listed as the treating physician for some of the women on the list who died."

I leafed back through the other certificates, noting the two other names that appeared on the Beth Shalom death certificates as attending physicians. "Who are these other two? Michael Bohm and Harold Rawling. Were they at Armstrong Bioproducts, too?"

"No," Flo said. "I called around, actually talked to Bohm. Rawling was out of town today. Bohm told me he was on staff at Mt. Sinai back then, and so was the other guy. They had regular rounds at the home, as did Armstrong. Each had their own set of patients, but whoever was there on the day a nursing home resident died would be the one listed on the death certificate as the attending physician."

"Did Dr. Bohm remember anything about the patients or the deaths?" Benny asked.

Flo shook her head. "Not much."

"Do you think he was hiding something?" I asked.

Flo frowned as she weighed the question. "Hard to tell with a doctor. A lot of them can be kind of squirrelly." She looked at Benny. "You ever handled any medical malpractice cases?"

He shook his head.

"I worked on a bunch my first years," she said. "Learned a lot of strange terms and got to spend time with a lot of strange doctors. It's hard to tell whether they're bullshitting you, but I think this Bohm was telling me the truth. I don't think he knows diddly about those deaths."

"What about the attending physicians on these?" I asked, indicating the Labadie Gardens stack.

Flo shook her head. "Pretty much the same story. I reached one of them: Randall Weaver. He was an emergency room physician back then. Split his time between Mt. Sinai and St. Mary's. Spent one morning a week at Labadie Gardens. No connection with Armstrong Bioproducts. Didn't know Peter Todorovich or Douglas Armstrong."

I finished my turkey sandwich and washed it down with a big sip of Dr. Brown's.

"So?" Flo said to me, crunching on a pickle. "Your turn for show and tell."

I winked at her and went over to my briefcase. "Here," I said, unfolding a large document and handing it to her. Benny walked around to look at it over her shoulder.

She scrutinized it for a moment and looked up at me. "What kind of map is this?"

"A treasure map, I hope."

She frowned at it for a while.

Benny asked, "Is this supposed to be St. Louis?"

"Actually," I explained, "it's supposed to be what's *under* St. Louis. The map dates back almost fifty years, but I don't think caves move around much underground."

"Caves?" Flo said.

Benny asked, "Where did you get this map?"

"From the Missouri Historical Society. That's where I've been for the last hour and a half."

"What happened to Clara Jacobs?" Flo asked.

I shook my head sadly. "The poor woman is really out of it."

"Senile?"

I nodded. "Pretty much so. I tried to ask her questions, but all I got for answers was gobbledygook. She ended up falling asleep on me. That's when I talked to her housekeeper. She was hostile at first, but softened up a little after I practically got down on my knees and begged. Turns out she was with the Jacobses back when they lived in their mansion. She doesn't think he kept any business records there, but she's almost certain he didn't throw them away."

"Why?" Benny asked.

I turned to him. "She claims he was a document packrat. Didn't throw any of his personal records away. She said that when he died she helped clean out the office in his home. They found stacks of canceled personal checks dating back thirty years. He had saved all of his utility bills. There were telephone bills from the fifties."

"So where did he keep his business records?" Flo asked.

"She's not certain, but she has a pretty good hunch. He owned a bunch of different companies. He used to conduct a lot of his business over the phone in his den. She overheard him enough to believe that he stored at least some of his business records in his cave."

"His what?" Benny said.

I smiled. "His cave."

"Hold on," Flo said. "Mordecai Jacobs had his own cave?"

I nodded. "It was known as the Gutmann Caverns, and at one time it was the most famous cave in St. Louis."

"The most famous?" Flo looked at Benny. "Is there more than one cave in this town?"

"How the fuck would I know?" he said. "I'm from New Jersey."

"There are other caves," I said. "Dozens and dozens of caves." I gestured toward the map she was holding. "According to *The Spelunker's Guide to the Caves of Missouri*, which I skimmed while I was over at the Historical Society, there are more caves in St. Louis than in any other city in the world."

"No shit," Benny said, impressed.

Flo studied the map. "There are a lot of them," she conceded.

"Where's his cave?" Benny asked.

I leaned over and pointed to the spot I had highlighted in yellow. "Right there."

They stared at the location.

Flo looked up at me. "It's still there?"

I shrugged. "As far as I know."

"How do we get in it?" Benny asked.

I checked my watch. It was only two o'clock. I looked at them and smiled. "Let's go find out."

We finished our dessert and headed out.

In our excitement none of us stopped to consider the implications of the fact that Benny had been able to find us. Nor did we bother to consider whether our actions that morning could have registered on the radar screens of my pursuers. Maybe it was because there were three of us. Three seemed so much safer than one. Whatever the reason, we certainly could have qualified as the rushing fools of the old adage.

# 28

CHAPTER

ST. Louis sits atop a thick bedrock of limestone. For hundreds of millions of years, surface water percolated through fissures in that bedrock and created a vast latticework of streams within the limestone, like arteries within a body. During the wetter millennia, the added water pressure drilled larger and ever larger tunnels through the rock. Gradually, those trickling streams became mighty underground rivers.

Then came the drier millennia. The water table dropped, the surface waters receded to the current channel of the Mississippi River, and the landscape became familiar. By the time New Orleans merchant Pierre Laclede and his fourteen-year-old stepson, Auguste Chouteau, clambered up the west bank of the Mississippi in 1764 to admire the fertile landscape spread before them, the underground rivers had long since run dry. On Valentine's Day, 1764, Pierre Laclede announced that he would erect a settlement on this good land—little realizing that this good land rested, like a massive green carpet, over an extraordinary network of cool limestone caves.

The caves of St. Louis were a provincial curiosity until Gottfried Duden arrived in St. Louis in 1822. Duden was, quite literally, an industrial scout, sent to America by various brewing and manufacturing concerns in the Rhineland who were looking for business opportunities in the New World. Back in the days before electric refrigeration, every brewer the world over dreamed of access to vast natural cooling cellars where the climate remained a dry, constant fifty-two degrees year-round—the perfect temperature for storing and fermenting beer. Accordingly, when Duden discovered what was spread out beneath the streets of that booming town along the Mississippi River, he immediately understood the opportunities it held for his German clients. I have found your Garden of Eden in the New World, he eagerly reported.

Within twenty years, St. Louis had become the largest beer-brewing center in North America. By 1860, there were more than forty breweries in St. Louis, most owned by German immigrants, each operating directly over a limestone cave. There was the Gast Brewery Cave and the Winkelmeyer Brewery Cave and the Clausman Brewery Cave and the Minnehaha Brewery Cave and the Cherokee Brewery Cave.

And then there were the celebrity caves.

There was the Bavarian Brewery Cave, which sat directly below Joseph Schneider's Bavarian Brewery on Pestalozzi Street. When the Bavarian Brewery went bankrupt in 1859, one of its major creditors, Eberhard Anheuser, bought the brewery and changed the company name to his name. A few years later, another German immigrant married Eberhard's beautiful daughter, Lilly. When old man Anheuser died, his son-in-law, Adolphus Busch, assumed control of the brewery and made one final addition to the company name.

And there was English Cave, nestled beneath Benton Park in south St. Louis. Used as a malt liquor brewery from 1826 to 1847, it was better known for the legend of the beautiful Indian maiden and her lover, who fled from the lecherous tribal chief and hid out in English Cave. The jealous chief posted a guard at the entrance to the cave to make sure she didn't escape. She didn't. The lovers died of starvation, and their skeletons were found wrapped in each other's arms. Or so went the legend.

And there was Uhrig's Cave, an underground saloon and nightclub near the corner of Washington and Jefferson, connected to Joseph and Ignatz Uhrig's brewery by a one-half-mile tunnel in which the brothers had installed a narrow-gauge railroad for movement of beer between the two locations. The brothers held concerts and plays in their converted cave and sold rides on the underground railroad. By the turn of the century, Uhrig's Cave was a prominent national entertainment spot and the site of the North American premieres of *The Mikado* and *Cavalleria Rusticana*.

But of all the caves of St. Louis, none approaches the fabulous story of Gutmann Caverns. In 1846, a German immigrant named Gregor Gutmann purchased a cave near Gravois south of Chippewa. It was an ideal brewery cave. Fifty feet below ground with a constant temperature of fifty-two degrees, the caverns included an enormous main chamber with tunnels at either end, one of which connected to another large chamber that could serve as additional storage space for the enormous casks in which the Gutmann Special Lager would age.

Aboveground, Gutmann built his brewery at one end of the cave. As business expanded and his fortunes grew, he erected a huge family mansion above another portion of the cave. By the turn of the century, Gregor Gutmann's wealthy descendants had bricked and smoothed more than two hundred yards of the family portion of the cave and had installed a variety of opulent underground additions, including, among other things, a full ballroom, a swimming pool, a gymnasium, a miniature railroad, and a theater.

Alas, poor management and constant shareholder battles among the grandchildren mortally weakened the company during the early years of the twentieth century, and Prohibition sounded the death knell. The Gutmann Brewery ended in a liquidating receivership. The last St. Louis remnants of the Gutmann family were evicted from the mansion in 1932, and the structure was condemned two years later. All that remains of the three-story

Gutmann Mansion are a series of stunning black-and-white photographs that hang in the main gallery of the Missouri Historical Society. The abandoned brewery building lingered on as a vacant eyesore until the city fathers, spurred into action by a newspaper campaign against urban blight, razed the structure in 1947 and converted part of the property, including the former mansion grounds, into a small city park named after Gregor Gutmann.

The old entrance to the brewery portion of the cave, which was just east of Gutmann Park, was used primarily as a neighborhood garbage dump until 1958. That's when a colorful local entrepreneur and history buff by the name of Mordecai Jacobs entered the picture. He purchased a parcel of property east of the park that included what the neighbors then called the Gutmann Dump.

Jacobs brought in a crew of men to clean out the rubbish and excavate the clay and gook that clogged the first fifty feet into the cave. To his delight, he discovered that the old storage channel was actually the front end of yet another large cave that meandered north and featured a dazzling variety of rooms of many sizes, each festooned with stalactites, stalagmites, and other formations. Even more incredible, two of the workmen exploring some of the smaller branches of the cave stumbled into a room that contained what appeared to be the bones of a large mammal. Jacobs was able to convince the Field Museum of Natural History in Chicago to send down a paleontological crew, which identified the find as a large saber-toothed cat. The crew spent six heavily publicized months in the cave and exhumed more than two thousand bones of prehistoric animals, including three full skeletons of an immense, long-extinct species of saber-toothed cat. As part of his deal with the Field Museum, Jacobs selected one of the skeletons and the museum reconstructed it in a ferocious attack position. Using the lighting director of the St. Louis Muny Opera, Jacobs dramatically spotlighted the skeleton in the original excavation chamber, which he renamed Saber Tooth Cemetery.

Jacobs had the soul of a carnival barker. He installed electric lights and advertised heavily, not only on local radio and television, but on billboards on every major highway within a 300-mile radius of St. Louis: COME SEE GUTMANN'S CAVERNS—THE EIGHTH WONDER OF THE WORLD! He lured them in from all over the country. During its brief but brilliant heyday, Gutmann Caverns was in the top ten of St. Louis tourist attractions, right up there with the zoo and the riverfront. A visit to Gutmann Caverns included guided tours of all the natural formations (with Satan's Waterfall as the highlight), the family portion of the cave, the beer storage process used by brewery, and, of course, the Saber Tooth Cemetery.

Unfortunately, the reborn Gutmann Caverns lasted less than a decade. In 1965, the Highway Department purchased the above-ground portion as part of the parcel needed to construct a section of I-55. Gutmann Caverns closed on December 1, 1965, and highway construction began the following spring.

One normally would have assumed that the entrance had long since been sealed off, and perhaps it was. But given the recollections of Clara Jacobs' housekeeper and the fact that I had absolutely no other leads on any relevant Beth Shalom or Labadie Gardens medical records, it was definitely worth a trip down to south St. Louis to search for a way into the cave.

We dressed optimistically, i.e., for cave exploration. I wore my running shoes and my jogging sweats—the closest I could come to appropriate attire given the grabbag of outfits Benny had selected for me. Flo put on jeans, a Kansas City Monarchs sweatshirt, and hiking boots. Benny had arrived wearing a Chicago Bulls T-shirt, baggy khakis, and high-top Converse All-Stars. Although the T-shirt wasn't warm enough for cave temperatures, he had a windbreaker in the trunk of his car.

On the drive toward south St. Louis, we stopped at a hardware store for a high-powered flashlight, plenty of fresh batteries, and the sorts of odds and ends that three rookie spelunkers thought might come in handy in a cave, including metal cutters, twenty-five feet of rope, several rolls of film for Flo's 35-millimeter camera, and a backpack in which to carry it all.

Flo drove while Benny and I tried to navigate from the backseat. I had a St. Louis street map open on my lap and Benny had the old cave map on his. We got onto Gravois and stayed with it past the Cherokee intersection. We went several more blocks, turned left at the light and weaved our way through several more intersections as the neighborhood changed from purely residential to a shabbier mix of bungalows, two-flats, and an occasional warehouse or storefront.

Flo slowed the car. "Here we are," she said.

There was a city park up ahead on the right. I looked down at the map for a moment and then back up. "You're right. Gutmann Park."

We peered at it through the windshield.

"Drive around it once," Benny said.

Gutmann Park was, by any standard, entirely unexceptional. It was a rectangle three blocks long and two blocks wide. There were two ball fields, each with a rusting backstop, and a half-court basketball blacktop with several bent and netless hoops. The picnic area consisted of three picnic tables, two metal grills, and a small shelter with restrooms in back. There was a playground with a set of clunky, old-fashioned equipment: swings, slides, jungle gym, merry-go-round. Unfortunately, the one thing we didn't see was a huge flashing red arrow with the message, "This Way to Cave Entrance."

The three of us got out of the car and walked the length and width of the park while Benny and I tried to coordinate the surface with the cave map. Although it was hard to be certain, since the map predated the park by at least a decade, it appeared that the cave ran directly beneath the middle of the park. We hadn't expected to stumble across an actual entrance, of course. Nevertheless, given that the Gutmann Mansion had stood roughly between the two ball fields, I had hoped to find some evidence, although faint, of what had once been. We moved carefully through the entire outfield, but found no sign of the mansion or the cave below. Just the patchy grass and weeds of a poorly maintained field. We even checked out both restrooms, but found nothing to suggest any subterranean access.

"Where was the other cave entrance?" Flo asked. "The one the brewery used?"

I checked the map, got my bearings, and pointed east. "A few blocks over."

Across the street from the park was a row of rundown bungalows. Visible beyond the bungalows were several warehouses and, rising above the warehouses to the right, the long, looping exit ramp off the highway.

We got back in the car. This time I sat in the passenger seat up front. As we drove toward the warehouses, I tried to trace our path on the cave map.

"Stop here," I said.

We were midway down a narrow street. There was a warehouse to our left and another to our right. Visible in the distance and slightly to the right was the descending curve of the exit ramp. The highway itself was beyond and above the tops of the warehouses. You could hear the sounds of cars and trucks rumbling along.

I got out of the car with both maps in my hands. I handed the cave map to Benny. Flo came around to study them with us.

"Nu?" Benny said, studying the street map.

I compared locations on Benny's map and mine. "Come on, guys." I walked toward the end of the block.

"Where are we?" Flo asked.

"Here," I said, pausing to point to the spot on the street map Benny was holding. "The tourist entrance was off Grolier Avenue." We were almost at the end of the block. I checked the cave map again, then the street map. "That means the entrance would have been—let's see—about a block further east."

We both looked up slowly.

"Shit," Benny groaned.

Exactly one block further east was the descending curve of the exit ramp. The ground beneath the entire length of the exit ramp was paved with broad concrete slabs. There wasn't even a hint of what had once been there. It was all covered by cold gray cement.

"Rats," I said in frustration. "It's gone."

"Not gone," Flo said. "Just covered."

"Great." I gave her a look. "Unless you have access to a twenty-man jackhammer crew, it's as good as gone."

We stared in silence.

"Come on," I finally said with a weary sigh. "Back to the drawing board."

The three of us walked slowly toward the car.

Benny paused as he opened the car door and looked around. "This area is the pits," he said. "Talk about urban decay."

I looked up at the warehouse across the street. It clearly was long abandoned: half of the windows were broken, and the rest were filthy. It looked like a rundown building out of a horror film. The sign above the door was battered and grimy. I squinted, trying to read it.

"What do you know," I said with surprise. I could barely make out the legend:

M. JACOBS & COMPANY, INC.

Flo turned to look at the sign. "How about that? Old Mordecai must have owned it."

We got in the car to leave, but as Flo started the engine I grabbed her arm. "Wait."

She gave me a curious look and turned off the engine.

I pointed to the exit ramp in the distance. "If that's over the cave, then so is this warehouse."

"So?" Benny said.

I looked at him impatiently. "Think about it, Benny. If Mordecai Jacobs was storing business records in the cave even after the Highway Department sealed off the tourist entrance to Gutmann Caverns, then he had to have another access to the cave. Maybe that access was through his warehouse."

Flo looked at the warehouse and then back at me. "Let me see that cave map."

I handed it to her.

Benny leaned over to look, too. After a moment, he grumbled, "How do you read this goddam thing?"

"Here." I pointed to the area that appeared to be located below the exit ramp. "You see, the cave splits down there. One branch runs due north, the other runs northwest. Look at the position of the warehouse. It's due north."

They frowned at the map, and then Flo turned to stare up at the warehouse.

"You're not serious, are you?" Benny asked incredulously.

"It's worth a shot," I said.

Flo turned back and winked. "It sure is."

"Hold it," Benny said. "Are you saying you actually intend to go in there?"

I looked at Flo. She smiled at me and nodded. I turned to Benny. "Come on, stud. Let's do it."

"Jesus H. Christ, Rachel," he growled at me under his breath as we got out of the car, "and you actually have the nerve to wonder why I prefer the company of bimbos."

# 29

CHAPTER

WE didn't need the metal cutters to get into the warehouse. The lock on the front door was rusted and broken. Benny pushed against the door and it creaked open. We stepped inside after him and glanced around.

"Creepy," Flo said.

I nodded. Chunks of plaster hung from the ceilings. There were large cobwebs in the corners and along the edges where the walls met the ceiling. The front part of the building, which had partition walls that divided up the space, must have once been the office area. It was hard to be sure, though, since there was no furniture or equipment anywhere. There were large, jagged holes through several of the partition walls, as if someone had taken a sledgehammer to the place. The floors were filthy and sprinkled with rat droppings.

I walked past what I assumed was the front offices and into the main portion of the warehouse. It was a large open area, vaguely divided at regular intervals by rusted support beams. Here, too, the floors were filthy. As I moved around, I saw signs of occasional human habitation: several empty beer and wine bottles, many of them broken; ashes from cooking fires that had been built right on the floor; two empty cans of baked beans; the front page of the sports section from the July 9, 1982, edition of the *Globe-Democrat* ("Redbirds Dwarf Giants in 10th; Win 4–2").

"Over here," Flo called. She and Benny were standing by a partially open door near the back of the main area.

I walked over to join them. "What?"

"These stairs go down," Flo said. "Let me have the flashlight."

I turned so that she could remove the flashlight from the backpack. She clicked on the beam and started down the narrow stairs into the darkness.

"Hold it, Rambo," Benny said to Flo. He turned to me. "Don't you think we ought to call the cops?"

"Benny," I said with an exasperated shake of my head, "what are we supposed to tell them? That we'd like them to poke around in an abandoned warehouse with us?" I took his arm. "Come on, boychik."

"Great," he said with a sigh of resignation. "I thought I was just the caterer for this event."

The air grew cooler as we descended. There was a vague odor of rotting plaster and moldy wood. When we reached the bottom, Flo moved the flashlight beam around. This space looked much like the one above, although the ceilings were lower.

"Shhh," I said, touching her arm.

"What?" she whispered.

"I heard something."

"Where?" she asked.

"Down here. A rustling noise."

We stood motionless, and then the rustling started again. Flo quickly swung the beam around toward the noise.

"Holy shit," Benny said as the flashlight momentarily illuminated a fat gray rat, which scurried into the darkness.

"Gross." I shuddered.

"We should have brought a shotgun," Flo said.

"Shotgun?" Benny said. "We should have brought the fucking marines."

"Let's work fast," I said. "Look for a subbasement."

We moved cautiously around the area, blind except for the beam of light from the flashlight. There were three small rooms along the far wall. The first one was a men's room—two urinals, one stall, one sink. The second room was smaller and appeared to be some sort of utilities control area: there were fuse boxes on the wall along with rusted water, gas, and electric company meters.

I pushed open the door to the third room. It was even smaller than the other two.

"Ah," Flo said as the flashlight beam illuminated the trapdoor set in the floor.

The trapdoor was surrounded by low guardrails on three sides. A lightweight chain hung across the open fourth side of the guardrail. I unhooked the chain and leaned over the trapdoor. It was about three feet square, with a door handle on the near side. As Flo shined the light, I tried to pull the handle down to unlock the door. The handle didn't budge.

"Yank it hard," Flo said.

I tried, but it still didn't budge.

"Okay," Benny said. "Out of my way, Earth girl."

He leaned over the trapdoor, put both hands on the handle and, with a grunt, yanked hard. The handle jerked open and the door swung down. Startled, Benny lost his balance and almost followed the door through the opening.

"Whoa!" he shouted in panic.

I grabbed his arm and Flo clutched his belt from behind.

"That was close," I said when we got him steadied.

He looked at us wide-eyed for a moment and then forced a smile. "Good work, girls. Just thought I'd test your reflexes. Now, if you'll excuse me, I think I'll go back to the car for a change of underwear."

We turned to watch the heavy trapdoor swing back and forth, squeaking on its hinges. Flo moved closer to the opening and shined the flashlight down. She looked back at me and winked.

"I think we found it."

I peered through the opening. There was about a twelve-foot drop into what appeared to be an underground tunnel. Holding onto one of the guardrails, Flo leaned over the opening and pointed the flashlight down. On the tunnel floor near the wall was a metal ladder lying on its side. The ladder looked long enough to reach through the trapdoor opening into the warehouse basement, but there was no way to tell if after all these years it was still strong enough to function as a ladder.

Flo looked at Benny and then me. "Who wants to go first?" she asked.

I looked at them and shrugged. "I'll go," I said.

I tied one end of the rope snugly to the guardrail. Benny pulled on it several times to make sure that it would hold and that the guardrail was strong enough. We tossed the other end of the rope through the trapdoor opening.

"Hey," Flo said, "just pretend we're the Hardy Boys."

I sat on the edge of the opening with my feet dangling through. I grabbed hold of the rope with both hands and frowned. "I never liked the Hardy Boys." I looked over at Benny. "Did you?"

"Fuck the Hardy Boys," he said. "You people are nuts."

Flo clicked off the flashlight and stuffed it into my backpack. I lowered myself into the darkness, my body swaying as I descended. When I touched down, I shouted up, "Okay, next."

It was creepy standing down there alone in complete blackness. As Flo descended on the rope I removed the flashlight from the backpack and turned it on.

"Whew," she said when she reached the bottom. "Haven't done that since grade-school gym."

I pointed the beam up through the trapdoor opening. Doing my *Price Is Right* announcer's voice, I said, "Benny Goldberg, come on down."

"Yeah, yeah, yeah," he grumbled as he lowered himself slowly.

Once he reached the bottom, I moved the flashlight around.

We were at the end of what looked like a man-made tunnel. It was about fifteen feet wide and thirty feet long. Directly behind us was a solid wall of rock. In front of us, off in the distance, the tunnel appeared to intersect with another tunnel. Except for the ladder against the side wall, our tunnel was empty.

"No files," I said as I moved the flashlight around.

Flo was kneeling by the ladder. "If there are any," she said, "they'll be somewhere else in the cave. Down there somewhere." She pointed toward the far end of the tunnel. "There's too much moisture here. Look at the floor."

I moved the beam along the floor of the tunnel. She was right. It was slick with water, and there were several puddles.

"This ladder looks okay," Benny said.

We positioned it under the trapdoor opening. It was long enough to reach up into the basement. The top end rested against the side of the trapdoor opening with at least three feet to spare.

"Let's test it," I said, handing Benny the flashlight.

Moving cautiously at first, I climbed up the ladder through the trapdoor and back down. "It's perfect," I said.

Benny turned the flashlight beam toward the front end of the tunnel. "I say we try to find those documents and get the fuck out of this hellhole."

We walked slowly down the tunnel. It connected with another tunnel, which ran perpendicular to ours, like an intersection of two roads. As we stepped into the main tunnel, Benny flashed the light toward the ceiling.

"This is the real thing," Flo said.

The ceiling was fifteen feet high and festooned with hundreds of little, pointed stalactites. Benny pointed the flashlight down the cave to the right and then to the left.

"Which way?" he asked.

I removed the cave map from my backpack and tried to pinpoint our location. Unfortunately, the short tunnel from the warehouse to the cave wasn't shown on the map, and I couldn't align the warehouse layout to the caves on the map.

"I don't know," I said. "We may have to try both ways."

"Let's go this way first," Flo said, pointing to the right.

"Okay," I said, "but I want to go back for a moment."

"Why?" Benny asked.

"Because I"m nervous," I said. "I don't want leave that ladder standing up like that. What if someone came along and removed it?"

"We'd still have the rope," Flo said, and then thought better of it. "You're right. The rope, too. Let's go back."

We went back down the tunnel, untied the rope, lowered the ladder, and placed them both against the side wall of the tunnel. Then we returned to the cave intersection and turned right. The cave was much narrower than the warehouse tunnel—roughly six feet wide. As we walked, Flo moved the flashlight beam from the floor to the sides to the ceiling and back to the floor.

"Hey, look," she said.

The beam illuminated an empty light fixture overhead. We could see a dark electric wire that had been threaded through the stalactites to the light fixture. The wire continued along the ceiling past the light fixture. We came to another empty fixture twenty feet further down the path. As we walked, I noticed that the floor and the walls were moist.

"What's that up ahead?" Benny asked.

Thirty feet ahead our narrow corridor appeared to open up. We quickened our pace until we reached the opening.

"Holy shit," Benny said as Flo moved the flashlight around.

Although the beam only illuminated a narrow area at a time, it was soon apparent that we were in an immense underground room. It was at least two hundred feet long, fifty feet wide, and thirty feet high. There were large stalactites overhead, but the floors were smooth and level. Even more unusual, the walls were bricked from the floor up to at least fifteen feet.

"What's that?" I said as the flashlight beam swept past a huge object on one side of the room.

We walked over to see. It was an enormous wooden cask. In front was a sign that read:

> THIS IS A GENUINE GUTMANN BREWERY FERMENTA-
> TION CASK DATING FROM 1873. THE GUTMANN
> BREWERY STORAGE ROOM, WITH ITS CONSTANT 52-
> DEGREE TEMPERATURE, PROVIDED NATURAL COOL-
> ING CELLARS WHERE THE SPECIAL LAGER COULD BE
> STORED WHILE FERMENTING.

"We're on the tour," Flo said as she swept the flashlight beam around the room.

"This ought to be a dry enough area to store documents," I said.

But there were none. At the opposite end of the room, however, we did find an opening the size of a double door. On the wall beside the opening was another sign:

> THIS WAY TO THE GUTMANN FAMILY CAVERN

How could we resist? We walked through the opening and down what could have been an ordinary, low-ceilinged corridor, except that instead of drywall and plaster there was chilly limestone. The corridor ran about fifty feet and opened into a much larger area. The sign at the entrance read:

> WELCOME TO THE GUTMANN FAMILY CAVERN
> PLAYGROUND OF THE SUPER RICH OF ST. LOUIS

Like three gawking tourists, we moved through the perfectly preserved playground. We passed the theater that had been constructed, according to the sign, for young Augustus Gutmann, who fancied himself a great actor. It was a real theater, with elevated stage, floodlights, wire-and-plaster scenery, and seating for fifty. We passed an Olympic-sized swimming pool. The pool was drained, and there was a skeleton of a small mammal at the bottom of the deep end. In the middle of the pool was a cast cement grotto tucked beneath a fake Greek temple where, according to yet another sign, "the decadent Gutmann grandchildren scandalized genteel St. Louis society by holding bacchanalian orgies."

"Look at that," Benny said, gesturing toward the sign and shaking his head sadly. "Maybe Rush Limbaugh is right. The old-fashioned core values are dead. It's hard enough to find a decent orgy these days, much less a bacchanalian one."

We passed the gymnasium and the dance studio and eventually came to the "gracious marble staircase, carpeted with genuine Persian rugs, that connected the Gutmann Family Cavern to the bounteous extravagance of the Gutmann Mansion." The carpets were gone, and the stairway now connected the Gutmann Family Cavern to a giant slab of concrete that formed the ceiling at the top of the stairs. If one could bore through the concrete slab and the several feet of dirt above it, you would emerge somewhere in the outfield of the Gutmann Park ball fields.

Although we had found no documents in the Gutmann Family Cavern or the Gutmann Brewery Storage Room, by marking the two spots on my cave map I was finally properly oriented. We retraced our steps back through the Storage Room, pausing several times for me to track our course on the map. We got all the way back to the intersection with the tunnel to the warehouse— the spot where we had chosen to turn right. This time we moved in the opposite direction. After about twenty feet, we came to a fork in the path as a channel branched off the main cave tunnel to the right.

"Well?" Flo said as we paused.

I checked the map and found where the smaller tunnel curved away from the main one. "If we stay this way," I said, pointing down the main path, "we'll come to what was the tourist entrance when Jacobs had it. That's the part that's under the highway ramp. I'm not sure about the other direction."

Flo pointed the flashlight down the smaller channel. There wasn't much to see, because it curved sharply to the right. She aimed the beam down the main tunnel. There were guardrails on either side.

"Let's try the main path first," Flo said, and off we went.

Thirty feet down the path there was an opening to the left, in front of which was a sign that stated: "The Throne Room of the Gods." The room was dominated by a humongous stalagmite that rose twenty feet off the cave floor in roughly the shape of a throne. It was surrounded by other smaller, similarly shaped stalagmites. It didn't take much imagination to envision Zeus and his court seated on the limestone formations.

We kept on the path, and soon came to what the sign announced was the Spaghetti Chamber—an outlandish room that was literally filled with thousands of long, thin, strawlike stalactites that hung from the ceiling and reached almost to the floor. We stayed on the path, which took us past other striking formations, each bearing the name Mordecai Jacobs had given it. There was the Curtain of Creation, Satan's Waterfall, the Bottomless Pit, the Executioner's Playground, and the Aztec Sacrifice Room.

Although several of the stalactites or stalagmites in each room had broken off (or been broken off), the rooms were otherwise in great shape. Out of curiosity, Benny tried to pick up one of the broken stalactites. It was about the size of a baseball bat but, from the strain on his face, obviously much heavier.

"Feels like a sledgehammer," he grunted as he let it drop.

We also saw living animals—weird, colorless versions of animals on the surface. In the pond in front of Satan's Waterfall were dozens of small, pale fish that appeared to have no eyes. Elsewhere along the route we came across pallid, eyeless salamanders, ghostly millipedes with elongated antennae, and spindly white spiders.

Another fifty feet down the tunnel brought us to the Saber Tooth Cemetery, with the reassembled skeleton arranged in a ferocious attack stance. The placard in front of the skeleton boasted of the importance and sheer volume of mammal bones from the Pleistocene era that had been discovered in that portion of the cave.

"You know what's almost as remarkable as these formations?" Flo said as we returned to the main path and kept walking.

"What?"

"Look at these signs and markers. This cave has been closed for more than thirty years, but these things are in pristine condition."

"That's not surprising," Benny said. "There's no wind, no rain, no sun. The climate stays exactly the same all year round. Remember those Stone Age cave paintings in France and Spain? They were still in perfect condition after twelve thousand years. Compared to that, thirty years is barely a heartbeat."

I pinched Benny in the side. "Thank you, Mr. Wizard."

"Hey," he protested, "it's true. That's why a cave is a good place to store documents."

"Apparently not in this branch," Flo said as we stopped. She shined the flashlight in front of us. "God."

We were staring at what had once been the broad stairway entrance down into the cave. The highway construction crews had dumped construction debris, old bricks, excess cement and concrete, and other junk into the cave mouth as landfill before they sealed it off on top with several slabs of cement. The rubble reached to the ceiling and completely filled the passageway. With all the flotsam sticking out at odd angles, it looked almost like a work of modern art.

"Well," Flo said as we turned to retrace our steps, "that's strike two."

"Three's a charm," I said. "Come on, guys. I bet the documents are down that other branch."

"*If* there are documents," Benny grumbled.

Once again, we retraced our steps. "That beam is getting weak," I said when we got back to the branch. "Let's change batteries."

We did it as carefully as we could, getting the new batteries ready in my hand before Flo turned off the flashlight and quickly unscrewed the bottom. Nevertheless, the resulting thirty seconds of fumbling in total darkness as we inserted the new batteries was so eerie that even after the flashlight beam returned, it took a few moments before my heartbeat returned to normal.

"I definitely did not enjoy that," I said, my voice still shaky.

"Me, neither," Flo said. "How do these animals live down here?"

"Be careful with that flashlight," I said. "I wish we'd brought a backup."

"Let's just find the fucking documents," Benny said, "and get the hell out of here."

We started down the narrow passageway that curved sharply to the right. Once we got around the bend the cave began to widen a bit and curved to the left. We followed the curve. As we came around the corner, the walls opened onto a large chamber. Flo swept the flashlight beam back and forth.

At first I thought we were looking at a dramatic stalagmite formation that consisted of a several dozen large, brown, flat-topped columns, each about six feet tall, lining the sides of the chamber. But then Flo held the beam steady on one of the columns.

"All right!" Benny hollered.

They were boxes. Columns of boxes, neatly stacked six high, each stack sitting on its own wooden pallet. There were at least thirty stacks, arranged in groups of two or three columns each along the walls.

We ran toward the first stack of boxes. Flo shined the light on the top box. There was a neatly typed label taped to the side of the box:

*JACOBS CADILLAC—SALES RECORDS: 1/1/64–12/31/64*

The label on the box below it read:

*JACOBS CADILLAC—SALES RECORDS: 1/1/63–12/31/63*

Below that were boxes for 1962, 1961, 1960, and 1959. There were two more stacks of boxes grouped together with the first one. According to the labels, they contained more financial records from Jacobs Cadillac.

The next two stacks of boxes contained the records of his dry cleaning business in Belleville, Illinois. Then there were three stacks of boxes of records from his tarpaulin manufacturing company down in Crystal City. We kept moving from stack to stack, checking the labels on each box. The first group of three stacks of boxes on the back wall contained documents on his warehouse operations.

And then we came to two stacks of five boxes each. Flo shined the light on the top box of the first stack. The label read:

*BETH SHALOM—1972 TO 1984—DECEASED*
*MEDICAL FILES: ABRAMOWITZ TO BRAUNSTEIN*

"At last," I said, exultant.

"What's the significance of the dates?" Benny asked.

"Jacobs bought it in 1972," I explained, "and he merged it into the Jewish Center for the Aged in 1984. The medical files of the living residents would have been transfered to the Jewish Center for the Aged in 1984. The rest would have stayed."

The label on the box below it read:

*BETH SHALOM—1972 to 1984—DECEASED*
*MEDICAL FILES: CHOSID TO EISENBERG*

And the box below that:

*BETH SHALOM—1972 to 1984—DECEASED*
*MEDICAL FILES: EMMERT TO GILDEN*

I turned to Flo with a big smile. "We found them."

Benny reached up and grabbed hold of the top box. With a grunt, he lifted it off the pile and set it on the ground. Straightening up, he said, "Ladies, let's get busy."

# 30

CHAPTER

ONCE again, the starting point was Ruth Abrams.

We found her medical file in the first box of documents. Her papers were in a brown loose-leaf notebook that had ring binders at the top, so that it opened from the bottom up instead of from the side. The cover had the patient's name and, in Ruth's case, stated that she was allergic to penicillin. As Flo held the flashlight steady, I paged slowly through Ruth's file.

The first page, entitled ADMISSION AND DISCHARGE RECORD, contained the basic biographical information: Husband deceased. Two adult daughters, both married, one living in Los Angeles, the other in New Canaan, Connecticut. One sister, Rose, unmarried, alive when Ruth entered Beth Shalom on March 4, 1969, died July 29, 1972.

The medical portion of Ruth's file began with a routine exam two days after she entered Beth Shalom. During the next three years at Beth Shalom, Ruth saw a physician roughly once a month. Based on the signatures on her charts, four different physicians saw her during that period. During those years she had what seemed like typical complaints for an elderly patient: arthritis, occasional constipation, indigestion.

Beginning in 1973, the frequency of her physician visits increased to the second and fourth Wednesday of each month. Most of her symptoms remained constant, although she was having more and more problems with arthritis. During this period she saw two different physicians: John Montaldo and Harry Silber.

But on Wednesday, January 16, 1974, two noteworthy changes took place in Ruth's file. First, she began seeing a physician once a week. Second, she began seeing a new physician. His name was Douglas Armstrong. I flipped through her medical records for the remaining eight months of her life. Throughout that period, the only physician whose name appeared on her file was Douglas Armstrong.

I looked back at Benny, who was peering at the records over my shoulder, and then over at Flo.

Flo nodded grimly. "Go back to her first visit with Armstrong," she said.

I turned back to January 16, 1974. As had her prior physicians, Armstrong used the same format for taking notes of patient visits. His notes of the January 16 visit were as follows:

*Problem 1: Indigestion*
*S—"stomach ache," "heartburn," Pt. complains of "gas"*
*O—BP: 160/90, P: 73; Abd: soft, nondistended, no organomegaly*
*A—Dyspepsia*
*P—Maalox PRN; Upper GI X-ray if no response*

"Do you understand what this S-O-A-P format is?" I asked Flo.

She nodded. "It's the standard format used by physicians. The 'S' stands for 'subjective.' That's where the doctor records the patient's description of her symptoms. The 'O' is for 'objective.' Here"—she pointed to the chart—"is where he recorded her blood pressure and pulse and the results of his examination of her belly. Those are the objective descriptions of her symptoms and condition. The 'A' is for 'assessment.' That's where he sets down his diagnosis of the problem. Finally, the 'P' is where he records his plan for dealing with the problem. So for this one," she said, pointing at the "A" and "P" entries, "his assessment was that she had dyspepsia, and his plan of action was for her to start taking Maalox."

I skimmed through the rest of the notes for that first visit on January 16, 1974. In addition to indigestion, Ruth Abrams complained of constipation, and arthritis. Armstrong seemed to pay the most attention to her third complaint:

*Problem 3: Arthritis*
*S —"right knee is swollen," "can't get my ring off," "having trouble with buttons," "difficulty getting out of bed," "sore and stiff" in morning*
*O—Rt knee: decreased range of motion, effusion present—general swelling and heat*
*Lt wrist: pain with movement*
*Rt and Lt PIP joints—rheumatoid deformities, pain with motion, decreased range of motion*
*Neuro: reflexes 2/2 thru out—*
*sensation normal*
*A—Rheumatoid Arthritis—severe, appears to have accelerated*
*P—Start Rx treatment*


"Poor gal," Flo said. "She had it bad."

"What's the 'Rx treatment' mean?" Benny asked.

"It means some medication," Flo said, "but it doesn't say which one."

Slowly, I paged through Ruth's medical records while Flo and Benny looked on. Although there were occasional notations by one of the nurses on other days of the week, every Wednesday we found the S-O-A-P notes in Douglas Armstrong's increasingly familiar handwriting. From January through May of 1974, Ruth Abrams' constipation and dyspepsia seemed to fluctuate in random fashion—better some weeks, worse others. During April she developed insomnia, which Armstrong successfully treated with Valium; by early May, her sleeping problems were gone.

But the rheumatoid arthritis—Ruth Abrams' most painful and seemingly intractable medical problem—began to dramatically improve in the middle of February. By the third week in March, her arthritis S-O-A-P notes read:

> S—*less pain—"feel great," swelling gone, "can play piano," "can get dressed by myself," Pt. able to walk without pain, "can fit my wedding ring back on my hand"*
> O—*Improved range of motion—decreased swelling; no effusion and decreased crepitus*
> A—*Rheumatoid Arthritis—marked improvement*
> P—*Continue same Rx treatment*

"Amazing," Benny said.

Flo nodded. "Her symptoms have practically disappeared."

By the end of March, they had completely disappeared. Under "A," Armstrong had written *Rheumatoid Arthritis—complete remission.* From that point forward, there was no further mention of her arthritis.

During June and July of 1974, Armstrong focused his efforts on Ruth's mild constipation and dyspepsia, neither of which seemed of much concern to either the patient or her doctor. Nevertheless, Armstrong continued to see her every Wednesday. Perhaps that was just standard practice with a patient her age.

The first sign of trouble came on Wednesday, August 14, 1974. Armstrong's S-O-A-P notes for that day focused on a new concern:

> S—*"feel weak," "hard to brush hair," "dropping spoon," "tingling or numb in hands and feet," "tripping—foot dropping," "vision blurred."*
> O—*Tachycardiac; Neuro: reflexes weaker, right Babinski reflex decreased sensation to pin prick and light touch; strength: distal 4/5, proximal 5/5*
> A—*Weakness—possible peripheral neuropathy*
> P—*Check Vitamin B-12 Level*

"What's happening to her?" Benny asked Flo.

Flo studied the notes. "I don't know. He doesn't either."

I pointed to one entry. "What's the Babinski reflex?"

"It's a simple test," she explained. "The doctor scratches the bottom of your foot. The normal response for an adult is to curl your big toe down. A Babinski response means her toe went up instead of down."

"Which means?" Benny asked.

Flo shook her head. "Not good. Back at my old firm we once had a malpractice case that involved an abnormal response. It's a sign of a potentially significant change in the patient's nervous system."

I flipped to the next visit, which was on Wednesday, August 21. The S-O-A-P notes showed a deteriorating condition:

> S—"hard to get out of bed," "can't lift head up," "can't move legs," "short of breath," "coughing."
> O—Neuro: Reflexes 0/2; ↓ sens. to pin and light touch. Strength: distal 3/5, proximal 4/5
> A—Ascending paralysis and numbness, peripheral neuropathy getting worse, markedly affecting strength
> P—Observe closely—transfer to hospital if conditions worsen— Is this Guillain-Barré? Is this lead poisoning?

Two days later, Ruth Abrams died.

I closed her binder with a puzzled look.

"There's that goddam Guillain-Barré again," Benny said.

"What do you think?" I asked Flo.

She shrugged. "Let's look at the other files."

Forty-five minutes later, we had two piles of medical records: one for all the Beth Shalom residents who were listed under the P/S column and one for all the residents listed under the P/A column. Although we had reviewed the files fairly quickly—we were starting to get concerned about our battery supply—we found definite patterns:

1. All twenty-four patients on the Beth Shalom list were women, and all suffered from severe rheumatoid arthritis.

2. On Wednesday, January 16, 1974, all twenty-four got a new physician: Douglas Armstrong. From that point forward, he saw each of them every Wednesday.

3. All twelve women under the P/A column began showing dramatic improvement in their rheumatoid arthritis by the end of February, and all were apparently cured by the end of March.

4. All twelve women under the P/S column showed more gradual improvement in their rheumatoid arthritis by the middle of March. Although the symptoms never disappeared completely, by June of 1974 all twelve under the P/S column were experiencing much greater range of movement and much less swelling.

5. Ten of the twelve women under the P/A column (including Ruth Abrams) rapidly developed symptoms of Guillain-Barré syndrome during August of 1974. Eight died. Two were hospitalized and recovered.

6. None of the twelve women under the P/S column developed any symptoms of Guillain-Barré or other form of peripheral neuropathy.

7. Although Douglas Armstrong continued to see the two surviving P/A women and the twelve P/S women through the end of the year, by October all fourteen of the women had begun to suffer again from increasingly severe symptoms of rheumatoid arthritis.

"Summarize, please," Benny said when we were through.

"Well," I started, "if we're right about those abbreviations—the P/S and the P/A—then the first column of women were secretly given Phrenom and the second column were secretly given Primax. The first group did okay—the drug helped alleviate the symptoms. The second group did terrific, until a horrible side effect killed almost all of them. Assuming that Armstrong's associate, Peter Todorovich, was doing the same thing during the same time frame at Labadie Gardens, the same pattern must have held. Remember, six of the twelve women in the P/A column at

Labadie Gardens died during the same period, while none in the other column died."

Flo frowned as she mulled it over.

"What?" I asked.

"There must be more in those files."

"What do you mean?"

"How was he keeping track of which woman got which drug?"

"With that list," I said.

"Maybe," she said skeptically, "but he didn't have it typed before his first day there. Moreover, what if he forgot the list one day? Or what if he didn't want to refer to it? Don't forget, if we're right, the man was conducting illegal drug tests on unsuspecting human subjects. He would have more than enough concerns without having to worry about pausing at each patient's bed to pull out his cheat sheet, especially with the risk that a nurse might walk in on him."

I reached for the Ruth Abrams binder. "But where?" I said, opening the binder. "He kept it totally opaque in his physician notes. Look at this entry. 'Continue same Rx treatment.' That's what it says in every one of those files." I lifted the page to the next set of Armstrong notes and pointed to the entry. "See?" I lifted that page to reveal the next set of Armstrong notes. "Same again."

Flo held the beam steady on the page of notes. Then she squinted and leaned forward. "What the hell?"

"What?"

"Look." She had moved the beam up slightly, so that it was shining on the back side of the page of notes from the preceding Wednesday's examination. In the upper right corner were pencil jottings in Douglas Armstrong's handwriting. I leaned close to the page to read them:

*Primax 25 mg IM.*

"Oh, shit," Flo said.

"What?" Benny asked.

"We've got him," she said.

"What does 'IM' mean?" I asked.

She turned to me. "Intramuscular. It's medical jargon for a shot. This is his note. It means he gave that woman an injection of twenty-five milligrams of Primax. Holy shit, Rachel." Flo raised her eyebrows. "We finally nailed the son of a bitch. Check the next page."

The same note was jotted in pencil on the back of that page: *Primax 25 mg IM*. And on the page after that. And the page after that. By March, he was using the abbreviation "Pri," and by June he was using the abbreviation for the generic drug that appeared on the Beth Shalom/Labadie Gardens list, "P/A."

We quickly checked a sampling of other medical files. The pattern remained constant. The files for the patients receiving injections of Primax had the same back-of-the-page notations as Ruth Abrams' file. The ones receiving Phrenom had a similar notation, except that the entry started as "Phrenom" and by March became "Phre" and eventually became "P/S."

Two of the files contained additional corroboration. The nurse notations actually made reference to the injections. On April 29, 1974, Anna Mittelman told the nurse that Dr. Armstrong was giving her "magic shots from the fountain of youth." The nurse's comment: "Pt. seems disoriented." Four months later, Anna Mittelman was dead. According to her death certificate, the immediate cause of death was "respiratory failure," and the underlying cause was "acute ascending peripheral neuropathy."

The other patient was Freida Perlmutter, one of the Phrenom recipients. On November 4, 1974, she complained to the nurse of the recurrence of her arthritis symptoms: "Pt. claimed that R.A. symptoms returned after Dr. stopped weekly shots." The nurse's comment: "File shows no IM treatment. Pt. must be confused over recent flu vaccinations."

"He must have carried them in his doctor's bag," Flo said.

"Carried what?" Benny asked.

"The shots. He'd visit the patient in her room, do the examination, and then give her a shot before he left." Flo shined the flashlight on her wristwatch. "Let's get out of here."

"Should I take some of these files?" I asked.

Flo looked at the stack of files and then at me. "How many can we squeeze into that backpack?"

"Four or five."

"Do it. We can send a crew back later for the rest. Wait. I've got my camera. Let me take some pictures down here. These'll go great with the story."

Flo shot through all three rolls of film. She took pictures of the room, of individual stacks of boxes, of me or Benny posed in front of the boxes, of the piles of medical files, and of individual pages from the medical files. When she finished, we stuffed four files (two Phrenom, two Primax) into the backpack along with the camera and film. We changed the flashlight batteries one more time and headed back.

"This is unbelievable," Flo said as we started back toward the warehouse exit. "A United States senator may be heading for jail."

"And you may be heading for a Pulitzer Prize, Ms. Shenker," Benny said. "Fame and wealth await."

Flo snorted. "We'll see."

"You know what I still have trouble believing?" I said as we approached the short tunnel that led back to the warehouse. "I just can't believe that Douglas Armstrong is actually the one behind the recent killings."

We paused at the entrance to the warehouse tunnel and Flo turned to me. "Maybe not directly," she said, "but he must know what's going on."

"How many others are involved?" Benny asked.

Flo shrugged. "Sherman Ross? He's been Armstrong's confidant for more than twenty years. And Lee Fowler sure sounds suspicious. Also, don't forget the current R and D guy at Chemitex." She looked at me. "Didn't you say he got uptight when you mentioned Primax?"

"He did."

"Sounds like guilty knowledge to me," Flo said.

"Believe me," Benny said, as we started down the tunnel toward the trapdoor, "there have to be several others, too. Hell, they've been sitting on this secret for—what? more than two decades? And then along comes their worst nightmare: a due diligence bloodhound named Bruce Rosenthal. He starts poking around, asking questions, looking at documents, asking for additional documents, and all of a sudden they start to get worried. It looks to them like he's picked up the scent. So what do they do?"

Benny paused as Flo pointed the flashlight toward the ceiling. "Oh, shit," he groaned.

When we left the warehouse tunnel, the trapdoor was open and the ladder and rope were on the ground against the side wall. Now, the rope and the ladder were gone, and the trapdoor was closed.

"Oh, shit," Flo said.

"It's them," I said in frustration, trying to control my anxiety.

"We're stuck down here," Flo said. "Oh, my God."

# 31

CHAPTER

FLO trained the flashlight on the trapdoor overhead. The door was at least twelve feet above the ground. I was five feet seven, Benny was five feet ten. Even if I stood tiptoe on his shoulders and was able to reach the trapdoor with my fingers—a fairly doubtful proposition in itself—the effort would have been futile. There was no knob or locking mechanism on the tunnel side of the trapdoor. Nothing but smooth, cold metal. Moreover, it didn't take a rocket scientist to conclude that whoever had taken the time and effort to remove the ladder and the rope would have also made sure that the trapdoor couldn't be opened from below.

"We'll never get that damn thing open," Flo said, peering at the trapdoor. I could hear the rising panic in her voice.

I stared up at the ceiling, my mind racing. "How many more batteries do we have?" I asked her.

"Just one more set."

"Turn off the flashlight."

Flo turned it off.

"We have to conserve battery power," I said. "Here," I said, reaching for her arm, "take my hand." She grasped it. "Benny, take Flo's hand."

"Got it," he said.

It was totally dark. "Let's go," I said.

"Where?" Benny asked.

"Back down the tunnel."

"In the dark?" Flo said uncertainly.

"It's not far, Flo. Come on. It'll be good practice for later."

"Later?" Benny said.

We walked along the right side of the tunnel in the pitch black. I kept my hand lightly against the wall until it curved into the cave. I stopped. "Now you can turn it back on."

She did. "What are we going to do?"

I slipped the backpack off my shoulders and unbuckled the flap. "See if there's another way."

"Another way for what?" Benny asked.

I took the cave map out of the backpack. "Another way out of here. We are not going to let those bastards get away with this." I unfolded the map and held it up.

Benny studied it with me. "Jesus, it's a fucking maze."

I nodded. "They run for miles underground."

Flo stood next to me as we studied the map. "Okay, Becky Thatcher." She sighed. "Show me where we are."

I pointed. "We're here. Over here is where the brewery and mansion portions are. Here's where the highway comes in."

"No exits there," Benny said.

We examined the map together.

"Maybe here?" Flo asking, pointing her finger at a spot down the cave to our left.

There appeared to be a narrow passageway that connected our cave channel to another channel. I moved my eyes slowly along the parts of the cave that we had already explored. I didn't see any other links to the rest of the network of tunnels.

"I think so," I said. "Let me have the flashlight."

She handed it to me.

"We don't know how long it's going to take us, so we better start on battery conservation."

"Terrific," Benny groaned.

I pointed the beam down the direction we had chosen. "Take a good look."

We stared ahead for a moment, and then I clicked off the flashlight.

"Oh, shit," Flo muttered in the total darkness.

"Give me your hand," Benny said to her.

"Ready?" I asked.

"Yeah," Benny said.

Just as we started forward in the pitch black, I heard a distant metallic thunk.

"What the fuck was that?" Benny said.

"It's from back there," I whispered. "By the trapdoor."

We were only twenty feet beyond the entrance to the warehouse tunnel. Quietly, and without any light, we moved back to the edge of that tunnel. I peered around the corner. At the far end of the tunnel, the trapdoor was hanging down. Through the opening came a thick vertical column of light, like a powerful spotlight trained on the cave floor. We could hear deep voices. Someone started lowering a metal ladder through the trapdoor opening. Down it slid, until the foot banged into the floor. More voices.

*Please let it be the police,* I prayed.

Someone started down the ladder and stopped after three rungs. He was visible from the waist down—faded jeans and brown construction boots. There was a walkie-talkie in his left back pocket. We waited. Two more rungs down, and he stopped again, visible from the chest down. He was wearing a black long-sleeved shirt. He reached up through the opening with both hands. When his hands reappeared, one was holding a high-powered flashlight and the other an automatic pistol. I had already started backing away when his long red hair and familiar face came into view.

"Quick," I whispered to Benny and Flo, pushing them back toward the direction we had picked.

We pressed forward in the darkness, moving as quickly as we dared. I kept my right hand against the cave wall. We had already been this way once—this was the section of the tunnel that passed by the Spaghetti Room, the Curtain of Creation, and Satan's Waterfall. According to the map, the passage to the adjacent cave tunnel was through a wall in the chamber that Mordecai Jacobs had named the Aztec Sacrifice Room.

The sounds of our jagged breaths seemed deafening as we walked and then trotted and then walked again. I tried to keep focused. Our pursuer didn't know the caves any better than we did. If he turned left at the end of the warehouse tunnel, we'd be in trouble fast. If he turned right, we'd have a shot at reaching the passageway.

We hurried forward in the total darkness with me in the lead and Benny and Flo right behind. To make sure we stayed together, Flo had a finger hooked onto the back pocket of my sweatpants. I had my right hand against the wall. I moved my left hand back and forth in front of me, like an antenna. The only noises were the scraping of our shoes along the path and the rasping of our breaths.

When I couldn't stand the blindness any longer, I whispered, "Wait." I stopped, and Flo and Benny did, too.

"What?" Benny said.

"Look back," I whispered, peering into the darkness, straining for the sign of a flashlight beam. "Do you see anything?"

"No," Flo said.

"Give me your flashlight," I told her.

We fumbled in the dark as I took it from her. I clicked it on. We were in front of the Saber Tooth Cemetery, the skeleton frozen in its attack stance. The flashlight cast weird shadows against the back wall.

"Not much further," I said.

I pointed the flashlight down the path, took a moment to fix my bearings, and then clicked it off. We moved ahead slowly, me in the lead, my left hand out front. We'd covered about fifty more yards when I paused to look back. Way in the distance, I thought I saw a faint flash of light. I strained, trying to spot it again.

"Did you see that?" I whispered.

"See what?" Benny said.

"A light back there."

"Oh, shit," Flo groaned. "Let's hurry."

We moved quickly down the tunnel toward the Aztec Sacrifice Room. Every ten steps or so I clicked the flashlight on and off to keep our bearings. When we reached the room, Benny stayed at the entrance as lookout while Flo and I moved inside. I flashed the light beam around the chamber. In the center of the room was a massive stalagmite, far thicker than a tree trunk. It rose four feet off the floor and ended abruptly in a flat, slightly concave surface that was large enough to accommodate a prone adult. A group of large stalactites overhead circled the slab in an oval pattern that mirrored the shape of the stalagmite.

As Flo and I moved further into the room, we were careful not to trip over the dozens of smaller stalagmites that were poking out of the ground or lying broken on the floor. We went around the sacrificial altar to the right and picked our way through the field of stalagmites toward the right wall. I moved the flashlight beam carefully along the wall as we maneuvered our way from right to left through the stalagmites, searching for the opening. We made clumsy, slow progress. We couldn't find it on that wall, so we made our way toward the back wall.

After what seemed like a long time, I spotted the opening on the left side of the back wall. It looked like a large mouse hole. I got down on my hands and knees and pointed the flashlight inside. The beam lit up the first twenty feet. The walls didn't seem to get any narrower, which was good, since the opening was no more than three feet wide and maybe two and a half feet high.

"Well?" Flo said. She was kneeling behind me.

I pulled my head out of the opening. "The map says it goes

all the way." I shrugged uneasily. "What other choice do we have?"

"None," a male voice said as I was suddenly illuminated.

I spun toward the voice, startled. The man was standing maybe twenty feet away. He had the flashlight aimed at my face, and the powerful beam blinded me. I squinted, trying to discern his features, but he remained in silhouette.

"Stand up," he ordered. "Both of you."

As we got to our feet I heard a crackle of static from his walkie-talkie, and then he said, "Hey, John, you read me?"

More static, and then a voice over the radio responded, "Any luck?"

"Yeah," the man said. "Two of them. Her and that other broad."

"Stay there," the radio voice said. "I'm coming. Over."

"Yeah, over." The man clicked off the walkie-talkie.

*Two of them*, he had said. *Her and that other broad.*

*What about Benny?* I wondered. *Where is he?*

The man was still shining the flashlight in my face.

"I can't see," I said.

He chuckled. "Tough shit, lady."

*If Benny's still out there*, I told myself, *you need to keep this guy talking.*

"Who are you?" I asked. My eyes were adjusting a little. He was standing just to the side of the sacrificial altar.

"None of your business."

"Who hired you?"

He laughed again. "Forget it, lady. You got lucky on me before, but this is all she wrote." He waggled the flashlight beam at me. "Time's up. Down on your knees."

"What for?" I said, my voice shaking.

"Just do it, goddammit."

I did. He shifted the beam toward Flo. "You, too, chubby."

As Flo started to bend down, there was a sudden smashing

noise, followed by a grunt. The flashlight beam swung wildly. Another grunt, then a dull crunching sound. The flashlight dropped; the lens shattered. Total darkness. Then the sound of a body collapsing.

"Damn," Benny gasped. "Rachel, give me some light."

My hands were trembling as I turned on the flashlight. I pointed the beam toward Benny's voice.

Flo gasped.

Benny was standing over the red-headed guy, who was flat on his back and twitching. Benny was breathing hard, and he was holding a chunk of stalactite over his head like a club. I trained the flashlight on the body.

"Oh, God," I said. The man's forehead was caved in—a bloody pulpy mess. One eye was open, the other smashed. As I watched in horror, his body gave a violent shudder and then became still.

"Benny," I asked, "where were you?"

"I was out there waiting," Benny said, still panting. "I saw someone coming. You were still back there looking for the opening. He would have heard me if I tried to warn you. I wasn't sure what to do. I looked around and grabbed one of these things and hid on the other side of this slab."

I came over and hugged him. "My hero."

"Yeah," he said distractedly. "We got to move. You heard that radio. Someone else is heading this way. Where do we go?"

I turned and pointed the flashlight beam at the opening to the passageway. "Here."

I kneeled in front of the hole and handed Flo the flashlight. I slipped off my backpack.

"What are you doing?" she asked.

"The opening isn't high enough for me to fit through with the pack on my back."

Flo peered in and leaned back with a shudder. "This is freaking me out."

"Just get down low and start moving. You want me to **go** first?"

"Definitely," she said.

I looked back at Benny. "I'll take up the rear," he said.

I slid the backpack ahead of me into the opening, took a deep breath, and bent down until I was resting on my elbows. Ducking my head low, I scooted into the opening. I pushed the backpack in front of me with my left hand while I held the flashlight in my right.

I purposefully kept the flashlight off. In addition to conserving energy, I just plain didn't want to see what was ahead of me. It was plenty creepy already. I was moving through a cold, wet space that was so narrow I couldn't turn around. Darkness was just fine. My claustrophobia was bad enough without the added jolt of suddenly coming upon one of those ghostly white spiders or blind hairy millipedes.

I slithered onward in the dark. There were no other options: it was either forward on your belly and elbows or wait for the second killer to catch up to us. After what seemed like an eternity, I paused. "Are you okay, Flo?" I whispered

"Yeah."

I could hear the strain in her voice, the edge of hysteria. As distressing as this was for me, it had to be even worse for Flo. She was at least thirty pounds heavier than me, which made the fit that much tighter, and the physical and psychological strain that much more intense.

*Poor Benny.*

"Benny?" I called softly.

"What?" he snarled.

"How do you feel?"

"How do I feel? Like a pig moving through a snake, for chrissakes. I'm on the verge of a fucking mental breakdown back here."

"We're almost there," I lied. I had no idea how much further we had to go, or even whether this narrow channel would stay large enough for us to reach the other cave channel.

The air seemed to get heavier as we moved on—probably

more a factor of our growing fatigue than an actual change in atmosphere. But another change was definitely real: the floor was getting wetter. When we had started through the opening, the floor was cold and moist. Now it was actually wet. We were sloshing through water. I was soaking wet and exhausted. My right arm was starting to cramp from holding the flashlight off the ground, but I couldn't risk letting our only light source get wet and short out on us.

Flo was wheezing behind me. "Rachel," she gasped.

"What?"

"I can't go on."

I stopped, trying to catch my breath. "We'll take a break."

"What?" Benny asked.

"Let's rest," I said. "Then we'll go on."

My elbows were scraped raw, my back was sore, my thigh muscles were throbbing. Gradually, my breathing returned to normal. As the ringing in my ears faded, I became aware of another sound: water trickling. Somewhere up ahead there was running water. I didn't know whether that was good or bad.

"Ready?" I asked.

"No," they both said.

"Come on, guys. We're almost there. I hear water."

"We're *in* water, for chrissakes," Benny said, "unless one of you is taking the goddamdest piss of the twentieth century."

"Flo," I said, "you still with me?"

"Oh, God," she said wearily. "I'm with you."

"Benny?"

He growled. "Someone ought to Vaseline this place."

We slithered forward. The floor got wetter. Each time I paused, the trickling noise was louder. As we continued crawling, the ground began to incline slightly. We were moving uphill, and there was more water now. It was moving past us downhill. It was getting harder to hold the flashlight above the moisture. The sound of running water was much louder.

I stopped and fumbled with the flashlight. The beam went on, illuminating our narrow passage. I peered around the backpack. The end of the passageway was just fifteen feet away.

"We're almost there!" I said excitedly as I turned off the flashlight.

# 32

CHAPTER

BECAUSE of the incline I couldn't see what was on the other side of our passageway, but the trickling noises and the sight of water sloshing into the opening told me what was up ahead. I elbowed forward until I reached the end of the passageway.

I poked my head out of the hole in the cave wall and clicked on the flashlight. The passageway opened onto a cave tunnel that was about eight feet wide. The entire floor of the tunnel was moving water—an underground river. The floor of our passageway was less than an inch above the water level.

I scrunched my body around the backpack. Flo was right behind me.

"It's a river," I said.

"How deep?"

"I'm going to find out. Here." I turned off the flashlight and handed it back to her.

I pushed my arms and head out of the opening. My hands dipped into the water. It was icy cold. Cautiously, I crawled head first out of the passageway and into the river. I couldn't see a thing. Now my upper body was through the opening. My arms were in the water up to my elbows. I kept inching forward, telling myself that sharks didn't live in caves, but then wondering what exactly did live in these rivers.

The water didn't get any deeper as I continued to move forward. That was a good sign. I pulled the rest of my body out of the passageway opening and splashed into the water. I scrambled to my feet in the pitch black. I could feel the current at my ankles. Leaning over in the darkness, I touched the cold water with my fingertips. It was just below my knees.

*Thank God.*

"Turn on the flashlight, Flo. It isn't deep."

A few minutes later, the three of us were slogging forward down the middle of the river. Before leaving the opening, we had shined the flashlight back inside. There was no sign of anyone coming after us. It either meant that we were several minutes ahead of him, or that he was still back there searching other rooms, not yet realizing where we had gone. Either way, we knew we had to keep moving.

Flo was wearing the backpack now. I had the map and the flashlight. Assuming that I was still correctly aligned with the map, the current was flowing northeast. We decided to follow the current for two reasons. First, there appeared to be more branches of the cave northeast. Second, smaller rivers flow into larger rivers. One of those rivers, roughly northeast of us, was the Mississippi River. If our river was headed for the Mississippi, it might eventually reach the surface.

I left the flashlight on. It was bad enough walking on solid ground in total darkness. Wading blind down a river was far too much for me. I checked my watch. It almost 7:00 P.M. We'd been down in the cave for more than four hours. My clothes were soaked and the water was freezing.

"You think we can drink this water, Rachel?" Flo asked, her teeth chattering. "I'm dying of thirst."

"I don't know. Benny?"

"You're asking me? I thought you were the one who took cave law."

I shined the light into the water just in time to see a dull gray water snake slither past my right leg heading upstream. I caught my breath but kept quiet. No sense freaking out Flo even more. A small pallid fish circled in front of me and then darted away. Snakes and fish could live in it, right? I leaned over and scooped a few drops of water into my mouth.

"It tastes okay," I said.

We each drank several cupped handfuls. I studied the map as Flo adjusted the backpack.

"What's that noise?" Benny said.

I clicked off the light and listened, turning back toward the direction we had come. There was no sign of a flashlight back there. I listened again. The noise was the sound of rushing water. It was coming from somewhere up ahead. I turned. "I don't know," I said. "Rapids?"

"Down here?" Flo said.

"That's what it sound like," I said.

"Fucking unbelievable," Benny said. "All this, and now rapids? Who designed this miserable goddam hole in the ground? Stephen King?"

We walked on. The sound got louder. The tunnel, and thus the river, curved toward the left. As we came around the bend we saw a fork in the cave where it seemed to split into two tunnels. The sound of rushing water was much louder. As we got closer to the fork, we saw that both tunnel openings were actually positioned above the water level—the one on the right at least five feet above the water, the one on the left about three feet above. It was as if some huge drilling machine had punched two large holes into the wall. Both tunnels appeared to be dry.

The river seemed to disappear into the wall below the two tunnels. And as we got closer, we saw that the river did indeed disappear into the wall. The sound of rushing water was the sound of water falling. The river was literally funneling through a wide opening in the wall and cascading down what sounded like a significant drop-off. Seen from below, it must have been a magnificent waterfall. A Kodak scene. But we were way beyond Kodak scenes. We could have stumbled across the Taj Mahal down here and none of us would have given a damn. All we knew was that we were somewhere underneath St. Louis with a weakening flashlight beam and a growing sense of desperation.

The water current was much stronger here as the river funneled through the hole. The current dragged on us, too—pulling us toward the edge of the waterfall. Our only option was the tunnel on the left; the one on the right was too high to reach. I clambered up into the tunnel first and turned to help Flo. Then both of us helped Benny. Once we were all up in the dry tunnel opening, I took out the cave map and studied it as we caught our breath.

"Where are we now?" Flo asked.

I shook my head. "I don't know. I don't think this part is even on the map."

"You're kidding," Benny said.

"Look for yourself."

He leaned closer to the map. "How can you tell whether any of these caves comes back up to the surface?"

I shrugged. "You can't."

"So how do we know where to get out?" Flo asked.

I looked at her. "We don't."

"Oh, brother," Benny said.

I pointed the beam forward into the darkness. "We just have to keep walking. We don't have any other options."

At 8:10, the batteries in the flashlight died. We put in our final set. Having lost our sense of direction, the map was totally useless. We just kept pressing forward. In order to avoid doubling back, we decided to take the left fork every time the cave tunnel split.

Ninety minutes later, the flashlight was starting to fade. We had just reached yet another fork in the cave and were about to go left when Benny grabbed my arm.

"Look." He was pointing at the other tunnel.

I flashed the weak beam toward the tunnel on the right. "What?"

"Isn't it sloped uphill?"

"Really?"

The three of us walked into the right tunnel. After several steps I said, "You're right, Benny." I tried to hold back my excitement by reminding myself that what goes up must come down. I prayed that the rule didn't apply to cave tunnels.

We continued on. The tunnel was definitely moving upward. Our budding hopes made it hard to keep from running. The flashlight beam was almost worthless now—just a feeble glow. The ceiling was getting lower and lower.

Before long we were walking in a crouch. But still moving uphill. Definitely up.

The tunnel got narrower and narrower. We were crawling. But still moving uphill.

Gradually, the ground seemed to level off. By then I was crawling forward on my hands and knees, my head scraping the ceiling. The flashlight was dead. I tried to block from my mind what would happen if this passageway kept shrinking until we could proceed forward no further. I tried to block it out but couldn't. If it got too narrow, we'd have to crawl back blind, all the way back to the fork in the tunnel. Then we'd take the left fork and we'd move on in total darkness and we'd just keep going and that was that. We'd deal with it then.

As I crawled forward, my head occasionally bumped the ceiling. Suddenly, though, there was nothing overhead. I stopped. Flo crawled right into me with a grunt.

"What's wrong?" she said.

"I'm not sure."

"What's that?" Benny said from behind her.

I reached over my head in the darkness. Nothing but air. Carefully, moving both hands around in the air over my head, I got to my feet. I inched forward very slowly. My hands bumped into a wall in front of me. It was a curved surface. I felt it with my hands. The wall curved toward me on either side. I realized I was standing in a vertical shaft. I kept my hands against the walls as I turned slowly in a circle. My hand touched a cold metal bar. I grasped it, felt around, grasped another metal bar.

"Oh, God," I said.

"What?" Flo called from below.

"It's a ladder." My voice was shaking. "It's a metal ladder. It's attached to the wall."

"A what?" Benny yelled.

"She said a ladder," Flo answered.

"Hot damn!" Benny hollered.

I went up first, followed by Flo, and then Benny. We climbed in total darkness. I counted the first fifteen rungs and then lost track. We just kept climbing and climbing.

My head banged into the ceiling.

"What was that?" Flo asked from below.

I felt the ceiling with one hand. "It's wood." I leaned out from the ladder to touch as much of the surface as I could. The wood felt damp. I rapped it with my knuckles. It sounded hollow.

"Let me up," Flo said.

I moved to one side of the ladder to make room for her. When we were even, she reached up to touch the wood.

"It feels rotten," she said.

"It does," I agreed.

"One way to find out for sure," she said. I heard her take a deep breath and I felt her tense, her knees bending. Then a grunt and a quick thrust upward with her fist. The wood splintered. She did it again. More splintering, pieces dropping down on us. Again. More splintering.

And light!

There was light coming through the ragged holes in the wood. Moonlight.

I laughed. "God bless you, Flo. Have you been pumping iron?"

"Karate."

I kissed her on the forehead. "You have brought great honor to your teacher, Florence-san."

"Cut the crap," Benny said. "Come on."

Flo and I were able to reach up and yank off pieces of the rotting wood. The hole got bigger and bigger until it was large enough for Flo to climb through. I followed her, and then Benny followed me.

When we got to our feet, we were standing inside a small Greco-Roman gazebo. The gazebo was on a tiny island in the middle of a large round lake. Off in the distance, we heard the coughing roar of a lion.

"Where in the hell are we?" Flo said.

I peered around. Rising above the weeping willow on the shore of the lake was a broad, grassy hill. At the top of the hill was the unmistakable outline of a commanding figure on horseback. It was the statue of St. Louis at the top of Art Hill.

I gave Flo a big hug. "We're in Forest Park. We made it. We can wade across." I turned to Benny with a big smile. There were tears in my eyes. I gave him a hug, too. "Oh, guys," I said, "we made it!"

# 33

CHAPTER

IT was an English Tudor with a circular drive and a giant pine tree on the front lawn. A slight breeze made the upper branches rustle and sway in the moonlight, casting menacing shadows on the freshly mowed grass below.

It was a big house surrounded by lots of land. Just like all the other homes on the grounds of the St. Louis Country Club. There were no lights on in the front of the house. Just like all the other homes on the grounds of the St. Louis Country Club. After all, it was nearly two in the morning.

Flo's sources said he was in St. Louis tonight, not Washington, D.C.

He was. The kitchen was around back, and the light was on. He was seated at the kitchen table with a cup of tea. Alone. He was wearing pajamas, slippers, and a robe.

It was his second cup of tea. I had watched him drink the first cup while I stood in the garden near the kitchen window. His girlfriend had come in—the tall, beautiful redhead. She was wearing a silky blue bathrobe and her hair was in curlers. They spoke briefly. From where I stood, it looked like she asked him if he was coming to bed soon. He shook his head, distracted. She poured herself a glass of orange juice, drank it in three gulps, left the glass and the juice container on the counter, and went upstairs. When he got up to make more tea, he placed the juice glass in the dishwasher and put the container of juice on the top shelf of the refrigerator.

While he brewed his second cup of tea, I crept onto the back porch. That's where I stood now. More than fifteen minutes had passed since the redhead went upstairs. I stepped back to look up. The second floor was dark. She was probably asleep by now.

I moved forward and peered at him through the glass of the back door. I rapped lightly on the door. He didn't respond. I watched him through the window. He seemed a thousand miles away. I knocked harder. He looked up with a start and squinted at the door. I realized I was invisible, standing in darkness. He stepped over to the door and turned on a switch. Overhead spotlights lit up the back porch, as if I were on stage. In a way I was.

He seemed startled at first, but then his features hardened. We stared at one another, both of us motionless. By now, all my fear was gone. Vanished. For the first time in weeks, I felt invincible. There was nothing more he could do to me. After a while, he seemed to realize it. His shoulders sagged a bit and he reached to open the door.

I stepped in. He moved back to the kitchen table.

"Tea?" he asked in a hollow tone.

I shook my head. "No, Senator."

Slowly, almost painfully, he sat back down. Taking his cup in both hands, he looked up at me with tired eyes.

"You changed your hair," he said dully.

"Did you think I was dead?" I demanded. I could feel my anger build.

He said nothing. He sipped his tea, his eyes steady.

"You know what's almost the worst part?" I said.

After a moment, he shook his head.

"The negligence," I said. "The pure stupid negligence. Right from the outset. It's unforgivable."

He frowned. "Negligence?"

"The way you and your cohorts tried to conceal what killed those poor women. You botched the coverup from the outset, didn't you? You thought you could eliminate all links to those women by destroying the Primax files. But that wasn't enough, was it? You failed to destroy all the key documents. You overlooked some, and Bruce Rosenthal found them, didn't he?" I shook my head in disgust. "Negligence. If you'd done it right the first time, Bruce would be alive. Karen would be alive. David would be alive." I was shaking with angry frustration. "As if those poor dead women weren't bad enough, three more people died because of your negligence."

He studied the pattern on the saucer.

"It had to be more than that list of names from the nursing homes," I continued. "Bruce found something else, didn't he? The list wasn't enough. For him to understand the real meaning of that list he'd have to have found something else, too. Right?"

After a moment, he nodded.

"What was it?"

Armstrong leaned back in his chair. Crossing his arms over his chest, he stared down at his tea cup in silence. "When I came back from Costa Rica," he said in a slow cadence, "I brought two species of the Peloto plant—one that grew on the Pacific Ocean side in the Monteverde Cloud Forest, the other from the Caribbean side, near Tortuguero." He picked up the saucer and turned it over to read the writing on the bottom. "A tribe of Indians lived near each species, and the local women ate the tubers from their version of the plant. None of the women in either tribe suffered from rheumatoid arthritis."

"What's the point?" I said impatiently.

He looked at me. "The fact that there were two species." He paused. "That's the whole point," he said, the intensity returning. "That was the essence of our dilemma. We had a choice. We had to choose."

"I'm not following you."

"We isolated the active ingredient in each plant. We named

one of the drugs Phrenom, the other Primax. We started conducting animal tests to see which performed better."

"What did Bruce find?" I repeated.

He shook his head, staring down at the saucer. He turned it back over and placed it on the table.

"Senator, what did he find?"

He continued on, as if he hadn't heard me. "We did animal testing on both drugs." He paused again and slowly shook his head. "We must have overlooked the earliest animal test files for Phrenom."

"That's what he found?"

He looked up and closed his eyes for a moment. "Apparently," he said. He opened his eyes and looked at me. "He must have found cross-references to Primax in some of the old Phrenom files. That's what must have made him curious."

I stood there, seething. "It's your fault."

He leaned forward, his right fist slowly clenching and unclenching. He stared at me, his eyes narrowing. "I assume that you fully understand those women were not supposed to die."

"But they did."

Armstrong breathed in deeply and exhaled through his nose. "There was no way to predict that." He spoke slowly and deliberately. "Can you imagine my horror when I realized what was killing those women? Can you imagine a more cruel irony—a wonder drug with a fatal flaw: it cured the disease but killed the patient." He frowned and shook his head. "There was no way to suspect that flaw. The animal tests showed no adverse reactions whatsoever. None." He stared at me for a moment. When he spoke again, his voice was filled with emotion. "Do you think if I had had even the slightest inkling of any risk that I would have ever used the drug on those women? Good God, Rachel, we were looking for a cure to a terrible, crippling disease. We were saviors, not killers."

"Not anymore," I said with disgust. "And don't try to rationalize what you did to those women. Properly conducted phase one tests on healthy people would have detected that reaction. That's the whole purpose of those tests: to uncover hidden flaws. Healthy young people would have recovered. You killed fourteen innocent women, Senator."

He sat back in his chair, his arms crossed over his chest. He shook his head as he stared at the table. "We never suspected it could happen. Never."

"Why?"

He looked up and frowned. "Pardon?"

"Why break the law? Why secret tests?"

He gave a patronizing chuckle. "Why? The world isn't black and white, Rachel. Surely you're old enough to understand that."

"Then you help me understand," I answered angrily. "You did it. You tell me why."

He sighed. "When I returned from Costa Rica, I brought back two possibilities for easing the pain and suffering of millions of women. I had no idea which version would make the better drug. That was the problem. We had to choose. Unfortunately, we didn't have the luxury of making a mistake. We were a tiny company. We couldn't start both drugs through the FDA approval process. It takes tens of millions of dollars to bring a new drug to market. We had barely enough money to finance one. We had hoped that the animal tests would make the choice for us, but they didn't. We were back where we started. We still had to pick one. Can you grasp our predicament? If we guessed wrong, we'd run out of money and never bring any drug to market. It was all or nothing—for us, *and* for all those women." He paused, his gaze narrowing. "Since we were going to have to bet the entire company on one drug, we had to find a way to pick the right one."

"So you cheated."

"We bent the rules."

"You cheated, Senator, and you killed fourteen innocent women in the process."

He seemed to think it over. "Perhaps," he conceded with a smile. It was a stern, unapologetic smile. "But let's not pretend this is Mister Rogers' Neighborhood. Fourteen women died. Was it worth it? Of course it was. Look at the big picture, Rachel. I had the courage to push the rules, and because I did, I was able to keep my company alive long enough to bring a drug to the market that has significantly improved the lives of millions of women. The price to make the drug possible? Fourteen elderly women lost a year or two off their lives. Balance that cost against the benefits. Millions of women versus fourteen old ladies in a nursing home. I think that equation more than balances."

I shook my head fiercely. "You don't have the right to make that equation, Senator. You don't get to decide who lives and who dies."

He gave me an indulgent look. "Rachel, I'm not claiming a divine right. I'm just telling you to take a broader view. Did we have the right to drop the bomb on Japan? Those who say we did point to the millions of lives that were saved by terminating the war. Did we have the right to invade—"

"Spare me your philosophy," I said angrily. "What about Bruce Rosenthal?"

He shifted in his chair but said nothing.

"What about Karen Harmon?" I continued. "What about David Marcus? What's the cost-benefit analysis there? The lives of three innocent people to preserve one man's presidential ambitions? If that's another one of your moral equations, Senator, believe me, it doesn't balance anywhere in this world."

He stared over my head toward the wall behind me. "Obviously, none of those three should have died. That was terribly wrong. Tragic. Unfortunately, certain individuals, acting out of a misguided sense of loyalty to me, got carried away by their own zeal. They did stupid things."

"Stupid?" I repeated, outraged. "You call three cold-blooded murders stupid?"

"I totally condemn their conduct." He lowered his gaze to me, his eyes narrowing. "I did not plan the deaths of those fourteen women, and I regret each one. I certainly did not plan or authorize the deaths of those three young people. I learned of all three after the fact. I abhor what was done."

He paused.

I waited.

I could hear the ticking of a clock somewhere in the kitchen.

"Rachel," he said, almost casually, "you understand what's at stake?"

I looked at him like he had lost his mind. "What?"

"I'm boxed in. I can't bring the killers to justice without destroying myself in the process."

"So what?"

"Life goes on. I can't bring the dead back to life. If I could, I would. If I could make the killers change places with the victims, I would. But I can't. Neither can you. What's done is done. All we can do is honor their memories."

"What are you trying to say?"

"There are more than two hundred and fifty million Americans out there." He waved his hand dismissively. "For a moment, put aside sentiment. We are poised at a crucial point in the history of our country and the world. I can make a difference. These are not the ravings of a loony megalomaniac. You know it's true." He paused. "But to achieve what I can achieve, I have to be president. It can't be someone else. There simply isn't anyone else on the national scene. Look at the polls. You know it, and I know it."

"So?"

He stood. "You can be part of it, Rachel. You can have an impact on this country beyond your wildest dreams. I can make it happen. Name your position. A federal judge? A position in the cabinet? Perhaps you'd like to be attorney general?" He stared at me intently. "Help me become president, Rachel, and whatever you want you can have. I can put you in position to make a difference in the lives of hundreds of millions of people."

I'd heard enough. "Forget it," I said. I turned toward the door.

"Wait," he called.

I stopped, my hand on the doorknob. I looked back.

"Why not?" he asked, obviously baffled. "Consider my offer. Consider the impact you could have."

I stared at him, unmoved. "We're different, Senator. When lives are involved, I don't believe in cost-benefit calculations. In my religion, we're taught that he who saves one person saves an entire universe." I opened the door and paused to look back. "Senator, you've annihilated enough universes for one lifetime."

Flo was waiting in the car. She started the engine as she saw me approach.

"Thank God," she said as I got in. "I've been dying out here."

I reached into my jacket pocket and pulled out the portable tape recorder. I popped the cassette into my hand and looked over at Flo.

"Well?" she asked, eyebrows raised.

I nodded solemnly. "He's finished."

The *Trib*'s Washington bureau chief didn't take any chances. We drove straight to the airport from Armstrong's house, arriving at quarter to three in the morning. Waiting for us there was a chartered jet and an armed guard. Four hours later, Flo and I were safe inside the *Trib*'s D.C. office on L Street, where we remained for the next twenty-four hours. I organized documents and outlined facts, Flo wrote the story, and her bureau chief edited the first of what eventually became a series of thirteen exclusive front-page stories.

They faxed us that first front page directly from the printing plant in Chicago. I remember staring in amazement at the huge bold headline that covered the top third of the page:

U.S. SENATOR ARMSTRONG TIED TO ILLEGAL
DRUG TESTS, CRIMINAL CONSPIRACY, AND MURDER

# 34

BENNY looked grim. "We got big trouble here."

I glanced around. "Not necessarily."

"Rachel, these fuckers want to kill us."

I gave him a plucky smile. "We're still alive."

The umpire stepped out from behind home plate and yanked off his mask. "Come on!"

That was all the encouragement the testosterone-crazed runner on first base needed. "Yeah, let's move it, you wussies!"

Benny looked over at him with disgust and turned back to me. "I can't stand that obnoxious turd."

I banged the softball into my glove. "We're up by a run. All we need is one more out." I gestured toward first base. "Go on back there."

As Benny walked back to first base, the batter called time and stepped out of the box. He signaled to the guy on first, who trotted halfway back to the plate for a strategy huddle.

I looked around the infield and outfield to check everyone's positions. I felt a slight pang as I looked at our right fielder. The last time we had played these macho maniacs from Crowley & Gillan, David Marcus had been out there in right field.

It was hard to believe that so much had happened during the

two months between that game and this one, which was the first round of the league play-offs.

Flo's articles on the Armstrong conspiracy—a scandal which quickly, and predictably, got labeled "PrimaxGate"—astounded the nation and triggered a massive criminal investigation. The FBI moved in fast, and within days the lower-downs started fingering higher-ups. To paraphrase William Butler Yeats, the center of the conspiracy could not hold. Things fell apart, and they fell apart quickly. Eventually, someone implicated Armstrong's long-time attorney and confidant, Sherman Ross. By then, to borrow again from Yeats, the falcon could no longer hear the falconer. Darkness dropped.

Douglas Armstrong resigned from office. Lee Fowler was found dead in his garage from a self-inflicted gunshot wound. His suicide note admitted his role in the original coverup of the nursing home deaths and implicated others. Last week, Sherman Ross and four other men had been indicted for numerous criminal acts including three counts of first-degree murder for the deaths of Bruce Rosenthal, David Marcus, and Karen Harmon. The Douglas Armstrong investigation continues. In Vegas (according to a front-page PrimaxGate graphic in *USA Today*), the odds are 6–5 on whether he'll do hard time.

Meanwhile, Flo has become the frontrunner for a Pulitzer Prize, and her series may finally eclipse the *Chicago Tribune*'s other moment in the center ring of twentieth-century journalism, namely, its banner headline proclaiming Thomas E. Dewey's decisive victory over Truman in the 1948 presidential election. Not surprisingly, Flo herself became the celebrity of the moment. The feature story in *People* magazine ("Say It's So, Flo") included pictures of her in a Georgetown bistro, at the *Trib*'s office, and jogging past the Jefferson Memorial with her big St. Bernard, Max. "The *Tribune* has given us Woodward and Bernstein combined," commented a dour Ted Koppel on *Nightline*. But when Hollywood agents starting calling with proposals and packages for the next

*All the President's Men*, Flo changed her phone number, bought two plane tickets to Bermuda, called Benny Goldberg long distance, and made him an offer he couldn't refuse. They weren't in love yet, Benny confided to me when they returned, "but we're definitely in lust."

While they were down in Bermuda, I flew out to Arizona to visit David's grave and say kaddish for him. I met his parents at the cemetery, and they invited me back to their house for dinner. We looked through old photo albums and scrapbooks until after midnight. I saw more of David in his mother than his father, but I liked them both. The trip was good for me. It helped finally close that chapter of my life. When I returned from Arizona, I was ready to move on.

"Play ball!" the umpire shouted.

I glanced over at the runner on first base, who represented the tying run. A stocky redhead, he stared at me defiantly.

I looked at Jacki, who was crouched behind the plate. She hadn't had much luck at bat today, but she was a superb catcher—a position she had played for years on one of the steel mill teams during her days as a Granite City man. Although she had on too much makeup and lipstick for a softball game, she had wisely elected to add a pair of baggy Umbro shorts to her tight Spandex outfit in order to conceal certain decidedly unfeminine bulges that would have otherwise been quite visible in her turquoise bicycle shorts and leotard.

The batter was digging in at the plate and waggling his bat. His teammates were shouting. Behind me I heard my infielders start the chatter: "Hey, batter, hey, batter, hey, batter." Jacki gave me a target and I lofted the first pitch toward her.

"Ball one!"

The other team started whistling and chanting.

"Ball two!"

More noise from the other side.

Then a pop foul back and over the backstop.

Then a line drive foul down the first base line.

The count was two balls and two strikes. Two outs. Bottom of the last inning.

"Hang in there, Rachel," Jacki shouted from behind the plate. "Just one more."

I glanced over at first base. The runner glared back. I looked around the infield and then back to the batter. Jacki was giving me a target. I took an underhand windup and arced the ball toward home. The batter swung hard.

*Crack.*

It was a whistling line drive down the third base line. From the pitcher's mound I watched as the play seemed to unfold in slow motion. I saw Diane Corre-Valdes dive to her right. She was able to knock the ball down with her glove. As she scrambled to her feet and picked up the ball, I glanced back to see the batter sprinting down the line toward first. Jacki was lumbering behind him in foul territory to be in position in case of an overthrow. I turned toward third as Diane released the ball.

"No," she cried.

Benny jumped up at first base, but Diane's throw was way too high. The ball sailed over his outstretched glove and went bouncing into foul territory. The rightfielder and Jacki gave chase. I turned to see the lead runner rounding second and digging hard toward third. I spun toward home. No one was covering.

I ran from the pitcher's mound toward home, turning my head to track the ball. Our rightfielder had picked it up deep in foul territory. He straightened and heaved the ball toward Benny, who was standing on the edge of the outfield about ten feet behind first base. As Benny reached for the throw, I took up position on the left side of the plate. I glanced quickly toward third and saw the runner round the base. I looked back toward Benny, who had just caught the relay throw and was pivoting to throw home.

I could hear the approaching footsteps as I followed the arc of the ball. Wincing, I caught the ball and turned toward third base. The runner was three strides away. I saw him lower his shoulder and put his elbows up like an offensive tackle. Flinching, I pressed the ball into my glove with the other hand, held the glove in front of me, and closed my eyes.

The impact knocked me back and literally head over heels. There was a moment of silence. Dazed, I opened my eyes. I was flat on my back. The umpire was leaning over me, staring at my glove, which I was hugging against my chest. I opened the glove. The ball was still there. He gave a quick, solemn nod and turned to the runner with his thumb in the air.

"You're out!" he hollered.

"Shit!" the runner shouted, kicking up a cloud of dirt.

Cheers erupted from my team.

Benny pushed past the umpire and kneeled next to me. "My God, Rachel, are you okay?"

I nodded. "I think so."

As Benny helped me into a sitting position, Jacki came charging in from the outfield. She ran right up to the guy who had knocked me over.

"That was totally uncalled for," she said to him, her voice shaking with anger. "You should apologize."

He looked at her with contempt. "Huh?"

Jacki pointed at me. "I said you should apologize to her."

He snorted. "Right. Fuck you, bitch."

Incensed, Jacki put her hands on her hips. "Excuse me?"

He thrust his chin toward her belligerently. "You heard me. I said 'Fuck you, bitch.' "

Jacki's expression changed from outrage to something far more menacing. "That is not nice," she said, her voice now a full octave lower.

He didn't seem to pick up the ominous change in expression or voice. "Is that so?" he said with a smirk. "What are you going to do about it?"

By now they were less than two feet apart. They stared at one another. Jacki towered over him. With a quick movement of her left hand, she grabbed him by the front of his shirt and, to his obvious astonishment, lifted him off the ground. Before he could react, she slapped him in the face with her right hand. Not a dainty, prissy, ladylike slap. No, sir. This was a solid, open-handed, head-ringing, vision-blurring, jaw-rattling slap. She did it four times—deliberately, forcefully.

Forehand, backhand, forehand, backhand.

*Whack! . . . Whack! . . . Whack! . . . Whack!*

The umpire and all the players stood motionless, mesmerized by the scene.

Jacki lowered him to the ground. Still grasping his shirtfront in her left hand, she yanked him around to where I was still seated on the ground. She took two steps toward me, dragging him with her. She faced him toward me and let go of his shirt. His legs were a little wobbly, his eyes a tad unfocused. He glanced back. She was standing right there, glaring down at him, her powerful arms crossed over her chest. He turned back to me, his eyes averted.

"Sorry, lady," he mumbled.

"Her name is Rachel Gold," Jacki said.

He stood there for a long moment. Slowly, he lifted his eyes until he was looking into mine. "I'm sorry, Ms. Gold." He spoke softly but clearly.

"That's better," Jacki said. "Now get out of my sight, punk." She shoved him aside.

As the other team quietly packed their stuff and left, we celebrated our victory. I was a little stiff, but nothing was broken.

"Jacki," Benny said as the three of us walked back to our cars, "you are totally awesome."

She giggled. "Oh, Benny."

"Hey, babe, I mean it," he said.

We had reached our cars. I'd given Benny a ride to the game. Jacki's car was parked right behind mine. I opened the trunk of my car and heaved the bag of equipment inside.

"Listen," Benny called to her, "when's your sex-change operation?"

Jacki paused, her hand on the door handle. She looked at Benny and blushed. "Next March."

"Well, when you're all healed and open for business, you just give me a buzz. You are going to be one awesome broad."

"Oh, Benny," she said with tears in her eyes. "That's sweet."

I waited until Jacki had driven off before putting the key in the ignition. I turned toward Benny and shook my head.

"What?" he asked.

I rolled my eyes incredulously. " 'Open for business'?"

He shrugged. "In a manner of speaking."

" 'One awesome broad'?"

"Hey, you think I was blowing smoke up her ass? Well, I wasn't. That stuff I told her—that was from the heart, Rachel. I meant every goddam word, and she knows it. The woman was touched."

I started the engine.

"Am I right?" he asked.

I looked over at him.

"Well?" he asked. "Was the woman touched?"

I sighed and nodded. "I don't get it."

Benny grinned triumphantly. "See?"

I shifted gears and pulled away from the curb. "I swear, Benny, you are living proof of that line from Hamlet."

"Which line?"

I paused to get the quote right. " 'There are more things in heaven and earth, Horatio—' "

" '—than are dreamt of in your philosophy.' Yeah, ain't that the fucking truth? Hey, you hungry, Rachel?"

"A little."

"Excellent. I'm buying. What do you say we head for Steak 'N Shake and put on the feedbag? Maybe a couple of double cheeseburgers with extra onions and Thousand Island dressing. Goddam, I'm getting a woody just thinking about it."

We drove out of the park and got onto the highway.

"One more thing," Benny said.

I looked over at him. "What?" I asked suspiciously.

"Jacki may be one awesome broad, but don't worry. In my book, Rachel, you'll always be the awesomest broad of them all."

I tried staring at the traffic. I even tried frowning. But no matter how hard I tried, I couldn't keep from smiling.